AFRICAINING A GORY GLORY MORNING

Mash Bangerz

A catalogue record for this book is available from the National Library of Australia

Bangerz, Mash (author)
Africaining a Gory Morning Glory

978-0-6451115-0-7 (paperback)
978-0-6451115-1-4 (ebook)

FICTION / Action & Adventure
FICTION / Humorous / Black Humor

Typeset Minion Pro 10/14

Cover photos by Mash Bangerz

Partake in the common hating of the odd off black sheep;
Obey political stars from Adolph to Ulyanov and Pol Pots!

Thus you shall be insulted in your irrelevance heartily deep;
as your existence will be historically not worth of accounts.

Have your ever inquired who is capable leading black sheep?
Shall we be ignorant to asking if black and black gives white?

There are many options to seed fear over an evolution leap,
but only unwitting wittingly greats appear in books that bite!

Long live education, freedom of speech and personal liberty,
Critical thinking will survive guild's fond of moral bribery.

THE PROVOCATIVE PATH TO REDEMPTION

1 A SOUR TASTING BREAKFAST COCKTAIL

The Upper 95% Fractile Drowning

All eyes are fixated on to the holographic media portal depicting the world's political, religious and social united leader, a gender free yocto* (for asterisks refer to the appendix, but warning it might impact on mental health of brains padded in first world seclusion rooms) cell transfusion technology developed plasma elastomer coated robot dressed in a beach sandy colored light yellow suit top, brown metal wheels replacing legs and decorated with darker caramel flower shaped tie replica. An important announcement just has concluded. The abstraction's essence is similarly to declaring that flies will never ever eat feces again. The vastly spread out sophisticated communication outlets are hooting, blinking, strobing flash lights. All gadgets on trying to visually show excitement, which given the large population size and the urge to control matters within respected boundaries does not leave much room for any disinterest. A few seconds past. The masses have gained physical momentum. They are digesting the message's importance. The multicultural merged coordinated race of excellence has obtained a small spark of intelligence which is absorbed towards igniting of a loud momentously seemingly endless applauding and chanting to satisfy the ruling political class! "Roofah Raajah, ruler of Boodja! Roofah Raajah, ruler of Boodja! Roofah Raajah, ruler of Boodja!" And as his name suggested, the schizophrenic lust of exercising sadistic leadership towards ensuring society's wholeness in form of a perfectly created hermaphrodite-king-bot is perceived by the generality as a divine tool for the greater wealth; well surpassing the taught and continuous repeated phrases of alienation towards the political alignments of those fiendish in thick impassable vegetation hiding societal jihad theory whispering squirrel hypnotists. Yes, a cunning publicly open run governing body existed on the other side of the fence where the grass is brown, dry and should be released from its pain by being burnt down. Just unfortunately this could not be done quickly due to the action perceived as unfair on those evolution left behind mentally disfigured primates where mercy should be given as their brains are of silky snot covered solidifying omitted fluid matter resulting in the miserable organic souls all worshiping a failed direct democratic experiment which survived through hardship of its outer continental origin's whereby crumbling post inheritance of the greater good's illegally hoarded rare metals, making the newly declared blood thirsty exchange stocks dysfunctional, dismantling any sourcing rights including that of magical and healing herbs. Access to agricultural commodities is limited through introduction of indoctrinated centralized affirmative access and inclusion action plans. But at today's wide spread over several continents covering speech and associated post reaction it seemed like the planet had gone towards reviving the search for Canaan* through praising trancentradelic short, wild rushes of excitement over a fundamentally sad briefing where albeit warnings from the global council a pair of unlucky children lost their lives in one of the few remaining isolation seeking rogue outposts. Due to the lack of any drugs, may the clerical sober promoting mind set of reality twisting to depression overcoming antipodes' coordinated frivolous behavior serenade end as quickly as it began. As the outside weather condition was already negatively impacting on the bodily operational reliant bionic substitutes, they all united drank a celebratory glass of water with two and 3/4 drops of high molecule containing lemon scented olive oil to keep the machinery greased. Afterwards everyone is hushed out of the brutally shining sun towards a return back in to architecturally monotonous designed, structurally contained fabrication of low-dim light producing plank elements, which however as evolutionary commitment to arts were painted innocently by very young children to brighten up the usual rhythm of following clear described work and leisure activities. Voluntold* is seen as the fair agreement between you and the basic social godly needs including those of others. It depends on discourses told by sarcasm and pragmatic incapable robotic leaders. Being erratic is in fashion! However there is the lower 5% fractile, the clustered ungregarious raw meat munching ferals! Why are those hunters and collectors not being forced to get the foggy mind cursing white middle aged man jam* stains removed from their frontolimbic neural circuit with a radical vegan friendly vapor laser? Personal independent choices purely based on human instinct only bring bad luck to common evolution society.

May Doom's Day Welcome the Lost Souls…

The event is happening at an exotic place where a folk of artificial intelligence avoidance losers congregate, for whom the robotic establishment could not give two hoots of care due to lack of human emotions. Yes, the evolutionist reformers incapable of cooking a home made meal are keen in following the commandment towards habitual genocide. The organic hate spreads all the distance to frowning on gardening own fresh produce of imperfect shape harvested from naturally fertilized soils containing worms. Further they carry a deep bolted shock that people still consume milk and eggs from real life animals. Further to their annoyance a mixture of atheism, animism and old religious practices had been chosen as life's path way over the national soul cleansing dogmatic spiritual unification; defying the true love that all humans are contributing to worldly wealth where individuality is purely honored as a sacrifice and not a right. Nobody from the mainstream is desiring to know details, nor exercise any cultural interest in showing respect how this minority was capable to get themselves in to this unavoidable fatal concluding situation. And to no availing surprise there was never a question raised of the why. The religious pool containing damned disease carrying fried chicken loving toxic waste bigots is an annoyance exceeding mathematics calculating irrational numbers. It is widely unimaginable how after so many decades and centuries these pure graded biological human matters are still resisting participation of the mundane terrestrial over arching ritual in being skin carved, scanned and up-charged with health promoting quadrupling human life extending micro-electronic components. How can somebody behave like a full scale scum bag infidel? How can you do this to your children? Why are you not striving to maximize productivity efficiency? How can you justify your actions to society's bulk? How can you be so backwards to give up the chance for you and your family to win the lottery prize of being allowed to maintain your genes on one of the external exploration receiving planets when finally the colonization plan comes in to agglomerate joyous fruition? Your selfishness will not only kill you, but also the future and the past ancestry!! The family tree will die out and its rotten roots will decay in to the oblivious space of non existence when Earth runs out of bionic, and yes organic too sustaining batteries.

For the cyborg configured homo flopians the actual climax of disgust is related to the radical separatism seeking aka violent terror force consciousness digging mental disturbance that a commonly portrayed betrayer could evolve in to a re-configured, hilariously foolish declared re-born spiritual leader! Yes, a former hugely and highly beloved golden child turned herself in to a trouble maker by believing some Denisovan* rooted mythology. She was destined for being a prime representative of the cross blood fondling soul consciousness incarnating value believing principles which after a tough fight won the upper hand against the former corrupt polygamy endorsing, bibulous celebration seeking misogynists led horde who enacted the war by declaring social etiquette process adherence as misanthropist jealousy. Her background and intelligence gave the big boost to topple the positive advancement bill board chart. Super star status was guaranteed! Not only is she an extremely dark skinned girl from the dried out Inner Niger delta or by the mass biological wired programmed human intellect known as The Macina Martyr Mess, and as such interpreted as a mythological romanticism through hypothyroidism* exposed growth delay impacted female who was referred to as the last fluently Xaasongaxango language speaker, but by the eternal Saharan wandering desert sands of evolutionary sameness and conjoined pride stretching such a large land catchment, she was also widely known as the one armed queefing* pygmy Lesbian warrior! What an ungrateful, egoist bitch! Was having a secured spot in society's top of the ladder not good enough? For this kind of social status popularity hungry Asian girls would go insane by inserting an entire selfie stick up their rectum while white chicks would hack each other's blue eyes out while exercising their old drunkenstein underwear avoiding Neanderthal habit!! However, she betrayed in cooking up some dopey soup kitchen bigotry with a thieving leader who added unbearable hot spices burning the intestines of common minion munchkins.

And thus when the guardianship dispiriting news surfaced of innocent children freeing themselves from their adultery partying supervising parents, followed by entering their religious eagerly in isolation kept protectorate and ultimately terminating their lives due to disbelieving the very rare shared conception that the forbidden zone depicted the domicile of the upmost malicious otherworldly phantoms; people had to cheer, "we told you so". For the majority it is the center of resistance breeding against human progress, for the followers it is the final place accommodating the foundation of the universal key holding holy spirit, and its density of power meant that only the destined could survive and provide value of its eternal summary wrapping up of all sophisticated interstellar benefits towards the greater goal beyond humanity's capabilities.

As an unworthy puzzle piece, the lost minors who wandered in to the deep jungle, crossed the infernal necropolis separating river, climbed up in view of farmers attending to their insect farms towards the for centuries untouched tomb located past the appreciated bush savanna serving as erosion protection in to the mist cloud surrounding the respected, feared, worshiped element's resting place on a mountain which was formed on top of a disbanded mine through a minor felt earthquake missing its target between the Golf of Guinea and the Rift Valley where additionally a spirit ensured no tree growth. The young devout rebels are to be never seen again. It is accepted that the godly soul took them. In the championing case view the occurred event is a sacrifice to the almighty planetary reigns or as for worse just another waste for nothing; suicide at its best. However even with birth control in place the ceaseless population growth of the majority and their through repressive power exercising elders are continuously pushing and squeezing the liberal freedom seekers or also labeled swellhead terrorists in to smaller sized autonomous segregating areas with unfavorable agricultural conditions exposing them to starving. But who needs to eat like a fat kid in a candy store? Combined with their individuality bonding in defending staunchly the pleasures of sex, drugs and rock'n'roll against the majority, their shared superior perceived multicultural propagandized view of real diversity made them realize that life can sometimes be better short and intense rather than long and boring where death is bluntly said limited to being worm indulging cream cheese crackers. Yes the infidels believed that a person is either buried or the ashes strewn out to avail a feast for the thought free and happily digging around invertebrates where with luck the final conclusion of your meager existence ends up as a squat pack from a flesh tube's ending.

The funeral speech

In view of the brokenhearted rainbow culture comprising congregation behind Sao Episapo cathedral's altar, a mahogany table carved with African animals fronting the church's most impressive Gothic styled designed window depicting a classic heterosexual black and white couple intertwined similarly to the yin and yang symbol with a separating light red and yellowish gray zone while high above being noticed by a cross eyed sun shining while laughing down by showing its teeth incorporating a gap in the top front row, holding on one side an ugly brown-greenish stone with red mumps looking sprinkle topping and on the other a circle cut like a pie in pieces replicating the 7 enjoyable sense alterations which are alcohol, drug containing foods, trance music, smoking, physical feelings from minor teasing pain to full blown out ejaculation, mental euphoria through chemical imbalance up to and inclusively of schizophrenia plus the unknown pleasure reserved for theatrical boredom playing dull goofsters. One last cough emerges from the in psychedelic colored robe with green slippers wearing Admiral Banter Cheng.

"Dear people from the chosen tribe of homo sapiens refinement who believe in our Suspercasparism* ideology of our humble founder while striving in pride like a lone hunting leopard avoiding peer corruption and sucked in by the global council's generational alliance promotion of "Make mine a 99" with its glorious stupidity enhancing message of "let them eat ice cream!" If it would only be ice cream made of real milk from a cow's udder!! Their grieving honesty was once again sprung* in today's visual high frequency transient wave communications; it was as hard baked and with inspiration colored like a Lamington*! I'm tempted to show them my middle finger and tell them to sit on it and rotate! Yes, one could get hot under a gagging cloak's collar, but unlike us those loathsome anti-fouling pesticide infused encephalotromanics cannot obtain refreshing enlightenment with a lager slab*. So please all crack up a carton* and hold up an honorable frostie* of liquid gold* for the grommets*. The grieving congress shall repeat my words, "We, the greater spherical conscious and guardians protecting the democratic warrant of individual personality who respect the physical phenomenon confluence of earthly limited life giving hydro-oxygene with its partnering galactic traveling electricity to breed ballyhooed* benefits for its messenger to collect and one day to release the transcript to the almighty beyond the cosmos' transformation ecumenical limitations. And so shall the lost sook* conquerors ones chosen to the vulnerable gambling of finding the 7th pleasuring sensationalism by visiting the consecrated resting place of the earth's story capturing medium with powers to disturb a heart's beat be forgotten until proven worthy for resurgence. In what form that shall be, shall be to the discrete of the unknown almighty and to ours in cracking up another stubbie* with aim to finish on a ton of goon* until all ass over tits!

Dear sacred imaginative cloud of nothing I know you have no time for this, but please consider all lost stories when then one day you have collected all the dusty remnants of this planet and wonder off alone towards eternity to unlock your gathered chromosome collection in front of some more sophisticated alien spoof* spillovers. We know that we are not even a decorative slash of paint worth on the coach's boot of your slap stick soap opera comedy show. Therefore for those on the other side of the fence, your pictogram shows might be more commercialized similar to the goggle box junkies many years ago; they still remain crap! And neither will your artistry emotional bullshitting raw prawn sales tactics convince us to partake in growing bionic scales. I can only wish that you look after yourselves as your body's are so artificial your boogalahs* have become hairy onions guarding tamed half mongrels. Yes, you are not even allowed to call yourselves men, so take care as who knows one days the council labs will produce a rabid breed of cloned ostriches, emus and nuclear sized dodo birds equipped with love rods bigger, fatter, longer than a witch's broom stick and as horny hot making any esky* implode through burning beer! And not to forget they will then be able to fly your missus in to a place called flaporgasdicka. Their rooting will be kicking your shit houses down the hill where one day you will harshly come to the conclusion that your efforts will be greeted by an even bigger dick sticker* being pulled down for a brown eye* flashing to please empty space! While the worms have now our dill witted drongos*, with having you in mind they will sadly most likely get the runners*! And if you want to start compassion based on new found empathy I recommend you to build a bridge over to your local Australia themed virtual holiday destination for a stoking snag creation laid in barbie sauce on top of the mean Children back's breaking slippery portion of sweating onions! Yay, better than wrestling a deadly Taipan snake! Ah right, you cannot as you'd have to do manual labor like chopping up wood or dragging a gas bottle to the cooker… Leave us alone, we here are happy as we can at least afford a beef twinkie*!!

Dear congregation, how many more times does the tomb containing the only galactic messenger has to theatrically reiterate its strength and how many times do we have to elude that when you die, followed by the rapid vanishing of your to others known 95% fractile, to be then inherited by those who remembered you to die and another 95% of this goes and on and on... Conclusively in all honesty what are the chances that your bones, your making, your who ever you are will survive? Are the chances the same like being reincarnated as a roasted quaggadagga*?! Even when the planet inevitably blows up and thereafter in the next 5 billion years the sun turns off its own lights, you the believers of ever continuously ridiculing monolithic atheism know it well that only the knowledge kept in the tomb will survive and the captive held intelligence with its disliking towards the human race might not even temporarily for a short moment allow a fluffy fart of the leash to the outside realm of reality. The hard rock bastard knows that we are doomed. It knows that we will never invent time travel, nor find the resources or life span needed to relocate our children to a new planetary home. It knows that humans will not partake in any real long time deal, nor it can be questioned that any other biological mass will ever do so! And looking at our digital implants running most of today's entertainment it is most likely laughing its shiny African spider barking ass off! Therefore, why do people still desire following the only two known souls who were ever considered to be destined for eonian acceptance? And not even they, our yin and yang of modern quim* escapees nor their messenger have a warranty for eternal historical recording. They might as well end up like the fairy floss addicted unicorn couple who while enjoying the sugar fix missed Noah's boat's departure! Have you ever calculated the fractile percentage of baby batter fried fractiles of multiple man tears in a sexual act absent bukakke session over a bird who seeks every Saturday afternoon at her leisure baby cream treatment and hence creating an even more freaking messing up fractiles!! Therefore you godly underprivileged, evolutionary hopeless, manners deprived, but sane tribe of the Feralites, the children of the black sheep and justified ancients of the Gazankulu* warriors, get high as long as you can as there is no afterwards. Afterwards is not even a dream, it is just fucking nothing! #Banterline replicates having sex with air# The by our vicious party pooping opponents celebrated collective happiness is ultimately a betrayal to your individual soul. It is kidnapping you of your own life. Yes, you can be together happy, but it should be as per your own free will and not an orchestrated load of Teletubbies repeating corporate communism infused hog wash*! They make you feel to belong, just to be dropped like a hot potato. Poor little African children, we love you so, but hey then one day when getting bigger, bolder, older to the degree that the interest of ironing a wrinkled shirt is quickly replaced by purchasing a fresh shirt instead. In short, promote your self esteem as one day you are back in the psychological desert all alone. Oh, may I find the strength to squeeze a tear from my left eye! Or even worse, they give you a phone number of some sort of mental sense sanity coaches to keep you nice on the short leash as a continuous mean to sell hope albeit their cotton farms further upstream are siphoning all the river waters away before reaching the basin of native original life! Yes, it does not matter who you are as evil comes in all shapes, colors, smells and sometimes as a rogue kicking around daffodil flower. Hence the diverse political orientations managed to merge very nicely with each other as the bad unified them beyond a triple chocolate cake. Look at the western world in the early Millennium when the former glory of Europe was rapidly crushed by new geopolitical muscling around like little kids on steroids, to just get its full scale implosion because of bitching against the separation seeking Anglobots, so you might ask why as many are known to be keen back stabbers? Well their humor beats the continent's beat! Then the voddy brothers in Moscow regained on influence in the Mediterranean occupying the ports of Latakia and Tripoli with only the frogs* giving up a fight to defend Algiers, but their arrogant colonial past biting them bitterly towards total destruction of their liberties. The West's final defeat was being financially and military disinterested to oppose the corrupting regenerated revisionism alliances in the Pacific where one stone by another fell, first slowly and then rapidly. Yes it was not the good hawker food which made the developed world not give a rats excrement worth on Macau which made its neighbors honker out loud, but the self chosen deaf refused to appreciate god's gift of eyes. Then came the surprising invasion of Kinmen where the big red propaganda machinery stepped up to a fully sick awesome firework. It literally stopped all naive sleepers. The rising empire not only lacked compassion, but for many decades beforehand it already exercised snobbish attitudes to ethic variances. It was now happily enjoying the smell of barbecued meat coming from the American fried up onion ring dipped in the Pacific. When one boiled island was guzzled, then the next was put in to the oven: Palawan, Jeju, Kyushu, Taiwan, Okinawa and finally the over zealous jealous move in to invade Borneo to destroy the united efforts of establishing an egalitarian spiritual Bahasa Sultanate. And up until then what did those first world counter prescription drugs and soap opera streaming addicted fatsoes do…? Well they got a home robot to deliver food directly to their comfy lazy boy* while switching on an app showing a peace making candle. Great solidarity they thought. But when it got dark over Saipan an army representing over 1 billion people jerked over that flame. While the crumbles of the last fast food feast weren't even properly wiped away from their stained undergarments when one more ass crack scratch was done and bang, the next fort of democratic resistance fell! With the annexation of Guam the new world order rose to equal status. It could now promote on a wide scale that humans are only a number, rigidly control Aquarius' age game rules of self enjoyment actualization is limited to your thoughts, that is if your bionic implement allows this else you have to wait for death, meaning activities outside professional life are either home bound or fulfill collective expectations. No hanging around, no telling of black humor jokes, no sun bathing or any informal chat! Even sport events are now banned as who knows what seductive elements can take control of you with suffocation by this unproductive behavioral parasite. You are to be constantly monitored. Your right to free information is only possible if you can afford frequency isolating walls, but not even reputable deemed new world order complying journalists can ensure common happiness to all costs, meaning any extra cash earned is taxed! And for what? It is just like those poor gamblers who could not understand that your luck's worth is part of a growing organic waste component, or more positive said fertilizer for a worm to dig its gummy teeth in or for a plant to grow and be nuked by some pesticide loving mentally unfortunate who is able to think as straight as Quasimodo was able to stand! Our chosen life stile of opposing these bullies is only done verbally. In peace which we also wish those who we are grieving today. The poor buggers are just too damn fucking stupid in acknowledging the potential one can have to enjoy life. However our opponents are incapable to compassionately feel sorry to our youngsters who only harmed themselves and not tried to chastise the different minded. Real empathy goes against their deep rooted theocracy, but has to remain on paper as not all anthropoid elements can be exterminated or the robotic system loses itself in code language before its own extinction. Yes hypercrits! Our youngsters went to sacrifice themselves and not others making them where vegetation ceases angry as it makes selling their grass as greener more of a challenge. There is only a certain amount of lip stick which you can put on a pig! Sadly reality flies over their head. For the narrow minded majority, human peak evolution success is merely based on the abolishing of physical inadequacies like race, gender, religious garments and physically like visually detectable disabilities all while critical thinking is continued being vilified and perceived as an alienating witch craft requiring to be ridden. And for what? And why? It is bloody wrong like a stool stack of freshly shucked gut bikkies* in a urinal! Therefore, we all need to inhale another big gasp of holy peace making herbal smoke and peacefully accept, respect the youngsters decision to seek the trail of early self destruction and disappearance as ultimately there is nothing anyway! Nada if you are a moralist. Nada if you are an egocentric influencer or social media selfie publishing dumpy dumb fuck!! With a few very special exceptions you cannot recall any names of 568 generations before you. Maybe you might still know Caligula or Nero, Stalin, Ivan the Terrible, Jack the Stripper Ripper or the dude which stuck those wooden pylon spears up peasants buttocks, but what about when it comes to the more exotic kinds like let's say The Babylon emperor Nebuchadnezzar the Second's favorite eunuch's mother's best friend's daughter and her 2nd autistic sibling?!?! Which by the way might have been a real smart boy with mathematical talents but because he had Tourettes making him constantly swear cunt shit in Assyrian his fate was sealed by being dug in the Arabian peninsular to his neck and was the first person where stoning was unsuccessful due to the lack of on site materials and hence was left out there to serve as the clowning entertainment for the soul fuming alcohol savaged king's court evicted nincompoops*, until they are the first ones to find out that a person's ghetto bootie can shit upwards when buried in bad draining soils and drown themselves in their own shload! And my dear patient listeners, readers, side show masturvacors*, are you aware that is how the first thought of recycling occurred? The mass unit dirty limbaugh was then invented as well as the first imaginary scenes of a human centipede! No, well no, no, no, because it is no and beyond the memories of today's speech nobody, no-bot, no duke nukem of an alien ass bursting exterminator, not even a compassionate conservative conservationist nor the most talented tushy coughing flatuloquist* will ever care about this non relevant nothing! Just like Sao Episapo's final life reflecting marvel on the window regarding our real own existence destiny, the good and the bad exist now, but both will ultimately vanish. Even the smiling sun above us has shown a liking to being mordacious when it comes to the human race's future as it simply will not give a boswellox* when one day our evolutionary steps hits hard on divinely crapped dog art*, as ultimately this soulless piece of hydrogen and helium will too stop full mooning its big hot lentigines* out in to the wide universe and hence ultimately is part of the bigger fucking nothing! So repeat me by raising your filled glassed, grab either some emollient injecting constrictor or a pair of juicy jumper stretchers and get to human monkey business as so long you can! May you proudly never be remembered!

The Below 95% Fractile Gutter Dead Beat

Hurt in their emotions and following chauvinistic traditions of disrespecting opposing views due to continuous fear of losing face and being perceived as weak nillywillies, not even their artificial implants managed to halt the small angry mob back from their knee jerking reaction to launch a nightly attack up the sacred mountain, burn what remainders could still be destructed, raid the tomb on the peak and loudly celebrate their win like the obnoxious cowards they are; too afraid to stand next to each other at a urinal or pee in the bush, but not too afraid to molest young girls with dick pics. They tried to mock their enemies, but to no success and when observing the ignorant attitudes one could hear deep laughing smirk sounds ringing the bells of death. Those to be offended are too busy in engaging in a lack of boundary confining orgy where the fortunate mingled in partner exchanging pleasures while cash less males engaged themselves in sexual acts with house dogs, stalking goats and cock suckling cat fish. Their compassion hungry, pecking-juiced but visually displeasing female counterparts, mainly fat marshmallows on stilts exposing their red pancakes* for cooling off like hot genetically modified reaped field strawberries just gone a touch rotten, waited a few seconds nervously, horny excitingly, legs crossing that hot bun for the freshly deceasing to come rolling down the slope, to then proceed to bitch fighting each other for the offered chances of securing half warm, semi conscious pickled corpses, massaging blood in to their single barreled pump action bollocks*, followed by tying a cotton thread around the little Adolf's root and then off it goes, corps or nor corps, necrophilia does not hurt the dead nor does it matter in the larger scheme of this event!

When a bright, glory shining morning dissipated the clouds high above everyone and fully opened the view for all to see each others demon driven ceremonious doing; the revisited view made the retrieved decision maker to accelerate its ultimate gory decision. Once for all it is clear that its followers seemingly found salvation through their bodily openings' constantly releasing ptyalism* gravy even replicating its own proud rather limp spectral colors, all while the political correctness promoting, aggressively dictatorial pushing and via data harvesting for reprogramming purpose ensuring wide spread social common codex mechanabalism pudding-heads had unfortunately lost their prudence guarding immunity as their cabbage containing b-spots* were eaten by aphids, moths and zomoebas* resulting in ignorance towards the power of drugs, especially those strongly boosting interpersonal social humorous engagements. Sadly the influential guild prescribing collectively the glory of the faithful loving their confinement to dull entertainment, even laughing at some religious nutcracker announcing how funny it is to believe in Abraham, proclaimed ironically The War of Enlightenment against all happy mind altering substances like alcohol, LSD, weed and more in total amnesia of their seducing, calming and maintaining passivity power towards assuring compliance of people's actions similarly to what the Soviet Communists did, remains a never ending pursuit of the jealous. Thanks to these sober bastards the towers of Babylon were replaced by a wrongly estimated force releasing highly contagious deleterious radiant powers. However to all surprise, the by artificial intelligence designed rays formed a slow start to a quick exponential human cataclysmic speed thanks to all bodily inserted bionic robotics following destructive algorithms which are making mathematical logical sensible equations overheating the programmed code and wiping every chip carrier out. The exception is a few animal trough protein stealing sewer rats which comprise largely of careless annihilated souls engaging in the wildest bestiality behaviors! The dark Admiral was never seen again neither… And the Saharan desert was allowed to return to its natural glorious unwritten plan by reintroducing the cycle of virgin life giving fertility to vegetation growth, enabling fauna to follow and thrive; subsequently providing a new developing environment where a revived organic driven creationism will be attempted.

2 2010 AND THIS AIN'T LIFE

As a good 21st century cyborg our hero of this story Shoetef joins every morning the grand army of blue- and white collar workers making and pushing themselves like mind numbed creatures of suburbia towards another day of unmotivated exercise to be able to obtain blue heelers*, red backs and pineapples* for survival and a buck or two for a pokey machine. The days of having the odd off sickie for a mid week one dayar* are also slowly vanishing, as the living dead do not require them anymore. Your brain waves are only for bits, kilobytes, megabytes and explosively more data harvested information to comprehend. Life is getting more complex and the buggers know how to milk a busty cow! Catching daily early morning buses where thanks to lack of driver motivation and planned maintenance even the first scheduled services run late, followed by missing the train and having to wait for the next one, only to see that it is already fully overloaded and then waiting for the next one while it commences to rain.... Looking at the female work force is only in summer time enjoyable. In winter some of these creatures venture out either dressed in million colors resembling parrots or classic stylish modern wearing hand gloves while simultaneously sporting $2 thongs. After the strenuous peak hour public transport navigation performance the brokering office management expects their human animals to get on with work instead of trying to look after the coffee machine's health. And the damn coffee itself has also gotten worse. 10 years ago nobody would have thought that such a work moral nose dive could happen, but honestly bad coffee purely promotes declining of productivity. This is even worse than being a intromittent organ lacking cyborg in London or New York. Operational savings is the new magic word, after sustainability, optioneering and privatization, making Shoetef think daily of puking up all this shit. But the final acidity in the choke brine comes from establishment's preaching of responsibility while stripping you naked of human rights with the assistance of brutal bonus hungry senior managers who are busily and actively avoiding any accountability while covering their asses with all possible strategies. Alcohol and drug testing has also been introduced, albeit being contradictory of reinvigorating to save money. But hey, they too are just high contaminated organic waste licking anal buds of the politicians who again are licking the hemorrhoids of the new rich like the construction and real estate mafia, unions, mining gangsters and the continuous bigger growing law manipulative breed of moralistic preachers of all shapes and colors; similarly in fade taste and oily like the a major shopping center's mayonnaise selection. Stop downloading Hollywood made movies from the internet or the government will get you!! Bitching slaves of Hollywood enjoying having their jerky dried wrinkle purses* being kicked at! Keep your kids safe, drive them to school and make them fat spoiled little bastards. TV cooking shows and life style magazines are still advertising lasagna and burger as healthy food choices to enhance the darn critters getting even fatter. Good fiber from beans is unheard of; better to be a carbivore*. Plus stay at home to not causing public nuisance or god forbid trouble. Additional benefits are public infrastructure savings while making it easier to brain wash the people in a similar fashion what Scientology loves doing or those evangelists who like to hang around in the central business district trying to rape your ears with their stories which are as soul saving worth like dating a person who was as a youngster mistreated and has not dealt with it. Shoetef just thinks, "Do not drop the f-bomb*! Or even worse, the c-bomb*. You damn mental waste facility operators! Love your company, promote it openly and annoy all real friends in doing so. And dob them in as high level traitors if they are not complying to your rotten feelings!" The show runners do not give a shit on you, as they are now your new parents, friends for leisure times and lovers where one should be dreaming off while spoiling the bed sheets; with sleep promoting milk! And what would this wonderful paradise containing green lawns, kids drowning promoting swimming pools, one story buildings on streets named after the chopped down native vegetation be without coppers. The blue heelers are here to protect you, even when an aboriginal citizen dies in their custody, the intrinsically modified cyborg mutants never breach any duty of care. And we are not going to talk about what porn do to you or zombie movies or anything hiding in the dark web; for many those sick minded have to be identified and isolated… Even making jokes about the Kiwis* is deemed as racist! Yes, we are indeed truly a lucky bunch which after a hard day of work has the honor to watch the action packed news containing socialist bloke hating bitches, twilight monkeys* and more religious nut cases of which some national leaders even follow. Another area where hate is forwarded: The tobacco industry. Oh, they are awful, first step to harder drugs like mean ass marijuana. Although it would not surprise if one day this is legalized, what then? The poor elected dictators will have to find a cure to harvest yummy tax flows from bush growth! Following another so hearten theory flogging by a Dirty Sanchez* exposed line manager to think above the line whereby his is low enough for an infant to crawl over, "Shoetef you should consider modern society as humanity's lucky bunch". Shoetef's mind answers silently, "hey we are still out there in the Middle East to ensure that our number one toys can still be filled up half way economically for some hooning* around including burn outs and killing any marsupial or other protected species in our way. Even the kids shall do drag racing and quad biking; and if killed then they are celebrated as martyrs." Shoetef himself has just realized that he's now standing in front of the entrance portal to professional hell, hassling around with his swipe card while fanatically trying to obtain entry to the beloved concrete catacombs; one of many caves where 21st century hunters have to dwell.

Days Ahead

Today is the final day of South Africa's world cup tournament and to celebrate in stile Shoetef takes his Missus for a weekend out to the country side. Well, it was sold as a romantic getaway… but on the other side of this rotating wet ball with mud patches, stadiums are being loudly enraptured by vuvuzelas. Thanks to attention spamming boxes aka televisions the hooting is spread out to far away corners including the high in the sky floating weaponry arsenal of Kang and Kodos*. The tranquility of being in a small town above a the bar and dining room of an old hotel is providing Shoetef a much sought short-term temporary escape. Booze and a feed are within intoxicating stumble distance to the lands of horizontal pleasure, plus after a day roaming through the outback at over 40 degrees Celsius, a pool awaits, which should make the missus content. She, the so called innocent dragon firstly wanting to go to Africa and then getting the better preached by her over protective mother, who to what ever freaking reason collects elephants as she has never gone overseas, of which she could have learned a lesson or two, like there are gentle giants out there…? OK, the Indian counterparts are more chilled, but that would have not changed her notion of opposition! It was scheduled to be a romantic weekend trying to find a common goal of exploring this highly different continent, but it ends up of her exercising dribbling incontinent verbal pudding from her cake hole* instead of stuffing it with a creamy bush pig* eclaire*! Finally, like relieving the Zimbabwean cricket team from a bashing by India in front of the local greedy merchant expats on the Salisbury* grounds she shuts up on moaning and complaining around. Mainly thanks to beer overtaking nerve system commanding. The world is so nasty to her and Shoetef represents mastery of Lucifer's puppet strings and further what ever is making her molasses under the skull bone go inferior like the smell of a warm sausage coming out of a dog's ass. Freaking female tool*. Spoiled mid aged girl who still knows how to milk her daddy for dosh*. He still pays for her when she wants to go bonkers* in Bali or is in need for a new car thanks to driving the previous given old lemon* to smash face all while hooked on all sorts of consciousness altering pharmaceutical goodies. Bamboozle! The nice fact of the nights is that thanks to the god of Medicus the angry puss requires more sleep than Shoetef, meaning he can stay up late watching the soccer. It is same lame as AFL or NRL which all his friends think is the cream of sports entertainment crop. But an appreciated relief after a day driving through "yay, yellow and red, everything's fucking dead" territory. The Saturday to Sunday madrugada* game is a vicious play between the vuvuzela whingers of Uruguay, which in those days is not yet allowing the legalization of cannabis to calm down the ridiculous South American boiling attitudes including usual soccer player habit of being plain ridiculous Snow White pusscake* show offs. The opposing pale Teutonic pimple faces turn the game around in the 56th minute. They win 3 to 2. This will make a new generation of crouts* swim in some resurrected arrogance and worship a new god: Soccerella* Schweinsbesteiger*. When driving back to town Shoetef continues describing his nomadic preparations. The final conclusion is that romance is definitely something only played up on in goggle toons* where the marketing attracts those unattractive 50 percent addicted to 50 cent noodle soups who also to love 50% low mental nutritional value cooking shows where they can fall in love with a particular manners lacking chef who constantly tosses food with his freaking hands while selling the dream that he is a sexy garlic tomato face pongstar* desiring to make love with a lonely smashed crab corpse.

Day 1

Another sleepy day in the office. Counting the days in escaping bull-shit-castle* has commenced, but the need of catching up with Hubert is turning slowly in to a high urgency. Hubert, the amateur stylish dressed septic brained cap shaven intolerable Teutonic boss. A man with no idea of the game rules, no back spine of his own, top notch in spin doctoring and terrorizing his subordinates. Some cope, others fail feeding new stories to mental asylum therapists. And Shoetef, the sorry ass who tried to build this revisionist son of a doberman, only to see him trying to promote himself and his 50% percent affirmative target fulfilling wife sitting annoyingly just two desks down the aisle. As funny and as like some characters in South Park, this couple bends over when they fart to enjoy their own defecating smell of greatness. For them it smells like perfumed roses! On her first day at work she hands over a business card to Shoetef while complaining all about the highly educated academic theorists in this world with all their doctor titles, all while her own professional title is astronomical longer than the her triple worded family name. In Shoetef the feeling urges to ask the Black Forrest bitch cake how many in hundreds of sexual relationships did she have with former Hitler Youth leaders?! Ausziehen Schlampe*!! Jetzt Mal schoen brav lutschen und danach die Rahmsauce geniessen!* But then comes a no no... She mentions their gene pool is the same. Shoetef stands up and reaches for help with his coffee mug in his hand stretching over and past the cheaply together glued plastic cubicle wall in direction of the coffee machine in the hope the darn thing can liberate itself from the plug and make its way to him.

Where are the allies. Hasn't the western front yet been established? Hubert got the job due to the senior Catholic head honchos choosing one of their own altar boy's. Those canine's must have done preheat testing butt sniffing. And for sheilas, bums containing less fluff means more square inches for the dirt to spread! Speeding up the arrogant Nazi son is not proceeding to all parties satisfaction as the so called godly creation thinks the knowledge was laid in his mother's womb. A few days before the grand trip shall commence there is of course the ordeal of processing performance discussions. The last two year's this exercise worked well without Hubert. It seems dealings are easier done with conservative Christians while using a delicate balance of misusing the pencil rubber as voodoo puppet replicating a low level of a devilish response. Christian bosses' biggest enjoyment seem to limit on Sunday's passionate choking of tedious Kum-ba-yah my lord praises and then smoothly glide in to the week's first working day to roast a poor soul on to the electrical chair; just like a Texan governor running for presidency! Their hearts speak; "Brother loving high voltage!" #Ding, ding, diiinnggg# "10 am and the third world war may commence."

Hubert: - Ah yes, well, well, lets have a look at your performance over the past 12 months ending in June. Any comments?
Shoetef: - Yes, the agreement was drafted with both parties expectations defined, which before you was between me and the senior management. I have provided comments to reflect that I have achieved beyond the scope and therefore should be seen as exceeding and hence a provision of an appropriate bonus should be conducted...
- Ah, yes, should be considered...
- Wrong! Shall be conducted as per company guidelines!!
- Aeh... Well... Aeh...
- Do not tell me that you have not reviewed any of this and are sitting here with the aim to renegotiate the outcomes so that you can sack in the rewards!!!
- Aehhhh...
- Look my dear line manager, you should feel fortunate that I am not attempting to rate this year's performance as outstanding regarding achieving throughout successful excellence!!
- But... Aeehhh....

According to Shoetef's mind Hubert, the bloody gas spigot technician sperm waste is only capable to produce Humbug*. Priorities are set wrong. No thoughts done regarding a planned succession hand over. The poor guy who volunteered to act for the next few months will be spewing on his first day of work. Amateurs! 20 months ago our hero was himself the lucky promoter of stupidity wanting to step up and reshuffle a small part of the company as the previous entire group left by running out of the door within 4 weeks due to a nut case of management supporting mental buggery; yes, this is seen as good Christian practice to those surviving Monday's grilling. Then hope of an afternoon surf vanishes as the psycho chick from two cubicles next door bubbles out like a reprogrammed prodigy of some new idea of awareness crap... Yaddee, yaddee, yaddee, Azazel's children's delivery of lovey dovey is seemingly never stopping. She is close to roaming the office with an innocent look like simulating a cat after killing a mouse and offering it as a birthday present to you... "Oh, donation, no worry." #fake smile# Shoetef is slowly but surely annoyed having to shuffle and search, shuffle and search in his pockets all in the name to demonstrate a theater that the pockets are empty and she shall get back to her desk to do for god damn sake once in a decade some freaking work! But the feline beast gets inpatient and starts whinging and whining about everything is better in the holy land of Nether-never-lander Zion, where that suits in a Prussian peat pit! But luck is needed in these kind of situations and it arrives in the form of a soda bottle being popping off its top and #bang# the girl is quickly distracted with a non trivial action targeting her vanity and the lid donation is the tin. A grin smile from Shoetef and the day is saved. Just asking himself why a first world country cannot afford to look after its people. The elected Qaddafis in Canberra should cough up the bill and provide its people an appropriate health service, not only bureaucracy and Idi Amin aligned talk. The government is so heavy bogged down with official-doom like incapable saving indigenous children from the violence of mind altering substance abusing community members. But even mentioning this and you are in the bad books. However humans are undoubtedly still stupid enough to re-elect the greedy bunch again and again and again; the shepherds for imbecile sheep. Further giving any money to the so called needy is hypocrisy in perfection as the receivers go back to vote the damn pink dressed communists into government again and again, only to get the working mainstream their butts kicked for higher taxes!! If you think this is right, well it is the blue collar worker coughing up his wrecked body for tobacco taxes to relief himself from a day's hardship.

In hard psychological times like this Shoetef seeks comfort in attending the coffee machine to conduct some minor maintenance to prevent accelerated corrosion until more boredom kicks in so that a good sleep at the desk is of help. However these episodes are sometimes a bit too short lived. Ring, ring… the stupid locked in telephone setting awakens the toughest office chair slumping viking. On the other side of the cable is Bruce informing the arrival of some Euro dudes who are interested in conducting some binge shlucking. Nice. Shlucking is always fun. Their own private German word for drinking. Shoetef introduced Bruce this word after he saw an 80s gangbang flick where a dozen of guys stood around a big kahuna equipped Gina Wild, rubbing hard their erection to proceed wanking off over the girl while barking in a wolf pack, "schlucken, schlucken, schlucken!!" And the Lord gave birth to a new English word: Shluckaluya! Education in a foreign language would do many sport hijacked Anglo-Saxons good. However many remain lazy fat pigs where blubber has pushed away any spare arm, feet and belly button leverage. To get from one bum cheek to another some folk require a Holden Commodore drive including being lifted up by a crane on its utility compartment! They also tend to belong to the suburban tribe breed known as bogans*; basically urban back water cockroach egg frying hilly billies. They love wearing beige ugg boots to black track suits with white US related inscriptions when visiting Maccas* whereby the girls have put the dot on the "i" with smearing themselves with $2 chemist warehouse stolen lip stick. And when they need a pap smear the doctors consider requesting asylum in an Ebola infested Guinean forest! Making the office environment as soon as possible history and calling the day before 4pm, Shoetef is psychologically already on his long march towards the life saving mental refreshment. "Stubbies-he-likum*!! Stubbies-me-likum!! Stubbied-we-likum!!" But not before a final bump in to the golden girl, who at once pops out a raw egg for Shoetef to keep as thanks for his donation. "What the ffffff…?" As if this world would never stop with being detrimental to common sense. Shoetef grabs the egg #fake smile# while hurrying out. "What did her mother feed her with? The Marburg Virus? Or stuck a contaminated Ruhrpott* down her throat? Something went wrong with her lactating avoiding mother as how else can you explain somebody giving you a raw egg???"

On arrival in downtown a big round of relieving excessive executed cheers and the bells are rung for binge drinking. After several coldies* and some fries Shoetef decides the timing is superb to heat up the night with some doobies*. The bouncers seem to be bored, which could make up a psychology students doctorate due to them forfeiting their last functioning brain cells to steroids and the triggering elements to activate nerve cells of these muscled up gorillas. Happy drinking and smoking for a few hours is always worth to lock in as means of leisurely pleasure, at least until that one particular importance overlooked political correct fanny wet wipe receives the urge of dodging in peaceful customers. Within a few short seconds, less than the time required to remove all ingredients of a mafia tart's* human cell destructive programmed enzymatic heat waves emerge seeking a worse fate than falling in to a sewer plant's aeration tank. The guys immediately split up and shoot out on to the streets in varying directions with the mentally disabled security guards running behind them. As next a cop car speeds around the corner; one intellectual cripple calls upon another! The escapees change direction in hope to avoid personal contact with the law reinforcing plaster saints. However over-zealous doughnut eating mongrel* releases his young athletic junior female copper to pursue Shoetef. "Fuck that shit" and the chase ends only a few kerb stones down the road where hearts are still thumping. In acknowledging the factual truth that an enforcing power is desiring to dictation a night's agenda detour the boys revert to wrapping up a hairy fairly tale case of marketing worthy innocence. Like fast food chains promoting healthy eating options. First lesson in urbanized jungles of civilized wannabees; always try to ignore the junior copper. Also be aware of chicks in blue as they are working in a male environment where proving themselves is extremely high on top of their dried plum agenda. Avoiding political correct crafted Frankensteins prevents having to take post event head ache defeating aspirins. Also never share with them private stuff as they will forward the info to anybody who can get your sorry ass kicked. In the early 21ˢᵗ century society people desiring a normal peaceful life are driven to satisfy ego driven rights of meat lacking samosa fritters including wiping up new master's grease stains. But it could get worse. Feminism neither unites all women. There will always be a career cougar versa a small titted tom boy versa the hairy primates refusing to use shavers versa that poor soul opting for a secret intimate relationship with her adopted dugong. For men the problem is their ease to mingle and share a few hop smoothies; preferably in a man cave causing a tsunami wave of disgust to the gender bender rights disciples.

- Gentlemen, why are you running?
- Well, there is that big guy trying to kill us!

The bouncers catch up. One of the doughballs* starts jumping up and down while shouting, "arrest the gang, arrest the social disrespecting bunch of druggoes*".

- Excuse me officer, what is the problem?
- Hmmmn, routine control Sir. Please stay with us?
- Not a problem, but I'm afraid of the security guy. He looks like
a pit bull in full rage having foam dribbling out of the corners
of his mouth.

The good old senior officer turns over to the jumping monkey and informs the banana deprived chimpanzee to go back up the tree. The point is scored; the problem has gotten a kick up the ass to mind own affairs.

- Well gentlemen, I would like to make you aware that the state
law allows the police to conduct searches without the need of
any hard evidence based suspicion. Therefore we deem a search
of your body and belongings as a necessity in protecting others
in enabling the society to enjoy a night out here in downtown.
We can do it either here or at the police station.

Modern society's leaders do not only eagerly harvest people's earned cash, but also dignity through forwarding big mutual interest promoting promises and hijacking them with moral dysentery. Keeping people stupid is high on politician's agendas and is sold sexy as stability. Making children chasing an artificial pig skinned leather ball instead of learning a second language is like misplacing a biro from a boring hand job to up your rectum! May the narrow minded attend to god's sent areal ping pong while the rest of the world gives not a white hardened ungathered dog shit about it.

- OK officer, I am willing to have this formality done as soon as
possible, in this case please commence immediately.
- Alright if you all agree I will start with you.

And bang the junior copper grabs Shoetef's bag without any respect of potentially fragile elements within. The action reiterates his opinion that if they would be smart, they would occupy themselves as medical doctor's rather than being roaming street bums!

- Hey constable, please take care of my bag. There is a highly
breakable product in there. Do you understand?!?!

No reaction, just ripping the bag open while the senior walloper commences body search to fulfill his soul wanking desire of feeling important. All the young years of being bashed by his mother are for a short moment forgotten. He is now the king of the turf and respect must be. But not is all bad. A lively feeling Shoetef is enjoying the view of the sheila's bum dreaming of her in tight leggings jumping up and down in an aerobic 80s stile Jane Fonda flick.

- Please lady, take care! Retrieve the raw egg from the bag and
allocate it at a safe resting place. You are responsible that it does
not get broken or I will be forced to take legal litigation against
any disrespectful behavior towards my belongings.

She looks at Shoetef in total disbelief as if the sky has fallen down hitting her so hard that not only the last bit of personal operations center has gone in to administration but also causing accelerated gravity making her tits hit the ground. His thoughts continue wondering off towards satisfying this cheeky bimbo piece of angry meat with a neat shag. "Maybe she likes it with an odd off small clapping on the bum while doing it doggy style? Or more kinky, 10m second choking flashes? Any other main meal condiments?" And then, behold, a scary moment arrives as the egg starts rolling down the authority's car; a scream emerges.

> *- Catch the egg! Catch the fucking egg!.... And now, bloody hell listen once to me. I have not said anything wrong, nor have conducted anything wrong and being arrogant will lead you into serious trouble. So please retain my beloved egg appropriately. I am a hobby farmer and a rare breed baby chick's life at stake, so please switch on any remaining motherly instincts!*

The words puzzled the unpleasant woman even more. The senior officer finishes the body search; his inner ejaculation culminating to a full body fever attack. A red rash on his bat ears appears.

> *- Aaaaahhhh #cough#*
> *- Yes, only keys, some bucks* and no cigis* in my pocket! #loser accuser stare#*

The nightly neighborhood watch is still requiring an hour of heavy duty investigations in to the drug deprived bag while the owner's minds are silently repeating the last song of the police car's radio they heard just before the action: Pass the dutchie* to left hand side…

> *- OK gentlemen, you are clean. Thank you very much for your corporation and patients.*
> *- And by the way gentlemen, do you know why we were called.*
> *- Nooooooo.*

- Marijuana is forbidden in this country.

"As if we are unaware shmucks*..."

*- And the possession and consummation can be prosecuted
resulting in heavy fines and in repeated cases jail. And your jail
birds will be decorative flashing peacocks!*

"Yes, typical in our modern society where it is a question of time
until everybody outside of their private 4 walls will require to wear a full body
condom."

*- Well Sir, it seems that we are innocent and therefore this
ridiculous late night sermon is beyond unnecessary. Earlier this
evening I believe to have observed the bouncer dude who was
beforehand jumping up and down like an excited ADHD grilled
sugar loaded marshmallow popping a few pills down his rabbit
hole before heating up to crackling salted caramel. You might
get lucky with checking him out. Lift up your kpi*, heh? You
should know that half of them are underworld bikey* associates
on bikkies* and they are not necessarily known to be children of
melancholia and...*
*- Sir, sir, sir, please mind that is our business. We do not want
any unnecessary trouble here. You are a shit stirrer!!*

For Shoetef the cheeky bugger can smack this crap into somebody
else's face.

*- Well Sir, to my knowledge, when authorities like you hold
people up to ransom making them missing the last train home,
you should supply adequate transport to accommodate this
undesirable solution. I might be a smart ass in your limited
world's view of a woodpecker jumping out of his cuckoo clock at
full hour, but one who knows some basic game rules including*

Big blue bear is now more like a little social anxious pink love heart striped zebra onesie* wearing care bear. Shoetef feels the goodness of power flowing through his veins and is in the mood to do naughty things with some sexy dream emanating female authorities, "bring on those hand cuffs!" Conclusively the lack of capability in finding mull does not come from nowhere! After heated arguments about a foreign provided address and the unprofessional attempts of whinging themselves out of the misery, the power hungry losers finally hand out the requested taxi vouchers. One each, humiliating like a publicly caught out group sex scene exposing herpes infected anal gapes! But the night is not yet over. Poor buggers will have to guard the boys a bit longer as a real good night out in downtown ends in China town, all while most probably somewhere in a beer can strewn backyard somebody gets stabbed to death suffocating from his own blood. Soon a nice place for some dumplings, Tsing Tao and of course a few more lovely herbal lumbers is found. And the gobsmacked blow flies are unsurprisingly continuing with their unsuccessful attempts in finding a reason for arrest. Signs of smartness start to shine, but any associated light reflections remain dim. They inaugurate a cervical numbing commitment of circling the boys in an exact rhythm of 20 minutes turn around. Even the scruffiest alley way cat beats in IQ. Not to mention potentials of a propped up dunny* seat; it would easily outplay them! But, the approach is appreciated as beer orders and joint roll ups can be planned until being inherited with general mass dizziness at 4am.

Day 2

A day to do a sicki* leading to a big fuss on the phone as the morals of the Prussian empire are under threat, siege by the enemy worse than a wrongly twisted pretzels and near catastrophe of having the Black forest painted pink. The alternative will still get his testies squeezed; but in the larger scheme of bad behaving managers this is just a drop in the ocean. The time is used over last nights big booze bash plus to look around for new professional challenges. In this day and age companies love employing short term view operating spin doctors, meaning they are content of losing staff, which ironically are disturbed by them moving onward which often results in a big whinging and whining about employee loyalty. The solution is to employ more foreigners from another corner of the world and not necessarily suited to the down under's down under the rubble work environment causing businesses having to pursue cultural education to keep all cheaper labored munchkins happy. At 11.58am resume and an incomplete opening letter are sent off; 12am is reserved to head towards the local hopberry juice factory. And as a nice coincidence Bruce is reading Shoetef's epiphany scrolls. So may the barbarian tormenting Colosseum be seated and the games begin! Again. May the lions never be deprived of hunger. A new day needs new beer. Friday's are always good, as they are deemed as blokes night out, providing ease of bypassing psychological exercises from a girlfriend who is unleashing her dissatisfaction of the proposed travel intentions. The psychological annoyance factor has increased from an orange warning to red high alert. But not that it is an official Friday, but also a Thursday or a Tuesday for that mater can count as a Friday; it is all about convincing others that time continuum has bent itself over for a deserved spanking! Knocking back the offer of a life's trip does not mean that others have to follow and live the rest of their lives in dull suburban mayhem of driving kiddies to sport events on Saturdays and doing gardening on Sundays while Missi goes out to spend all the cash on clothes and shoes. Especially marriage was invented by the vixens to cull male spirits and have their male bonding level reduced to rubble stomped Violet Crumble*. But society is an apple strudel overloaded with raisins hoping of gaining some attraction through a milligram of cinnamon but instead get puff party served while a simple normal person, even if feeding an entire footy team is usually just happy for their medicine to be served cold in what ever sized glass, a boot of 2000 mills being to dream of all hop stars.

Day 3

Damn! Shoetef is caving in! This is indeed rare. This is promoting some near dead flesh to make the way back to the unholy office's concrete catacombs. But first watch some Perverted Stories retro porn as vaccination against Herr Arschlecker*. Plus to learn details of the peat pit drilling trade. But not is all glory as this neck twister deems it of importance to write his personal notes of mental challenges in dealing with his ignorant employee, but for post coital hindsight observers just shows what a poor drama queen Hubert really is. "His missus must be catching him out wanking as no way he gets sex! This will come and bite the moron's tail one day." Shoetef allowed the day to come and now is letting it go; at 2pm in the local piss shelter with Bruce who commences with letting him know that the cops knocked on the office door in search for a pervert who steels vibrators, licks balls and likes it up the rear entry, "shall we now pretend that nobody knows you?" Some people urinate, others take a shit and then there are those bloated cartoon characters. Avoid the latter as this is the only animation sporting powers to become factual. And an explosion ends messy.

Day 4

Shoetef's environment is rapidly heading towards global warming gang buster when his missus phones in and starts again with accusations of him being something like the monster of splatter beach or the slimy disfigured worm popping out of Terrorvision's idiot box*. By informing her that she has no grasp of the real world plus she is too frigging frightened to enlighten past shopping malls the chances of ending this episode without introducing a refreshing destructive ice age vanishes slowly like a fruit sorbet grilled in the sun to ugly cordial whereby not even an added double shot of Vodka would appease. Buddhism is a very flash thing with the some misconception which first world daddy's only darlings seem to use while seeking a gravitational lensing of life's purpose as reality hurts too much. The hard ship of convict ancestors are well historical and if not forgotten, then often glorified to ridiculousness rather than just paying respect as a breath later they regain focus on leaving electrical devices and air conditioners 24/7 on, eating meat over lower environmental footprint producing greens, avoiding public transport as it would mean to study a timetable and purchasing plastic Buddha statues limited to the head piece and then placing them with a disrespect on to the floor. Those religious insulting artifacts are sold at retail giants with questionable promotion of universal positive karma while disrespecting any potential disgust of true believers. The kids want and get a blissful Balinese setting, albeit many never venturing much further out than the resort's pool and the Australian themed pub around the corner. No mentioning that many of these products originate from labor by families living in utmost poverty, needing the children to work too, just to ensure the first world can continue finding their little yard ape* sized dramas. For Shoetef the question to be asked is, "do these devoted people who believe in reincarnation put bets on if their visitors get reborn as stinking raccoons?" Dinner ends in a disaster as excessively consumed bubbly* water is transporting too much air in to nutrition lacking brain cells transforming the missus towards hyper anger rushes until two hours later tiredness finally shuts down the control systems. Her swearing turns in to wall cracking snoring meaning finally time for Shoetef to sneak out for an enjoyable cocktail, bucket bong and zombie movie session at Bruce's joint. A pleasant stumble into next day indeed.

Day 5

A real gem of a hangover greets the day with a nice touch of pungent ethanol smell in the air. Shoetef himself is slowly getting used to this type of awakening and has started liking them. The first deed of the day is trying to conduct a warmhearted reattempt of calming down the Missus and offering her to reserve the day for romance. The man of the rough seas takes up the task of doing a nice continental breakfast with croissants, home made jam from the markets, ham, egg and cheese and a bottle of bubbly*; with Ozy lasses booze never runs out of wonders. At least in most cases. She cranks up again the mind fucking crap in total arrogance of his efforts all while she is dressed in discount store clothing looking like a cigi* addict which usually with age comes in a deep drowning throat scratching voice. Women, leopard stile colored tights are just dreadful and makes a man wanting to poke his eyes out! Please let Peggy Bundy take them to grave. Back to Shoetef's missus who continues living with her old aged parents. Life can be economical through keeping the retired mother occupied in cleaning up behind her. Shoetef even goes so far in offering her to live at his place for free, with the condition of being maintained and no open door invitation for wandering thieving suburban fuck wits. Oh bang, at once the sheila is calmly listening and showing a high level of alerted interest. She just wants the place; it is glittering in her eyes while avoiding direct contact. Shoetef is somewhat surprised. He continues with explaining required chores and that maybe a rent inspection will come up requiring the place to be neat and tidy. No bloody deforming Chernobyl or Hiroshima noodling soup exercises.

And also the garden requires attention as the wrong weeds tend to feel a slightly too homely out there. #Bang# Gardening is the magic word flipping the switch right back to mental disrespect. Shoetef just sighs. At this moment concludes why the fuck would anyone want to marry an Australian sheila representing pure white trash attitudes. They are just after your money and bubbly* water while truly believing they are stylish with wearing clothes which were burnt in Europe in the 50s! Anything older and she would have been a candidate for the burning witch stack! As next step he decides it maybe would be nice to contact her parents by phone, but throws out that out as they are too one sided positively biased towards their spoiled critter; some go so far and pay 30 year old kids backpacker packaged tours through Europe! Packaged shall be reiterated as many are incompetent to read public transport time tables! After conquering that weak moment it is slowly getting serious timing to enact on the last opportunity to get hammered before a new working week commences. If that matters in this demotivational professional setting at all. Quick sneak past the aggressive foul mouthing and furious Missus, a sharp left turn towards the local billabong*; may heaven's gates open! The day's concluding reminder: Bro's before who's!

Day 6

Another gruesome wake up at 5am. A hangover and an angry Missus who was up for the entire night greets the day turning the attempt of going peacefully about the most rational way to work in to communications slaughtering of the decipher continuum past a painful crab fart stuck underneath the shell. Constant nagging and shouting of garbage from her tooth brush deprived oral cavity is making the already existing mental pain worse by each passing second. Bloody schizo nerve bashing of paranoia infused imaginative stories. Within a few minutes he has enough of the bull shit; decides to scratch his scrotum followed by getting on with life through a wank under the shower followed by a quick escape from the larger than Large Hadron Collider bad mood accelerating poltergeist. The mission is to enjoy a more amiable environment outside this torture chamber. Buddhists believe that suffering is part of life, but why does the world produce mental dominatrices desiring to inflict pain by opening the doors to Sodom, Saddam and Gomorrah. At that moment an obnoxious chime tune comes from the mobile phone phone informing that Colonel Klink will be working the entire week from home, but for any urgent matters still available via mobile phone. "Well…. Not of relevance; the only relevant priority is to somehow get the fuck out of this all." And of course Hubert's fangita* is pulling the same game off too. Not at all suspicious! A minor cheerful sigh of acceptance keeping in mind Conspiritus' saying that there is no beer too strong, just weak men. Subsequently Shoetef starts work by commencing to save all professional files onto the company's central filing system, just like an obedient minion, which as an action itself is in accordance to the brain washing mob's policies, but ultimately a decision is done to hijack the real intention by allowing only a very small hand full of people file access. Not that it will ever matter with their destructive behaviors which will throw the business back 10 years anyway. In a Death Star environment nobody will be ever as innocent like a chained Princess Leila resting in front of Jabba the Hut. And surely not the German Sheppard dog, who just poorly tried to back stab Shoetef in front of the general manager a few weeks ago. The viking delivered a multi million budget project within less than 0.1% cost variation and the overtaking lane thinking autobahn autocrat had the damn arrogance to polish his guts up to claim the success as his own!! Lucky that Shoetef had a good line with senior management who in return told the chutney tunnel* licking Goebbels sister that the success was achieved independently from him and he is lucky that currently redundancies are off the board's books. What a wonderful piss off. Albeit it would have been better if more than an odd off tear came down that stone face, but nope he is nearly as neatly and hard as a minted flag pole swastika. But for Shoetef it is a delightful moment replicating a shower of golden juices being squirted over the asshole's fallen pie face, while still trying to gurgle before swallowing. The fourth Reich of Hubert's own world has taken a small dent, maybe his after-world greatness preserving achievements might be scratched in rotten wood close to its final decaying stage to humus. Yes, he would even molest the dead by poking! And may heaven will be spared, at least for a while, of somebody attempting to show off their greatness at the wrong moment and Godzilla suddenly surfaces with a vicious Kohldampf* hunger for a small Bratwuerstle*. In what ever kind of hell his final destiny will be, hopefully the pickled cabbage stays at the correct right level of sourness! And so when Lucifer takes a break for a shit, Hubert goes in to overdrive when another senior manager forwards an email with a request for a report by end of the week. The opportunity to brush up the ego is eagerly taken by Hubert while Shoetef decides to embellish his face with a devilish smile, waiting for the moment where the real deal comes in to effect, that is giving an objective introduction of the project complexities, challenges and proposals to tackle them. Just simple, stupid, accurate English language to defeat the mumbling of a spineless aggressive hog who would still follow like a little dog the next messed up Austrian messiah in to a new world war. And no Hubert, Santa has not came past to give you written guideline or process chart or anything else to assist your limited capabilities which are consistently erased through irrelevant engineering talk targeting a total different specialized field! God damn it, who the fuck sits in HR allowing this mess to happen!?! A rational person would think that people with tertiary qualifications could use their brains to achieve the outcomes, but no, once again Shoetef is being made disappointed. Slowly but surely Shoetef is ready to smash the sucker luncher's face to pulp worse than a passion fruit exposed to a stampede. But the shit us too soft to get a grip on, "shut up and just let me do my job!" *Bang* At once, no fuss and no moaning. Unbelievable rare silence. It is like screaming and creaming off in space and nobody realizes. Well the concentration camp leader sits at home, hopefully with a wide open mouth acknowledging that his Latin is insufficient to respond. Maybe the dark episode in tasting the licorice is after all sweet rather than salty. With the great feeling of fuck them all penetrating all bodily hidden corners Shoetef decides that it would be a good day for an extended lunch. The brain is hoovering back in to a mood post sexual depression and thus thirsting for excessive booze. And hey, good news is that the local whore house is just around the corner and a lovely French bakery too. And what a nice first world problem he hears at the down under loft; the lovely young sugar sweet brothel babe starts complaining of how she had her vagina once waxed causing rashes which her vulva is still in need of some TLC, tender, love and care. Aaaahhhh yes, until… bloody phone has to ring! At least it is not the Medusa back home. And he had a breakfast wank which has calming attributes too.

- Yes.

- Hey dude here is Bruce again, you old fucked up stoner! I've got today a roster day off. And am dead shit bored. Wanna go for a game of golf?

- Hmmmnn, you lucky sales pitcher, worse than a second hand car dealer. I am right quite busy in organizing stuff and so for the trip you know.

- Come on mates are mates forever while women are only interested so long a wadi has water. For the sake of Pol Pot, Ayatollah Khomeini and Hillary Clinton, we are in the 21st century where you do not need to blindly follow the Australian dream of marrying your high school or in your case university love with 22, buying a house with 23 and have her before 25 spurting out 3 hyperactive brats. Anyway lets just leave the exercising bit away and hit the pub on the half way.

- Stop it right here now. You have no idea what, where and how my dire Shakespeare's play is trying a successful return down the slippery red velvet carpet path!

- Hey bro, I also promise to show up on Friday for your last drinkies.

- OK, OK, no worries mate, but firstly give me some lunch time and secondly please do not call me bro. I'm not a Keen Individual Without Intelligence. I know that Tassies* are the god's heavy handed proof that Kiwis can swim, but mate you are not even from there!!*

- Alright, I hear you, Professor Shluckinsky.

- Easy going, everything is cool. My missus has her yoga class today, that if she is not too fucked up in the crannies nest as she hasn't been bothered to cook, clean, iron or anything else for a few weeks now.

- Yeah...?

- Eddie has locked it in, catch ya at 4pm.*

- Cheers

Golfing is such a nice thing when you get over the frustration of being a total ball hitting loser. As a survival guide to avoid these kind of first world psychological problems, you have to organize enough piss*, at least one stubbie* per hole, better make it two plus a spliff* on every third! And the associated name is trek pack or in short trekkies*. And an Ozy never forgets that dehydration is a serious matter!! It gets even better if you agree that each counts as a favourable minus score point!

Day 7

Another awakening with a hangover. 4am. The place looks even worse. Nothing cleaned up and again a new session of psycho terror by the missus, "it is season 128?" And then they say you have to show support for women like the white ribbon initiative which should be renamed in to psychotic gibbon; like the Nazis overcooking discrimination just replacing the chili sauce with raspberry coulis. If Shoetef would be a doctor he would announce this case as mental rabies where the infection has spread to the further organs, namely the seemingly never ending mouth moving muscles. Instead of venturing in to subsiding the world but still being hated man theory, the story ends quickly with a plain get fucked! Exorcism is over. A final "the relationship is over" scream and the cyclone's eye can now be directed towards questioning of the brutality relating to tomorrows' hangover. Or will it be limited to a subtle sour acidic smell of the own breath? At least no more squealing sounds of slaughtered pigs. But there is one more challenge. It smells like all duties must be done to the satisfaction of an annoying sweet mustard smelling curry wurst dog miserably attempting to sell itself as a culinary delight. Barking but not biting. Ultimately he is anyway only waiting for the moment Shoetef leaves the doors to rip up all his work, followed by pointing out some good night story fairy tales of how messed everything is while supplementing them with some half baked tongue twisters as method to pleasure more asses and with luck have his own sniffed at. At least it looks like Shoetef manages to maneuver through the day without conducting any major set ups or mistakes and as the machine's oil slowly loses its ferocious velocity, there can be even a lunch scheduled. Noodle Soup and beer shall just be fine. It is a great combination and stretches the zero alcohol policy of the political correct spastocrats*. A phone call to the Human Remains section to inquire the stand of job application processing and kindly to inform them about the intentions of the few weeks leave awaiting soon, so that the lazy asses finish their beauty spas and crank in to gear. And like sticking a magicians wand in to a honey pot, luck strikes two hours later. Good news. Interview invitation. Time to cheer up. Time to attend to a pro-drinking Indian rain dance in the half nude!! Tonight's beer will taste even better. But, but, ring, ring... It is the missus. Or better said the disease foaming wildebeest!

> *- Hi, is it still possible that I can look after your place while you are gone.*
> *- No.*
> *- Ooohhhh please.*
> *- No.*
> *- Don't be so mean.*
> *- Not mean. You cheeky bitch ignored and terrorized me over the past few weeks.*
> *- I'm sorry, but...*
> *- But you silly thing misused all the great offered opportunities such as free flights justifying nullification as spirituality and women's rights campaign. Guess what. Bad luck hun* I am not as stupid as the 95% male population majority which do a uie* when they smell pussy. And by the way gender equality should endorse female topless bathing, just like the way men do. But no, all you want to do is pick and chose while avoiding any associated responsibilities. Get fucked with that attitude, I am taking my life back in to my hands by returning home alone. And thank god to porn, we don't need you anymore!*
> *- Don't talk like that to me.*

What a pity. Before listening and getting sedated by all those wannabe gurus she was such a jewel herself. Thanks to crap like Gnosis, books from Wayne Dyer and other beasts of modern spirituality taking her down a so called consciousness evolutionary path. Although the local girls are largely incapable to sew a button on, cook beyond a tub of micro wave lasagna and do basic house holding, they at least can do appropriate piss ups with their men. "Respect! And now get off your pink unicorns!" The drinking part can be massive and some girls can well shred their male counterparts in to crying dysentery causing tape worms!! Yiiihhhaaaa, unlike complicated Euro chicks who only want to visit museums and cafeterias serving dick art on the fluffy milk foaming cappuccinos, while talking themselves out that it is a cup full of tea oxidants with the blessing of some dolphin riding angels sucking off Van Gogh's dead dick while listening to atrocities from Chris Isaak and who else in their world qualifies as an extraordinary bittersweet man. The real sad reality is that many of these dream princes prefer dipping their prime beef in to the chutney of other dudes. Oh and adore almond milk containing magnetic good feel transient waves, Hulk strength promoting bio-power, g-, q- and arm pit hair growing vitamins. Further they join other hypes like congratulating parents to ugly babies. Over are the good old days of shifting your one-eyed wonder weasel from the left to the right showing what a man is made, thanks to idiots who unhooked the panting bulls too early. The evening concludes with a few happy hour blues rhymes, enjoying the peace, tranquility and having a chuckle with other local booze cartridges in their own right followed by a dozen oysters Kilpatrick, a bottle of Vodka and an enlightening cruel session of Texas Chainsaw Massacre. It is a blissful night home alone.

Day 8

A bright new day and a new wake up with a never ending hangover; but this time all in a peaceful environment as for the only source of sounds is from outside birds. The idea of wearing a tie for the so shortly scheduled interview is soon dismissed and all thoughts are directed towards getting greased up with a bacon and egg burger. From an unknown and not responding number he receives a quick message that a country lad and an English aggro have been invited for an interview. The contender does not look good regarding qualifications and is known to wear worn out jeans. Needless to know about the latter. Further brush up your soft skills! "Is this tip off legitimate? Is that suavely enough said?" Showing good behavior is always important, but it will need just that extra fat dollop of HP sauce on the burger. Lucky the interview is later in the morning, so there should be enough time to get rid of the tired face and work apathy. During the first hours of the morning Shoetef does nothing else than rehearsing fashionable words such as creating mutual benefiting sustainable solutions, supporting management driven innovative business improvement, positive customer influencing, tailored communications, open collaboration and so on and so la la la, lets make this Lady Gaga show go woohoo towards googoo.

Day 9

And... again a golden awakening with a hangover, but with a chatter box gut emptying spew up where half of the acidic gravy infused mutton jambalaya lands on the floor instead. The stomach is slowly getting emancipated! A nice review of last night's session with self made Shepherds Pie and enjoyable execution of an entire 4 liter Chateau de Cask. Shoetef is feeling as lucky like an anorexic chick having the honor to enjoy dinner twice. Later a new low leveler makes his mark in the office and albeit most probably bloody keen to prove himself and that with an age older than 10 year's difference, a coffee or two and he is already slowly getting corrupted. Nice. Therefore the decision is made to conduct the final work scheduling meeting to discuss perceived formalities with el acto the poor facto* at the pub, but only after inquiring about the job interview performance..... #SUCCESS!!# "Getting away from the gulag, yay!!" Amateurs like Hubert and many of his peers leading thoughtless obeying minions truly believe in intrinsic rewards as if drag queens ride cotton ponies*! And compared to all worldly tragic figurines, Shoetef not only maintains his ethics, defends the values of a viking who in war buckles steel with his knuckles, followed by having the god damn guts to get anywhere in the world smashed!! Lucky the handing over the reigns is as quick as Speedy Gonzales on salsa verde inflicted diarrhea, so that soon the downtown pub could be timely inspected regarding its customer service quality and more importantly assessed on its value per capital delivery on its 5mm froth serving. Even more luck strikes as the corrupt bouncers are having shift, so bar daddy "Long Breath" gives them free smoking treats… Yesterday's cute human resourcing recruitment chick is also there and a bit wobbly on her legs. And when seeing Shoetef a happy half moon shape over her face emerges, from one ear to the other. "Just the way we like it – head down, ass up." Then he sees her smile and approaches elegantly teasingly in slow motion, breaks the ice with a few harmless jokes, pretends that she is one hell of a smart cookie while he is a stupid monkey, ready for a ride without having to do too much talking, tame enough to not stick the finger up a bum and sniff on it. And even better when the monkey is a single venturing out ape on the hunt for juicy fruits, as it cuts out tedious dealings with drunken stupid friends believing that there intoxicated infused needs shall be accounted for too. Some guys are just painful jealous knob heads who then attempt to cock block their way past you, capture the lined up future pride, totally disrespect you by pushing past to talk themselves up and still believe there will be no consequences; unfortunately they are sometimes so freaking annoying right in their beliefs. Yes friendships usually outlive a partner, but that does not mean you can act as a full scale mongrel injected with Viagra. Hence the philosophic change of stalking the prairie alone and keeping those parasites at bay.

Day 10

This morning's hangover has the sweet taste of a female body occupying the other half of the divine horizontal heaven.

- Good morning gorgeous, how are you?
- Aaaaahhh, Hi!
- Would you like a coffee?
- Aaaaahhh, no thanks. I think I have to spew.
- Feel free, the dunny has recently collected some jolly reverse munchy experiences.*
- Oooohh, I usually don't do this.
- Oh neither do I my little princess!… I feel so sorry for you, my shining gem of love. Let me fetch some Aspirin for you. That will help. Maybe a glass of warm turmeric and apple vinegar to get those digestive organism charming again?
- When do you think we can see each other again? Saturday night would be nice.
- Yes, well…… I think that is actually a good idea. Give me your phone number and will call 5pm. Would you like to go the cinemas? There is a French movie session going on and would surely be something really romantic. I would like to invite you for dinner beforehand at one of those new modern Australian restaurants.
- Oooohhh darling, that sounds soooo sweet. You are such a nice man.
- Oui ma cherie et ca c'est bien alors?
- Ooohhh, and you can speak French. How sexy. Makes my headache feel much coushiere. Looking forward to meet you on Saturday. No wonder I chose you my honey bear.*
- Grrrrrrowl!!! #oh, smile, she did the tip off!#

After all this sweet talking Shoetef makes a runner and lets the little angle sleep out her yesterday's work out. Well actually as usual it was him doing the work! Back to make mine a 9 in the office; as expected with the attitude that the shit sniffers really cannot really assume that he is going to be the most productive cyborg number of the day. And the new guy who should be acting in his position has sent in a notification that one his kids is sick and cannot make it. At least one plus point of being an Australian parent next to perving off on MILFS when the brats play Saturday sports. Mr. SS is still not showing himself and in the end that pusscake* will never do anyway. Looks like the former fort of fascism has colored itself pink. And those remaining narrow minded in their traditions caught conservative value defenders are anyway on the losing highway. Nature's approach that only the strong survive is over or else the outlook would be bad for metrosexual* cappuccino chocolate sprinkle drinkers adoring a love heart shaped foam; although they have surpassed skin headed idiots in evolution. And Hubert, the Kirsch punch lacking Black Forrest Quaker baker can look forward to the apostolic news of his minion changing through a surprising automated email. The cream has gone sour. One should never forget that life is a giving and taking; whereby oblivious actors deserve a serve of fried karma! 12pm, ring, ring, ring.... Time for the pub. At least the girls in the office want to join in for lunch. They are powdering their noses as enabling agent to go beyond the smelling of free piss. A yay on good old crazy Ozy sheilas! And the day gets better. Bruce is also on his way doing the obligate afternoon piss up at the local. Right time to commence with some shots. At 4pm 2 chicks and Bruce transform into a polygamous bunch of Chukky's new best friend or new found romantic gut drenching love. One of the girls goes gutteroo by lifting up her dress and places a nice Mr. Hanky on the outreaching pub's window ledge. Thank god the lazy and grumpy bar diva is having a belated lunch break. Then the other commences to projectile coughing all over the bar, a nice line of orange poppy cake ending the final chapter as a carried out exit. To put the cherry on top of the cake, the behavioral antics occur simultaneously when a vicious Ex-Missus rocks up wanting to "discuss" things. Fuck that shit, waste of time, Shoetef leaves. And after an hour post waves ebbing pops in again for round two! Peace is back and happy hour is on. A nice thing for the man of the modern jungle barfing days. Good luck has it when a bunch of local bar residents rock up to his gracious honors. And that with a present for the viking!!! Like a little exited kiddo the usually rough and rogue man goes screaming like watered down jelly; Show, show, show! He then quickly rips the large in newspaper wrapped up parcel apart like a wild wolf having a bite in to the first fresh reindeer for months. And bang there she is, sees the light of day for her first time: Fat Slapper Porky Pauline!!

- Oh mate, thought it would be lame if you take something like a fuzzy soft toy with you on the trip. Man up and take this fat plastic bitch with you instead!

Nice, all the locals are laughing and have to look that none of them starts giving slapper some fisting love up her muck hole*. Shoetef decides to put 300 buckaroonies* tab aside to enhance the piss up towards a hard shlucking exercise. 11pm and a few drinkies, a carrot* or two later and the god damn hotel lighting forfeits! No more piss!! "Hey and what about the tab? Still enough for a striptease dancer there!" The issue is however that everybody is too smashed and worried about driving. Bloody 120 days of Sodom and Gomorrah again. But hmmmmnnn, Bruce is sleeping in the back of his car. Time to grab the keys of him and do some drink driving, yiiiihhaaaa. What a feeling and the kiddo is whinging that we will slam his tuned up kangaroo killing Jeep into a tree. "This ain't a roo hugging outing!" Not on the first day of Shoetef's holidays!!! The political correctness swines have brain washed the poor bugger too much and it is time to perform an appropriate spirit dispossession by driving out these dybbuks! At least one of the office chicks is still playing it right in the belief it is snowing outside. After two stops in convincing her that no crystal angels are falling from the sky, it is time to hit up the next bogan* joint the refueling port of call. And the poor little fruitcake still cannot grape it that there is no fucking snow falling down on this deserted suburban shit hole which everybody so loves. GOLD. Bruce is left behind disguised as Mr. Sleepturd gone wrong doodle in his car while the party hits the bar for more enjoyable intoxication exercising until the by their mothers beaten up retarded bouncers decide to evict the serious folks from the billabong*!! Damn pantie spoilers!

Day 11

Early wake up. And it is dark like hell could be when taking an outing to a gardening show at the cemetery. A big yell of Shoetef greets the day with a aaahhhhhhrrrrrrr, the brain is slowly getting exhausted from all the nasty actions against the body. Time to go, go, go!!! The next step is evacuation by ringing the taxi, followed by a Mr. Singh guy rolling down the highway to the airport where as a last lucky grab a lotto ticket is purchased, followed by drowning a cup of coffee and a double whiskey to smooth the early hours. The overseas path to Johannesburg includes a flight over Antarctica, however boring ice and snow and ice prevails a boring view which is only disturbed before and after with those of the ocean, but the mind is set to happy vegetative mode.

3 LET THE SAFARI BEGIN!

Day 12

Johannesburg or Jozy? Shoetef decides to call the smog pot Joe-Banging-Bad-Hoes as the common part of the place is that nobody voluntarily stays in this dump longer than required. The city's outskirts embrace a smell of death, burnt coal and biltong on opiates. At the airport's tourist office Shoetef receives the recommendation to hit the road to a place called White River where he will be greeted by a guy called Cristian Cristianson or in a short snort CC; a local safari operator from the lands where insulin is produced, but albeit in need avoiding it. The plan of attack develops nicely by commencing with an ego celebration at the airport's Keg pub; traditional Australian breakfast containing high quality protein exploding fried eggs, vitamin B aka beacon and three healthy pints of Castle Lager. With some wobbliness in the legs the task of managing to catch the bus just succeeds and the following reservation is back to snoozing past the excitement lacking eastern Transvaal's wheat belt. Shoetef even misses the steep descent through the gorge in to Lowveld. The grannie* next to the modern Vasco de Gama is not so amused having to enjoy the mobile brewery emanating fermenting process gas wastes. She is not happy and getting angry as like most old birds her liking of talking is not being shared. After a few unnecessary obnoxious complaints a loud responding "hang on to your floppy tits and shut the fuck up ouma" response is made. The world swiftly reverts to peaceful days again. It is 3pm. The trek arrives safely in White River where while everybody is being greeted by a family member or friends, Shoetef feels is left alone in the savanna. "Damn, should have been nicer to the old birdy and now I am a baby Impala without the mother and its protecting herd. Where the eff is this CC dicktopian cuntogolist!?!" After 30 minutes Shoetef decides to roam away. A few meters around the corner awaits a sports bar where he reenacts the 1818 Zulu chief declared Mfecane massacre by murdering an elected assembly of cool fresh Black Label stubbies also locally referred to as the wife basher*. 2 hours, 3 hours, 4 hours and he remains the bar's only guest. No sign of that Danish hurenson*! At 8 pm finally a meticulous beautiful young white bird walks into the place looking for a pick up and she is eyeing Shoetef! Will he be lucky? "Oh cucumber gone tzatziki!" The sheila is CC's rootatoot; at least he does get picked up. CC the 75 year old pervert excuses himself of being the entire time playing poker at the casino. "Fucking idiot" Shoetef could have drank there instead of trying to make the homosexual waiter happy at the sports bar! "Alrighty, alrighty, better than nothing." As next the new team hit the road and to no surprise it is directly back to the freaking casino!! Lucky that CC is a royal platinum card gran puta* meaning that his guests receive free tucker* and piss for the rest of the night. "Fuck, again why not earlier?" While the gambleholic is well in to losing money his Afrikaner bride commences misusing Shoetef as her psychologist. A few beers and whiskeys later, he flees for the top level bar where some Swazi sheilas are doing some illegal stripping. Just getting away from the nutcase is a big relief which no nomad should endure on his peak season of traveling. It is definitely time to get to know some local Tsonga mousse au chocolat avec confiture* fraise* delicacy!! Just a damn pity that Shoetef cannot lay his testosterone lubricated blood veined hands on these cute little African darlings, no no no Apartheid is not over in this royal Danish made open sandwich... Today only old boys are scoring. Especially CC's fat meat head is slowly transitioning from healthy pink color to a pale yellow. By the time where Shoetef gives up his hopes of venturing out in to a soft velvet cushioned dark cave expedition adventure by returning to the interested folk amalgamating table of intense increasing play off between CC and some pirate style dressed up Al Capone imitator, the bets have exceeded the price of a normal house. There is a tension gathering like electrical sparks in mist before a thunder strike releases the accumulated tension through a crisp relief making all air composition including organic life form being squeezed between the voltage loads. Shoetef gains the perception that a final bladder emptying is on the radar and a few seconds later gets shouted at with, "footsak*, footsak, footsak, vinnige vinnige*!" A final defying ohm surge and, "what the Sharpeville drama now, I ain't here for vinegar you sour pusses!"

No response, some random black girl wearing unnecessarily over sized sun glasses and a blond-blue wig grabs the piss head and a moment later he is sitting between the new found pestilent African mardi gras phantom and a happy grinning Boere girl. He is enjoying the rare event and avoids any complaining while unsuccessfully defeating sleep while listening to the fat bag's "life is so fucked, mean and hard" moaning…

Day 13

4am, more hangover and..... time for the first safari! Oh man of the underworld, this is a tough call for the Viking. Especially the honor of eating fried liver for brekkie. Shoetef is not amused and is wondering where did evolution go wrong with these people? Then as the dot on the "i" he meets his driver. Stone age Tom, 78 and bangs a 23 year old white cherry blossom making him the paedo bear picadore of the savanna... First action of the day is driving to the game park gates and obtain an entry pass for South African residents. Unfortunately the security guide smells the attempts of gaining a cheapy and so must the honorable black gentlemen be bribed with a few Safa* rubles while him blaming the whites to have ruined the old strong Rand! But all goes good and the morning turns out to be very enjoyable. Zebras, wildebeest, elephants, lions, hippos, rhinos and so on. Shoetef would have liked to catch one to make a dinner feast or brai as they say here. Like a big bonfire with the animal roasting over it to cowboys getting silly on cheap flask juice. But a man can only take up with a certain amount of this and with these thoughts 10 o'clock is just the right time to hit the local bar for some drinkies, lunch and a 4 hour siesta. Of course Tom has to be filled with enough juice too so that he buggers off with the desire to drive around the entire day. Later in the arvo* the bush pigs hit again the road again and this time, it is paarrrtty. And when Shoetef sights his first lion the mad man jumps out of the car in attempting to give the big pussy cat a big hug. Tom remains in the car screaming ballistically while trying to find a gun or a knife or just anything to defend. Shoetef manages to get a touch of the road kerb sleeping animal, then runs back and jumps into the car just before the lion gets the chance to yawn. Good old Tom just manages to dodge the bullet of his second heart attack. And now of course hell is happening in the car until Tom gets remembered who the client here is followed by forwarding the wish to hit up the next water hole worthy for a viking's soul. It shall not be forgotten that drink driving makes also a lot of fun, not only in Africa, but especially in Africa!! In this neck of the woods, the serving of stupid brain washing ads and glorifying coppers as Hollywood wanksters on television is innocently rare.

Day 14

4am, nice try guys, but not today! When Shoetef finally conquers the difficulty of getting up, Tom greets him at the porch with a huge smile on his coupon.

- Good morning Gek?
- Gek?
- Crazy mother fucker!
- OK, knock out, what's on the stove boiling?
- I think we are going to do a different program today. No safari, too dangerous with you.
- Prefer two legged springboks anyway.
- What about digging and washing of gold?
- Albeit some gold being handy, hold off with any dirt digging thoughts.
- As said grasshopper I am not not going to open any doors for you to go on a radiant away from normality. If there was a tribe representing you, I would call them the Menecoptomians! By the way you did over zealously flirt with Natalie, the bar girl from Mozambique last night…
- Thought she is from Angola?! Never mind, my imaginations directed me towards desiring to suck her milk jugs in the hope of extracting some Milo out of her.*

- He, he, he, yes sexy and also very smart that one. She speaks a few languages fluently and seems to know a fair bit of varying cultures with a weird interest towards anything Indian. Else given the chance I'd fuck her too. But for some reason she only obeys CC and thus he uses her as a spy at the casino.
- Great Tom, I am not into swinger parties with dirty old bastards. Although she might not refuse being done as a spit on the roast?! But bah, not with baked wrinkles as side dish! Anyway before having to spew up how the heck do you please your leveret? It is not like Viagra is cheap for you.
- Yeah Shoetef, you just stay in naughty boy corner while watching the professionals having a meat piling dinner...
- OK, respect to you old Trannybag!*
- Well my dear fried, until you are ready my grand mother would have gotten out her wheel chair and ran a marathon! So we shall venture to nearer pastures.
- Sweet, let us include Natalie!?
- Shut the f... up! Deal is we leave her out and she stays out! Verstaan, understood? Behind my back do what ever you like with her, but your gob zipped up in front of my cherry blossom or I'll drop you off at a township full of revenge hungry black warriors infected by some prawning virus making their dicks grow in to the heaven like Jack's bean stalks!!*
*- OK, Wikus van de Merwe!**

After grabbing a few coldies*, they head up in to the Drakensberg past hundreds of wooden shacks selling in some cases beautiful hand crafted artifacts which are for Shoetef as nearly as nice like grabbing the next stubbie*. The tour along the escarpment separating Highveld with the Lowveld, high above the Blyde River canyon is in cruise control speed including the visitation of some tourist ripping off highlights like Gods Window whereby even Shoetef acknowledges the small hike being pleasant. A picture is taken of some roundish shaped mountains which are sold as some kind of royal stone tribal huts stretching his imagination to some place of humorless stone aged dinosaur sized fierce amazon rug munching* guardians protecting the canyon from the loopy shaped below lying potholes eating away their rocky foundation. Shoetef is reminded that they are neither big deep rubbish bins and thus not a place to dispose any gifts to mother earth! Not even from the cliff or bridge above! But as the day continues and more beers are drowned the gold washing becomes Tom's next touristic sales attempt. The adventure lasts a mere 2 minutes until Shoetef decides that it is not giving him the ease to earn a quick buck. Tom immediately instinctively knows that his customer's patients is running low and is slowly acknowledging that his Gek could transform in to a hydra hyena. The afternoon's program diverts to Pilgrims Rest's church, a place which Shoetef thought he would only enter at his old girl's* funeral! The structure was not only being built a few hundred kilometers to the east in Mozambique, and then dismantled and re-constructed, but also serves as a haunting bar for locals with potential of converting a masochist atheist back to a punishment seeking Catholic altar boy. Ironically the afternoon crowd includes a priests, who manages to weirdly mumble something thanks to a few peach schnapps shots while swerving towards the door, "evil has many faces at many places, but some are here beyond a cold beer". The in a content world dwelling punters respond, "ya ya ya, froggy, au revoir!" The way back to the lodge is undoubtedly a touch less smooth. A burping driver capable to ignite an earth quake while night is rapidly befalling. At once the phone rings and it is Natalie…? She is in need for a ride. Her friend who should have arranged the lift is happily getting intoxicated at a nearby shebeen, and even with the biggest protest and safety scares coming from Tom, this opportunity is not to be missed out by Shoetef. "Hey gray beard, my way, verstaan!?" However there is a pass where the climbing stops and downhill riding wind is enjoyed just a bit too much making Tom in need for a sugar fix. In true stile there is a small barbecue with chicken skewers happening in front of the beer hall. Tom never thought to appreciatively dip any meat in to this rough burnt capsicum with chili tasting sauce locally known as chakalaka. The universe is saved! Whether the concerning phone calls from CC nor the weeping of poor Natalie are noticed. The man is sitting in front of a cold beer, so shop is closed!

Day 15

Baaahhhhh.... Not even fried liver and boerewors* for brekkie can cure this hang over. It looks like the good run might end and a relocation might be of advantage; maybe to Ka Bula Bula? No doubt this Kalahari bush hole myth must be busted! The old boys are not too happy and neither is Natalie, but they will get to the local hardware store, buy some wood, hammer and nails, build a bridge and get over it. It is time for Shoetef to follow his own animal instinct driven migration. The savanna offers a variety to feed on beyond meat and potato diet of the albino wildebeests while many of them also believe their diet leads to being a bigger stud than an elephant bull. Shoetef sadly admits this is the case for Tom and CC. But as not being a man of habits, he makes a final run by jumping on a passing direct express luxury bus to Jobandagesherd. But still had to do a detour around a crime scene between him and the bus station while also attempting to get a few roadies* down his gut, while two black fellas* are lying splattered around; freshly chopped up game meat with guts hanging out. Additionally one is missing the upper half of his head with the remaining ear trying to grow legs making a runner before being stolen, but is being held back by a string of muscle making the beetroot colored blood being the final bonding glue to the rest of the lifeless human composition; plus to gift gravity its last bet on dislodging the gristle. A true fresh zombie meal up for grabs! And you would think the coppers would put blankets over the guys. But you cannot educate the genetically useless born. The thoughts of this garbage dressed in blue is obviously directed towards obtaining the next bribe as with the emergence of shocked people their hands turn swiftly in to nervously reaching out open palms; all while Shoetef himself is hoping that the market fresh corpses wont resurrect as living dead a la Manchester Morgue keen on a radioactive brain flesh munching trip. The brain juices running down the side of cheeks of innocent victims, preferably naked virgins kept fresh in a slime bath like in the 80s Breeders flick. On arrival in Go-hooker-splurge Shoetef follows dirty old Captain Stabbing Tom's recommendation regarding a safe location or as near as possible as Shoetef's intentions are still on a diversion from the ones of his partial hero banging a chick a third of his age. However while remaining in this lung killing hell the taste for some B-stile movies arise. Like the zombies from Buttcrack, or human munching animal mutants of Splatter Beach or even better brain eating aliens of Bad Taste or Killer Clowns from Outer Space or or or.... It just tends that places with some poor social etiquette are exactly those where decent entertainment is offered unlike Khartoum, Mogadishu and most of Australia where fun either means drunkenly swearing before concrete diving or lost in bumfuck marveling dried spinifex overgrown nature while realizing that everything in then outback is yellow and red, and bloody dead!

Day 16

Hangover and what suits better? Thinking of last nights' hotel bar staff having to help pressing the elevator button must be god's sign to return to the Keg Pub to grab more fruit juice lacking fried'n'fucked up critter offal breakfast grub screaming for an accompanying wash down loading. A premature shit face condition is doing an early door knock and is slowly promoting a lesser sane dose of paranoia towards airport authorities. Perception kicks in that his walking stile is imitating two caught out copulating wolfs incapable of a timely separation. Howl! However, zero worries exists regarding Air Botswana's attitudes, "they must surely regularly transport fat sweating loud and rude Boerewurstis." After maneuvering through the Joe'sgangerbangers' airport, even passing a Firearms check in followed by the airport bus nearly being hit by a South African Express Airways jet Shoetef finally ends up on a quite amusing flight. Sitting next to a drunken lad who connected from a flight from the other side of the Indian Ocean! Wonderful food, free cold St Louis Lager and an Ozy fellowman... The thoughts start wandering off to...

- For fuck sake Bruce what are you doing here?!?! Stop masturbating on soul porn, this ain't a guava seed separating juice machine. Are you seriously wanting to participate in drinking all bush bars from north to south empty!?

Shoetef's mind nudges him, "sounds like the dude has a plan" changing his opinion towards a liking of having a mini guide at his side. And a proper pissed up piss head reflects pure ginya binge-ya professionalism. While the flight takes less than 2 hours or 4 cans of shit brew, but hey to many other airlines 4 cans! The following wait for Mr. Customs in Kasane turns out to be an exercise demanding patients to the degree wanting to follow Jamie Uys' small boys in "Gods must be Crazy", just merging his scene with Animals Are Beautiful People's marula fruit party. And as booking accommodation encroaches in to boozing time combined with none of the two having a bed or anything close to a hay laden stable corner, not even a spot to a lactating hippo morning tea party, a mental executed rain dance with beer offering is done with the subsequent phenomenon that to the front of the two savanna pirates a lovely lady ceases showing off her to maturity perfected buttocks and offers an unbeatable value package including a godly present of a cold beer. As the dot on the i, the milfy* also has a dead drop gorgeous daughter who will accommodate them all after the boat trip to one of the two local pubs for steak night. The only thing is, it turns out that Bruce sometimes might be Mr. Happy, but not necessarily Mr Smart and ends up having with the customs officer an issue relating to a white man's cock size because of being incapable scribbling a fucking damn cross at the right spot on the immigration form; obviously unaware of the golden rule to not challenge honorable want to be corrupt free African gentlemen. If a problem arises so shall your wallet; the rule is easy as that. An hour later after all the hassles the dudes dump their junk at the guesthouse, grab more cans of St Louis for the blues on the boat, which itself offers a bar with more pleasure enhancing tinctures, making the cruising past elephants, giraffes, crocodiles, roe semenator colony containing Nile perch very wooooshhh, especially when fluid mosquito repellent aka Gin and Tonics are on service. And more Vitamin B as wash down while appreciating a wonderful sun set with the dust breaking the light. The colors match so nice with Margaritas, only bad luck that the drinks comes from the cradle of mama boys rather than humanity's first step away from the wilderness. When evening greets the Oechsle* captains are well and truly tired from looking at the lively roaming meat and it is time to ensure that their carcass counterparts receive some attention. At the local pub first all goes well with meeting the owner and sharing a few stories of glorious 3rd world country conquering, but things slowly get sticky after getting served a piece of chewy steak. A lighter sided comment is forwarded. The owner looks backed perplexed and then turns in to an imbecile arrogant rabies infected yarpie* desiring for a spitting face bashing exercise as lame excuse of his kitchen not being capable to cook a freaking piece of cow! The steak is worse done than compressed elephant dung with monkey brain. The offering of some training to the chef accelerates the bugger towards a typical ever better knowing patupap* face. Whinges half of his life about the shit around him, however when uneatable stew is thrown around below the kitchen ventilator his fried ego boils over to the degree that he will for sure be booking nightmares of raw steaks chasing him over the paddock for the next two months. It is like a belated Bittereinder, a remembrance day where instead of a signing a peace deal in Vereeiniging two rogue shlucking generals retreat of not giving much further a "Botha" as the sought gold could be obtained at a different spot and the pub itself is anyway a replicating the hate against foreigners as if it is a dedicated deconcentration camp.

Day 17

What a deserted grub pooping and minerals thieving place Botswana would be if you could not rent a jeep including a driver who rocks up with a highly appreciated esky* to store some little lovely bubbly Windhoek Lager babies. A whole day on St Louis would strenuously stretch any taste bud's physics, even of those proclaiming home brew as the beez neez of their microscopic back yard universe. Soon thereafter they are on the tracks to Ka Bula Bula with an appetizer when leaving the bottl-o* where the else wise rejected sons of Livingstone encounter a group of monkeys gang banging their local hairy ape calendar girlies. Click!! Lovely picture to take home. But the ultimate decision is aiming for capturing moments of crapping animals. Especially elephants eat loads and therefore extra large shining droppings. But also others are highly appreciated trophies. Zebra turds too can make a camera reach limits! The next observation is an eagle squirting a fountain from the a tree branch. The day slowly goes by, one peaceful beer tag teaming the next until an old desire awakens again; the cuddling of a pussy cat. Luck strikes later in late arvo* where a leopard crosses tracks. Even more luck comes alight as Bruce turned Mr Imbecile could not eat all his polony*. The first two slices go well, but then kitteh gets greedy and makes the attempt to jump on to and into the open aired jeep. Little freaking aggro tiger's attempt result is not only having the hell break out in the local Botswanian guide's life worse than his cheating wife in Maun, but the absolute catastrophe of dropping a stubbie. The poor driver thinks he is next on fur ball's menu list, but the boys calm him down, "mate wild cats eat wild meat, chill now and we let puss come up for a cuddle." But as the goddess of Nyx gives migraines to young girls as a convenience to avoid sex the local tour guide goes beyond menstrual insane. He flicks on the anti-climax switch by cranking up the speed rapidly to madness, hovercrafting over the dirt track as means to free himself from danger. "Silly stupid man, everybody knows that most deaths out in the African bush are caused by hippos!" And all what Bruce as Mr. Dumb-snot has to contribute is to inform that the word for cat in Czech lingo is cocka, but possibly they say it more like cotshka, but cocka definitely sounds definitely more of a sexual harassing nature suiting the needs of the day. However, one plus point of the evacuation equates to swindling a free ration of boredom panacea fighting liquid. Dangerous low levels are being reached and on return some mozi* repellent in the form of Vodka bitter lemons is enjoyed as the sun goes under at the Plan B pub. But the protecting angels buzz off for a smoko*, meaning Bruce decides to play Chucky* as Menier* Kotskop*! In front of the clapping of local girls who are actually performing some form of hypnotizing dance. Lallalala Lallalala, yuuuuwiii!!! This all however deprives Shoetef from the opportunity to get close to any bouncing geminis and even more disappointingly neither a root from the guesthouse's daughter on return, who bluntly deems him as sexually inhospitable. "Or not black enough?" #Smack# Not necessarily the anticipated dream ending of the day; but things can get bigger, better and wetter!

Day 18

With lacking an entertaining Plan C it is time to leave the mentally challenged town of Kasane. The boys too need rehabilitation. The taxi ride takes them towards the Zambezi river via passing several kilometers of queuing up trucks to finally board the river crossing ferry in to Zambia. This place is one of the few spots in the world where four countries meet and which can be seen simultaneously, all while enjoying a final departing St Louis under a large boab tree. A similar place is the Red Sea where Egypt, Israel, Jordan and Saudi Arabia meet. Of course there are also alpine mountain tops existing with views covering several countries, but they do not meet as such at one point. For real geographobics the ultimate point is where Australia meets New Zealand, Chile, Brazil, Argentina, Russia, United Kingdom, France and Norway. Just unfortunate no flights go to the middle of Antarctica and good luck with peeing in ice cubes! Weirdly enough the border between Botswana and Zambia is not even world's shortest. This honor belongs to Marocco and the Spanish enclave of Penon de Velez de la Gomera where a majestic grand stretch of 87 meters separates the two. Historically the Spanish enclave was an island until in 1934 a massive storm disposed a sandbank. Another place which possibly could count with a very short border would be some fish meal regurgitating pelican resort island on Adams bridge between India and Sri Lanka. Continuing with weird short borders, originally only 340 meters divide Macau from China, but reclaiming lands is gone fashionable. Lesser known country borders are for an example are between France and the Netherlands on St Martin in the Caribbean which is the smallest island of the world occupied by two sovereign countries. Spain and the United Kingdom share a small 1.2 kilometers border length too which separates Europe's only natural monkey haven from the continent. Favorable to keep those all inclusive holiday package soccer shirt wearing dead beats away from Andalusian's culture largely originating from African Moors.

Back to the Kazangulu ferry crossing where the islands to the west belong to Namibia, the field in the east is Zimbabwe or to make some tough Afrikaner readers a bit more content it was also known as Africa's prospering wheat basket Rhodesia of which the capital was known as Salisbury and not Harare or more suitably Hazema*. While in front of them lies Zambia or former North Rhodesia, which gained independence two years before the Protectorate of Bechuanaland. To the surprise of many Westerners this ferry has been the only access point of Botswana to the so called freed Africa for many years and in the early 21st century trucks are still waiting to 2 weeks to cross. It seems that the so called Africa way of doing things does not necessarily include building a bridge!! But it could be worse as shown by the neighbor where Robert Mugabe clearly demonstrated that ruining an economy is easier made than developing as for many of the continent's leaders a preferred way forward for developments is stitching up their own pockets to harvest cash without offering any returning investment security. But there is hope as Bruce is paying this time nicely his taxes with an undetectable silent mumbling out of his feed tube, sufficiently in giving the customs officer the hint to arrange cleansing ear buds. The previous nights' exercise removed some feral genes making him tame as a fat house cat relying on lasagna hand outs. However the question of will he survive the ordeals of traveling in Africa remains. After arriving at the new hotel in the early arvo* Bruce hits the sack and is not seen for the rest of the day... That absolutely does not have an impact on Shoetef's plans. A happy man with a mission, vision and value can entertain himself skillfully lazy a tropical haven with a cool pool and an adjacent bar serving chilled drinkies*. The big relaxing may commence with a few not so brightly delicious, but purpose meeting Mosi-o-Tunya long necks. As no further guests emerge desiring to use the pool the ego party goes in to overdrive as all yellow waters originates from one source only. The rest is also allowing Shoetef sufficient time to read about the local swamp monster, the Nyami-Nyami. The critter has a snake body and a fish head and roams the waters of the Zambezi river. It is believed that Nyami Nyami gave an extra ordinary revenge to the locals while building the Kariba dam in form of a heavy flash flooding; just nobody is inventive enough to sell it as world's largest bladder emptying. But thanks to the good old tradition of slaughtering animals, the river god got tamed or fat as an American fast food enthusiast and it also washed away any forgotten dead bodies towards crocodile infested waters. Even now in the modern days the villagers still pray to Mother Earth and her pet Nyami Nyami in the hope for good rain falls, so that their crop fields can prosper, the animals have sufficient water to drink and the locals can finally wash their smelly genitals. It is an hour before the sun goes down and there is still no sign from Bruce aka Mr Snorrebroed. Shoetef takes on the task to head alone down town to the supermarket which is to no surprise located next to a cocktail bar. A good safari enthusiast keeps on observing and observing... His mind plays sweet ragga tones while smashing drinks over a resuscitating dusk while keeping an eye on passing tourists eager for bread, beef and potatoes. As the silence of Mr Happy continues an uneventful feeling of time wastage nudges Shoetef. He makes the decision to leave and to grab some indigenous grub; fried baby fish, mopani worms and frog legs. All served with n'shima on a table next to a huge xylophone with hanging down different sized nuts which are purposefully echoing different tunes, but do look like massive wooden testicles. "Nyami-Nyami might also be sex monster!? And when Zambian girls date, do they use testimeters?" For his perception it could well be that a chief wants to ensure that his prettiest daughter receives the most potent Jungle Jim swinger and sperm bringer. But all good things end when a bunch of three admitting pretty Norwegian girls enter the scene, but beauty can often mean stupid and hence they start annoying the crap out of Shoetef with their silly talk while believing the damn Lonely Planet is describing the biblical truth of nomads playing with their gonads. But they are still stunners good enough to make a horny bloke get in the mood to hit the nightlife. Most men in this situation would at least ask the girls out to go and hit the decks, but in Africa the rules vary and sometimes to the bad for a white man. Firstly 99.9% believe in the right of free drinkies*, but be aware of white girls as they transform in to bitches leaving you for a black fellow as they are here for black mambas and not albino cave dwellers. And for their partnering men, free drinks only for free weed! Therefore the smart savanna sailor decides to have another drink, but limits the scope to sharing the fluid fun with African princesses. Just unfortunately the first one turns out to be a drunk Big Momma containing a package of bad breath, hanging tits and a buttocks requiring star ship Enterprises' beamer transporter to get from one cheek to the other. There are times where alcohol loses its sorcerous' potency. And without having a burka handy the only way out of the misery is to jump in a taxi back to the hotel. May luck shine tomorrow.

Day 19

A 9am knock, knock, knock, knock, sadly not against any horny bum cheeks, but on Shoetef's door. As unsurprisingly yesterdays Mr Soul-Retriever-Yogi- Bear is full of bursting popcorn.

- Come on dude, time for the Vic Falls.
- Fucken' hell, get me some eggs and bacon and a Mosi-o-Tunya
or you can hit the road on your own.
- But the hotel bus leaves at 10 and if we take a cab we are before
the shmuck faces there!*
- OK, quite like this approach, especially if those stupid white
bitches from yesterday are thinking of doing the same game.

Finally the day has come where a judgment needs to be done on one of the world's most famous waterfalls. Although the visit is conducted in the dry season where low water levels make it a safe home for the local crocodiles, the falls still impress and the modern warriors take a hike along the top edge for some jumping fun off the cliff where after a flight sharing with migrating feathered birds the drop down the rock face concludes in one of its a pimples; a pool to allow for chilling with views down the gorge and over the steel bridge linking the two Rhodesian brothers, who most probably now live in England instead. Time to celebrate; today's choice of a real drop is a sparkling blind making red can of Castle Lager, cheers! However with the time more and more hobbits flock in, mainly again silly Europeans more worried about the functioning of their modern gadgets than a submerging flesh eating reptile. Shoetef's mind is asking itself if Nyami-Nyami could go devious by doing an experiment by pushing the tourists over the edge to check if these new modern avatar critters could fly?

Just like in the movie as most probably those cyborgs can connect themselves directly to a memory drive stick which was with help of an everlasting active anesthetic forcefully hammered in the back of their heads, whereby thanks to consuming canned raviolis containing anti-depressants remain unconscious of their biological abnormality. While his thoughts are floating around those nearby have already posted their ugly faces on to a social web page saying, "hello, I am great, I am the hero of you losers, I am now here and now there and now shitting bricks"; softly followed by spewing over the local tour guide making him feel even more agony beyond being an educated third world country resident exposed to spoiled failed miscarriages! Shoetef gives a miss of emptying his stomach contents and leaves the pool to avoid any effort investment towards the ill-breds.

After maneuvering themselves through the local rip off market, the next planned destination is found: Sun-downers at the bar next to the supermarket to strengthen mood and revitalize fiery hearts! "May some good vibes crank up! Look, three local girls who might be keen to join?" The girls are readily and happily to take part. A beers and a few Mampoer shots and feelings go through the roof resulting in the ladies desiring to show and host real men a good old local downtown night out! And what a pleasurable surprise, the bars are overflowing with black beauties, making birthday merge with Christmas and as present Easter bunnies are awaiting. More beers, but now with dirty dancing where Shoetef and his princess attract views of jealousy from other men, including lost tourists from the old continent. They are sweating, rubbing their legs, her bum against his crotch and towards the final dance lips softly touch seeking for some added caressing. Nature's temporal order prescribes a return to where the girls live; outer suburbia or in blunt lingo* expressed a temporary made permanent squatter camp. The last meters the taxi navigates over a few narrow twisted corners on a dirt track past shared toilets and a laundry block to its final destination, the shack where the girls call home sweet home. Although Bruce is getting a little bit nervous and turning in to Mr Scary Care Bear requiring a tranquilizing effort from one of the girls who makes an altruistic move by allowing some nice views of her goodies. And luck strikes again like Luke Skywalker's light saber befalling down on to his father. One room only, meaning it has to happen African stile. After a further literally heart warming beer, the girls commence massaging the two pairs of testi bros following by engaging Jon Bon Condomi for a neat little tag teaming group orgy. One serve of banger is not enough and the mash too must be whipped up with enough added cream!

Day 20

Somewhat after 7am the Gucci adoring princesses fall a sleep and by 8am the adventurers finally free themselves from the embracing meerkat's. The way back to the more comfy hotel beds is a bit tricky. First they both give the night's favorite, Princella a good night kiss on each cheek as a farewell. Absolutely hot student chick from Lusaka demanding unexpectedly cheeky a final fingering and kissing of her sensitive nougat praline. Lucky Bruce kept his punk spunk in the take-away container. After fulfilling this mission she hands over her phone number to Shoetef asking for a promising of getting in touch again. The home way evolves in to a Super Mario Land navigation exercise through various levels of passing township butchers executing their trade in the open to the amusement of flies, bakers marveling at flat bread due investing money in bucket beer rather than yeast or the mentally insane wanting to discuss some Peter Pan matters. Compared to the southern neighbors the Zambians seem to be quite amused with the two lost tourists while allowing them appreciated solitary and not having to worry that any Kwachas go astray. The morning is just getting more enjoyable; women are singing loudly lord praising songs while selling stolen goods from South Africa. 10am and hello hotel bed! Subsequently it is the last time Bruce shows up for the day. Fine for Shoetef as some sleep can revive the thirst for another crazy night out where in front of the sun-downer spa a fresh round of ATM abandoning Kwacha millions are retrieved to allow Livingstone's downtown jazz bars, discotheques and drinking halls' doors open without the need of pushing. And tonight Shoetef has all three girls for himself and thus starts grunting through to dawn like a spoiled pig owning his own bog pit, just as muddy as Zambia's other big swamp, Bangweulu. Oink, oink, oink...

Day 21

Another day and once again Bruce aka Mr. Fuck-go-back-to-bed-seriously-Knobhead knocks on Shoetef's door at a ridiculous time point.

- Hey Dude, today's plan is to visit Zimbabwe, stay the night over there and jump on tomorrow's bus to Windhoek.
- Aaaahhh. 8am!! Go and have brekkie and then we shall somehow reach the other side of the falls.*
- But dude, I have had already brekkie. And ooohhhh.... The girls again?
- Quite down you eponymous shoebill face. Did you know that Zimbabwe is a cash society, so are you actually properly prepared? #rubbing fingers like cash counting#
- Oh, well, no.
- Then what about going to the bank first! Leave me alone.
- Yeah mate, no worries, just... you took a new batch to bone!?
- Not really, but rolling up like a pangolin sucking its own twinkle twinkie while compulsively fist rubbing the prostate gland does not only make you feel alone, it makes you to turn in to a real splitter fitter spitter shitter! Now get out of my way. Need to arrange Princella a taxi before releasing more anus sphincter muscle relaxing crappy promises. Plus you will also have to give me some minutes to get rid of the vintage smelling cheddar downstairs and then after the advertising break we will be back with plugging more or those double dipping vibrator free highways!

On Bruce's return Shoetef has surpassed the coma stage. He is even smirking while giving the cute, lovable African honey bird a final good bye kiss, including the obligate smooth worded promise to phone on a regular basis and that one day he will marry her back home. Albeit knowing well that it is a lie, she still departs with a wide smile on her soft face knowing that the short term relationship could have been worse; for example a racist derailed rich farmer from down south piously devoted to replicating Fritzel Schnitzel's* dungeon games.

> - *What? Do you think while I am on holidays I stay home?!?! Missing amusement is not a goer, sorry mate.*
> - *Oh Shoetef, you are right, I for myself just miss a flaky crisp meat pie with tomato sauce dollop.*
> - *Fair enough dude, they might be good in mincing meat, but they are useless when coming to gravy. Here to lighten up the day a good old joke. A man visits the doctor and reports that his anus got raped by an elephant. The doctor tells him to bend over, checks for a minute the mammoth cave and remarks that when elephants have sex with humans their rear entry cavity is 2 foot long and five inches wide, but his bio-solids deposit facility is only 5 inches long and over a foot in diameter, so hence there is something wrong with the story. The patient replies that the blimey elephant was sensitive and wanted foreplay with fingering!*

And at once some sun shines through the shrine of soberness. Even the taxi drivers offers a special price for the drive over in to Mugabe's paradise. The phone numbers of the girls are thrown out of window in to the African breeze with final resting on the bank of the mighty Zambezi. May a love seeking willy wagtailing* reptile phone up for an adventure beyond his species' limits! On arrival the Zimbabwean customs officer jumps off his chair like a hyperactive child an ADHD drugs.

> - *Mister, mister, I know you. I know you!!*
> - *Huh??*
> - *I have been surveying you a little bit!!*
> - *Huuuhhh?*
> - *We go daily to the shopping market over in Livsteyn. Right next to the place where you sit with beers and your friends. Very*

pretty girls by the way. You are a man with high level of taste, you know what I mean.

- Oh, oh, well yeah, I like to have a beer and two boobs to snack on in the late afternoons.

- My dear friend, first big honor to welcome you here in Zimbabwe. No visa fees for you!! Secondly please enjoy plenty of Lion Lager and Zambezi brew. Wait, wait, I will draw you a map of all bars here in Vic Falls. You must visit them all!!

Finally Shoetef receives a well deserved majestic greeting. He is imagining walking down the red carpet; hopefully not all too heavily stained from the blood of slaughtered farmers. As a gift they receive a master of disaster pleasing guide! It feels like the lion is being served a prime piece of Chateaubriand.

- Well now that sounds exactly what a world adoring traveler needs. As you are a great man of honor, you surely can provide us further rapport regarding cuddling lions or a nearby lion park or what ever is seemingly offered in the travel promoting magazines? They say all this yearning jibber about Victoria Falls and as you are the utmost friendliest gentleman of this continent we would appreciate some therapy doctrine to re-align Bruce with his second personality, Mr. Happy.*

- Yes, mister. They offer town lion walks a few kilometers outside of town at 6.30am, 10am and 3.30pm.

- Hmmmmmn, what time do we have and how safe are the taxis.

- Oh mister, it is too late for the 10am walk and the taxis are friendly. I have a friend, he can drive you around 1pm out there for lets say return 80US.

- Sounds a bit over priced.

- Oh it is. The few tourists which come over here must pay big money as Zimbabwe needs the cash. And for your information they do not even sell Lion Lager there.

As if the world would be imploding a tear drop appears on the edge of Bruce's eye socket. The bastard even gets the strongest Viking heart soft scoring an offer for a lunch shout and another visit to the falls where well jack in box stile meteoric springing elbows are needed to pass around diabetic old age Contiki* cribbage rollers, who in today's case of hell bells take a liking to preaching some kind of conservative religious lovey dovey scripts written with diaper feces on bog rolls* preventing by all earthly means any fun for the party mob.

After an endurance of over two hours Shoetef manages to convince the reborn porn prankster Bruce to hit the local casino to tackle Africa's toughest ever served steak. "Stiff dung beetle excretion, even worse than Kasane!" Additionally the casino is as empty as a spinsters' funeral lacking any roulette, poker or black jack promotions nor a bar where some girls could have danced and earned a few worthless billions in cash! After a lone pricey drink at one of bars the decision is made to escape Mugabe's failed utopia experiment. Bruce aka Mr. Centrelink* or Mr. Social-Welfare-Services hands out scraps to beggars and Shoetef obtains a set of Zimbabwean dollars making him instantly a trillionaire. Thanks to the old freedom warrior rubber neck turned liar Mugabe nobody visits Zim anymore. With an intelligence resembling a Mohrenkopf* he managed to ruin an entire country and that albeit having 7 degrees, well maybe less as what the heck is a Bachelor in Arts?! "Sketching that dung beetle excrement in pink?" The calculations still require the subtraction of the fact regarding to the English heritage originating attitudes where poor manners are justified with sport as it is also done as excuse for a career in medicine, science, law and so on and so forth with languages detected as major road blockages. "Sports. And now who earns a golden wage by throwing a stupid javelin around?" Before conducting any further education related thoughts, the nightlife at least returns to moon wandering expectations, that is mucking around out of sight on the dark side. Bruce, back as Mr. Skulleroo ordering drinkies* for more cum hungry darlings whereby at the one bar, #bang#... Mr. customs officer sits at the back table enjoying a little private striptease performance and he is enjoying throwing around those money notes. Shoetef's Confucius conclusion of the day is, "lucky that inter racial body fluid exchanges do not result in children ending up being striped like Zebras!"

Day 22

Like any other day in Africa, the waking up is combined with the taste of being an extraterrestrial smelling brewery and the only cure against it is more, more, more... Bruce too is gaining momentum of individualism. In his soberness this modern day Watson already has organized the bus tickets to Windhoek. A nice 22 hour freaking trip in a crammed up bus is ahead. But that ain't the vikings big issue. Nope the early rush to organize sufficient anti dehydration medicine provides the modern Sherlock O'Beer more headaches than his hang over. After some patient maneuvering past street vendors and their underworld associates while avoiding a franchised Wrestlemania event the bus stop is finally found. However, as per African way of life the damn coach is of course late and the nightclubs down the road are closed, thus depriving a last ass wiggle for Nyami-Nyami's new found friends. No cold beer. A stash of useless 100 trillion Zimbabwean dollars are being waved by vendors in to the faces of our two ghost looking Shona warriors. At some time after 12pm the news is giving of the new timing. At least the delay can now be planned with a hearty lunch at a nearby n'shima joint where the lack of tasting self brewed home made maize beer is annoying the viking. The keg was emptied a few days ago. "Correct me, a few days ago?" Bruce comes and comforts him, "dude, there will be for sure another opportunity coming."

With the bus departing last views of Zambia are captured. They consist of clay, hay and dung huts along the highway to Sesheko where finally a small achievement of the bush dwellers can be seen: An actual bridge over the river! After the crossing border formalities are done on a higher level of professionalism than the customs of Australia who are only interested in selling their hero set ups to commercial channels with attempting to scare the already chicken afraid Australian's from traveling further aboard than their colony on Bali.

The communists of Canberra with their unholy alliance with zealous religious leaders do not want people enjoying themselves. And the interstate customs are even a bigger joke with their lies of random explosive testings and warnings that no fruit flies exist outside which ever jelly bean governed Zahiristan* prefecture! Australians boast about living in midst of full mean, aggressive and deadly animals as it is a good excuse to get drunk every weekend. But some would honestly crap their pants if they knew more. It is not like, "hell yeah that Mulga snake gave me wink for some glory hole action!" Plus boozing up helps the elected dictators to reside away from the workers in hidden places such as ocean kissing mansions, tropical seedy bars or the Snowy Mountains while subsidizing ski lifts as uplifting tools for their slippery propaganda slopes! When coming to racist, many aboriginals are not better by any means. They can swear at you in a high pitched voices as if a five year old is trying to explain that syphilis does not inflict pain! Sadly moralists win again here by limiting the purchase of alcoholic beverages; but still keep an odd off door open to redeem income through taxes. Apartheid in Australia makes spiders desire to catch a comparable supersized animal for dinner, "but now imagine how big they would go on a carton!? Bye bye kiddies..."

Day 23

No news headlines to report from the northern Kalahari. And it is not because of the Lozi people's desire to test out their newest toys while sporting uniforms of the Caprivi Liberation Army! It is rather Shoetef who is considering swinging fists towards the soberness preaching bus driver some 200 clicks west of Katima Mulilo on the river banks of an Okavango feeder. Thanks to the eager diplomatic efforts of a cock fight disinterested Bruce the level of verbal enmity is quickly reduced to dust, as who else would get this sun ray emanating ass transported to the next hotel bed! Peace returns to the barren booby trapped fields surrounding this national park squeezed between Botswana and Angola. And as night slowly takes place and neither of the two warlords are in the mood of falling prey to some local partisans the trip continues without any further flares of mistrust. Shoetef still manages to finish his liquor, but keeps a low profile during the entire night including avoiding a request for a toilet break in the open. The following morning upon arrival in Windhoek the travelers are greeted by a group of top less Humba queen, passionately introducing new earning tactics from the photographing addicted tourists. And for the boys a pair of real flash fleshed out Masters choco milk containers do neither represent an unworthy shot to show off home! The subsequent surprise is the harsh reality of zero available accommodation requires a Plan C. Plan B is already being redeemed over the ten hour pit stop! Killing time in a city not necessarily known for touristic highlights like is a small challenge, especially to not be relieved of any valuables. Ten long hours for wussy* pussy Bruce to visit the swimming pool to wash off the cheddar slice from his ramburger* while Shoetef's preferences are visiting the National museum with all the Herero and Swapo freedom stories where leveraging out both sides of the coin, which actually has three, a subsequent interest is shown towards the depicting enemy via a more delightful lunch at one of the former colonial masters' brewery. Impala knuckle with red cabbage, accomplished with a Bavarian potato salad and a liter stein of wheat beer. What is worse, surviving a day without a shower or a day without mind numbing fun raising substances? While the Germans may be a pain outside their country, they still honor an exceeding level of service when it comes to not only engineering, but also hospitality where as icing on the cake the bus picks up him up right behind the beer garden's rosemary bush! Win win and cha-ching; Shoetef can slam down another two pints and the owner earns another few savanna shillings! And priceless to mention Baby Bruce's face when it takes a few unknown reasoning minutes for Shoetef to finish the cuppa and pay. After 5 extra traveling hours and past a short 40 kilometer desert strip a quaint German town makes itself visible on the horizon, Swakopmund. A Prussian town in the desert kissing cold ocean waters where even the black population has blue eyes. "Freaky!" By now Bruce is showing again signs of hop craving.

After throwing the luggage on to their single room hard bunk beds the beautiful girls at the Grüner Kranz bar convince the boys in to excessive enjoyment of the local specialty: "Oh, yeah baby, serve us some devil's rejects." Shots of Austrian Strohrum and Tequila are the perfection medicinal cocktail the Namib Naukloft roamers need. "Kill the fire. More, more..." But there is a minus point: A truck load dumped white girls whinging and whining to the two for an invitation. But remembering that a white bloke in Africa who pays drinks for white girls is a conscious lacking imbecile, the strict answer is a no. The value gaining potential is about that of Monty Python's holy bunny killing grenade and thus making an investment a 100% sure loss. Weisswürstel* are again not the sought specialty. It is black pudding what they crave. Just stupid this means for them having to pay for once the drinks which seemingly goes against some lady's spoiled social codex beliefs. Bad luck! The boys are not Namib Desert's Centrelink* branch, nor Worldvision and neither stray cat caring vets from WWF! It gets them even more outrageous when a beer is bought for a black guy, but he has sweet gansha* which would even get resident's of Fraggle Rock in to raving mode!

Day 24

Revenge time for Shoetef. #bang#bang#bang#

- Hey Bruce move your fucking lame ass out of the room! It seems you have an orkhund instead of a sarkhund*.*

Hardly any sound escapes from inside, with the odd off exception of a whinge or two. A depressing reality hits the poor amateur as no normal functioning homo sapiens lives three days or more without booze. "The bed is so hard, how can he even think about more sleeping?"

On the outside back wall of the hotel Shoetef observes an advertisement to rent out a luxury apartment and decides to crank up his merciless full blown desert fox Rommel replicating violent wood breaking exercise until the softie Bruce is out of bed for good. Still no success. The sleeping autocrat wins the battle, again. Bad luck results in a brekkie* beer. Still no life signs from Bruce. The lovely young dark smooth polished skinned waitress working at the neighboring Italian restaurant turns out to be the angel of the day in allowing Shoetef to use her phone, plus agrees to a date! As the apartment owner is of Pomerania decent timing is vital towards ensuring that not a second battle is lost within the first hour post awakening. 15 minutes is 15 minutes and not eine Staatssicherheits* Minute später*! Perfectly on time the older owner picks up the sour pickle and drives him down the Brücken Strasse. However as per usual African money wasting desire the real street name is after some twisted cast iron pan handling story teller representing the typical regional important PR gag ceremonies of the new ruling crooks which is of higher priority than feeding their own people. 2 big bedrooms, 2 bathrooms, each with a spa, big TV with DVD player, luxurious large kitchen, huge fridge for a cult gathering of Shluckenlagers* and a massive balcony with view out in to the dessert and the surpassing ocean behind. The final a surprise awaits Shoetef when he realizes that home sweet home has a sugar coating; three stories below is a conveniently located bottle-o*. Shoetef is already imagining that Bruce would approve; and if not who gives a rats ass as the pad could also very well be used as a private little harem. Girls are plenty and so are drugs! Plus a short period hope did resurface towards transform Bruce back in to a proper drinking buddy. Not all blokes get taken away from sadness and eternally locked in to lonely fanny* desiring dreams. Of course there are also the gay dudes existing wanting to have none of that! The next step is to get the price even further down. The trading efforts are making Shoetef act as a gentlemen of unknown territorial dimensions with a warm smile shining through his unshaven face while practicing some of his upmost polite Weimarer Republic lingo*. Abracadabra, half price secured with the promise of cleaning the joint before leaving. Wunderbar und wunderschön*. Fourth attempt of getting Bruce out of bed succeeds with the cafe girl sweet talking in a variety of calm and adamant Prussian tongues while inquisitively knocking on the door. Although not receiving the expected morning blow job, the apartment entices Bruce to new levels making it time to get their third travel companion out of the treasure chest. Yes, time to release Fat Slapper Porky Pauline for a walkie*! All through town to a nice beer garden on the ocean promenade for some oysters and meat loaf. And of course Porky is old enough to have her own chair! As many locals and tourist alike stink of evangelic conservatism, some shocking anti praises will do those goodie gooders good!!! The first reaction is half of the guests depart as quickly as possible while others turn their backs, which with those animal lard fattened pigs saves gracefully pain infliction on to their eyes too. Usually these kind of cases result in eviction, however Africa does it the African way. Relaxation, laziness, less annoying Nazi behaving guests and the place begins again to laugh rather than chasing business from self righteous playing up white supremacists. In the evening the boys return to the bar to meet previous night's local hotties where a high level of fluttering flirting commences to proof that profs are at work and not jellybeans*. Although the red one is everybody's favorite beer bottles come in green and their smoking bananas in white! Beyond the free drink scammers, the guys find camaraderie with the only bloke who is worth paying a drink: Francois, a white bloke owning a car boot filled with green whakky tabacci*.

Day 25

It is past 3am and the bar has ridden itself from the triple nuisance. As the town center is dead the three roll towards a northerly located township searching for illegal brewed cacti juices. At the first junction where they decide to stop, a local drug lord introduces himself, but with seeing only white fellows he starts hassling. The verbal kept skirmish goes quick in to over drive resulting in dogs being let out. "You sneaky vag badge!". Before guns are retrieved they continue driving another kilometer down the road in to deeper Bronx where the next player awaits; already warned but at least keen on business. A crazy little Latino lost in Africa, but on arrival greets Francois as if he knows him. Juan Armada Cortez swiftly transfers the ownership of two bottles of cheap ass sherry and cocaine in anticipation of what was to become; the armada's rapidly cessation as some el Senior J.A.C ass enters the scene and releases few rifle shots, this time towards the car of the three! Plus some added yelling as a reminder to avoid the area in future. The only place deemed to be safe enough for the early morning hour drinkies is a school playground. After the initial burn outs on the basketball court the triplets turn to the swings in attempting to fly over the top metal bar. The event concludes with Bruce falling off from over two meters height requiring more healing smoking and drinking until he decides to engage in a fluid coughing competition which he wins due to lack of competitors. But in hindsight it was a classic of a face dive! The final shot is taken when Francois ties the entire swing construction to his car where during the thieving attempt the damn thing lands on to the vehicle itself fully smashing the front passenger's side. Slowly, but surely the pendulum swings towards a more sobering motion and the kindergarten cops return back in to their luxuriously concrete built tree house.

Later in the arvo*, after a big fat South West African stile meal of diced gems bock chunks swimming in gravy, Francois returns with dodgy car number 2 for a ride out to the dessert. Of course it had to be a vehicle without 4 wheel capabilities…. People get older, but not smarter. The golden rule of driving through sand dunes is never stop at low points, go slowly over crests as often behind them is a steep drop and being aware when exiting the cabin while exercising content drunken attitudes as side winding snakes tend to be grumpy teetotalers, especially when an empty bottle is dropped on to their heads. "Duh!" as Homer Simpson says. Instead the guys hunt down and catch a thin long black Namib snake, a few geckos which it refuses to eat and even capture a chameleon whipping out its tongue making good camera shots. The reptiles are very territorial and eager to fend its catchment, even if this means walking to Etosha. And like any other dry place the dessert gives the adventurers a bigger than Ben Hur thirst, while neither forgetting that the local girls are always keen mingling with cashed up jellobusters*, whereby on top of the pops is competing on being the master of devil's rejects shots.

Day 26

What a bloody lovely hang over again! Shoetef wakes up awfully, but it gets worse when he turns around in bed and having one of the bar maids next to him snoring her god damn face off. She is neither the prettiest one, but the associated mind fucking brain hammering is not allowing any contest rating like those pedophilia American judges at beauty pageant events promoting the pimping up of under aged girls and their pre-mature slut exposure by their low self-esteemed white trash fat, sweat dripping in cheap perfume engulfed mothers. "OK, I won't get blind neither; and no time for shmuck*." Shoetef's thoughts are heading astray with a big virtual skull stabbing when further asking what the heck is next on the sick menu? It seems that Francois is sleeping with one chick in Brucie's spa while having a burnt out cone between his fangs and Bruce, well his door is locked and I guess it will be like that for the rest of the day. But the sexual innocent buzzing upstairs' tranquility ceases quickly when Shoetef shouts to Bruce's door,

> *- Get up you nose picking Ogre!! Are you man enough to have*
> *a girl in there too?*

Silencio…

After a rapid extortion of strenuous hover crafting down to the juice shop where having to listen to the manager in his finest Afrikaans disrespecting them as a cluster of rogue hobos* a new batch of precious Schluckenlager* is safely secured. Breakfast needs to be refreshing or else the day ends up as a drag. And there is even cheap, urine tasting Nestle coffee powder to pour in. No toast or stupid stuff like cereal is bought as eating is cheating. And then, and then, as if the almighty does scratch his balls in the rare event of decency shown on a Rupert Murdoch's owned publication, Bruce's door opens and a sheila joins the merry berry morning party bunch. One could well imagine it happening like a cheerful family outing picnic! Thanks to the good vibes, some sweet talk and hydraulic generosity a dinner invitation is made. "Yay, to the mother fuckers!" is all what Shoetef is capable to think off. Feeling sexually aroused like a naughty chook wanting to plug its back room storage space with her own freshly laid egg!

The initial meeting place is a bar on a remotely located southerly located beach, well hidden from any pork chop drooling tourists. The venue's wooden decoration has seen better days and so has the pirate themed Ronald McDonald statue boasting a partial ripped off head with a torn skull flag as covering scarf, plus a faded wooden parrot looking like an obese gray haired Caucasian fowl. "Most probably has a striking imitating bad breath too!" However, such dives offer value for money which promotes desert lions to happily roar loud out and then retrieve to quite purring just as what kittens do. Thanks to Francois they avoid walking and he promises to return with a friend. "Juan?" As written by the wandering landscape swallowing Namibian sand dune saga, Francois did not return. "Ha! Good bye! Forever?" However, Shoetef dedicates himself to keep his eyes open as seemingly Francois is a famous photographer for airline magazines. Yeah maybe for Kalahari Kaminazi Aviation!! Alcohol, drugs and the one off root does stimulate the artist in you where all can rock'n'roll so long you do not get winded up the little finger of a jealous sheila. The afternoon ends up quite nicely with the girls who beforehand arranged a roast to enjoy, plus they are keen letting Shoetef and Bruce know that the kiddies are hand balled to some poor aunties while some local male friends have dropped off a barrel of home brew. "Finally some maiz brew!" While the waves of the Benguela current thunderously drop their cold water on to the beach, the Jaegermeister shots start thrusting warm feelings to the ever-greedy mouths and hearts. The afternoon ends up with a rust colored sunset over the beach and as usually in Africa it is a jewel of an accompanying dusk. Around 8ish a taxi is ordered and drives them in to deepest Bantu Bronx. Compared to the Zambian girls here they share a big house, well contains over twenty residents. Many people in the developed world have no idea how real life happens in poor countries. There are continuously large parts of this ridiculously spoiled society promoting crap like veganism, socialism, religious extremism, spiritualism, political correctness and many other modern world seemingly relevant crap, but globally on a large scale it is junk as the majority of this planet struggles to get enough to eat. The first world remains morally dysfunctional as it was 50, 100, 3000 years ago! And the worst of this hard reality is, many lack consciousness beyond the modem's cable socket. Getting a bad belly is about the biggest foreign catastrophe many gather. Their talk often resembles to stupid people letting you know how smart they are. As for Shoetef's perception these narrow minded moralists should come out and join in for dinner: Roasted goats head, baaehhhh!! Aaah, even the glassy shining eye balls are intact and it is the guests' honor to master the small culinary burden of eating each the beast's goggles. "Somehow gooey, somehow could use more sauce, somehow lucky that there is enough Namibian bush champagne available to swallow this delicacy. A proper French man would ask for a piece of bread to spread the binoculars on!" The evening heads into the right direction, with the exception that later two of the former husbands' rock up drunk while playing Samurai with their machetes. With some luck and jumping over empty dishes, an escape like ballerinas on cow hoofs is done via the back door and a lengthy 3 hour walk back wraps up a rather busy day ending as shoe-less lion kill hunters.

Day 27

Bruce decides it is enough of which his intoxicated peer is agreeing to. Time to get out of here and that rather quickly. Came, saw, conquered and leaving a decent mess back. Word of their anti-social behavior is spreading around; to the degree that Shoetef hears a taxi driver gossiping with the downstairs shop owner. When the shop owner notices them he grunts in disgust disbelieving that any positive intentions exist from the two. "Another arrogant sedater showing scorn for inferiors!" He agrees that maybe over the past eventful days the apartment has transformed from a luxury pad in to an Angolan civil war hand grenade impacted trench, "but that is none of his business!" The cool sea breeze is taking a break while the boys are taking a deep breath while considering their next step. But thanks to a hand full of Namibian dollars the taxi driver turns his traitor neck away from the shop owner and a new friend is speedily secured; aren't we all prostitutes! A statement which Bruce seems to disagree, however the counter argument that volunteering children over a pedestrian crossing gets blown away with the wind to the next daisy patch. 99% of these people are elderly who have grand children making it again a form of whoring, just this time for society. A real true altruistic example would be letting a homeless lady move her hairy unwashed ass from the kerb to sitting on your face! A fetid walrus fart or two later they are rolling past the former South African held enclave of Walvis Bay, which seems to be more of an ugly deep sea outpost than anything else and thus it is no wonder that the airport is not more than a shed containing two competing ticket offices. One representing the overpriced Air Namibia and the other the neglected South African Express. However, for an hour's flight to Cape Town the latter is chosen and to Shoetef's delight at least a few cans of beer could be obtained as substitutes of an offered inedible news agency sandwich, which made him forgive the impolite airport staff service at the bush airport, who believe that it is appropriate to lecture upon a person's free speech declaration that the place is a shit hole. "At least clean the god damn lavatory you lazy Fffff......" To extend their annoyance Shoetef commences catching roaming cockroaches and giving them names of African presidents, like Mubarak, Mobuto, Francisco Macias Nguema, General Sani Abacha...

Cape Town airport greets the travelers very pleasantly with its efficiency, cleanliness and quick immigration processing well above par with its more frequently used competitor Oliver Tambo. The arrival continues its smooth ride with the taxi trip to down town where soon thereafter our alcohol motorized organisms find themselves in a new-found paradise: Bobs Bar! What a great place to feel like Chacma baboons consuming sweet fruits in fluid form. Albeit not stealing their drinks, our good primates did feel like royal apes by highly appreciating the cheap price. But like the tide comes in and goes out, so did Shoetef and Bruce having to find a suitable tree branch to crash for the next few nights. And sometimes alcohol can result in changing a person's attitude from being relaxed to a full-scale nuisance, in this case giving Shoetef his first gray strain of pubes hair through Bruce's drama queen dancing like being seventeen but trapped in a body of a seventy year old spoiled grandmother! A normal person would think that when consuming hop tea that a normal bed would suffice, but not for Bruce. And thus, Long Street is becoming Shoetef's alley of torture all the way to the top of the hill where finally a place is declared as acceptable, just! And it is kissing Table Mountain's butt. The accommodation is so rustic that even a fart makes the wooden floor creak and the pool consists of a small concrete formed seat in a miniature sized roman stile fountain, where it is a struggle to fit a carton of piss in. But the pain does not stop here. Bruce demands for a shower, plus he desires to powder his nose. Shoetef is close to reaching boiling point, grabs Bruce's throat, chokes the sadomasochist's funnel of life until a squeaking barn yard pig's voice of defeat emanates; he pleads for mercy. That is however not yet good enough, making the poor fried flour face slowly turn in to a blueberry jam dunked doughball* releasing a final yelping of offering free shots and Black Label oral rinsing. The viking defeats his Anglo-Saxon knight, who should appreciate this striking episode as a lucky escape; hundred years ago Nordic pillaging was rough resulting in loss of limbs while occasionally maintaining an injurer's cock sucking abilities. Bob's Bar returns quickly and gloriously to universe's revolving center of gravity. With night approaching local nightingales commence chirping their way towards this sacred deemed place of amusement, where a few dressed up lasses are invited to join the drinking exercise. Sequentially the initial distilled batch starts sleeping on the table with one of the eagerly re-hydration souls falling off her chair. All funny games until when oh lord oh mercy, an African lady enters the bar with knockers exceeding the height of the mountain behind them! They seemed to be able to cause more damage than Twin Peaks' paranormal events. With the fermented juices their part of brightening up the day the thick cloud cover follows by disappearing; may smiling sun rays shine over Yodlers Peak and Champagne Castle!! And may some tittie slapping get the nipples hard enough to grow out like coat hangers. This command ultimately goes too far for the homosexual bar tenders and the boys give a good bye kiss on each over ripe nipple; they are so hard that they can carry Bruce's umbrella!

Day 28

Following a breakfast containing some ugly soft bikkies, Bruce sees an advertisement for the casino megapolis Sun City which lies 200 plus clicks* to the west of Joburg making him to annoyingly distract concentration towards spending (again) a few days in the Kalahari's back yard.

> *- Hey Mate, we could do a few days gambling there.*
> *- Ah Bruce, crap in a bucket, empty it over yourself and find the*
> *hidden clue of last night's dinner. I was not all too long ago in*
> *Mpumalanga casino participating at a depressing wank festival.*

Mpumalanga, Gauteng, Tshwane… typical full retarded African politicians, changing locality names matching whatever kind of last century memorable dwarf mongoose being sacrificed by a witch doctor, who caught himself on fire and hence the story survived a few years or some greedy chief who sold off his daughters in to slavery for a piece of shining glass or a town steeling the cows from a far smaller group of opposing bush bashers, decimated because they even sold off their wives, this time to fat walruses! Attitudes just like some African gentlemen leaders still exercise nowadays! There seems to be plenty for spending big bucks for new public statues, artifacts, pompous political rallies and shiny official correspondence letter heads while brothers, sisters and children are starving. In many cases the poor are being unconsciously sarcastically sold as African progressive development resourcing potential, while not allowing them to wake up from their dream and for critics, well nightmares are a product of white supremacists!

- Oh common you stranded Son of Thor! It would be a few days fun. And you could even have a game of golf between wild animals. How about that? Puss puss puss?
- At least the cream skimmers* do show sometimes some solidarity to others. When Somalia, Pakistan or any other Muslim country is raped it is usually again western countries who tend to take up aiding the poor buggers, who in some cases are actively breeding future fighters against those feeding them; there are ungrateful bomb chuckers* keen on being mean. Look at France! Yes, every society is rooted by some form of evilness including gambling....
- Hey Shoetef, enough diverging irrelevant yarning*; you feral moon face! Fuck you to Uranus with political correctness. I am just making plans for more fun after this place goes dry. Or after you have ruined all...
- Take it easy Fury! You sleep through half of the action. Nah, still not convinced about visiting an alternative desert septic tank.
- The whole joint seems to be a massive resort with heaps of stuff. As said world renown golf course, theme parks offering elephant rides and... of course lion cuddling!
- Hey, what about first finding out if there is anything burlesque on offer.
- Hmmmnnn, well...

30 Minutes later Bruce rocks up at the internet cafe and finally a day's plan of attack can be made. As the sun is still shining, why not jump on to a mini-van bus service and tackle the Table Mountain. Of course by cable car. This isn't a sports activity holiday nor any healthy fundraiser collection promoting marathon or an event where money spending grudges do not know of alternatives to pump up their adrenaline. The harsh local reality returns when firstly it takes more than a roadie to reach the valley station. Plenty of bends on a flattish grade sloped road. But then the downhill ticket's price makes the poor man's champagne rumble in their stomachs. "Verdomp*! Shall we really walk down that freaking mountain? What can happen…?". An additional back lash occurs when reaching the top of the mountain. The fog has not gone to lunch and is

screwing up any potential views including hearing disappointment coming from the nearby leper colony of picture taking addicted Asians fearing a loss of face, but the absolute environment ravaging fact is that no mountaineering lagers can be secured. "Verdomp*!" After the realizing the slap on to their thirsty mouths rain creeps in. "Fuck that shit, I don't drink with my whelping toupée*!" To make most of the situation they call the task of trekking down the 1000 meters altitude in Australian hiking shoes as the Prospectors' Trail to Golden Castle Lager… If the god of weather would have been around, the guys would have given the deity a proper dishing out of their thong's wet rubber soles, each smacking a facial cheek to purple fairy floss. Therefore it shall be written in the grand books of heroism this torturous hike is conquered on bare foot! Over big rocks. Over small stones. Through freezing cold streams. Through little canyons with high velocity flows. Actively playing a jump and run game, just without being able to collect any rewards on the way. At least there are no electrical escalators replicating the snake bypassing ladders to shoot a person up the god damn slope again! And instead of being saved with a full treasure chest, it is a rickety half occupied mini-van whereby lucky the gangsters kept to themselves down in the Cape Flats. When back in town poor Bruce is needing a prolonged beauty sleep while Shoetef takes up interest on street artistry interest at the Waterfront; but not without adjusting his views through beer while defending himself from crooks attempting to sell stolen goods.

Day 29

"Aaaaaahhhhh, my freaking bones hurt. Stupid trekking. Stupid tourist rip off mountain." Shoetef gets out of bed, releases his womb raider and assesses its functioning potential. At least this action distracts from the pain until… the door opens and god damn Bruce walks in. Like a mother entering the room of her teenage son and catching him straight out wanking!

- God damn you horny ass. What are you doing?
- Aaahhhh, I guess fucking nothing! Or shall we call it fuck all!?!?

- You horny ass, you could have released your hamstrung yesterday at Bob's bar!!

- What? Cats choking on Chewbacca's hairy sea urchins? I was there early and later. No sign of you. Let's go now and grab some fish sandwich!*

- Sorry was a quickie literally. Had within a few minutes an interested lady who took me out showing down town. Disco, dagga, back to dancing and so on and so forth until we ended in an upmarket hotel for some horizontal yoga.*

- You soulless egoistic piece of denigration! May your prick get a disease, turn black, disintegrate from your junk trunk and get eaten by a laboratory zombie rat with a human ear growing on its back to better hear you scream!

- Stop playing shingle face! You look like you're still freshly disembarked from a side door washing machine. Chewed up and spat out like a tough piece of beef jerky or biltong as they say here in some kind of Nazi lingo infused slang.*

- Ah get fucked.

- Ha! That has already happened!

In this moment Shoetef jumps on to Bruce, locks his jaws, bagdrags* the bastard, pulls up his pants down and leaves the scene. With a shock of the day combined with yesterday's dagga* Bruce is feeling queasy, wishing he had some kind of fury, fluffy, squeeze toy to hold on, but manages unharmed to crawl back to his bed and renew his license of rest where he concludes that Shoetef rips off quicker than water drenched toilet paper.

After leaving the accommodation and realizing that Bob's Bar does not open until late afternoon, Shoetef ends up stranded in front of Cape Town's Castle where after a few tiring meters around its perimeter medicinal beer is imminently required. It also allows obtaining some fresh local inspired ideas on where and what can be done without exercising the body strenuously. The sore limbs support his opinion that sport should be limited to television; preferably something easy to follow like lesbian mud wrestling. People can exaggerate sports, especially men thinking highly of themselves as competitive machines whereby often lacking average intelligence, often at glory's fading ending up immitating their spectators as fat apocalyptic couch potatoes with a never-ending hunger for junk food.

An hour later and Shoetef is on the train towards south-east dodging gangster paradise Mitchells Plain. On approach to Kalk Bay a majestic view opens, one of Earth's most spectacular infrastructure surfaces: Two pubs with direct entry from the train station platform!! And both squeezed nicely between the tracks and the ocean. The first an upscale brasserie, just right to regain hydration while the latter is a Cuban cocktail bar accommodating wonderfully savoir vivre* of watching the bypassing storm front while snacking on mojitos, spicy stuffed peppers and cigars. On he flip side, white sharks chase dolphins away so does the place go useless regarding picking up girls. He soon misses Bob's bar where at night's befalling it is time to check the aviary cage to see if a nightingale or two might have itchy wings to fly away on a short migration towards being discovered by an ornithologist offering an entire froth filled bird bath. And as Bruce is still not to be seen, the entire fountain of joy may all belong to him! Two B52s and luck strikes. Two nurses are celebrating their start in to the weekend. A quick greet and meet exchange is done followed by both joining in for a few fun drinks until one makes a runner before getting too heavy pickled. Some kind of husband and kid story is served while Shoetef remains ignorant as the prettier gazelle stays back for law and order maintenance in the Great Karoo, "booohooo!" After a few more shots the two head over the road to a club full of ladies seeking cashed up gentlemen. The disco light strobe flashes a pink light over the otherwise barren concrete walls and at one side there are two camping gear tables with very basic wooden seated chairs on slim steel frames while on the far end a bored bar maid is waving towards the somewhat unexpected guests as the venturing in to this dark space evolves tackling a flight of stairs promoting thirst whereby the relieving black label six pack is heavily overpriced. It seems they are the dim lit whorehouse's only income of the night whereby the room costs represent poorer value than the nutrition tag on a can of baked beans. Another few Rands out of the bands and both are inside their own tiny designated adult playground; a very basic room with a single bed, barren walls, no sexual simulating decoration and a shared squatting thunder box. At least it is clean, no bugs, no ants, no Zulu war dance performing squirrels and a bucket of ice for free to keep the valuable bottles of hop tea content. The lady herself is not anymore the youngest, but for 40 still in very sexy shape decorating a flat and flabby free stomach unlike some of the to be bitten desiring meat pies back home. Zero stretch marks, nor signs of a caesarian cut and it is Shoetef's first experience where a more mature lady has taken upon the efforts to cleanly shave her vulva bump plus carefully also removed any hairs along the flappers' brim. In the earlier millennium days what is perceived as the norm with younger girls remains exotic for ladies in their 30s. Some do it purposefully to dislike men whose preferences are a dry and clean desert over a moist rain forest. Plus flossing teeth belongs to the bath room! Some men do try to avoid getting an eye poked out when going down and who knows what organic material like decomposing algae can be found seeking refuge in her map of Tasmania. But Shoetef admits that men can do better here too and so is his hard phallus reaching to the sky from the stem breaking out of nature's growth removed viscera flats.

Day 30

"Clap your hands, Bruce makes an appearance!" After receiving an update that his new found love enjoys splurging money more than him and successfully relieved him beyond dick putty an inner urge to forgive provides Shoetef just sufficiently a good deed of the day.

> - *You silly poor bugger. Your parents must have been so smart that when they first bought a color teevee they ordered a red one.*
> - *You low ranging self-singing Soprano rub burner, beat it!! A sharp tongue is no indication of a keen mind.*
> - *Well I did have thoughts if your parents were alien siblings, just lower class than Clark Kent and Co, say rather like a pussy sniffing Ferengi*... and thus do desire to ask you what your outsider thoughts on human race are...*

- Well until a few minutes ago I was hungry for breakfast, but now I am fed up!!!

- Alright Brucey baby, shall stop being obnoxious and cease any tongue diarrhea before causing any thought constipation. Else will have to declare that in your case abortion would have been the solution!

Conclusively Bruce is not almighty. After highlighting Shoetef that affordable and regular scheduled circum navigating tourist buses exist he urges to hit the road to Kirstenbosch to satisfy a new interest in botany. As being in the rain season's back end the Mediterranean vegetated slopes are embracing spring life and like all good places beyond shopping center center bottled water hoarding suburban Hogwarts small shops too are offering travel provisions. When entering the gardens Shoetef's mind drifts towards the blossoming of virgin flowers and how they can be softly corrupted or less softly like a pasha pleasuring his harem chicks through one big reverse gangbang session. Reality returns when they climb up a steep slope to a small waterfall. Shoetef's mind patterns adjusts to, "lovely secluded place for a polygamist master's concubines to wash, brush and beautify themselves!". Bruce slowly realizes that his friend of nuisance is slowly showing signs of being stressed in an environment far too natural for his physical and mental condition. He retrieves a remedial beer out of his man bag. "Mate, don't grow long hair or you'll go full scale retard with an upstairs bun while the ego ride makes you go quite on the downstairs' gun!" To make the scene feel like a bush man's romantic dream come true, the water pounding down Cape Town's house mountain shows a yellow brownish color replicating a pigmentation similarly to malty Indian pale ale. Like Neptune jerking off with a loud ape yell in to the ocean the Castle Lager can lid is ripped off and consumed similarly to a fat kid having a fast food outlet to himself post a week long's diet. The juice of joy is funneled down faster than a cheetah running post exposure to truck full of energy drinks. To fulfill the initial part of the day close to perfection, the in the midst of the beautiful flora setting placed restaurant decides to serve the guys morning dew blossom replicating sweet smelling bobotie* with millipap*. As a rare moment the two guests showed decency by letting the waiter choose the accomplishing wine; a lighter Merlot from the Veenwouden Private Cellar produced in the nearby Paarl region. Albeit Shoetef afterwards returning back to a shlucking* hard habit by ordering a few Black Labels as wash downs.

First a smoke and then the two jump on to the next passing bus which meanders along the park's edge, over a mountain pass where passing a few small lush properties offering asylum to cozy homesteads the landscape quickly changes to shanty towns bonding on the hill sides like glue, but not super glue as the next heavy rain event will dislodge them exposing the residents already trying to make ends meet to increased struggling and deprivation to the basics of Maslow's pyramid. The next stop is the pier at Houts Bay where two smiling blond farmer's daughters, giggling twins talking in synchronization greet the travelers in a manner that they could well partake in a horror movie of murderous barbie dolls luring new victims with their artwork soap where nostril pleasuring aromas hide their evil agenda using body fat as soap founding material. Every stupid spoken word is on a bilingual polyglot dot sending a cold shower down the back of Shoetef. It does not matter that they are dressed in pink high heels, beautiful legs ending in sexy color matching small sized dresses allowing their busty décolleté* shine out in to the southern hemisphere's day light to allow for successful eye catching. Still the way they talk is driving Shoetef up a tree like a monkey escaping a horde of vicious hyenas. One beer and the next bus gets him out and away from any yet to go rotten tomatoes!

Day 31

Thanks to a few quite sun set drinks at Sea Point, followed by Shoetef showing Bruce a pub or two at the Waterfront where both slowly find positive stimulus through greasing the machinery to as the French say "à pointe" for concluding friction less wild water rafting at Bob's Bar; river levels went never beyond laminar flow conditions meaning the atoms behaved! It is now 4am and the two are ready to move onward to the airport. Cape Town is charming but its exposure to rainy, cold winter weather makes this corner of Africa rather a paradise for Siberian leopards, saber-tooth and fury mammoths; not as sexy as the free beer swimming ebony crocodiles. The quick movement of the two not only surprises the hotel staff, but also the taxi driver. Shoetef smells like an old barrel of aged rum left in the corner for a century. Bruce is still determined to experience Sun City and gets himself a cheap flight out, but the gamble goes sour as the roulette ball lands on zero. Two minutes after purchasing the ticket the flight's delay is announced. "Bruce, there you go with being a cheap ass and good luck getting in to Bophuthatswana by night! You might even bump in to some of the Waco* stile parading tears spraying Afrikaner Weerstandsbeweging (AWB) spawns while still trying to understand karma to what occurred to their land greedy leader's death while likely chucking a vicious giggle when commemorating the taring and feathering of van Jaarsfeld." However he remains clueless about taking direction. Shoetef is getting chirpy for a beer and thus is procrastinating to commence roaming the nearby airline offices. But this airport lacks a Keg Pub. Surprisingly quickly an opportunity to score a good deal is found with a soon departing winged vessel to Durban.

> *- Brucie babe enjoy your few days rest at the dice and card playing joint!!! Don't look too deep in to your chip bucket or else the one armed bandit turns in to dark skinned flesh and grabs your cock inserting oral cavity!*
> *- Shoetef, hope you keep your hands to yourself. Give those young berries a suave period to reflect on their innocence before enacting in being their soul dissolving lemon!!*
> *- In three days? Joburg? That is you don't start smoking ylang-ylang or do any other coconut crazy imbecile mischief with any collectors and having to live on brown gone mango tree fodder!!!*
> *- Yep, I shall be like a virgin in a chaste!*
> *- Yeah right you self declared Scandinavian dolichocephalic skull!! The brittle Lego construction of your socialist attitude is limited to hyperventilating on forest collected elderberry blossoms being squashed by Stockholm bimbos' feet in to cordial with an ending of receiving free blowjobs from those blond open sandwiches post getting soaked by a six pack of mid strength øl*. Honestly your fairy tales are worse than a troll mother believing that her son is handsome!!*

Bruce's adventure ride ends here. Well at least for a few days to allow Shoetef to retreat in searching his inner depth, which is bluntly put in words shitting out beer worms after a night out transforming himself in to a mutant adoring a cheese cake's passion fruit jelly top layer! Needless to say that Bruce is spending the night in an airport hotel boring himself to dead with free to air television due to being too scared investigating the upbeat nightlife of Johannesburg. Not even the music channel is screening any raving scenes from its one arm turn table machine DJ Black Coffee. And further Bruce's memories of Sun City are confined to losing money and sedating himself with top shelf spirits with some seedy rich animal trophy hunting oligarchs from Siberia. He did not bother spending any time in the water park, nor doing a safari in the malaria free Pilanesberg National Park. No visiting of a movie theater, nor a cabaret; just watching the ball rolling on the roulette spinning wheel while taking tag teaming bad choices between red and black. Here the Chinese are the looked after like masters; and that might be a wise choice...

Day 32

- Wake up! Wake up! You drunk stupid English man, wake up!!
- Huh, what the fuck? Where am I?
- Durban Beach, Sir. I want to clean the Marine Parade Loopvlak.
- Fuck, what is a loopidoopiii what ever thing? I thought bleached slang is not spoken here!?!?!
- Get up and stop ramming your boner in to the concrete crevice!!
- Ah for fuck sake, don't tell me I'm getting again Francoised!?!

- Yes Sir, you ran away from the dessert sands to make yourself a total freaking idiot in front of a new found Indian drunken com padre who drugged you and attempted to make millipapp out of you, silly fucking pommy heritage stamped foul mouthed ginger minger!!*

- Aaaaaahhhhh, first to start off, I ain't an island monkey!! Wait, I am neither a… Anyway I guess thanks for getting me out of a pickle. You said, Indian, hmmmnnnn would not mind some lime and chili pickle condiments on a curry or so. At least it would get the desire of a cheap scotch brandy infused diarrhea lose asshole squirting gonzo party over.

- Can do. Hmmmnnn, I'm in need for some camera work help…

- Explain. Spill the brainy beans!

- I'm on my way up north trying to find a good opportunity for wildlife pictures. Was thinking either a haai or a croco at St Lucia…*

- I like getting high! St Lucia sounds like tropical drinks on the beach, served by some yummi black momma manufactured honey booboo, hmmmmnnnn….

- You are an etterkop with a dopkaas* mind!!*

- Fok julle naiers, go kak in jou modders poes!*

#stun#

After some early breakfast bunny chow and a few local brewed frothies*, the challenge of finding Shoetef's booked accommodation comes up as next on the to do list. "But first more drinkies please!" Thanks to somehow remembering that he searched for a place downtown behind a few rows of skyscrapers lining the marina, just as he did unlovingly with Bruce in Cape Town, the memory of having a quick feed at Nando's surfaces. It had to be close to a Shoprite as cheap booze was safely secured before heading downtown for a sedated session with these unknown Indian guys. Finally after clueless navigating around the run down hotel is found. While grabbing his belongings and checking if all items with exception of a few Rands are still available he is considering having a shower. The idea is quickly dismissed. Lifting a loose tile next to the dunny* exposes a nasty cockroach hood, just without a basketball court! The hangover is well beyond normal pain threshold and as the tap water is brown the aspirin is swallowed with curing juices from the only surviving spirit bottle hidden in the mini bar fridge. After a strong verbal complaint by Francois, "jou vokken stink vuil geaborteerde fetus damduiker*!", both make a runner. They hastily dive towards north eagerly trying to reach the highway. Even Francois seemed to be nervous and restless. But for now he is clearly the master and Shoetef is more than happy in knowing that nothing is left back for any rats housing the big lavatory with a polished foreshore. No real nightlife and heaps of hidden gangsters as the city itself is able to fly below the radar thanks to other city's lime light position; and lime light in color they all were indeed.

Francois is keen to find any opportunities for law disrespecting actions in Richards Bay, as it is known by locals as the occult worshiping center of South Africa. Shoetef still experiencing sedating influences, but slowly finding his liking back to being numb in intelligence, liked the suggestion as it means that he might get a change of being lucky enough to get some white meat put on the plate. The Zulus might believe in traditional witch doctor bone chucking reading, dried gnu penis powder snorting promoting longevity health and showing their spears up their own rear ends as means to keep quite, but no way would they ever become Lucifer's naughty kinky daughters!! At the first petrol station post leaving the highway, Francois leaps out of the car towards a rogue looking obese bearded AWB lose moose jellybean* basher. It nearly seems that they knew each other, which somewhat is freaking scary. Slowly Shoetef feels in need for some breakfast. Well it is surely time to inform Francois that he is at least thirsty and retrieving to the unclean lavatories is deemed as first step towards physical recovery. While entering the ablution block, a pungent smell of spilled local home brew floats in the air towards him, followed by searching for an elephant sized toilet roll to clean up the mess. Welcome to Africa son, regain your squirting skills! Aaaaahhhhh, and shit splatters all over and out the toilet cistern. Lucky there is a knock on the door and a warm bottle of dark amber fluid is passed through. But not without some more Africans swearing, footsak*! Ag you hol man, blerrie boudkapping poeskak*!! Thanks to the hoppy survival ration Shoetef even manages to retain his hunger for a meat pie, which to his major disappointment had to be consumed without tomato sauce. Yes, some cultural aspects are similar to home, "but really no sauce!?!?" An hour later St Lucia appears, where after a short circuit through the town they halt at the yacht club to obtain another package of delicious cans. And to their luck they are also provided a free plastic bag filled with ice cubes to ensure the party goes on. As next Francois is hell keen to cross the river just upstream of the car park where he spots a narrow pass rather than taking a detour of several 100 meters over the nearby sand bank.

- Mate, narrow passage mean either deeper waters or quicker flows; neither all too great in our circumstance.
- Common Shoetef, take it easy with the piss. A drunken soldier is of no use in the war.
- Huh, mate one thing I don't like is crocs and this stinking slym sloot smell doesn't really get my ass in to overtaking gear.*
- Now be a bloody viking and not a stink poes!
- Spaiker yourself! Fucking crocs are advertised throughout this entire mosquito infested pielkop* kakking resort and I ain't sure you are knowing what ya doing.*
- Hey kotskop, don't listen to those jellybeans over there, I've got the camera and my light set, you grab the rucksack and time for you to show me how to wrestle a croc. You mad suig piels* tell the rest of world that this is your weekend time killer.*
- Yeah, but not sure if these babies are as nice as the freshies…*
- Shoetef, time to prove that you can whisper in the ear of a croc, you told me that you've done this shit before in some Amazonian swamp. Don't tell me that a croc came out of a women's rear!?
- You fucking annoying anus mask, those were ankle biters compared to the shit they are marketing at the safari joints here. Until the day it has been proven that there is plenty of piss in heaven, I ain't gonna be suiciiilI….*
#Gulp# #Splash# It is quite. Nothing is visible. "Where the fuck is Francois?"

4 A FEW MOONS AGO...

Francois' unexpected, fast disappearance makes Shoetef remember how he lost his own grandfather. The man who made him feel like a king with rights well beyond the average citizen, while the maid, gardener and stable boy lived in a sanitary lacking basic masonry building at the back of the property. They all shared one big room where in the evening they cooked up what ever tin food was given as reimbursement for their efforts, which one must say, was not of great efficiency due to tiredness, slackness, disinterest; generally attitudes which contributed to a lesser favorable reputation of many high flying and hoping European visitors whose perceptions were and still are often crushed brutally early. In the evenings the laborers sat in their dire shelter gambling and trading their thefts along with consuming moon shine, bong and anything doable for a bonking parties. Shoetef was a bastard born in to the racist Safa* society before Apartheid fell!! As the tides retrieved far earlier in other parts of this exquisite land mass, the influence of the outsiders ensured a wealth in South Africa while making their darker skinned genealogical brothers jealous long beyond return of being again the masters of the land. Maybe one day when the Eastern aid loses its golden shining, maybe then at least the under historical British occupied influence catchment's children might conceive that there were economic benefits existing of this admitting unfair coexistence. The French remain well in to the 21st century disinterested in mutual benefiting trade while Asian investors largely sport fake compassion.

Shoetef saw how the family's real estate vanished through dodgy deals, silly family decisions and a ruthless nascent establishment inheriting. The years post implementation of democracy reiterated fear of a new class arrogance. The new established political elite operated not necessarily with much cleverness. One president boasted having sex with diseased women and explaining that a good shower cleans off all organic mean traces. Some whites however managed to save their bacon safely through to the rainbow nation's birth years, but he could not give a damn about this decaying society. Whinging whites who have lost their privileges while still being paid by the lower seen castes versa an African population containing a lot of hate, not only against the formerly gloriously foaming whipped cream which is turning sour, but also against other tribal originating groups, especially any outsiders like Nigerian prawns. One of the family's ownership relieved property was basically infertile rock comprising a terrain incapable to allow a single bean stalk grow. Would be a waste to mention that the new land owners even considered doing anything other then mantling a tin shack to drink piss under cover. The new lucky bunch is more interested at lingering around the local chicken shack inhaling glue and drinking home brew. Neighboring Rhodesia highlighted clearly essential psychological gaps of Africans lacking motivation towards taking up initiatives like producing beyond own needs, meaning when a year did not evolve in a favorable harvest, famous artists were flown in to some European paddock to stage aiding concerts, where ironically groups like Queen could rise from the ashes and sell more and get rich and then direct interest to something with a touch more hope. However, also looking back to the private services which previously most families could afford, one thing Shoetef did acknowledge is that many women show keen signs in giving entrepreneurship a go, but the patriarch run society deprived any larger scale success. Again here, not only because of the black man, but also the white man not being interested in developing a mutually benefiting civil society. The rot is deep. In his younger years Shoetef's uncle joined the mercenary where the poor fellow lost his health in Angola fighting rogue Cubans. Now the grand children of the originally exploring colonists are earning good cash on diamonds while partying at a bar in Havanna or Lisbon for that matter. After the civil war and with the fall of major allies the victorious communist led government had to open itself further towards the exploiting keen Neo-liberal capitalists representing an unexpected great opportunity to seed corruption to blossom up maximizing personal benefits from oil extraction. Luanda developed itself in to the world's most expensive city while most of the nation still vegetates as a homo sapiens waste disposal facility! The final straw of hypocrisy was the fact that many Westerners avoided visiting Africa and mingling with locals while believing they had a right to shame apartheid. For Shoetef it is disgust of disgust declaring the disgusting as a disgust. In many countries discrimination still legally exists. Australia for an example is prone to political correctness going in to overdrive of positively marketing affirmative action as a better outcome than awarding market's best qualified, artificially and in full knowledge creating lower value with the majority's incoming tax money. It is still discrimination, but the narrow minded society are kept at bay with free to air sports and cheap toast bread. Catholic school boys are in charge and nope they are neither interested in creating more globally human intelligence. Equality as an example is best achieved through promoting discriminatory applied white ribbon accreditation exercises whereby women who desire a fair dealing of cards rather than giving narcissists and bullies the lime light are excluded and hey, maybe if just stick to the fact the best person qualifies for what ever, even if it is a golden raspberry! The rot starts at school with having to give all children a medal as false avoidance step against them having to realize that they are just an average normal puzzle piece of society and ends with depressed crispness overdue mothers acting rather like blue gibbons when drunkenly picking up those ankle biters from school. Not to mention that somebody has to pay for all this first world problem theater, whereby the Catholic school boys have advantage over the cigarette smoking, beer drinking blue collar worker. In summary many Western countries nowadays strives on redistributing the unfairness instead of setting equal education for all, for an example stopping to subsidize private schools whereby continuously twisting and turning goal posts to justify the fat cat's nepotism. Sounds nearly like African politics!? Just with increasingly female senior managers who dislike men because of many interests, but mainly the stupidity of perceiving sport competitions as the highest luck feeling abode and any potential female threats from the rare rational thinking breed while happily in the escalator discussing in front of Shoetef the fashion status of their high heels or who does the best manicures. To date Shoetef actually believes in equal opportunities as else it would be boring like talking matters to a brick wall. But in his younger years he really perceived that as a nice guy you could assist in the continuous development of this great country; the result is ending up as a sour gone cheese cake topped with rotten mullberries. Australia has lost most of its funny, larrikin alike nuts and bolts, while being replaced with soft jelly minded selfie addicted plasma brains who are forcing people in to a world containing ever stricter guiding processes. Wide scale changes sometimes only happen because a my-loving person wakes up with a migraine from too much sweet white wine, has genital discomforts indicting menopausal mid-life crisis, getting overly angry because on breakfast television a Beverley Hills psychic answers a viewers question wrong, a rogue cockroach not being killed by the useless husband or just being pissed off that the expensive avocado is harder than daddy's stiff one breaking the toast when smashed on… "Yeah, would neither be surprised if the sprinkler showering backyard rat is jumping because the bread contains too much multicultural grains!?"

The death of his grandfather occurred nearby, further south at Blythedale Beach on a group of rock outcrop where smaller cliffs reach in to the point pointer infested ocean waters. The gray haired stud was a keen fisher and believed the biggest catches were made during unfavorable weather conditions. Once he even got a lightening strike on the Vaal's river bank which catapulted him several feet back wards where he smashed his hard stubborn head on to a thunder egg containing an outer ring of blue agate and within a bouquet of pink crystals. On the day of the grim reaper's door knocking the family first visited Durban's sea world museum where after observing the sea creatures made him eager to view them closer; in a frying pan rather than letting them happily swimming in their natural habitat, which seemingly fondled the interest of death in a similar fashion. While the late afternoon winds took up on intensity the water fielding Hannibal's heart pumped those easy excitable blood cells more ferociously through his veins. He had faced many challenges from enduring the second world as a young man which deprived him from participating at the Olympics, followed by escaping from the spreading communism, meaning leaving life as he knew and all his possessions back. Together with his wife they traveled west wards where later his daughters were born, of which one had cold temperature promoting kidney problems resulting in searching for a brighter future in warmer conditions. In nowadays views a person could call it the wandering of a racist from a seditious nationalistic fertile ground to a white supremacy stomping utopia. But like a cat losing its 9th life, on this day Shoetef's oldest known boisterous personality lost his final life through straying out just before a swollen swale produced a thundering wave topping the sought refuge on the safe perceived rocky outcrop meters and swooping up the daredevil of a fisherman, dragging him down to the depths were he made his final kiss on

Neptune's barren rock ass! It was the moment where the deity's bung hole did a nasty fart smashing the human potato between floating debris and a human swallowing underwater dragging current with a marine geyser doing the final touch of death; he had saddled one his ancestral steppe horse to join the ride towards Nirvana. The family struggled to digest the event which took over 20 years to set up a barren wooden cross on top of his grave. It resulted in a drifting apart between the siblings. His uncle sought refuge to moan life's grievances through a decaffeinated social circle encompassing a life of slavery and acceptance deprivation by his wife's family who in return were always happily siphoning off money coming from the financially ruined grandmother. She in return converted to an evangelistic church which relished loving attitudes towards thee white neighbors while wishing the hell's gates to open for non worthy seen jellowogs*. Yes, these people truly looked up to leaders like the Bush family who cherished publicly Christian values on Sundays while returning to work on Monday to flick the on electrical chair switch to grill the next guilty by looks and race determined poor devil's possessed soul.

For the viking's soul, life is rather one of being playful than be eaten by some polycephaly conditioned ancient bush snake. And with races, it won't change in color like television's evolution many decades ago. Crap smells bad despite the characteristics of the owner's hindquarters!

5 BACKING OUT

A return to Day 32...

What the fuck, Francois…? No sign, just nothing. No visible crocodiles. No visible waves. No signs of blood. Shoetef runs the few meter and jumps right at the spot where Francois disappeared. To no avail, but to the spilling out of the Castle can and neither to any luck of jumping on a critter smacking with the feet its greedy meat cleaver, even better poking the darn things' eyes out. There is dead beat nothing, not even a cold drink in his hands. Slowly the song from the car's CD emerges in his mind; Die Antwoord's SOS album blurring, "wat Pomp's fok all yella, fok all, fok all, fok all yella, me being burned like a frisket with no biscuit and no bat from da cricket to smash any wildebeastsket… fok all, fok all, fok all yella!! And fok da system, dis is still my song!!" What ever mutant brought the party to a halt, it seems like something malignant is screaming from its underworld restrained position, possibly shackled in a dark corner of the universe asking for acknowledgment from somebody's ma's stink poes in a fish paste jar!! "I'm a rich bitch in need of a super friend", but Die Antwoord cannot offer an adequate answer neither, just more mind sanity insulting singing of "stomp around, stomp around, party is over, ek ain't vrot in a tronk*!" Conclusively some fancy dagga* puff on the way out of this joint could sweeten the day… "Well for fuck sake, first a fresh tinnie* is all needed to start relaxing those nerves!" Shoetef turns around and runs for his life out of the murky river waters. While he is finding means to excel in mutating towards a flying hoover craft, the local observing taxi guys are laughing their posteriors off while being sedated on petrol fumes. Could those blockheads be the next brick shitting curse or his divine saviors who won't melktert* him around? What ever choices exist, a reasonable alternative is not coming to mind. The guys saw the two wading out and could play up as fokking moerskonts* poeskaks rather than maagd dogter poeslekkers*. Lucky there is an older guy without hair on his head and a port wine stained birth mark visually resembling Gorbachev's titkop*. He appears fair dinkum* enough for Shoetef and as it emerges he is not giving a compost stamper's slym sloot's* care about anything to do with Francois' disappearance. However, he still argues for a case asking an exorbitant price to get to the nearest railway station, which is in a place called Mtubatuba, "don't you guys get enough oral sex opportunities to avoid inventing such freaking names?". On arrival he kindly calms Shoetef down through assisting him catching the correct mini bus; squeezed in midst of a church congregation on wheels, all lacking the application of deodorant. One old bird responds, "God's unconditional love has no time for this!" But too late to notice as Shoetef's concentration diverts to being now in war of not ending up as a kotskop*. An amiable extra 1000 Rand provides relief in form of an early drop off at the Swaziland border crossing in to Lavumisa. Signs of diarrhea are pushing hard on the intestines making him feel he could soon achieve Olympic gold in spyt kakking*. But first he cannot resist shouting back to dooms land "Spayker you self en suig my piel, you fokken draadtrecking goffels*!" Then the boogie woooogiiiee of the warrior gut explodes like a water filled balloon hitting the tarmac, just here on an already unclean border town toilets, followed soon later by renting and sharing an unmaintained room with mozis in a self declared clinic which is harboring cockroaches as nurse replicas. It is as dire as being a thirsty stranded pirate at Somaliland's alcohol free Hargeisa port.

6 THE BOTCHED WEDDING

Day 1, 2005

After several weeks overseas including missing out riding the nearby occurring large wave on 26 December 2004, Shoetef decided it is time to break his old habits all together. He had already walked out of the door of his employer, middle fingers stuck high up in the air and thus is surviving as good as he can on what ever jobs surfaced, but it did not take long to get enough of the current working stint in Dubai which itself actually eventuated as an Indian culture related relief or in more suavely expressed a pleasant light weight diet of it. "Dubai is Indian, no doubt, but it is functioning!" He had set his eyes a few days ago on to Mauritius which is known for a harmonious multicultural society while remaining under a healthy leveling influence from the French and English making it one of the more developed African nations. Post card pictures are resting in his mind ensuring the night flight won't awaken any further mental disturbances. For the meantime he is absolutely finished with drinking over priced beers while professionally dealing with Western folk who either remained disgusted of both India and Middle East or who actually changed in to frantically loving the places; mainly the religions are attractive depending on taste for colors and chaos or the strict rules clearly defining the society's participants responsibilities. What he found difficult to understand is the opposition of men against these Christianity differing religions which ultimately for one you exchanged booze with plenty of weed and four wives while the more openly engaging women refused to understand that a path away meant giving up on personal liberties on a volunteer basis, in most cases for a back hair decorating future husband containing the hidden risk of an abusive family history. The final relief is the departure of an older friend met on previous travels, who resurfaced unexpectedly and being with time annoying. Chongstar claimed to come from Honkers* and was in beginning a relief not only from tree hugging attitude pink glass wearing foreigners, but also exercised a more down to earth drinking and smoking companion towards rehabilitate any tedious bus ride emanating sore patches on his rustydusty*. Initially it was amusing to see a guy act like a funny comedian marketing himself as a 30 year old virgin imitating a freshly from the butcher escaped chook*, in this case a prestigious English college with subsequent inheritance of a tedious working experience in the financial market for a banking conglomerate prone to adamantly demanding voluntold* aptitudes all while in the back ground being micro managed by a tiger mum. While many seemed to be beyond their altruistic lip servicing aka still religiously believing that German rock bands had superior tunes, Scandinavian butter should not be used as lubricants, the further East you go the better the Vodka is and bland cheese filled schnitzels represented the world's number one culinary highlight, Chongstar managed to amuse with a funny yodeling which would make all Alpine slopes shed off snow quicker than an avalanche triggered by squeeze bag polka rhythms all while the local seemed to be pleasantly content of non cultural intrusive comments about their own terrible singing Bollywood film stars high on Himalayan fruit*. While the Westerners continued with their bullshitting open attitudes while maintaining an avoidance to try out any real local cultural experiences, Chongstar's worldly Neo-liberalism attitude was initially perceived as refreshingly progressive. But with time it slowly showed its real face; the pure love of greed and supremacy over what he called jaffers which replaced the racist word of kaffirs with intention to misuse a chocolate candy filled with orange flavored goo representing that inhabitants of Tamil Nadu are like black chocolate on the outside, that is not as sweet as the real deal combined with a bitter business making approach from within while lacking any nutritional benefits. His beliefs covered a wide range of hedonistic attitudes which did have some kind of resemblance to Shoetef's own ethic values opposing political correctness which mainly supported the conservative elite and associated attitudes of a continuous desire for a good time far away from these pathetic hypercritical snot slime licking porcelain doll heads, who upon his exposure tended to crack and seek healing with some egoism moral suiting glue! Or is it more like baking powder and yeast to get that sour cherry pudding rise again? To his astonishment

Chongstar went soft after their last night out drinking, squeezing some tears down his cheek and inquiring of Shoetef's travel plans to which there is no definite answer except for chasing the down any left back stains from the holy flying spaghetti monster. Shoetef is seeking a more peaceful setting to place his noodles and meatballs in a clean empty dish.

Day 2, 2005

The first laugh of the day arrives early, when a run down airport building emerges in plane window's view; it's length is insufficient to contain the entire location's name of Sir Seewoosagur Ramgoolam International Airport Plaisance Mauritius. Why the heck even try to attempt giving it such an arduous long name, which would have save some ink on the immigration cards. Although surrounded by ocean this commodity might not be so precious. "Do squids get a runny stool?" As a positive note the world commences to shine up when last night's cocktail memories surfaced and seeing the light at the tunnel's end indicating that more of those babies are awaiting! There is no hope for Shoetef; he is already a fucked up young adult. However, the level of trouble is still contained in manageable parameters. Also his manners are still within the reasonable expectations of his old girl, but leaving home has continuously given him a new meaning and context of life: Beer, bongs and boobs! The only shock is that the greeting came again from a person with Indian background including exercising the exotic head bobbling, making him think along the lines, "now here we go again and what on merry boysenberry hill does this really mean?" Shoetef admits he was too drunk and slept through any opportunity to gain knowledge through the in-flight magazine describing that over half of the island's population eats, thinks, talks, lives and scats curries as a national pride!

> - *Good morning mistah, whale cum to Mauritus, verrrryyy nice island.*
> - *Aaaahhhhh.*
> - *May I have your passport, Sirrrr…?*

The typical African contradicting white male self-esteem steaming attitude vanishes quickly enough to allow the Indian merged African bureaucracy regain contentedness to skillfully retake an undisturbed acting pace and opening the door for a warmer welcoming embrace by locals. Even the usually observed scam hungry airport located taxi drivers are offering reasonable prices for their service to transport the new arrival across the entire island's length from the southern sugar cane crops dressing its plains to the northern counterpart beyond the decline past the capital city plus Quatre Bornes where Shoetef indulges on an imagery tasting trip through the home producing local hop delicacies followed by a smooth checking in process at Grand Baie Hotel. The concierge and hotel owner's son is very polite, efficient professional, friendly and offers a free drink as a nice step towards feeling cozy abroad.

At a nearby beach shack a fresh popping sound emerges replicating decibel levels of when a young blossoms loses the integrity of her hymen; a cold Phoenix is cracked open starting the arvo session. Both, a dark skinned African lady and a white skinned lass with English heritage are providing good value for a well deserved gibberdabbadoo*. All goes good until their boyfriends make an appearance, which is akin to Shoetef saying, "damn, my A for Ave Maria is going to eventuate in to a B for Bye Maria!". Consequently he leaves for the next jungle juice bar on the main street corner with Papaya Road where he soon after taking a seat meets a matching drunken counterpart; a French speaking African alley cat on heat who graciously both after a few more cheap vodka brand containing drinks pukes pastel colored rainbows defying offering any invitations to gold digger as literally that pot headed serving chest is spewing golden juices in high reaching arches over the pedestrian path with a clear message to French tourists to keep their honeymoon to themselves or for those with children eluding that fairy tales can end badly when they don't shut their mouths for two seconds when told so to do. Further some of those poor souls learn that dirt cannot wash dirt, but dirt is not necessarily seen as dirt; just like manure is beloved by nature producing the fruits and vegetables which even negative thoughts exaggerating people consume. Although for some it is limited to a salad leaf in a burger at least eating has the potential for them to halt in hyperbolizing a drama from a non existent crisis and infecting others with their undignified distemper. To his delight on return to the hotel the entire kitchen staff knows of his Hansel and Gretel outing, feeling sorry for the poor bar tender having to be the cleaning up broom vroom bitch witch. The staff comprising of Indian expats received the update from the concierge, who was in hiding scanning the street while mainly the dish washers are playing rummy with the rule that the winner finishes the game in one stroke. Not as easy for an intoxicated warrior turned worrier, but there are worse events happening as the bets are low and the beers free. And the girl is stacked behind the beach bar where customers at night take a piss. Not very romantic but it is the safest option post 10pm. Self made bhajis, vegetable fritters and chicken lollipops are offered as the guys' mood is to celebrating a pre-weekend soiree. While hijacking the game as card cowboy Shoetef finds out that two of the staff have not seen the island beyond the hotel's roof terrace other than the freeway drive from the airport through the country's industrial belt and that at night. Well at least they would have seen the nation's most important land mark, the brewery! Thus, with some Scotch to finish off disinfecting the butchered taste buds and ensuring that the stomach has something more dense in its physics than beer to digest, a small plan for the next day is with unprofessional consultation chiseled in stone.

Day 3, 2005

The sun awakens the rum barrel made of flesh. He can hear the cars as his room is just above the main road circling the island with views right behind of the Indian Ocean shining its light opal colored blue with a minimal touch of green from shoreline dwelling algae towards a cloudless sky. The emerging conclusion is that yesterday was definitely a wonderful start in paradise! "Let's rock and roll!"

The late afternoon venturing out for few drinks at a beach shack just meters away reminds Shoetef of the simple things in life or better said, with not planning movements all too well ahead and letting the world take its pace including guiding an open-minded traveler who so far has avoided to fall treacherously on to his upstairs dome* and evolving him to some special kid syndrome, "in all honesty there are plenty IQ and EQ deficient psychos on this planet who seemingly can find new stupid annoyances like asking daily if you are OK as if they really would give a dehydrated white turned shit about you!" Freaking by imbeciles' bred doctrine of the first world attempts of verbally drugging you mental health resulting in making you then to actually feel depressed in a painful manner beyond perceiving loss of compliance allegiance with society as the sheep farming station owner is dressing you up as a herd betraying goat instead! These evangelist missionaries must be drugging themselves with the feelings of lords defending anti-Christ defamation acting gays while using their as weaponry designed words to in venture out towards lost frontiers where they continue finding means to analyze events negatively. Step by step configuring people believing that one day a nano mind controlling chip insertion is humanity's only cure; it will be the evolution beyond providing free bibles for the starving. The unappreciated mob must finally understand that words can feed, kumba-you-with-my-i-dot!!

To get the things cranking up, first port of call to enjoy some exotic yummy rummy mouth perfume is this morning's guarding front desk clerk. He is a nice enough fellow who introduces himself as Aadarsh while doing a motion of holding his hand high, flat with palm up moving it in the direction towards an older guy limping away eluding Shoetef with a retarded looking but proudly executed peacock dance that his pop is the hotel owner. Next he eagerly recommends a visit to the nearby memento junk house to meet his wife. It is not far away and some fresh air will do good. But before that he demands to serve breakfast. The rotten gummy bear taste in his room is not necessarily something he wants to expose the staff to; it for sure won't make them do a celebratory kuchipudi dance. The kitchen had already prepared two toasted ham and cheese sandwiches to ensure their English advocating guest remains content by having his gut thoroughly greased before venturing out in to paradise. But for Shoetef paradise does not necessarily contain cheap South African imported white toast bread and its commonly available glistening orange colored cheese. "Fuck, I know Australian cheddar is seen by many foreigners as a horrendous product, but it still dresses yellow, yellow, you understand yellow!?" Anyway, it is still a nice thoughtful gesture, appreciated rare customer treatment compared to the dismal service offered back home including beating a fry up breakfast where watery bacon goes along with tasteless saw dust spiked sausages, half green tomatoes and boring button mushrooms. "If you want culture in Australia, go buy a tub of yogurt!" With the day dreaming he slowly getting aware that the poor receptionist has been on shift since 6am while it is well after 12pm; thus prone to a lengthy suffering before death through the agony of starvation where the mouth dries up, the gear stick goes in to sexual parking and at late stage unsuccessful attempts to eat nutritious lacking tucker*. "Fuck those grainy pieces of dry soberness, I am after fluid bread to get my system going!! Phoenix, Phoenix shall make me rise like… Phoenix!! The brekkie* is all yours buddy, bon appetite mon ami. And don't fall off the chair when working hard! And next time get me some elephant road kill biltong, would ya!"

The perplexed concierge recommends to arrange a car. The current offer is 30 quid a day. While discussing Shoetef's eye wonders away desiring to met its counterpart pair, glossy shining soul gate keeping receptors circulating dark enlarged irises: Sanji, the house's shy daughter, but cheeky enough to swap the traditional sari and choli top with semi-tight blue jeans accustomed by a long sleeve lose silk blouse; depressingly preventing side boob views. Basically she is as minimally allowable dressed to not make her parents consider any strict virgin retaining measures. The unfolding seen of mutual liking development is not being unnoticed whereby the lucky man receives a few seconds later an offer to join for lunch consisting of traditional fish curry known as Cari Poisson including a French twist of mixing the coconut cream with miniature bread croutons to gain the sauce's thickness and using Dijonnaise mustard as the lime pickle base. Albeit all the nice talking, Shoetef's flirting skills are already known to be thicker and spicier than the meal's condiment, but which he fine tunes towards a smoother consistency when Sanji prematurely shows her good girl instincts aiming at teasing the bad boy… The air's swinging molecules are transporting her hormonal heated vibes unintentionally to furthest reaching corners in his nostrils similarly delicate in nature to a bloke farting while his albino cave dweller is inside her resulting in a small pleasuring earthquake! He is even allowed to accompany her back to work, but the follow up discussion is now remaining very superficial. He is doing some effort taking hard yard stints to not mention any perverted story text lines from Ron Jeremy or just simply swerve in to the overtaking lane by dropping his pants down and urgently relieving himself on a fangipanji tree or a hibiscus bush. He is holding back as albeit the existence of more flatulent acts, but it is not the right timing having to explain that fresh urine gives flowers an extra touch of blushing! For now manners must win! The final refuge de jour is again at the beach bar and as Murphy's law has it, last night's alcohol addict is there with darker eye rings than her African skin, but all in position for a healthy cougar prowling dash! Yes she would not get angry on any piss turding around.

As surprisingly like a Nubian tribal leader volunteering himself in to Egyptian slavery Sanji's brother pops up; and with him a rare drop of rum due to national sugar cane distilling prohibition laws. However, in the northern flats behind the beaches stretching from Port Louis to the mystic, in rough weather sailor men challenging Cape Malheureux and past the eastern cape of Lafayette where subsequently the dream beaches for upmarket tourist make their appearance hidden groves honoring of rummy-bummylicious have remained as historical part of a harsh island dwelling life; cheap grog soothing working class' pain. Going to buy expensive low quality brandy remains for many people not an option, but do it yourself with the help of a basic distillery is not unattainable and offers a welcoming numbing post a sweaty day in the sticks while maintaining hope of getting rich through finding the absolute last dodo bird. At a glance of a rare sober moment Shoetef reminds himself that maybe the concierge is on a mission to assess his behavior! Hmmmnnn, the Indians and Africans are neither known to be the biggest brother loving chum buddies. In midst of Apartheid South Africa there was a famous incident where the late Mahatma Ghandi refused to leave the first class train wagon for the racial allocated second class while all together avoiding the for blacks reserved third class. The division of these two ethnic groups was visually never as evident compared to the wider gap existing between Caucasian cheese cakes and continental locals, but it still lingered onward for decades with secret kept explosive potentials which is destined to unfold with Mao's children expanding national chauvinism through the yet unknown belt and road project where as part dragon blood is infused in to several African located economies to the cost of reintroducing a recreated two class system. The result will be wide scale suppression requiring dissatisfaction; an example will be the reinstatement of Kenya's Nairobi Mombasa railway line where construction, maintenance and operations are agreed as a foreigner run affair. With the revolving towards dissolving this mind cloud the previously relaxed African grog pig is slowly mutating towards an impatient swamp monster where a momentarily look in to her empty eyes indicates Shoetef to immediately pull out of the game by giving a mentally too quick to follow eloquent flick.

Shoetef is in need to overcome his love for strawberry mud cake. He returns immediately back to hotel and joins in to the session where two pantry fossicking* curry bashing nippers* are initiated. Soon after the lame ritual Sanji makes a leap away from her parent's value exercising expectations to partake in celebrations through ordering a cocktail over settling to a lesser spirituality tangy making mocktail. And she is not stopping at one resulting in the sun setting itself over a small cue of empty glasses. Then one of the Punjabi youngsters attempts to not only reduce the likelihood of having to peer drink his way towards torturous territory, but also as avoidance measure having to shout a wallet harming round. He directs the jolly discussion towards shit stirring and initiates a discussion which is known that Aadarsh will not appreciated especially if it originates from a friable mouthing co-worker.

- I have heard that your family has historical ties with deeper Africa far away from this mellow island life?
- Hmmmnnn, the beliefs of the stupid can result in anger; honor the belongings of the great minds and avoid remnants emanating from lesser gifted.
- Oh big mitr! I do not desire to build a union of wicked words, however not all are like coconuts; tough on the outside but when cracked refreshing and nourishing.*
- Just be made aware that you are entering a world beyond curry cooking where the honey of some tongues originate from a poisonous chalice. You are a Punjabi where coconuts do not grow, so shall you be made aware that riches should be treasured

as jealousy can lead to a person having do the biggest sacrifice one can ever do, that is your own life! And when going down slippery paths decisive and misleading hope will eat your soul.

- Oh big mitr! Please do not look downwards as your psychological state might make you complacent towards recognizing the good, but you should be humbly keep self-esteem to open yourself to the gift of being only a little puzzle piece on the game's board. If questions are not raised, knowledge can get eternally lost.*

- Yes, you might be right, but consider that patients is a virtue in gaining the truth which together with contentment and mercy is the path towards a great mind! Currently I do not desire to reach out to you as my forefathers' search for happiness led them in to the open arms of Vetala only to have their consciousness torn away like fresh flesh and spat out; just like what you usually do with your chicken lollipops!*

- Oh big…

- My dear jig! Look at Shoetef, being content with the surroundings. Our family tried their luck on the African mainland and...*

- Never say never…!

- Well, thank you Sanji!?!?

Day 4, 2005

After some late-night stomach churning, the own inflicted hunger games are resurrecting their reappearance and after hard laboring of choking up some urine, it is definitely time to stop sacrificing free food to Pancha Mama. A minute later there signs emerge that somebody has not forget him as a knock on the door is observed; one without any calling or reminding of "hurry up grasshopper!". When peaking out of the door, a fresh looking and exotic herb fragrantly smelling, spicy tomato filled idli dosa welcomes Shoetef while his two new found friends usually on kitchen shifts are already excitingly waiting downstairs in the lobby. Time can be rare at times where time is trying to kick some ass in a timely fashion. Time out!

The first stop is the Botanical Garden Pamplemousse; named to the same guy as they did for the airport. "No not Mr. International Plaisance; damn head ache playing with my mind." However, fact is too that the island government lacks fantasy or is over zealously loving the dude who due to poor performance lost an election including his own seat plus also resulted in his socialist mob ending up with zero representation in the parliament. But African politics would not be African politics is not his son inherits the show! Shoetef's thoughts wonder away from questioning if Sir Seewoosagur Ramgoolam's philanthropist's heart would be content to have his name everywhere or if there was a time that deep in his personality the animal's farm meaning of equal is like the gathering of the garden's big water liliaceous plant's leafs for a legume gathering without starving the surrounding algae of life supporting light. As for being a good social citizen himself Shoetef offers 100 rupees to one of the kitchen staff for the deed to attempt walking over the bathing plants. After even 1,000 rupees are rejected Shoetef concludes that Bollywood stunts men still had some educational adventure soul promoting work ahead. And no wonder Shiva is uncontested! One cool ass rocks a million to a billion aiming for a trillion! Walking down the alley with trees planted by people of importance to commemorate themselves is slowly boring the viking whereby neither are the aphrodisiac or psychedelic substances lacking flowers blossoming in the bushes behind going to roll the dice of high life today. His mind drifts towards Sanji; but in this culture being raunchy naughty would mean full scale offense to the family followed by disowned as an outcast. "Hell then I would have to kick my ass in to gear!?"

He drags the compadres towards the car. Next is Flic-en-Flac beach, which already on arrival is deemed to be a disappointment. While the hotel restaurant staff enjoy their cherry popping swim in the ocean Shoetef is forced being on lifesaving duties. Their chicken lollipops are too good to let them drown! Luckily the fun dip ends abruptly as the swimming instructor is fed up at perving on bangable untenable Euro chicks enjoying honeymoon with future wife bashers!! Unsurprisingly the attempt to visit the nearby bird park is subject to renovations, but some excitement did arise thanks to the kitchen hands being afraid of larger fauna. Even a freaking albatross gives the two shivers which conveniently is then misused as a hero sales tactic by kicking the innocent winged rat and subsequently falling on the backside. At least the day ends in mercy. The left back kitchen team has cooked up some South Indian fish curry and fried pakoras with a sour tamarind based chili sauce allowing the evening to return peacefully to the usual business of getting ripped off in rummy. To his appreciation not a word from yesterday's discussion emerges. It is bluntly said as bland as English tea competing against a fruity loonie tasting rooibos brew!

Day 5, 2005

Shoetef gets up early in morning without forgetting the previous day's breakfast. He is wondering if a door knock is to occur again. And he waits, and waits, until at once he hears a gentle rattle of a tea cup and immediately opens the door… where his eyes met the tight derriere* of Sanji!!! Well, well, lovely, Shoetef transforms himself quickly in to his rare gentleman personality by immediately forwarding an invitation to join. He made himself even look silly by additionally offering the plastic flowers on the small room table. As not being a big eater and two tea cups on the tray, there is a challenge existing to avoid a rude refusal. She grew up with manners and also lets him know that her brother is positively acknowledging his kindness with the parents being delighted that their kitchen staff adapted him so unexpectedly nicely. And the latter matters, as the Indian custom is…. "Holy macaroni and Jesus on a motor bike!"… Sorry love, just a thought bubble. His inner voice continues nagging him, "yes of course, in this culture the old folks exercise dictatorship in deciding their children's marriage, including the toll!!" After realization the crispy pan cake dough is gaining extra weight towards tedious chewing and swallowing, worse than 3 day old white bread roll with no water to assist. At least the lovely lass receives plenty of leisure time to pursue tightening the knot with this perceived well-mannered traveler. An exorcist is poking Shoetef to commence finding a nice day out program… But before the two can make a runner, her brother enters the ballet stage by dancing like a swan, not as good as poor Austrian choir boys prone to Vegemite on cheese sticks whipping, but neither uselessly replicating a waterfowl chook*, offering the two an invitation to his place for late afternoon. "Ah bugger, there goes the option to get blotto*..."

While his miraculously reborn lovey dovey is powdering her nose to his sorrowfulness in her own compartment, the idea of just heading towards Souillac for a surf and then giving a flick to soberness, a more sophisticated plan is requiring urgent drafting. What do women want? Yes, ears that listen to them, sometimes big hairy antennas which can properly capture all the space junk dribble and which are capable in filtering the unnecessary releasing data overload. It comes to Shoetef's mind that Chongstar mentioned Ylang-Ylang as a delightful yellow flower which releases a sweet female attractive perfume odor. Yes odor, something better than what some religious endeavors do with sacred cow urine, for an example yogis drinking the piss in beer mugs. Thus, as a modern noble man Shoetef takes his soon to be bride for a ride along the eastern coast past romantic bays with white, silt granular beach sand and light turquoise colored water to a garden where scented plants grow. A guide explains the production in not too hard core detail and more importantly they can be smelled up on like a fag restaurant critic treasuring the finest truffle aroma somewhere hidden in a small dollop of freaking vegan ass juice oil!! And all with squeezing a small cry from his left eye due to the missed chance of buffin' the muffin. Further the noble man buys a small flacon in the hope that the investment will pay off as the ham string on his back is not going to ebb away like a wave does; and neither is beating the meat on the program!

The late afternoon gathering partakes at her brothers and his wife's new pad, which is a basic second floor unit in a white color mortared concrete building, not far located from the hotel and the entertainment strip, squeezed like a sandwich with a rubbish dump behind and pig pens below. At least he is allowed to bring a few beers and dégustation of local rum is also promised which is calming karma for Shoetef. The high light is definitely the home made octopus curry, which sadly insufficiently masks the fact that Sanji is not allowed to stay the night under the protective secrecy of his bed sheets, but promises him to show some island secrets over the upcoming days. Shoetef is wondering if this promise package also contains gummy bears, revealing of an illegal distillery as dowry and then maybe unpacking of a delicate gift? To the beholder's eyes she definitely sported talent!

Day 6, 2005

The door knocking happens earlier than anticipated and breakfast is brought in by the mother. "What, the mother!?" Poor Shoetef is slowly getting annoyed from all the attention. She also has a present for him: A full scale formal wear bag from her deceased father including a white button down shirt and brown pants combined with a same colored long sleeved cotton jacket. Luckily she is not yet insisting for him to wear a tie. Almighty, his worst concerns are being confirmed. They actually have arranged an informal job interview with a poor guy having deformed lips with consistently dripping the sugar water from the right corner where before gulab jamuns swan in. "Great, a cousin having to show off wealth to gain respect." The signs are now unarguably set on serious red alert similar to the Australian bush bashing category of 1003 plus blow flies imploding in your mouth of which no matter how bitter the beer is, the catastrophe cannot not be washed away. Mum is all smiles, clatter farting* around where the babbling* is only interrupted when some ass talking* about how a morning glory can be gory surfaces. By the time his numb mind awakens to understand the thematic has changed to the high price super markets are now charging for a whole uncooked chook. As time is seemingly rapidly vanishing Shoetef is pushed towards and in to the waiting car where Sanji's brother is all freaking smiles too. "My smile costs a beer!" The back-to-front day or better said the ass-to-face situation is maneuvered with silky swift elegance by a bunch of people seemingly gone bananas! To prevail logic the appointment is held in a French restaurant where a lavish lunch is served comprising cured ham and croutons as entree, bouillabaisse, coq au vin, mousse au chocolat and then the salary discussions are scheduled to an accompanying cheese board with Roquefort, South African pepper lime infused cheddar and local made goat/sheep putty. Albeit the session being a beaut, it did not smooth Shoetef's wage barnie* as the expectations are long hours honoring a typical Asian's family values. And add to that generous subsidizing of rellies* and future wife's desire, which will go beyond her fake golden Tiger Eye rings. Shoetef persuasively requests a mental smoko* for a few days. Thereafter, he directs the discussion towards the real game regarding their alienation indicative family's past with all the fried batter remaining in the cooker. Sanji releases a whisper in his ear promising to specially address all the wants, except in Shoetef's thoughts most probably never give a blow job. Contradicting his hopes the next move is picking up another fuzzy cuzzy*, who manages a run down joint to the west of the city center and close to the beach. The by salty air chipping away white painted facade enclosing outdoor seating area still suffices for a few celebratory drinks of deskilled rum, which is tasting more like Siberian Vodka, meaning in real need of plenty lime and a dash of coke to give it a more pleasant old barrel aged brown color. The gathering is conducted in standing around a pool which has seen better days before accommodating a partying local mosquito population representing a great opportunity to collect a few diseases. Shoetef is in his comfort agitated as the drinks are not keeping the darn things at bay. When the first signs of cousin Prafula showing happiness and angering Aadarsh about what ever kind of driver duties he makes a move towards offering 500 rupees for Prafula to drink a glass serving of pool water. It is amusing the other booze cruisers, who then chip in; bang a deal as sealed. "Shlucken* hard!" The next stop is Cauldan water front. A fairly new development where even after a few years in operations is still searching for shop lessees as small rascals have been over the past exercising keenness on relieving the few visitors financially, especially lazy and uneducated cruise ship passengers are always appreciated income providers. However with the accompanied local business men Shoetef is safe. With the drowning of a few expensive European lagers masculinity capabilities are now competitively exaggerated to new highs including shouting prescriptions of potential treatments to anyone in hiding while considering any pick pocketing attempts. After the sun sets itself and the group's mutation in to a drunken gang, now including Aadarsh as a respected minion, a taxi is flagged down with Grand Domaine casino as destination. Upon arrival proactively seeking luck is in the cards to avoid overly scratching the security guards' patients and behavioral tolerance level. After gaining entry, the first spew session commences just far enough inside the building's guts resulting Prafula needing to clean up the mess on his suit in a heritage stile replicating rest room. His fat cuzzy steers towards seeking an argument with an African prostitute of how to spend his "one in a go" roulette win, unluckily near under cover police. He is arrested and under protest is carried away. As the night just has started Shoetef makes acquaintance of the newly developed situation and finds it funny seeing a black lady kicking an arrogant high rolling Hindustani's ass. He even has the red dot bindi on his forehead, "a third eye to cheat?" However, it is not the night where the wheel of fortune spins lucky numbers enabling a night of free booze flows. The bouncers soon find out that Aadarsh turned in to concierge wreck is part of the intoxicated entourage. It is becoming clear to pack up or face some unfriendly prescriptions of some mean sheikh certified owner who most probably was already gearing up with threatening to arrange his Russian contacts to change the casino games to snakes and ladders, where the ladders would lead to high above in heaven but not without first a ride down through a hidden torture chamber comprising snake wielding Chechen mujaheddin and nosy South African double agents who both would be keen to decorate themselves with new golden chains around their torso thick necks consisting of freshly chopped off fingers and ears conserved through plastification practices as done by their taxidermist inbreeds back home in some Caucasian mountain barn. Shoetef reminds himself that snakes are not very fussy and unlike a stoner seeking change from pepperoni to anchovy pizza does not mind which kind of rodent is on his menu listing!! While many Arabs back home, especially the Libanese wanna-be gangsters are more of full air sporting small weeniers* incapable of sexually pleasing their big arsed, high maintenance and sexually anyway disinterested sisters, tackling Russian mafia is generally not advisable and a Chechen mad man who terrorized for decades those already nasty enough commie cunts even less! Nope, it is not time to play a woop-woop wisecrack. Just right timing to be a wuss* and get the wimping* wally* out! In midst of the mess he finally finds in a hidden corner a crying Sanji; lucky she behaved, kept her innocence and is all good to get out.

Day 7, 2005

In good knowledge of the previous night, nobody is knocking on the door. When Shoetef finally manages to submerge out of his ocean of non remembered dreams walking over the plank back on to land Sanji and her parents are already waiting in hope that their new found, oh so polite and etiquette following friend is going to be capable to digest their intentions. The first task however is fighting off a heavy morning boner* and the sight of the house's daughter dressed in a tight body wrapping sari exposing her slim stomach with a diamond decorated belly button makes him first having to do some empty shluckings while imagining his last seen deep sea documentary series where an underwater frequency radar seizures mass baby shower* moaning sequences from ugly jaw exposing, pigment lacking blind fish. His thoughts continue going childishly astray by memorizing the son of a cetacean aquatic mammal finding out where he comes from while the father says "Your Welcome*". He is slowly feeling the need to sober up quickly so start recapturing a scene of his youth patching up the push bike's tire after a thorn bush gave it a puncture inclusively the tedious squeezing it back in to place... And as he'd expected the delivered news is a punch in his face: Sanji's hand. One week on the island and being nice is heading towards a wedding arrangement which is already taking part before even mentioning anything about a dowry! "Well bingo, surprise but not unexpected." With as serving of fine Darjeeling tea the half crippled old man gives Shoetef 48 hours to think about it. And it is not about the yes or no; it is about logistics in getting his family involved! #Air shlucking# The gods have gone crazy, but somehow they now have infected an entire blessing of single horned hoofed dodo birds. In all madness it seems the event is being exponentially multiplied by some form of genetic mutation with erratic behaving to the bones scared chihuahuas and love deprived boa constrictors on rabies! Shoetef's path has deviated on to a one way street tout la-bas et tout droit*.

In fulfilling the duty to make the deities content the two drive up in to the mountains to visit Grand Bassin where they lay flowers in to the Ganges replicating lake waters. After initial appreciation of the calming surroundings Sanji burns a batch of incense sticks underneath Mauritius' highest statue, Mangal Mahadev as believing measure to ensure the clan of gods around Shiva will guide her in to a blessed future. Unfortunately she forgets informing Shoetef about the temple rites' attires, "no, no, no, you are not right doing this" and the head behind the voice is never seen as Bhairo Baba* has discovered loudspeakers to bark through! "If I throw a bone in to Ganga Talao lake will the amplifier fetch it?" She looks perplexed at him, undecided if the comment is funny or insulting, never the less decides on the first in responding with a smirk while grabbing his hand, "allez a Chamarel." On the viewing platform with the waterfalls in front of them he gives her the first ever kiss to devour. It is a tender touching of lips giving her butterflies in the stomach and a side ways pressing twitch on the tips of her breasts. Due to lack of experience she feels a bit ashamed, but is admiring this moment where she could embrace the world, but is too shy to lay her arms fully around him, "what if he knew how much I really do feel?". Shoetef senses the awkward moment of his princess and retrieves back to holding her hand instead. It is a comforting approach to walk over the hills dispatching colored Earth, whereby he behaves and refers the scenery to the variety usually displayed in Hindi temples.

Mauritius well accomplished paradise island dream contains a dry coast for the sun seeking foreigners and a wet inland accommodating down pours of refreshing rain, silken the day's hot temperature and provide opportunity to seek refuge on a covered hill top bench with forest views to the coastline and inquire about Morning Glory. Sanji's big dark eyes look in to his while eluding him to the far reaching wrathful secret.

> - It likes to attract. It likes to play. It likes to be bad. Ultimately it will kill you. However, there must be a taming master code…
> Cursed castles, sanatoriums, islands, swamps, cemeteries and roller coasters can be dismantled or redesigned, so why not this piece of grim reaper?
> - What? That is it?
> - Yes, well, it does not talk neither. It literally bloody acts! And it is impatient.

The curse of Sanji's personal life's Veda scripts enacts with her car breaking down on the home way. While waiting her hand bag grows legs. Shoetef is trying to numb himself to quickly forget the stoner story lacking being stoned.

Day 8, 2005

A scheduled day out fishing. There is plenty of Phoenix stubbies wrapped up individually in plastic bags containing ice cubes and stored in a large hard plastic tray. Aadarsh and Prafula are batting in healthy happy attitudes. The first hour is just letting the weak current take them past Gunners Quoin, but just when Shoetef is ready for his fourth stubby a pulling of the net line occurs. The two locals jump up and start retrieving it; a net full of fish plus one mean shark. When trying to separate, it bites in to Aadarsh's arm #chomp#. "Fuck, fuck, fucking shit fish!", the shock needs quick absorbing and not losing consciousness. Now Shoetef is also in a sedated state imagining being Captain Stabbing of finned beasts. Unlike his porn counterparts who can enjoy post action relaxing on the deck, he is having to maneuver the boat in to the harbor while screaming at Prafula to phone up an ambulance. But he is not on deck, rather below cringing at stomach aches which he a bit too late indicates have been ongoing since the casino visit. "You both are useful as aquatic vertebrate podiatrists!"

In the afternoon the family gathers at the hospital, naturally crying, controlling to avoid a mental break down and still unaware of the new born curse beholding them. As Shoetef hints that their faith is aligning to some of the Morning Glory's related historical theatrical drama plays the best he can do is returning to the beach bar and meet up with the black lady. He picks her up for a hotel visit in Mahebourg, as far away possible from the shit hitting the fan.

Day 9, 2005

Lucky there is Air Mauritius! Au-revoir.

7 CHROMATIC CHRONOLOGIES

Day 33, 2010

The morning feels like having all bones broken by a Catherine wheel. The forwarded breakfast is also contributing towards the torture; two slices of burnt toast, dry as dessert scrub being deprived of water making it loose branches one by one aiming to have the stem act as sanctuary for the last vital cells purposefully ensuring hope of survival. Shoetef is slowly realizing that time is running out in catching up with Bruce plus in the current state of affairs a return to Yarpiestan* could result in a salutation opposing the rolling out of a red carpet. A vicious manbearpig is tearing his innards apart. No brotherly man hug feelings at all. The first step is to move away from the close border vicinity to lower the likelihood of being kidnapped by the SASS intelligence services. After one more rear releasing chocolate mousse splashing, all belongings are hastily collected, squashed in to the back pack followed by venturing towards the bus station. A few minutes after returning the keys the short happy run is interrupted by a second wave, which in this unfortunate situation means he is leaning against a large tree behind the border post office while spilling undigested bread crumbs on to the fence separating the countries. Yes, he is shitting from a secure haven in to the enemy's territory! Golela in South Africa is receiving an organic ammonia bouquet fulfilled herbal smelling accolade. "And the wet may take a little while to cure as new border crossing path!"

With some daydreaming nightmares or just pure nervous anxiety kicking in that some bad boys are on their way coming to get him plus dark clouds in the sky are nearing in, Shoetef manages to drag his heals to the nearby gas station where he purchases a healing packet of masala chips, followed by endeavoring them like a big cat ripping up its victim's stomach before licking the draining offal juices. However it is the only brand on sale making a bunch of fat South African rich bitches double unhappy as too no coke is available. The world can be a weird place, where whale watching success is best made at Maccas* by observing pods of homo sapienised balaenoptera musculuses* stuffing chemically modified nuked mashed cow uterus laid between sugar overladen buns accompanied with thin fries to ensure maximization of trans fats whereby in action imitating a scenario of wide open mouthed whale shark engulfing sardines. The misery is soon inherited with the shouting of mini van transporter employed boys and not long thereafter Shoetef is on his way towards north. The hopes that some half way decent airline serves Swaziland evaporate in a dust fart; his seat neighbor highlights the fact that the national airline is subsidized by the Safas, which is irrelevant compared to the doing of his intestines making the trip to finish a few miles up the road before the township of Big Bend with its banks hugging the Lutsufi River.

Now that is it. Shoetef is not happy having his bum fucking him. Thus, at a nearby country hotel a septuplet-tripling serve of local brandy is ordered in the hope that the stomach parasites might finally get defeated. At the next moment when looking up to receive a half pint full of fluid bug vermin, a shiny white smile from a pretty black face emerges.

- Natalie!
- Heiya sexy Sir!
- Holy bloody cow shit gurgling spread barrel bombing medicine man on DMT!!
- Yes my hidden bright star from the milky way... You do not look good at all... Help!

Natalie holds Shoetef while he slumps his head down on to the bar table.

> - *Shut up bitch! It's that alcoholic shamozzle* from a few weeks ago.*
> - *Fuck off! He was you client not all too long ago and one who was relaxed in attitude compared to the usual ones who crack the whip on you to constantly get better shots.*
> - *OK. And admit he was fun. Get him to the local witch doctor. Looks like an alcohol abstinence shock. Some pickled lion penis soaked in home brew will get that mad man back to being a sex pest!*
> - *Yarpie* Tom! By the way, where is CC?*

He hits Shoetef's unconscious face.

> - *It looks like you have twisted the poor girl's thoughts. Usually Schwarze Fraeuleins* are not like the Caucasian counterparts who stupidly fall in love, or have to fall in love before allowing a donkey's salami seek refuge between their samba chops! Be aware of her slutty attitudes, she is smarter than the best future seeing shaman floating on a divine healing trance trip flying on a cloud originating from earth's purest herbs. May the medicine man reinstate her racial boundary disrespecting mind!*

Now Natalie stands up, taller than Tom using the rare occasion to look down on him.

> - *Enough Tom. I'm a boa menina* not a garota podre*! You are a stale carrot. Old fag carrot! Old stinky moldy gran culo* plugging carrot!*

Day 34

Surprise, surprise, Natalie's help is immensely appreciated. It does not take long where a tincture containing grounded bones and witch doctor's nose boogers in ox blood followed by an hour long chanting relieve Shoetef from pain and shitty pants. Both CC and Tom are buffed seeing the rapid improvement. Natalie is not enclosing that she accompanied Shoetef during half the night, with her hands sexually pleasuring him, teasing his cock to near orgasms in hope to make him even more keen on recovery and thus smartly revitalizing his fighting heart to back up his body again. By lunch time he is up again for action!

In the afternoon in this remarkable little country packed full of natural offers where half naked virgins are dancing for the king's invitation to his harem, the boys are muscle promoting tiger fishing at a nearby dam. Shoetef's strength is more orientated towards retrieving lost fluids. The fun curve is heading nicely upwards. But by 4pm CC is urging them to visit a casino, but due to his bad record is acting agitated. He knows that he could end up in real trouble and therefore retreats to more intensive piss slamming while leaving some poor local teenagers to do the hard reeling work on a near unbearable hot afternoon. Soon CC's devine drop storage dries up, which to his anger cannot being restocked at the local Shoprite market. He screams for ideas towards a Plan B, "men this is serious"…

Day 35

"Yes, indeed a good feeling day ahead." CC hardly survived last night's outing. In his rage of being banned to punt and having to consume for his taste substandard alcohol, even the biltong on sale is for him compost stamping kack*. He then subsequently dragged the entire party in to the car to just fall asleep behind the wheel on the first kilometer. Those cheap last drops made him totally knackered and mentally exhausted thanks to previous executed all-nighter tantrums. Blerrie doosis*! Tom decides it is time to leave the scene. It slowly dims Shoetef that the only circus animal tamer here, is not here #damn#, that is his pale 25 year old bunsen burning bambi!

- Ah fuckaluya! Give me the keys you bloody old junky! And a shot of your spirit's last drop.
- Darling!
- Natalie? So all sugar sweet free to raise a voice when Tom is away?!
- Ah, big sorry my monkey scrotum. CC did not know that you were so desperate by only drinking Amarula!
- Let us head off, I might need to do a visit to the capital myself. And where I might be able to get a serving of eye candy by witnessing the king's newest wedding by the means of AIDS free incwala celebrations!*
- What!?
- Just joking love.
- Be careful my darling. Here in Swazistan Mswati the third is currently a bit ferocious about the by under-aged boys spanked missionaries ridiculing his chastity law while he drags a minor in to bed. But that is not all. As you can see the local dam levels are low, which as you saw is great for tiger fishing, well that is if you retarded wank waste products would have been capable in holding that kind of rod as well as your own (!), but this means there is a drought and some are dying, just like in my home land, which ah fuck, your stupidities are twisting my mind, means the ape of a local chief here had to buy himself a private airplane while people are starving. Blerrie swaksinniggers, oh mercy to my too petite to qualify as black bootie, even I am getting racist, anyway they are all swaksinniges*!*
- Ah my dark jewel feel lucky that you are not collecting that dry grass without flying high above the sky on Air Dagga and then having to fix up the mosquito breeding straw huts of the king while dancing and show casing yourself as a little horny portion of mash potato with a juicy shot of sweet gravy readily to be*

As the roads are fairly well maintained and Shoetef in his own Schumacher rage, the hectic drive along windy roads avoiding any school children deaths ends around 8.30am in Mbabane, the capital of this authoritarian ruled corner of the world. It is not CC's day as while left behind in the city center to wait for a bottle shop to open and enduring a dry chicken sandwich in front of hungry AIDS orphans, some of them obviously infected by come kind of rash producing parasite, most likely bilharzia, making him throwing up the precious food as his weird form of solidarity sharing. Nope this Safa* is not consider getting instead a plate of cheap fries instead and sharing it around. At the same time Shoetef visits with Natalie the High Commission of Mozambique, which refuses to open on time at 9am and pushes it out until some Portuguese swear words are launched, only to be then told to get some Rands ready or else privileged access is lost in translation; all without holding back any further crazy Latino fiery slang words making their way all through the brick walls whereby "Burro do preguicoso caralhos*" is answered with "Cala te puta enrabar!*". And albeit finding it weird that Natalie is refused entry, the disliking of Lilangeni is surprises due to being pegged against its neighboring regional major currency. Africa and logic do not necessarily hold hands... Plus there seems to be less friendly attitudes existing against anything he does towards obtain the sought visa; possibly because of the language barrier? Or is there some unknown nasty history involved?

Day 36

Getting dragged out of bed is one thing, but it is another story when a young African girl with neatly tied up braided hair runs through the room naked, not only having the actual need to maybe use the shaver once again to tidy up the downstairs' drawer, but has actually ants in her slim pants desiring to go to a place she claims is safe, makes her feel more like home and where the two are more likely to push the reset button. It is must be serious as the old stile alarm clock is doing a Shoetef's mood matching frown by showing of 20 minutes to 4am; still digesting the night out starting with a carton of Castle Lager under the local sugar mill towers, followed up by a barbecue feast with accompanying exquisite Cape wine at the Country Club while making jokes relating to the planned next day's golf game whereby agreeing to only use the putter and no other clubs, "Africa has time and so does Tom when trying to swallow a Viagra; and then still drops his balls well behind the bush in to the rough muddy bunker!" Yes indeed there are a few silly juice infused happy pickled minded ideas floating around like the ice in CC's scotch. Late in the night the tired bar staff took the expat bunch to a local brandy serving shebang until all went lose and Shoetef had the honor of drink driving back to the lodge while trying to suavely navigate away from an increasingly agitated mob showing a high level of disrespect albeit the visitors shouting them drinks! Dubul'iBhunu, shoot the boer; and further in Zulu that the land is theirs and that all African land is to be returned. Thupa eyetla, oa bona thupa – the punishment is coming, soon you will see and in scare pee!

- By the dollops of freshly squeezed monkey cream, I am scared.
- Wow, your lingo has improved!?! But no worries my crisp chocolate crunch.
- You do not understand. These guys yesterday were bad and...
I do not want you to turn sour like Greek yogurt.
- It is still in the middle of night, how do you think we are going to be moving any time soon?
- Don't worry some older taxi driver will be already waiting for a job. My deliciousa sponge cake I got you covered. The South African guys were generous gentlemen, but have changed to the worse. You have your mozzie visa, so all good. I have contacts. We shall pass the border before sunrise and make a swift run in to Maputo where you can marvel the beautiful jacaranda trees lining the Avenida de 24 Julho all before any officials have the option to get nasty. Plus look forward to a nice peri peri lunch!
- On the plane may I then scream for more cream?

The two quietly sneak out of the lodge and after good 15 minutes walking towards Big Bend a mini van is passing by, not without triggering a hoot sounding like an old fire truck's horn, unpleasantly loud for the early timing, but welcoming enough to offer a good run through the back roads winding past Manzimyame nature reserve, traversing grass hills already collecting dew giving the morning a touch of humid freshness, especially a touch of earthy smell, then zig-zagging through the lush vegetated gorges of the Lebombo range and entering in to Portugal's former colony. A large tree representing the final post of Eswatini is passed incognito. The neglected wooden customs house, just a mere larger than a hut to accommodate an army jeep followed by a reiterating sign of entering international disputable territory lacks any light. The border seems to be as low scale. Natalie mentions the cold war era and South Africa's influence was historically not necessarily appreciated by its neighbors, thus no Bienvenido sign neither. Only an emerging frightened taxi driver hinting that traversing a mine field half-illegally in to another country is not pumping sufficient content making adrenaline, but remains quiet. After leaving the most easterly growing local aloe bushes, civilization is emerging from the basic clay huts to greet the morning sun's mildly glazing from where then the trips itinerary changes its direction towards north. On arrival in to Maputo around 9am Natalie is already eagerly arranging a flight for Shoetef. But Shoetef urges that they are to first have breakfast; a dozen of Doz-M's on the Mira Mar shore front. Just a pity they missed the sun rise over the ocean. Albeit keen on getting as much Rands paid as possible, the taxi driver returns to cheeky attitudes by allowing himself the freedom to join in for a few cold Laurentinas while his vehicle is hiding two streets back to prevent nosy investigative police detectives finding a reason of treason. African authorities can be ruthless when finding artificial means to play up paranoia, especially against their own race. Then the so called legalized rule executioners with official unofficial permission need to protect the community with help of any cashed up person capable in funding repatriation payments. Therefore a new taxi is flagged down to ensure smooth passage to the lesser populated northern beach end while the one decorating Swaziland plates is used as distraction; precaution cannot harm to lower the risk that lost glory of Laurenco Marques revives its old nasty days of civil misbehavior.

At mid day the small Lineas Areas Mocambique air craft, an airline in those days banned from the European airspace takes its course towards Inhambane. On descend it flies over a wonderful stretch of wide pure white sand beaches where before landing a swerve over the turquoise colored bay is done allowing views to the sister city on the opposite bay's shores, Maxixe which pronounced as ma'sheish in honoring a former chief. Thanks to today's bubbly feeling of Aquarius the airline crew is not shy in dishing out plenty of stubbies* to make the bumpy landing against the north-easterly incoming ocean winds change from a doable to pleasurable event. And if one would imagine that there would be a greeting party awaiting; well not quite. But the shack is continuing with good mood vibe promotions by offering cheap beers to purchase. Shoetef is holding a weirdly pyramid shaped wrapped up parcel from Natalie. She mentioned nothing about its content. One more can and off he wanders to the car park where a rickety taxi driver is on the look out for a good earning through scooping up a lonely and lost tourist. However, it is not his eternal resurrection from Valhalla as the Viking has plenty of time to sit in the road side to wait and enjoy the nauseating feelings coming from the early heavy alcoholic beverage consumption stint. After the dust settles he continues with investigating the traffic flow. The poor gold digger deprived of any customers is eagerly gluing himself to Shoetef trying to break the ice towards creating a new friendship. His smile through the gold imitation plate of one of his upper teeth seems to only partly capture the awareness of the tired, but still mentally strong and in the heat astonishingly patient soul. "Você não é um bockie branco*?" The beers combined with the hot afternoon sun are slowly gaining traction towards a heightened interest in finding a lodge to rest. The haggling starts and soon the price is halved. The two depart for Praia do Tofo where to the traveler's surprise at road's end in front of the beach at a food shack harboring a friend is seen: Bruce! And he is all smiles while digging in to matapa crab stew with a fresh inviting metaphor calling coming from the side salad containing chopped capsicum, onions and tomatoes.

- Hey you retarded placenta waste, what ya doing with a god damn iced coffee!?!? I thought I educated you better!?
- Fuck me dead you pissy mongrel! We agreed to meet again in Jo's-stealing-bastardry.*
- Shut up you bush oyster eater! At least you are not wearing clacker doodle doo* cord togs* or I'd give you a merciless flick!*
- Alright you freckle face, you are as sober like a well fed carnivore in an African zoo!*
- Well sorry to the new born orphan! Been unfortunately busy like a cat burying its shit.
- Right, as I would believe you. Sounds more like a flat out drinking lizard on a concoction of hoppy champagne showers and female cum! Most probably behaving like an annoying, every drop licking lurk!*
- Umm, your talk is like somebody opening their lunch box through a wet fart!
- Alright, I somehow will try to forgive you. What is that funny piece of shit you are carrying?
- Don't know, but will unpack it when time allows. Not so important. Most probably some girlie bejeweled fanny wipes in a golden box.*

Day 37

The night at Luisa's is very pleasant and as a rare occasion Shoetef has the ability to peacefully sleep until lunch time. The little hotel contains only three rooms. His with twin beds while the other two have nice rusty, big, wooden king size beds hiding under big mosquito net umbrellas. It is basic, but the beaut is the location right on the beach. Today Shoetef can finally do a relaxing swim before observing the arrival of the third party; a lovely mid aged blond lady from Oporto Portugal, seconded on UN duties in Maputo. She is exactly that piece of Nando's chicken gone astray on Tofo Beach beyond the limits where most action occurs as the younger tourists tends to conceal themselves at the local backpackers further. But that place has its charms too as it attracts cute local lasses who very dark in skin, but gorgeous slim and compared to their European peers they have not yet discovered torturing other with stupid demands for vegan food while next door children are starving or whole meal buns whereby those children would even gladly eat stale white toast, soft toilet tissues for their pimple strewn asses, second pillows to lay down the carbivore* accumulated double chin, Bob Marley reggae music over independent dub while unrelentingly messaging their dislike of southern African dance music!

As Bruce is no where to be seen, the first action of the day is getting some flowers to gift the beach shack owner, similar in age as to her by far more sexy Portuguese guest, but sporting the typical mama small size with decent love handles and a short gray toupet. Nothing attracting as such, but hey she seems to be best buddies with the hopefully cougar to be! Shoetef's thoughts are directed towards reverse tag teaming, hoping that Bruce might pick up the vinegary smelling cabbage head while he devours on the sweet fruit! But the day ends hapless, a friendly smirk by the ladies and on they go out to Inhambane, sadly alone… The universal time clock makes a break. Plan B is enacted, that is off to a restaurant to enjoy crayfish sized peri peri prawns, barbecued butterflied with cool 2M wash downs.

Day 38

Finally Bruce warms up his soul by dragging Shoetef to the local dive shop which is offering nice, adventurous specials beyond hunting down stupid lame nudie branches. It is only on the boat, far out in the sea where problems surface; the engine hits a whale shark, injures it to the degree that the animal just sinks and causes mass screaming havoc. Additionally the tour operators don't have official recognized diving certificates while the boss himself is not giving two hoots. The gooseberry's response is, "close your eyes and you cannot see!" The first dive is developing itself towards a pleasure, although not necessarily that to an animal empathizing heart. The injured creature is attracting gray nurse sharks. Lucky that no white pointers arrive! Lucky in deep sea you cannot hear cries neither. After a quick execution of half warm beers the second bubble blowing undertaking is done; maneuvering exercise through some small cave formations which were advertised as new discovery. Explorations of the untouched is right up Shoetef's alley, however Bruce's continuously boasting of his own jewel grotto makes any detailed inquisition stale. The absolute highlight however follows suit when drifting upwards from 30 meters depth towards the 12 meter mark. At once a crushing sound is observed, halting the teams resurfacing plans and opening up the investigative curiosity box "from where do these smashing decibels come from?" And #booommmm# well above Neptune's sons' a hump back whale is enjoying the liberties of Free Willie by lifting its fat gut out of the water and thundering its weight on to the waves.

Later in the day Bruce emerges with the desire to buy himself a new pair of shorts and while his search is evolving towards a fruitless lunatic attack, it is giving Shoetef finally the welcoming opportunity in conducting some small chat with the lodge's female guest. She introduces herself as an accountant who is tired of shoving bureaucracy around eventuating in her wanting to just relax; and maybe doing an odd off good deed to pleasure heart and soul. But as per Shoetef's mind correctly identifies, the good deed does not necessarily involve her vagina! And as her reading of books desire is not matching with the hyperactive nature strangling Shoetef, he grabs a surf board to show off a bit during the moments she does decide to lift up her head to view the wider world.

At night fall she is still not showing much interest. Thus, Shoetef joins Bruce in his new 50 pence thongs, shorts on offer are too small in size. They venture to the nearby beach bar shack to mingle with local girls instead. On return the lady from Oporto is now showing interest, but not a positive one. She discovered the fact that spending the entire with the owner only talking about their home land does not score in any flesh pleasing activities and as such starts slowly showing more attention towards tasting a crumbled fried sausage over an olive oil cooked chook! However she does not this occasion's opportunity. Her night's destiny is giving tiresome attention to the lone accommodation soul and with some sadness in her eyes, she blinks her eyes in eager anticipation that Shoetef returns from his room, which becomes rapidly reality thanks to Bruce rekindling to his old extensive sleeping pattern. For Shoetef it is a waste of effort as a few minutes later she too is in all need for a trip to Lalaland*.

Secluded in the dark with a full moon guarding him, drinking a bitter tasting cashew distilled blind making spirit which is purchased off an under-aged girl darker than the night with finer curly hair tips, just too short for the usual head covering moss carpet. Due to poverty she is forced to sell illegal alcohol or her father's mood swings go towards an abusive freeway overtaking lane, where even her substance misuse addicted mother looks away in full horror gladly he does not lay hands on her. Shoetef retrieves the secret package and slowly opens the pastel colored yellow, beige wrapping from where within a shining, sparkle emerges; dark green in color with brown fissures and small red sparkles. Or bluntly described a varnish painted piece of fresh horse dung containing blood droplets. A raw gem stone with indications of unsuccessful cutting attempts. As for the limited knowledge existing it does not resemble the pale color of an Aventurine jade while its lack of white discounts for being a malachite and the brightness disqualifies nephrite. Lastly emeralds are not known to be related to Africa… In one heart attack promoting shooting motion, Bruce speeds out, runs to the ocean, has a quick swim in his male lingerie, comes back and mentions he just had a nightmare; one where he will find the poisonous ivy of love which will choke him dead and in to a grave where his bones will actually be dug deep under desert sand. Shoetef already half way joining the lullabies himself, sits up again vertically, opens his mouth wide up, watches Bruce grab a quick shot of the half full bottle containing the lethal mind altering juice. His glossy eyes are fixated to Shoetef's lap and the heavy weighing glassy piece of shining rock, He announces excitingly...

> *- A freaking diamond, a freaking diamond!*
> *- Nah mate, forget it. Too heavy, too ugly, it is just a big fat ass kicking quartz.*
> *- Mate, you, you, you...*
> *- Stop being intrigued. You are a worry on legs. Boa noite mulher de príncipe*.

Day 39

As like every holiday there are days where a sloth attitude comes with benefits. It only seems that Bruce is now behaving as if on amphetamines. He is attempting to drag Shoetef for a walk towards Tofinho Beach to search for a bigger and better treasure hidden in an isolated corner of paradise. And he is annoying the ladies, so maybe it is better to leave and redeem a smile from the ladies as an award as any other luck is unlikely to occur any time soon. Their morning mental attire is anyway replicating the national airline's attitude of better not crash in to the ocean as waves do neither provide life jackets! The previous days' obligate under the seat stretch revealed a very good reason why LAM is not being welcomed by the European Union!

The final drop in the cashew spirit bottle is eliminated and thus breakfast done and mind busted. Shoetef is now ready to go hunting with Bruce, that is he is keen to find the young girl to secure. A final twinkle twinkle little star stare to his La Primabella and off the two start wandering. Shoetef feels that the atmosphere between the two is slowly energizing itself with cordial affable protons, as a tease not yet contacting each other due to resisting electrons. And potential sources of nearby jealousy. Never the less Shoetef sees in her eyes, that the disliking of his chauvinistic perceived world view is in the process of being neutralized by his friendly etiquette. It might have been the flowers which started this unstable chemistry to develop towards a tighter bonding. After a few minutes they pass an outcrop of rocks and cliffs, followed by a secluded beach. 30 more minutes walking and still no signs of a hidden place fermenting hokeypokey cordial. Shoetef is getting itching feet for a bad yabber* rap of foul mouthing cascades to flow down on to dick head Bruce. As if he smelled it, he flags down a taxi to Praia de Barra. First cocktails, then lunch with market fish, stuffed calamaris and salada pera de abacale*. Shoetef mood pendulum swings in to positive towards el grande chefe maritime carnivore whereby his dazed mind makes beach represent Serengeti's Grumeti River; him being the crocodile eagerly munching on female wildebeests… But the dreaming is contained to his skull confinements as the servicing daintily delicate zebras are showing zilch interest to be caught in his hungry jaws. On full stomach with sign of alcohol causing an ictus, Bruce's mission changes again hectically by running off to the water, this time just with a surf board under his arms. Where the eff did he steal that one...? "Bloody hell, make up your mind you hyper active intellectual hindered spoiled first world kid!"

But in assuming when one door shuts, another one opens, Shoetef's liking is more directed to relaxing and chilling in peaceful solitary on the hotel's terrace... The day animates to continue pursuing a smile for his new found adoring target, who is has adopted a touching distance. This behavior attracts him more! In typical stud manner he decides to enact on a new silly thought of the day: Surfing on Fat Slapper Porky Pauline! A final check that she is concentrating her eyes accordingly. Ready, steady, go! Shoetef walks down the beach with the doll underneath his arms whereby a cute stray dog accompanies him, but does not enter the water. Shoetef catches the second incoming wave. "Yes!", he scores the desired smirk from her. It gets better and grows in to a real big smile unlike a group of conservative evangelists walking along the beach who post observing the event quickly and hastily attempt to cover their children's eyes from the views containing frivolous behavior. "Welcome to Shoetef's religion; now start praying to the almighty flying spaghetti monster!"

Day 40

The morning resurrects with a stinging headache and while Bruce is already exercising superiority towards the drowsing spirits by doing a morning surf on the small crushing waves. He is showing off to some boarding newbies from Sweden. For Shoetef a feeling of wanting to visit the local market to smell and taste spicy fresh food takes hold. He needs a contributor to improve the current personal feeling before ambient warning lights start flashing in his eyes. As like a puzzle game where pieces slot in nicely the lady from Oporto bumps in to him while setting foot in to the veranda; her eyes full of life and gratitude that she achieved a good sleep for a consecutive night. Sometimes even shit faced boys can unintentionally show empathy by gurgling on their vomit rather shouting around like derelict idiots! And sometimes also Fortuna wipes off the crust on her eyes as today his sugar sweet heart melting moment is sharing the desperation to visit Inhambane. Expectations are exceeded through her bluffing out the scheduled bus times. "Why not save on taxi fare?" Shoetef's mind drifts away to a critical thinking moment, but hey you can also caress each other on a bus' back bench! Imhambane is showing itself with a fresh dress on, it seems that even some mascara has been applied! But the show fades quickly when finding out that his mentally derelict bank advisor was born with an IQ of a Teletubbie on Retalin; his promise that all banks accept Mastercard is rubbish. Luckily a wad of traveler cheques is accompanying him; world's only really trustful money safety net and hence immensely unloved by financial cronies. The harbor too is clean and lacks of any sewer, waste or dead fish odors. The suave breeze through the bay ensures that the blue and black checkered local jail bait school skirts participate in synchronicity to natures' blowing; swaying the rim edges nicely above the beholders knees gifting Shoetef a breath of his acidic preserved manhood which steadily increases with passing old fading red and blue buildings while smelling her releasing perfumed scents. On return at the bus station's back yard they visit a big chaotic market where a pair of thongs decorated with the national flag containing AK47s is purchased while sitting on a stall's esky containing 2Ms watching mama busily cooking up spicy Zambezia chicken accomplished with a paozinho bread roll and pickled capsicum.

The day fades away, but not before buying fresh fish and potatoes. In the morning Luisa insisted that the Oporto lady meets some of her local friends, which later in the afternoon after a few refreshing Laurentinas evolves in to a rarity of a shy South African guy from Port Elizabeth joining in, however also an annoying froggy prick full of himself is on the guest's list. While the first rekindles himself to Bruce's liking sporting chum buddy, the latter purely advertises himself as a snail shitting beau of the tropics while skulling the girl's wine, which results in Shoetef thirsting for a walking break by arranging more bottles of fermented white grape juice. And the need for more breaks continues in to the evening, where he volunteers to act as the barbecue master while the ladies escape in to the kitchen to prepare salad and those potatoes; a real loved shared between the two cultures. Unfortunately he still desires to be be deaf. The frog just cannot makes a move in being a bloody talker stalker. The situation is as dire like searching for some smoothing music on a Parisian radio channel where too the verbal diarrhea never seems to end. But like a racing car on a circuit the spoken nuisance maker drives himself in repeating circles, just here anguishing the spectators. Shoetef is wishing for a repeat of Le Mans in 1955, just being more temperate as only one casualty is needed… The next victim is Luisa. She gets up, mumbles that she is feeling drained and starts to retract. The failure of her strategy by getting her annoying guest drunk with cheap bubbly* for the sake he finally makes a move homewards is unpleasantly seeping through her consciousness. After the poor exhausted South African guy leaves and Bruce is showing his own piss head success off by using Shoetef's bedroom bathroom for a final good night's bladder emptying to just get red handed caught out when stumbling around. Finally Luisa manages to have a quick private word with Shoetef for.… #bang# One quick hit on the back head and Monsieur Miserable says adieu and bon nuit. Luisa heads back to her own living space while Shoetef drags the obnoxious guest by the legs, along the beach away to the forest's edge and dumps his limp body in to bushes sharing the grounds with a pile animal feces. A well deserved spot for a nightly resting of this linguistic toxic waste producing butt face.

After clearing the event stage from the garbage the big birdie ears are freed and the softness of her legs incur the desired gentle smooth kisses; all the way up from the southern Algarve sand dipping spoiled toes to tidy vulva deforested hill. The moment is contributing to a tumbling erosion of morals ending in the swamp of feverish arousal. As if they have waited for centuries for this one day to occur. After all the affectionate eye winks tag-teaming with staring in to the opposite irises the couple can now action passionate love. Finally they vent inner pressurized steam vessels and let the stored up energy drive their engines for an eternal perceived period of soul pleasuring embracing while touching each others light salted, crusty skins. As next the two advance in the adventure of fondling the sexual organs together and exchanging all excitingly exiting body juices. Soon they ignite an exploding flame uniting their souls through melting as one form work of love beyond what words can describe or the messed up bed sheets can tell!

Day 41

After a final tight hugging of his warm, soft bolo de mel* she who excited him as the first more mature girl in ages and is equipped with a by him admiring larger sized labia majora. Her performance was commended as outstanding in both quality and quantity. With his loving words in her mind she wakes up feeling like a new blossoming rose plant which over night grew a new prickle to challenge any inheriting gardener. She decides to sit on top of him, grabs the Willy Wanker and runs her front teeth down the shaft. He awakens with her moist water slide touching his nose making it a pleasurable morning task of oral play as entree while remaining stuck in the soft loving theater setting of tranquil horniness which with a loud "Roaarrrr" is abruptly interrupted. The unwelcoming disturbance comes from a drunk mouth shouting French abuse words. The coq-au-vin has escaped the pot! Bruce is already up and about sporting out his fitness on the sand. Shoetef looks out and observes him now charging towards the predatory communicunt and *bang*, he too now strikes him down with one epic punch. The idiot flies over the wooden veranda railing in to a coral patch. That is it; the face is smashed beyond what pure alcohol can do. Bruce commences to play the anxious kid on the block by shouting and commences packing up his belongings.

- You mother fucking rogue beast. Worse than a rotten corpse in the morgue returning to life as a zombie…
- Zombies, yeah sweet, aim for the head, aim for the head, he, he, he…
- I had enough!!
- From what? Stop acting as a goon bag miscarriage!*
- I had enough, I had enough. Want to go home.
- Ah corpus Christi, hear what you say. Lack of Mon Cheris is making you go insane in your membrane!*
- Membrane?
- Yes your fucking intelligence is limited to the skin on your dead apple in the goggle box!
- Fuck off. You have no…..

As if Nero was burning down Rome the girls are too switching gear in to panic mode. While trying to digest the situation, the women follow with packing up desiring a return to Maputo to let the heat dissipate. Within an hour, the soft cock and the two anxious cats have departed leaving the entire place for Shoetef to master. Paarrrtyyy!!! Well first somehow he has to dispose the muppet who should have done an audition at the satirical Le Bébête* show. Now this humorless twat chasing drooling bozo is more pulp than a porn star fiction and lies there con comme une valise sans poignée*. He observes nobody on the beach. He drops his pants and pisses over the nuisance. Then he goes inside and searches through the whole place; up and down if there is something to get a real kick off. The old bird must have had something to smoke, swallow, snort or at least to buy that stuff….? Disappointingly the biggest sport on offer are eggs, frozen croissants and a "hell yeah" to Lucifer's arm pit smelling Manchego stile cheese! After the overly energizing breakfast he reverts to packing up. The signs are not good for staying back, but in the sacred name of the lord of coolness he cannot be bothered in following the hustle and bustle of the others. Coming to his mind he still had a few weeks spare and maybe making love to a sweet Negress on the Shores of Lake Malawi might be a good item to add to the bucket lists' shopping cart. Suddenly his horny thoughts drift towards Natalie and... The bloody stone! "Where is it? Where was it?" His heart goes in to erratic pumping mode while the mind is crying foul play, "who on earth would be interested in that piece of cheap glassware looking rock?" As next he sees that one of the stray dogs must have pinched a page from the Noticias newspaper. On second look it is two days old, but contains an article describing the death of two older men at an exquisite resort in Swaziland whereby both were brutally chopped up by machetes and dumped in Luphohlo dam as fish bait. Dizziness sets in. The world is moving towards a... choo choo train, next stop ahead is... #black out!#

8 A STONE PITCH'S BEGINNING

The birth of Morning Glory was anything else than a romantic prospecting outing by some lucky charm seeking mavericks. It happened on another dawn fulfilled morning with down pouring over an open cut mine, meaning the tents were shared during the night with bite lusting mosquitoes where any protective cover resulted in waking up soaked in sweat. While the flying army bastardy ate up the masters the local diggers are held under submissive rule of rogue militia bandits operating independently, astray from the main troops with their Chinese financier who coerced with anyone, anybody any humanity consciousness lacking African butcher or so called independence and liberty fighter. It was nearing towards 5am where a small group of men hit tedious, opposing, if alive vicious defending hard rock whereby in action one digger hit himself with the pick ax with the spear protruding deeply through his leg's flesh which immediately commenced to bleed and him to scream in agonizing high pitched tunes. The supervising under-aged soldier started to respond by screaming in a high pitched voice with a responding demand that he continue digging or else he will won't see his family after the night shift's ending. However the peers of the injured too cry that the blood stream wont allow him to do this anyway and that the human resourcing levels are already too low to meet the master's expectations; the young kid himself was not far from saying good bye to the world. In this moment the Chinese entrepreneur stepped up to the trenches edge to make his own observance. After a short preconceiving judgment orientated thought of money being sufficiently drained away together with his disliking of the rainy situation he takes out a gun and releases a shot towards the poor man. It would have relieved him from his painful misery quickly, that is if the shot had not gone astray by purely blowing off only his ear, half the jaw and some skull exposing the brain behind the eye; and then attempted to disinterestedly walk away where he then bumped in to the barrier forming young militia making him too fly in to a puddle of muddy water whereby informing all involved that money was still his. His supremacy is not to be questioned, never. He reverts to shouting, "zou, zou, go, go, zho, zho"; acting and sounding like an erratic farmer chasing away scare crows from his crop. With shock penetrating promptly deep in to their bodies, another digger pushes his shovel a bit deeper and retrieves a heavy clay laden rock clump out of its earthy naval hideaway. His first thoughts are, "nah this cannot be anything of value". In parallel anger was building up in his master's mind. It splashes out quickly with a new demand of the digger to pick up the found cluster and to carry the bloody piece of hard shit out of the trench which is without hesitation immediately obeyed too. However, the exhausted man slips out on his final step to the top. His upper body was looking out of the hole, but the soggy steep unprotected embankment collapses sending the poor peasant with an avalanche of dirt down in to his own dug out grave; ultimately also the grave of his fellow men plus the supervising kid with his assault rifle making the last swerving arm movements over his head aiming to protect the weapon before being buried alive. The recovered stone supersedes the unfolding event by falling out of the death destined man's leathery hands in front of the shocked foreigner's feet. That time elapse is needed to understand the magnitude of multiple deaths happening whereby the storm too is allowing a small break for some shimmering rays to emerge from the pressed conical shaped coal ball past its clay covering cocoon. The disgust vanishes quickly and his mood turns in to curiosity. The next to him standing sergeant lifts up the stone and polishes it with his wet shirt. More of the weird color combination is visually released. Their faces maintain the status of disbelief in what was found. Never the less the smize* through the Mandshurian master's eyes slits replicating a mean sounding tooth grinding smirk emerges from the side of his mouth while simultaneously he grabs the new found carbon piece. In return he hands a few silver coins to the sergeant, plus two cigarette packets to distract further interest. "Shoo, shoo, go and buy a goat or pig instead of bush meat shot down with medieval bow and arrows. Plus there is sufficient coin to buy grog to please the missus and who knows 20,000 kids, brothers, sisters comprising family in their tribal pecking order."

At night fall the stone is cleaned and its first glimpses of being again exposed to oxygen fulfilled air. A captain commissioned by the catchment commanding colonel arrives at the new owner's tent, exercising hatred apathy emotions towards the racist behaviors which are beyond that exercised by the white man. His sign language and in indigenous vocal chords roaring uptake only results that the rich outsider arrogantly reiterates his opinion of operating in midst of animals more primitive than apes whereby it was time he should consider change of tactics similar to what the Belgians did in Congo. Naturally the comments are not necessarily emanating friendly collaboration efforts, which increases the annoyance of the upper class modern saviors' Cantonese good will of cold war related brotherly help with a final snipping back and pointing out; "Cao, wo tsoa gou zaizisszzz*!" The answer comes promptly; Tai niu bi,...bi, bi., bi*!!! The words, the tone, the aggressive anger is just enough that the two militias jump on to each other where the sergeant fires off a first shot in direction of the Asian resource stealing intruder, followed by tripping over the jewel and in the motion of falling releases the gun a second time, a third, a fourth bullet shoots out while reattempting to gain tight grip of the weapon, but too late, both are clean and clear swiped from the living with blood splattered all over the 45 degree angel shaped green tent walls, worse than a zombie missing his bite for the brain and accidentally wounds the neck vein! The event including being covered with dirty seen human grease leaves the internationally educated foreigner increase his own desire to disband the African continental shelf all together similarly as his forefathers did from his developing ancestry's home town towards a city desiring to be among the flowers in the nearby hills rather than an open sewer swamp. And just like his people of origin looking to reunify the far flung islands to the north of his heritage country his eyes are magnified by the stone; a gift worthy to symbolize reunification of his African intertwined history with the Far East influenced troubled family past. However, this time with the clear ruling of their class representing the highest social bracket above the plebs who labored hard in the muddy waters of Yangtze River's delta area, who on a continuous basis of survival strenuously were aiming to tame nature's destructive forces. The newly found bonding's purpose had alignment. The stone was seeking a form of ethical domination opposing interbreeding like preserving cultural identity through executing a similar drive like the Aryan movement or the Ku-Klux-Klan; it was reborn from the ashes and keen to gain a status as a pure blood compared to the new friends who are perceived as archaic mentally mutilated fortune hunters desiring a reinstatement of an unjustified status above everybody else. The domination vision aligned to the expedition master's context of seeking glory beyond the deleterious environment of these woods and beyond a world which constantly attempted to humiliated him. However in case of the stone it went beyond world's limited cognition. It was seeking a prodigious far flung constitutional fascism representing a humanity unknown societal value! Could it be unfortunate that the rescued ultimate goal did not match that of the rescuer? Were those screams at its second birth representing an overarching anti climax of life? And will it decipher between human race and make a choice? Evil knows no boundaries.

The stone is gone and Shoetef awakens in a hospital to the whispers of a female voice welcoming him back to the realms of the lucky living. It is a nice and bright, white sterile room, somehow making Shoetef astonished that this kind of medical facility exists in Mozambique and, and... "what the god damn fuck?" Natalie is standing in front of him in a nurse's costume, bracing a sexy smile with her tongue tip touching those big juicy lips with her staring eyes indicate a determined desire for pleasure, plus a bloody damn whip in her hand!! When she realizes that he is truly on the path of awakening and regaining consciousnesses she makes a smile making the top row of her teeth shine in white color through more brilliantly as if sun rays are braking on crystals. But they are the wrong stone, "you are a naughty boy as my prize is not here". #Shwuuueeeee - bang# and the whip cracks above his head hitting the hospital bed's railing. "Oh wonder", is all that can chime through the dome's arteries. A second voice emerges, "Tranquilo, slow down, take it easy you black hare, yo se que tu eres enojado!*" On the opposite stands the Latino nutter from Swakopmund, Juan Tequila Dumpstar Guerilla with a typical dubious left side mouth corner lifting grin, while bending over the patient and wearing a doctor's gown!

- *Fuck me dead!! Fuck me dead!! Stop this freaking dream beyond rancid haaqarrll*!*
- *My dear friend, how are you? I know you are surprised to see me, however there is a reason behind the madness.*

- I bet! What next…? Pull my thumbs apart, drip fry me with hot wax or shoving a pineapple up my rear!?!? Come on, shoot me in the head and kill the disappointing zombie mutation.

- He, he, he, unfortunately you stumbled in to a messy story, imagine a French cook trying to do a flambe with watery chocolate mousse.

- So keelhauling through the chippie fryer?

- He he he, I didn't mention French fries did I!? By the way in your condition, keep away from them.

- In that case even worse à le chef de grand cuisinière, slicing an onion to perfection with Chinese infusion; lingchi death through 1000 cuts!?!

- No my dear friend even evil doctors prefer effective guns instead of wielding around with razor sharp knives, he, he, he.

- Or foul smelling Latino jokesters being denied a blow job from an African lass…

- Ha! Well amigo, guess what!?

- Hmmnnn… fire off and do the job properly.

- Without us you would be dead! You have undergone quite an extensive treatment.

- Again, please be professional and aim for the brain!

- Well amigo, I did do a funny selfie with you, that is your half dead corpse which might gain popularity as a bad tasting zombie flick containing some stinky tofu as main actor. And that to the anger of the actress who gave you a break from any painful female jealousy shadowing behaviors to only thereafter dive deep in her heart to do saddening deep prayers seeking forgiveness followed by bad thought haunting her, thus retrieving you from international money hungry corporations who dictate those governmental bionic machinery mutants operating those rewired secret agents…

- Você está uma babaca! Mas*, mas, mas, what the heck are you up to?*

- Sorry Natalie, but

- Tsss… Where is my stone?

- Your stone now again, huh? Actually not a problem, but only if you promise me to glue that sexy dress on to your body as you might need it when treating a chain's ending Leninist backstabbing Marxist but in reality Stalinist twat face's trauma with a golden shower after he rimmed some smelling turd caves of Western agents like some ransom bold South African muscle monkey, old thick glass wearing thin bodied CIA nerd with a graying moustache keen on pounding obese fat containing perspiration dripping chicks with popcorn crumbles all over them, in these times likely together with some South Russian emir so full of himself proudly wearing black track suits with false Italian designer branding stitched on matching to his white socks, yellow ice hockey jersey and San Fransisco 49ers baseball hat, all hiding the fact that he intentionally shat himself in his thermal underwear!

- Whoa, whoa, whoa, my sugar cube in gamy milk, all I knew is that they did not know and now…?

- My dear dirty play desiring mistress, my knowledge is limited to a curry pot full of surprises which gave a pinch of piquanté in my else wise escaping dull life being captured in the rapture of an egoism acting society!

- Tsss… unlike you, the stone is not a racist!

- Races, racist, and there run the horses down the track. So role play vice versa, welcome to sit on me instead!

- Sorry amigo, but the cold war too opened rifts on this continent between those who wanted to do good and those who are just purely after quick riches.

- So in this case you are defending the Commie cunts…?

- Basta! Stop right here! Those so called commies are at the moment your best muchachos. If it wasn't for Natalie you would likely be now rotting slowly away on a discarded urine and genital juices soaked mattress containing a smelly second

*breeding harbor for ants and insects with dirt stains stuck to
it like dried hydra merda* on toilet cubicle walls while being
munched by scavenging dogs...; and not here!
- Here...?!?! Does your wore basta mean the land of pasta?
- My dear amigo, welcome to Angola!
- Não merda sherlocoloco*!?
- By the way you had a stroke and we believe your body systems
shut down because of alcoholic ketoacidosis. We had to keep
you on life support for 10 days before returning you from the
lands of happy sedation.
- Ah yeah, so where's me beer. What brand rules this joint?
- God damn you, you, you...
- Boofhead*?
- What ever, no you won't get any booze, just try to be happy by
flying on these psychotic causing Russian anti antibiotics, which
by the way in this neck of the woods are rare as hen's teeth!
- So what are the upcoming plans...? I guess you want to retrieve
the brown massacre.
- You will get to know in a few days, you will get to know....
Anything else? A phone call to your parents...?
- I could do....aaahhh alrighty alrighty.... Where the heck is my
comforting love of my life, Fat Slapper Porky Pauline?*

Natalie makes a duck face, sees it is not bringing his attention, snaps
with giving the middle finger and leaves. But Juan manages to swiftly retrieve
the doll to allow Shoetef a whoring port of strength gathering while subject to a
lock down in a hidden world where utter poverty mingles with living costs well
exceeding those in more fashionable, world adaptable cities.

Angola's control of sphere is smartly restricted and so is the near dead
man's life until a few days later a social media entry notification pops up. Bruce is
bumming around in midst of the colossi of Memnon. A few hours later the three
are sitting in a limousine rolling down Avenida 4 Fevereiro with the shiny skyline
of the Ilha in the back ground kissing the setting sun over the Atlantic. They are
rolling towards Luanda's international airport.

- You are lucky not having to stay long here. As a memory to fondle in all eternity you can have a Cuca before departure.

- Cuca is that all!?! One only? What about a safari along the city's foreshore? Anyway what is the annoying story here…?

- As you can guess I'm not African, however there are still close connections between former allied governments. And then there is this race for international fame, greed and what ever a demon's horns thinks it can poke on. By the way this country is rich in tourism potential, but remains deep back waters. Its national beast, the orix is a good example of potential to make it beyond advertising on a shabby airline's rudder, but is pushed aside by more petite springboks. May the moon landscape of the Miradouro da Lua and the Quedas de Kalandula be only reachable for the mighty brave enough to sit in a local taxi keen on ripping you off every piece of Monopoly money!

- "Hey!", comes from a disgusted Natalie, "I'll report you to the Zé Maria!"

- Si, si, si my small esquinera with a big mouth! I wonder what flirtatious propositions your secret service head honcho has so far forwarded you? Este país está más interesado en hacer rica a su querida hija que en cablear un taxi*. Socialists are worse than hoarding clans of Soros, Rothschields and Zuckerbloomers! Thus, there is a never drying interest on low radar flying exorbitant quid making treasures…*

- Ahhh, so rightly coming back to the stupid stone which guessing Bruce stole?

- Who else?

Shoetef makes a sign with moving an enclosed hand towards and away from his nose.

- ???

- Fuck knows!?! Fuck nose amigo!

- You bobolito are actually muy funny.

- So how does this fit together with CC, you, Natalie, Francoise…?

- Oh, well yes, good question. I was in Namibia because of the diamond trade. Francois the idiot showed too much off and everybody knew that there will be a big bang. Natalie's involvement was smartly executed as she hid behind the hot headed fumes. We just do not know who is pulling the strings on the other side. What exactly happened to CC is unknown. And what I can gather Natalie was so scared that she let down her guard by helping a drunken world roamer.…

- Thanks, why now the hurry?

- Shit can be slippery and even more in Africa. Remember, eat plenty cassava porridge with moamba! As you can expect and appreciate we will fly something resembling a metallic falkor to ensure being undetected by any anglo-saxon bullies and believe me you don't want to use their lavatory. I recommend that you chose a decent lunch at Murtala Muhammed International. Maybe avoid soggy fried chicken…*

The next day commences early morning with prayer songs from the nearby mosque. What an exciting greeting after the days lingering in a secrecy kept hospital with talk avoiding doctors and disinterested nurses limiting any entertainment to sterile injections and now this loud awakening; a bit too early to Shoetef's liking, "but hey no freaking headache! What a great rooted feeling of being alive, able to hear drums beating the crap of eternal sleep out. There might be some ticklish action at the beginning when the worms eat your cadaver slowly out, but do you then still qualify as proper dead tissue to partake in a zombie apocalypse?!"

The Lotus Hotel located near the Tahrir square is nothing anywhere close to the shiny armor of the pharaohs, but its bar doors open Shoetef a return in to routine with his drinking habit. The Stella beer is not pursuing him to classify it as a worldly top notch drop; it is a more merry maker after the consumption. Slamming down a brekkie trekkie is charming the wait in front of the building containing the hotel's quarters in the upper levels; happily with a stomach full of tasteless, mushy, filling Ful Mudammas*. The recommended taxi driver is of course taking his time to arrive. Natalie remains angry resulting in Shoetef trying to forget any hope of pleasure and to be pleasured. At least she is standing next to him quietly applying final touches of blue mascara, "what a lovely color on ebony skin." Juan is rampantly walking up and down the entrance area, a bright white room with an unpainted high ceiling whereby the elevator is located in midst with emergency staircases embracing the sides. On the walls are a few paintings, one of a young boy dressed up as a concierge with an Osman empire Turkish hat on while another one is showing the upstairs wooden bar reproducing a cocktail party scene as the classy days of Paris have never ended, just the glasses seemed to be filled with brown liquor; coffee instead of wine, cognac and absinthe. The street in front of them is bustling, the shops decorating their sales pitch of western high end merchandise for ladies. While people are rather hectically passing by an old black Mercedes rolls in to the scenery and stopping in front of them. "Salamualeikum sadiq, welcome my friends!" comes as introduction from the local guy who introduces himself as Islam Moses. The intentions are discussed and the search for the thief begins! El Italy, University, Coptic, El Nada, Cure and New Cairo hospitals are visited, but the exhausted party's mood is only lifted at a hidden shwarma serving drinking den. "Two beers please, aka yalla yalla* min fadlik*!!" While Natalie is slowly heading towards happiness, Juan gets up angrily gesturing with his hand a slit being cut and mentioning the need to phone. At once two locals ask to join the party. One guys speeds up things by a nice clump wrapped up in aluminum foil; dark brown hashish. The following lesson learning is that in Cairo so long the bar tender is content drifting along in his own world smoking dope drinking beer is all jayid*. However with Natalie slowly sliding in to the land where English is forgotten and thus changing to the desire of only communicating in French combined with Portuguese it seems that the locals are slowly getting eager in showing off their language skills learned at the Sham-el-Sheik or similar nearby place on the Sinai peninsular. Shoetef is disliking, mistrusting the developing situation and reduces his inhalation loads when the qanb al-bakstani* cigarettes are passed around. He even starts to buy two additional rounds in hope that everyone's high flying altitude can descend towards a tarred landing strip, but when one of the local guys starts showing over zealous interest in Natalie by maneuvering his hands over her thighs, the plane is steered towards crash collision. Shoetef silently stands up, moves to his free right side, slides over the tiles and smiles; and then quickly grabs a chair and smacks it over the horny monkey. Shoetef's next move is throwing a table on a self-proclaimed rescuer want to be Egyptian Knight Rider, but ultimately also only a mug with back side hair protruding out his shirt's neck collar. Half of the bar is evolving in to a state of unrest. Shoetef gets hold of a bottle and breaks it, leans behind on to a local bystander and exposes the sharp edge to his neck. With the other hand he tears Natalie away from the remaining testosterone intoxicated punters, throws a few pounds on the table and vanishes with forwarded cries of some camel raping swear words.

The following second day is getting even more strenuous. Again no lucky strikes except in form of a tobacco brand. They decide that maybe a late afternoon detour to Egypt's nearby second biggest city Alexandria could be the answer. However riding on a sarcastic wave, Bruce in his anxiety got most probably cost conscious as too he should have returned home by now whereby the travel insurance could have run out of validity, making it an easy discounting of him seeking refuge at the upmarket Salam International Hospital. However, surprisingly soon after arrival at Sidi Gaber train station while walking towards the German hospital the first signs emerge where Bruce could be undergoing treatment. A South African doctor at a cafe over looking Stanley Bridge mentions that an inertly rotten rooted bio-wasted patient is still miraculously alive at the American hospital. The doctor further eludes to implemented security restrictions, something he is not allowed to disclose, but taking in to consideration the unnoticed stolen medications providing him a welcoming break from the bleak days running at nights through the paintings lacking white walled corridors, it for his opinion really did not matter if any information gets leaked. The question now is who of the three had the guts to go in! Less surprisingly, Juan forwards the demand to be dropped off at the railway station; as source of inspiration!

After enduring a damning headache the day before Natalie complied with Juan's desire and had by now fully forgiven Shoetef on their home way with a chartered boat. She even found some liking to the idea of Fat Slapper Porky Pauline destined Egyptian burial in the Nile. Although the idea attracts a loud protesting from the captain and it is not what a person would think of. He rather realized that the love doll could finally have a fulfilling sex life with his 15 year old son! "Really?", comes from an unbelieving Natalie, while Shoetef commences a ceremonial kumba-ya-my "good bye"* tire lord anthem and throwing the doll over the reeling in to the river. All good for a minute or two. Then a lost police boat speeds past chasing the oversize kiddies' floaty and retrieves the triple holed bloke's milking device. The fishing sergeant screams and wants to return the darn thing by directing their boat to follow. It is a frustrating adventure for a police vessel lacking competitive the horse powers, but as a positive note, they are able to keep the reward as a bad luck charm. Who knows, maybe an unannounced Arab spring revolution is soon going to strangle the authorities.

By now Natalie realized that her own search for Morning Glory might not meet her imaginations as being the future modern mother of universal crystal emanating power. Never the less the stone shall shine for her and she shall still attempt to be Earth's new matriarch goddess of fortune, love, humanity's conscious connecting chain in evolving towards a more sophisticated existence, but also fertility and a reign over female lickspittles* and lastly to torture those male borborygmooses*! Oh shit, the thoughts are making her horny and a weird returning transformation of love is taking place whereby Shoetef is perceived as the new religious master capable fulfilling all her wet dreams hormonal pounding expectations. Her pink knickers became misty from the heat, making them look like accommodating blood rather than thought promoting fecundity juices. All while Shoetef's mind is wandering off to accessing Bruce without being captured by the guards where he could use a funnel as doctor's tool, dress up like a Coptic priest, while passing healing hop and malt medicine right down the patients damn lying throat!

It is 3am in the morning where Shoetef is sneaking in to the morgue. Dressed up as a doctor using a black wig from Natalie. A nice wig which is in fashion with girls too impatient to have their curly hairs grown a decent length to plate, but he still is cutting its length to shoulder height; it needs to look professional rather than a slutty garment. He enters the venue through the back door in to the morgue where not even the toughest bear wrestling KGB agent is going to be on shielding duties. The plan is to move forwards towards the wards which are located on the opposite side of the building by using a stair case as remote as possible. He heads up to the top floor and descends down to the below level where Bruce is believed being held. Well that was what the doctor said...

Just walk around and where there are guards think of a tactic to distract them. "Maybe a piece of string with falafel balls attached? And then sliding them over a patch of garlic yogurt sauce?" But nope the answer is in of the morgues' attached examination room. Shockingly on the bare stainless table on a mattress lies Bruce, ready for his last rights of passage to the underworld. The hospital must have triaged him past any hope to unlikely survival and awaiting death. Or….?

- Oi! Are you a week cunt?!
- #Gurgle# fuck me dead.
- Save the hassles, not required. And neither that anybody thought to give you a first class ticket on the last train to Trancentral, nor a sound blaster looking like a pyramid chanting those Mu Mu chorus rhymes. Hope they are at least giving you some choo choo train releasing steamy pain killers.
- Mate, that damn fucking cunt of a stone!
- I hear…
- Went northwards towards Mozi Ilha, but then in to Beira where the locals informed me that the Renamo was gaining activity. Not good as further north some rogue Muslim bandits were fondling with ideas of separatism. So fuck this shit, as when in Africa rebellions take place they tend to be quite nasty. I paid an exorbitant priced taxi to reach Malawi, where as next my stomach started bloating up like a dead goat who had drunk from a poisoned well. It got worse, the excruciating pains were not doable, so got in touch with my travel insurance, which was a useless mob under management of some foreign disinterested conglomerate. The doctors in Blantyre could not hold off their swearing in Hindi, seemingly in mental agony opposing to Londoner do gooders with Indian heritage.
- So how the heck did you get here…? And where is the bloodthirsty stone?
- Let me continue, #gurgle gurgle# After a detour through some over stressed nervous Bollywood acting NGO medical amateurs in Kenya whereby the travel insurance mobsters

slowly got nervous. They were of course worried that their money is heading towards a walk about which was a tedious exercise in interacting with stressed up Asians who negotiated in annoyingly high pitched voices, the decision was made to transfer me here. But by now as you can see, my entire face is fucked up with pimples and sores. My inner organs have ceased functioning, but there is something you won't believe. .

- Tell me, tell me, it seems that Moses' cradle is navigating well through the sharp edged Nile river reeds...

- Since two days I am feeling like… aaahhh getting better!! And you would not believe to whom I ditched that piece of shit…! That soulless uncharitable bacterial nuisance parasite Francois!

- What…!?!

- That guy rocked up with a mixed bag of embassy delegates, like vultures flying off thorn bush aligning a valley of death with opposing cliffs pushing wind in to their wings, telling me all these nice words bla bla bla, but, #gurgle gurgle# you would think those bad asses could have brought me something like a freaking chocolate bar to sweeten my lost soul…!?!? Bloody tight asses with cold stone walled tits!!

- Oh Bruce sorry mate. I'm not better, got nothing underneath this silly carnival coat. But back to tight ass...

- Ha! Fuck you all. Ten dicks up your bongo bongo! I'm not allowed to eat anyway with exception of awfully bland baby food of canned carrots swimming in slimy porridge. But you would not believe it, one bastard laughingly joked that a meat tray resembles my look and that I am a slow cooking fat chunk of steak barbecued by a piece of hard pressed and impressed char coal. There was dribble coming down his double chin!*

- So I gather they know that your betrayal aligns with their attitude towards exercising compassion of exhaling shisha fumes in a smoke free restaurant! And coincidentally the tobacco contains that fruity tangy fruit smell of revenge. Well looking at

the mess you are in, let me tell you, I will pray for forgiveness. May at least your anus die as a virgin!

- Ha! Sadly your bad humor is the best entertainment since a while. Missed it. These guys are worse than robotic chickens. Francois acted like Darth Vadar supervising Emperor Palpatine's clones before destroying the Death Star while eagerly planning to avoid any traces.

- He, he, you will resurface like Kenny from South Park, but just looking like Karl from Aqua Teen Hunger Force...

- Nope! That perv will be you! And larrikins needing crystal meth to raise to your level will all be going with you to hell! There they will be sitting at Lucifer's camp fire where your hacky sacks will have their STDs roasted off to thereafter be bashed with rotting feet!*

- OK, ok, you lurk, stone gone, so what now? What shall I say to the fart catching commie twins?*

- Tell them that I hid the stone at some place. Anything or anywhere so long it involves locals. What I could gather is that Egyptians are seen as rat bags by all others including Arabs and guess what?... There is a reason!

- And I guess your weak broke mind thinks the same with me?

- You bet, when I return to stealth health, get the fuck out of my view as I might have by then hypnotized the stone to grow angry wings, albeit would not be surprised if that piece of evil shit would do seek soul friendship with you!!

*- Insh'allah ya sadiqu khiana saghiru!**

- When I return being a smooth running engine, please avoid your presence as my essence will not require biomass polluting lubricants full of shit covering dip sticks like you!

- Well, look at it as trip of a life time! Literally. Laylatan saeidat wa dae'aan.*

Shoetef returns and lets the other two know that a second visit is needed due to Bruce being highly sedated, but managed to indicate through a soft murmur that the hunted might be hidden near the pyramids. As the day is well in to its rock'n'rolling shacking and closely dancing with the Saharan sun, Juan vanishes again on another mysterious mission, this times' excuse being a spiritual need for Coptic churches, which for exercising a Marxist mask seems weird, but Natalie is dressing a smile when Shoetef suggests a visit to the Egyptian museum. #She takes priority# Plus it is a legitimate reason to do some eye candy shopping on local culture disrespecting Russian dolls sporting short skirts! Shoetef's mind patterns divert towards a horny party with petting behind the mummies, followed by fingering and placing his obelisk between thighs embracing hieroglyphic written tats*. It is like a 1970s b-grade movie inspired story of Cleopatra finally re-unionizing with her love Julius, fully awaiting to make love on the Khufu ship with slim 6-pack bellied Nubians playing the drums while female slaves waving cooling palm branches over them and muscled up brain amputees from ancient gyms serving them dates soaked in honey wine which they would lay in each other's mouths carefully to enable the release of all possible sensualities from touching, smell and tasting. A guard finds them sharing a female toilet cubicle and in anger chases the two through the halls to the large foyer atrium and out in to the park to join a pack of feral unclean dogs.

 Before getting back to work in retrieving the stone a visit to the pyramids and the Sphinx is deemed as a must. And a closer view than from this African monstrous, but generally doable city. And the sexual abstention is nagging the odd couple as neither is the hotel allowing unmarried couples to share a room at any time. Therefore, slowly the animal instincts are heating up to where after the obligate camel ride Shoetef goes down on to his knees and hides his head under Natalie's Islamic tradition complying black long skirt. But it too did not bring the sought relief. The guard's protest surfaces quickly. Their doing also opened a door to demand extra tip. It is becoming obvious that money requests a full day consuming annoyances until one guys has the guts to forward one for purely buying dried figs of him to which his dirty face receives a hand full dirt thrown at "Rat! Next time the pebbles will be larger. Now yalla yalla* and fuck off!" Of course the guy's self confidence is as strong as wobbly jelly, so the attention is redirected to arguing with a wolves pack of visitor targeting thieves only to be then hassled all the way to a shop's entrance by a local police officer attempting to mask his allegiance by telling fairy tales of his honesty towards protecting uneducated but appreciated, the stupid but looked upon tourists. "Bullshit; there is a reason that the Egyptians lost the Sinai!" Even more when abusing comments are getting forwarded that they are drunk Russians intending to destruct old sacred religious artifacts; and that with insh'allah in every second word coming out of the liars shwarma gap! The accusations step up a notch with lies that they even touched the smallest of the heavily weathered out pyramids, which are deprived from seeing any of the funds, at least not through any donations originating from the careless locals who are clearly only interested in milking off tourists rather than investing in to maintenance. The financial rip off continues; somewhat self inflicted by showing minor inquisitive interest towards a nearby jeweler selling gem stones. But, at once Juan surfaces. "That rapscallion might become beneficial!" All in pleasurable smiles as if nothing historically has happened. A seconds pass where the shop owner forwards them all an invitation to mint tea or Arabian coffee. The good intentions are purely a sales pitch for over priced junk where after a while the ultimate happening takes place; after one handler smartly recognizes their mission for a rare stone whereby in a rare move for locals actually admits having no clue nor anything comparable available. While this old man with a fully bold head is sharing his shisha the smoke gives Shoetef a break to think of clearing the smoke from a mirror. The host is giving some funny clues about women he met craving for more diamonds, literally seeing them as their best friend and often it does eventuate through premature death of their older lovers. OK, Shoetef now orders beer as this might take longer. While the hints are soaked up by two, Juan's patients on the contrary is wearing thin. All the small talk resulting in the business man swinging, smoothly like warm butter spreading verbs and consonants though the room to rise in to the carpet lined ceiling as if it is a dream catcher, makes the Latino go back on to the top of his league by soon standing up desiring to move towards the man to prevent further white washing his so called guests. He is held back by Natalie as the only real possible love story ending is providing buyer's commitments. Juan chooses laughable looking red slippers, but goes nuts by grabbing several glass bottles containing sand plus a papyrus roll cheaply crafted with his name written in hieroglyphs; palm trees, stones, birds of prey and a lion. "Hey mate, that could also well mean Lucy! Or shit, dick, fuck me with a strap-on for that matter!" Juan's take on his buying spree is being perceived as a possession acquisition hunger attack, worse than ravaging munchies and thus usually only seen by women keen on shoes. Neither is Natalie too impressed on her scarab, nor Shoetef with his golden can of Heineken beer which was bought outside but with an added commission to please everyone; however it is now a savior for buying anything more expensive and as time is running out, some empty beer cans are left back for the owner's sons. Due to fierce competition, meaning that there is no way to inquire all shops the story is radiating away along unfavorable patterns, which is increasingly frustrating, especially Juan seems to struggle.

Plan B is passing by the hospital again. The day is still early and plenty of time existing, just unfortunately the caravan's sleeping in hiding camels have been replaced by black German sedans with tinted windows, like big vicious super detective bugs luring in front of the main entrance. Juan's inner Latino raging heart now takes control. He drags the other two to a nearby drinking den, where they meet a local business man and his entourage doing a living on directing drugs between North Africa, the Middle East and Europe. And again it comes down to the fact that the local bar owner, the brother of the mob is desiring to take a bigger share of earnings above his entitlement. In midst of all the guests smoking hashish and going silly on King Browns*, soon bottles of Stellas are flying over the place as if Captain Spock is defending rationally a heart attack on irrational assumptions of figuring out how this all could happen in happy orbit. Natalie jumps and hides under the table while the guys are cranking themselves up for pub wars part 2. The bar tender's unfortunate fact is actually for once using his pygmy sized brain cells. Just it is worthless ammunition against the roguishness acceleration in the heads of the two piss bots, where the final act of aggression is him being thrown over the counter; midget tossing!

Next morning is an early start where Natalie is attending her beauty sleep while Juan and Shoetef are departing with a headache and dry mouths. Running down half Egypt from Alexandria to Cairo at night with train rides either way taking over 2.5 hours and fully fed up from another bland breakfast of beans plus the luxury of an accomplishing plate of black olives. Shoetef's comment of the day is, "not even the shit beer motivates here!" A few meters before exiting the building the ceiling starts to produce a crackling cracking tone whereby a second later plaster pieces liberate themselves. The structure is preparing itself for total failure, making both turn 180 degrees and jump towards the lift hugging building's core. During that motion Juan grabs the hotel's cigarette smoking concierge and protectively leaps on to him. #thraddaddaaaaduummmmmmswooooohhhfffff....# It takes less than 3 seconds and half of the ceiling is now on the floor. Just millimeters away from where three heavy chunks of debris fell they lay all covered in white dust. The concierge frees himself from Juan and instead of offering free laundry forwards the demand, "bakshish*!" Juan's persistence brakes while giving Shoetef a helping hand for retrieval;

> *- Get fucked you annoying goat raping rejection! Get fucked and go and fuck yourself, hard, quick or I stuff a camelus dromedarius up your stinking pig cock sucking ass. You are less worth than a piece of dog shit! That is it. God damn shit. I had enough. Out and over. See you in another life. Mierda, mierda, mierda...*
>
> *- What the heck. What about Natalie? What about the diamond? What about your commie spy friends?*
>
> *- Those putas* can all get fucked too. By all four of canopic jar protectors; the baboon's cock and Imsety's fist as turkey stuffing, the apple being replaced with tongue kissing Duamutef the jackal while covered in the falcon's squirting dung glace! But not me. If you want to avoid your own cavities being spiked by mummified dicks of beasts, then escape too before the gyps get you.*

Shoetef is astonished to see so many people at an international airport looking forward to leaving a country lacking any war, high crime levels or natural disasters, which it mastered exceptionally well with the construction of Aswan dam. After buying a ticket out he observes an article in The Egyptian Gazette of an Australian aggressor passing away through an unnatural death caused by political opposing devious fractions. The story continues that the poor patient was brutally glassed. The autopsy found thick convex lens pieces below his skull; it seems that there is more entertaining verity existing in Egyptian state disciplined media over a tabloid containing a top less girl on page 3. "Not!" Like the truth keeps continuously insulted feeling political correctness movement away from sleeping so too has this page been a lively painful awareness reminder of human instincts. The replacement is more putrid written diarrhea. Undoubtedly not even an umami sapid salami stick between their legs would save them! "Yes Juan is right, Cairo is worse than mutilating young girl's genitals."

9 A HARD STOOL EPISODE WHERE TOUGH BEHAVING EMANCIPATION MEETS OVERLY RELAXED CHAUVINISM

As the continuous fight for quality and quantitatively sufficient supplying land was not enough hardship for the small village in midst of the Southern Chinese brackish black back waters, the average population was also subject to rough social conditions and tough implementation of Neanderthal leaning values. Men not only regularly worked as free labor, but as peasants they were subject to paying hefty taxes to leaders showing no empathy towards their hardship of wringing pastures off the sea. Life's physical grating wore out the patriarchs at early stages resulting in wide scale of abuse beyond themselves; the bad behaviors engraving in to their children's psyche as if a cow's ass was branded. Post a traumatizing year consisting his mother's giving birth to not only an unwanted girl but with adultery accusations coming from the wider community which only left her forced suicide as rescue beacon from own worse plus more global executed punishments. They were lying dogs as her action did not prevent his father receiving glossectomy* by a blood hungry, opiate addiction driven greasy greedy colonel, without anesthetics. The forwarded script of justification was misleading information relating to harvested rice quantities as naturally a parent first wants to fill up their children's from hunger bloated bellies than feeding a murderous machinery where history has shown that any trust, empathy or good will will never emerge. Not tomorrow. Not in a decade. Not in hundred years. Damn to all rotten eggs ruining what is already ruined as if the infection could penetrate any hard shell. After several years' of floods tag teaming with droughts the crop was in one year a real treat. It gave society hope. False hope as soon thereafter it became clear that it was a rare occasion well fed young lad's turn to serve the aristocracy as soldier. Japan was continuously defeating the Qing kings; first along the Korean peninsular, then they crossed the Yalu River in to Manchurian territories whereby now actively threatening the nation's political heart land. The colonel did not forget to ensure that all young men from the town were enlisted in to recruitment. The selection process took place south-west of Shanghai in front of a few rural wooden shacks along the urban fringes which nowadays is known as Pudong. As it was a glorious morning the nearby operating mistrusted Gweilo* merchants crossed the river just after the dawn to give their horses a good cardiac exercise. The early wet grass maintained the resting cavalry with that touch of challenging gallops. The meeting between the two worlds represented a good opportunity for the foreigners to secure a racially more evolutionary seen Sino slave for their admiralty friends who were hunting further south in defined lands of lower class citizen also known as being rebellious coolies. And purely based on the arrogant perception of being in closer proximity to the heart land they desired a more purer blooded "chien chinoise*". Soon the boat departed the Concession and with it the ordered labor supplies who mostly were subject to the code de régime de l'indigénat*, which was later passionately enforced by the freight's receiver.

Madagascar's 350 year monarchy was freshly abandoned and anger simmering everywhere. Queen Ranavalona III had to be carried on her deportation. On a wooden luxurious stretch she left her country, but not before she took up the last opportunity to call upon a last gathering with islands spirits, fairies and talking lemur trolls; an act involving looking deeper in to the glass than viper fish can swim. As sure as the earth circles the sun and the moon the earth, on arrival their treatment went worse than what stray dogs receive making survival in the coastal mosquito infested back waters hot pot tedious. One soldier was destined to be tough, maintain wit with the aim to be honored an alpha male status, but this made hope even a more miserable thought. As distraction he soon took up the liking to torturing others all while it was his soul being eaten by the remnant existing spiritual maggots. The awarded status supported further demotivation as it made him fall between the table and several chairs, also a big strong European aristocracy reserved couch was there. His wish to remain to his secretly held atheism beliefs was granted as the missionary inputs were deemed as good contribution to the larger picture of gaining wealth and him serving up some Taoism lies would not grow feet. Ultimately everybody saw their destiny as an abortion blown to hell!

Chongstar's ancestors who were already plenty drenched in all sorts of criminal blood arrived on the first boat crossing the Indian ocean from China. The new challenge was not only defending themselves against colonial master's devaluing attitudes; illness and sickness ceaselessly worsened. While the French were diseased, the by locals lesser respected shaded colored aliens were left detached in their camps to die from mosquito bite born fevers; breaking the last straw of the hard labor exposed bodies. Pookake became a common site; and smell. This first imported wave lost its fight when trying to establish a port. The masters brought in swiftly relief as if people where stored on shelf in a nearby warehouse. Cantonese speaking dare deviled dragons, just like our man from further north carrying the strength of mangrove dwellers resilience commenced with constructing the highland connecting railway. And they too started to convert to Catholicism giving our Shanghai rascal an extra unaware by him demoting social status, but compared to others he maintained pride by not touching any local girls. When desperation starts to kick in as weirdly nowadays many Asians dislike dark skinned people. He lone soul was aware that misbehavior would be a wet slide in to a pool full of monkey business bathers where harmonious relationships was as abundant like the ex-queen's talking lemurs. His acknowledgment as a group leader strengthened through the hard handling of these deemed lower class chameleons to a degree where they just diminished to die; death is nothing new here. Soon thereafter Indians and Swahili speaking Negros arrived as the new preferred manual suppliers which catapulted our Sino fascist to a degree similar that to a colonel and allowed him to engage with one of the very few tidy kept Cantonese women, who were not only as rare as a Delalande's coua*, but he knew her cooking could bring them prosperity beyond gaining freedom where an ugly snot snorting and spitting person with similar origins still represented a better deal than being on the social status of a piece of human garbage. With dobbing in a few bullying rogues from Bihar he gained even more acceptance and offered liberties, albeit being the drunk thief himself! This story of betrayal began a century old feud between his family and those of mogul's expats. Racism exists everywhere, just for some social utopia believing idiots it will take longer to realize than rational thinking humans to accept. Life was not meant to be easy, but an objective person will still conclude to live and let live. The dire consequences are heart breaking for the lesser fortunate when they learn that nowadays most left wing fraction rubber necks practice yuppie upper class chauvinism rather than showing interest in the worker man's troubles while still persisting on incoming union membership fees as it enables them to feel fairer free and as supportive incitement to invade their poorer client's neighborhoods with a drive to change the demographics towards multicultural artistic societies excluding any coal dust coughing leather faced laborer who can harshly disturb the newly created political correctness colon pudding capturing container with its lid rimming harmony of pink glasses on for everyone's attitudes. Yes, in the eyes of this new socialist elite they are not worth a dime nor a shout of a cheap, low quality, bitter tasting and sweat dismal relieving pony*! And if it does result in some form of interaction, the misfortune horse fodder payer is forced to listen to awful seismic pitched lesbian feminist voice or for that matter of a gender neutral declared R2D2 while doing fund raiser speeches of a helping conjoined albino platypus triplets!

Even after breeding a family the self proclaimed zhuhou* continued maintaining distance to the cattle ticks*. They knew that the chances ever to be seen as "first" class whites was impossible with those racist, self loving, continuous merde de vache* talking, stalking and acting bourgeoisie rêver d'ânes de campagne*, but neither will they ever be fully accepted as a local. And nor was there a desire to descend in to their foreign value based social hierarchy as it was seen as lowering themselves even beyond the untouchable shudras* from the big mountain hiding lands where human carcasses were sacrificed to an almighty river. The first success came after several attempts to amalgamate the method of quick Chinese cooking in a wok together with the found spices on the island, mainly pepper and cinnamon where with time turmeric was added to please the Indian community. In true Asian business mentality, money does not stink; from what ever hand it comes from, or grand mother's untidy foot if it had to be. When the French decided to enhance the importation of goats the clever guy immediately knew that cloves spiked up the meat nicely; hitting the bulls eye of the importer's taste buds. The new business venture grew with a healthy pace towards a small empire of catering to the matching clients able to afford the sharing of eating food pleasure. The fortunes only increased when not only vanilla arrived the shores of Tametave, but additionally the knowledge of a 12 year old Reunion boy who found out a methodology to pollinate the precious blooms in its narrow window of less than 24 hours. The success was allowing it as the sole orchid to develop a fruit for harvesting what represents nowadays the origin of the world's favorite ice cream taste. For the continuously increasing world's population hunger for the creamy treat the pod had to be replaced with vanillin, the biological or chemical synthetic counter product of 4-hydroxy-3-methoxybenzaldehyde. But back to the roots where the family business evolved and was never short of passing these tales through the generations. The attitudes did neither change, but their home land did by experiencing an ever increasing tension; the emperor's were replaced by army generals, then came the Japanese, followed by a civil which culminated in to a separation between a national Kuomintang government maintaining presence in Formosa versa a distinctive communist ruling under chairman Mao with creation of two buffers, Garden City's* back yard island swamp and Honkers*, both places where the family could set foot in a more stable territory, but now either being exposed to frivolous and corrupt Portuguese or drunk back stabbing Brits. The last interaction with the homeland occurred in the early 1950s. On the contrary the new found life in the tropical setting became more stable and prosperous, however here too they were still subject to others creating the future road which was unlikely seen to be as sweet tasting as an adventurous rocky road* with marshmallow cushions.

In 1960 the tide turned. The colonial masters left. And the in superstition believing remaining foreigners feared a return of the in early 1900s defeated black death, this time with a never heard or seen revengeful fury! And rightly so as still well in to 21st century the majority of world's reported bubonic plague cases are linked to Africa's largest island. With the knowledge that the French are in language and behavior similar to the Portuguese occupiers, Macau was the first port of call, however in the 70s realization surged that possibly Honkidoori* was a more political safer haven. It offered better international connections and properties above Stanley Beach were still in financial reach to afford. The city was on the verge of booming and thus the remaining commitment to Macau was to accommodate a smoking mirror business address where with the gained island expat business friendships a secretive ivory trade could be developed. They even gave it a go to sell lemur penises as the potency furball ginseng! But the world on these small islands was very small, a bit too small and conflicts simmered below the surface.

With family linkages to the English speaking port of Fort Kochin and malicious perceived dark skinned people's harbor of Madras, the history of a lost Indian soul in Africa begins as it ended on the sub-continent; one of being a minority like his alien roots from Pondicherry which was a melting pot for outsiders. Just as was Goa, a similar state occupied by an exotic mob. Generally people in this part of the world have never been treated as equal or respected by those calling themselves locals and those who desire to flee the place as quickly as they came in. Even well in to the 21st century those with deep roots still remain where Indian natives are discredited for being asylum seeker smugglers albeit their history of entrepreneurs partaking strongly in the development of local with international merging business markets. And the level of wide spread interracial disgust simmered on a low temperature like cooking a curry where the aim is to capture as much nutrients and proteins by remaining the pot of mixtures on low heat, but like the love of many for deep fried foods, the boiling point can hit quickly before the dough is removed from the scaling environment. One big eruption occurred when Chongstar's father was subject to black mailing for a bribe attempt by a former Goan liberation fighter from the Praja Socialist Party while actually being a political guest from whom the soon to be victim was trying to betray!! It was his escape, nobody's other story. But he also had to admit while the larger scale plan was as strong as coffee making swimming impossible in it, it was still in the execution as weak as one could not walk over the coffee. The previous weeks were a horrendous head ache pain inflicting cocktail of navigation efforts through inhospitable terrain of bare exposing savanna hills and dense jungle growth in the valleys past demon worshiping locals showing a high level of distrust towards the open cut mining, well knowingly it was all to satisfy a greed hungry elite hundreds of kilometers away enjoying life on the beaches of a city's ocean reaching peninsular far away from the painful in hunger fighting and lack of decent sanitation surviving poor. A friendly classified mob damn good in neglecting the entire country through bureaucracy, dictatorship and installation of mutilating land mines aimed at their too ruthless operating enemies, the UNITA.

The nightmare already started in obtaining the permission from Beijing, but how many Chinese in the world can speak fluently several Latin languages, English and swagger around the knowledge of playing an African culture trumpet. Angola was not necessarily a happy cosmopolitan melting pot of Bantu cultures; no it was a play ground which the Soviets stupidly showed little to declining interest, the currency starved Cubans hanged on to mummy's tits like a 7 year old maturity defying hobbit, offering the Chinese People's Republic a new and safe venturing environment to allow them gain their first African experiences before even the West would gain knowledge. However as rare as a pregnant nun they were subject to a half or quarter decent soldier who understood the previous conqueror's mentality, which in those days unfortunately demanded resourcing complexities as their first port of call whereby the triads from Kowloon Walled City failed miserably by showing more interest in scum bags conducting illegal animal material trades. However they lead the government agencies on to the path of mastery in disguise. They were inclining in the world's economy quickly and nobody was being fussy with whom they did business. It was all about the how. Never the less he was seen as a defector; a born and bread capitalist will never be an ideology sharing socialist. He knew well how to make means to his advantage when they became available.

And now the two were standing in front of each other and both needing, but neither trusting each other… The Chinese guy caught out in fleeing the wrong direction away from the safe territory crossing Kwango River and the rebel. Both standing lost in a city changing the charging hands. Soon it will be enemy territory held by UNITA rebels with the MPLA hiding in unknown surroundings with rogue operating Angolan Military Resistance Committee filling the buffer between. It was now 5 years past the colonial masters' departure and things were getting not only sour, but the men were having goosebumps on their skin while sweating off an unbearable heat. The lack of a refreshing wind at 100 percent humidity is demanding and else Kwachas were rare, political leaders killed or extradited and sub groups forming terror cells at their liking. The political roots and language skills proved an advantage for the Malayam blooded partisan and he managed to convince some fishing peasants to direct them for two days along a stream flowing downstream in northerly direction past dead bodies with associated smell of gun powder and rotting flesh. It was here where through a mishap the diamond liberated itself to the view of all. The Indian tried to bend over and grab it while one of the local men took out his machete, but he received in the last second a blow by jealous town's folk who immediately and without a second thought smashed from behind his skull with a wood plank. It was one sufficient strike to make the Chinese guy somersault, grab the machete and hack it in to the attacker's leg. He fell down over the victim, his blood just adding that one more touch of extra cerise color to the brown, green murky waters while screaming in pain, just like the diamond would have done if it had an inner voice to protest against its own rape of being removed from its the righteous owners. With some odd temporary jungle leafage breaking sun rays both water and stone aligned visually in a teaming agonizing status. When it came to defend interests, it seemed that the genetic, heritage and human strengths originating from a shared desire to leave hell bonded the two men. And they were aware that as foreigners on a continent where betrayal was not only existing for the purpose of tribal self-confidence and survival when resources were scarce, the modern history of human life disrespecting leaders commenced in the very early days where Egyptians royals influenced their Nubian counterparts in the realms of the Kingdom of Khush to release human laborers for the construction of its temples including the horrendous retrieval and transport of the sought after materials in the upstream regions of the Nile River. And soon children emerged, playfully replicating front line infantry foot soldiers. They too were chopped up with the inherited machetes, however two were instead captured and tied up for bailing purposes. By the end of the day the applied tactic allowed the escapees a well earned break in a bunker underneath a government disbanded mansion well to the north of the district's main town. Their strength seemed endlessly and a protruding perception by the locals was gained that the two were not normal humans, but freed animal demons who gained power through an ugly shining talisman.

And from thereon the next few days were easy navigated and the sparse food, mainly maize porridge sufficed the two who on one glorious morning after a harsh rainfall thrashing night in a cave managed to descend down the steep lush green hills overlooking the Congo River. They had crossed the border through dense forest. Well before they left the bloodied stream's water way as it did a bend towards the Atlantic coast. The Indian mercenary was smart enough to read the sun's patterns of descending in the west. It would have been an unfavorable outcome as the government was deploying forces towards its northern border along the coast line in enabling a supply line for troops in attempting to suffocate another rebellious group, the Frente para a Libertação do Enclave de Cabinda, FLEC who were accused of kidnapping and killing not only local militants but also East Germans and Cubans. However the Zaire was neither hospitable terrain, but in comparison Africa's equatorial heart was managed efficiently by a long term dictator. And his greedy mob, who during the cold war era easily changed political sides as often as their own underwear and hence were capable to safely accommodate the two lost souls in hope of financial gains in return. And there they stayed as honorable guests in the Hotel Metropole with a view over the harbor and the train station, where coffee, timber and fish from the nearby factory were loaded for the European market in exchange for imported goods which due to the nearby rapids could not be shipped upstream to the markets in Kinshasa, Brazzaville and beyond. Compared to a later stage, the railway was still functioning making the city a tradesmen hedonists' outpost comprising leisure time options of nourishing on exquisite French cuisine, drinking cheap self burnt brandies and urban hunting of small pygmy women who were as exotic in their looking, behavior, but with some fear were challenged by many to act as standing blow jobs while the crafty one could balance a glass of liquor on their heads during the act! Some even claimed that when tamed they were even capable of performing the sexual act while a man could free up his hands to lighten up a fashionable, rare cigar made of Nigerian tobacco. Their main challenge was to remain incognito from the sight of the nearby Angolan consulate...

10 KNOCK, KNOCK, WHO'S HERE

Usual life is back to full scale nepotism and discrimination against anyone who is not acting like a drag queen. Business managers are behaving like them on rags whereby continuously finding means to change for the sake of freaking change. The newest attempt is side lining lesser productive specialists to alliance partnerships, which is from the start deemed to fail due to their hunger for variations. Over the past two years the missus returned in to a temporary being nice attitude, but is rapidly deteriorating to the degree of being a whistling tea pot brewing some ugly evil tincture mixture of jealousy driven micromanagement. The days are not pleasant. The nights neither. When a new position to gather fresh air is offered no acceptance hesitation is executed. Not only does a new job substitute the good vibes of a holiday, it also gives a break from the usual bull shit eating your poor soul. No doubt Lucifer changes his visual representation. After an initial acting period, the new and old business entities come to an agreement to share the employee through weekly rotations. This makes the missus' mental health accelerate downwards in to a wild raging gully seeking the gutter for relief. She is not only turning in to a full scale chaotic raggabrash* violence but neither is she realizing her worthiness of being pillow grinding subpar. It all ends with a final war of words requiring the police to assist in chauffeuring the alcoholic wreck to rehabilitation. One problem solved. Next, Hubert and his change to being a devoted Evangelist foozle*, just like George Bush loudest song singer at Sunday's mass, but on Monday turning over that big black handle to grill a death row inmate. Shoetef's question is when will relief come for this pediculous rakefire*. But rather it is getting worse. During a secondment opportunity Hubert engages a new manager. A chain smoking, coke drinking addict with Tourette syndrome; nervous facial tick just above the nose moving the neck along with every itch. A psychopath who polishes apples with door mats. And he is efficiently pulling the corporate line over zealously by attempting to change industrial rights of employees including Shoetef's car parking allocation, declaring a shared coffee machine as unwelcome, banning the listening to radio. Concentration camp attitudes where only head down and ass up is accepted. Rewards are non existent for this kind of self loving managerial waste. But the real rage is born where Shoetef gains knowledge of and reports to Hubert the rubbish dump humping tool's past being a prosecuted fraudster. The following week Shoetef's mood swing goes in to daily before work protein spills* mode. But also this gets worse when his brain washed hypercritical work colleagues ask him if he is OK. He is caught in a mentally challenging world surrounded by abdominal canals who are all ignorantly pushing his life towards misery. The only light at the end of the tunnel, is is to make his seconded position his primary professional occupation as soon as possible which would be a good move to leave back his bonkers gone lunatic ex. But the Nazi is not letting lose, albeit releasing an obsessive-compulsive haywire for him to leave. The following day he even covers Tourette cindarella's ass in front of the general manager with an objective discussion only to receive a returning response of a back stabbing full metal jacket stile. It blows his boiling pot's lid off; transforming him in to the angriest, raging claw chopping and foul mouthing swamp crab resulting in firstly the general manager leaving and secondly finally the face wanker losing his job. Beyond this Hubert takes up thee liking of molesting young female co-workers which is resulting that half of his department is leaving crushed in tears! Inconveniently Shoetef is now seen as their priced jewel as he actually does some work, which with correct prioritization could be done on a 50% pension, highlighting waffling senior managers' common incapability. They give him an own office with sweeping lake views and the CBD's* skyline as backdrop. But it is feeling like an imploding social submarine pressurized by a spoiled ignorant figures deprived of showing any heart as if they were Libyans smuggling economic refugees aiming to be either caught by authorities or death by vessel capsizing. Unsurprisingly the mother in law has too commenced finding means to exclude him from the family; no Easter invitation, hiding of the Missus' mental history and lastly sabotaging their overseas holiday proposal. "I don't understand why you don't get your exotic kick in nearby Bali?" KLF's song "Fuck the Millennium" describes short and sharply the theatrical interludes at play, but there is still unfinished business to be done. It is Friday afternoon and unsurprisingly top of the billboard charts is the need for a real heavy base swinging weekend motivator. Surfing and golfing? Possibly a road trip up towards the warmer north? Just getting out would be nice, but money seems to be a bit rare. The missus' preference are expenditure rampages instead of working, paying rent or car maintenance. The monster queen is exercising values of a potty hole! However frustration vanishes quickly when a cute blond haired, very light reddish skin tan girl from human resources materializes.

Her face turned in to stone like Rapa Nui's Mo'ais. Good timing; Hubert pops in to inform that he received an unexpected phone call to approve the request and is now demoniacal agitated of executed political powers against him and believes he cannot deal with it and bla bla bla. Finally he leaves with a surprisingly polite, have fun next week and see you then in 9 days time…?! A hand softly but decisively grabs his chin and directs his eyes to her. Damn, steer away from the boobs!

> *- Mate, I am here on behalf of two gentlemen. One will be your future boss of which I have an agreement, the other your immediate after this conversation.*
> *- Huh, has the soggy pumpkin head turned back to Halloween clowning around? We all knew that Ronald McDonald was an old captain stabbing, but it took time to evolve to that with all the other kiddie dumb toys those burger moguls "gifted" in happy meals. Like happy tree friends slowly reacting on Rohypnol!*
> *- Ok, honey, my sweet diddledidooo Winnie the Poo making adventures with big boobed piglets! You are so sexy as nobody else in the dire i-robot cyborg producing factory… The man hugging crap which these catholic school boys pull off here even distastes your CEO and the upcoming generations are so corrupted by promoting their shitty kids on Facebook albeit the back ground is a miniature yard full of poop.*
> *- Yeah, Michael Jackson showed them how sterile a "threat" worm can live in kiddies penis'! Not to mention their mission to pray for total human obedience to society's codes and behaviors. Drink driving comes from Lucifer and leads to hell just like the frivolous behaviors of the forgotten pagan, but romanticism blossoming empires of Greece, Rome and Alexandria!*
> *- Oh, Egypt, very good, you are slowly getting in to the right mind set I am here to influence you towards. Like an honorable knight winning a blood looting battle, smeared with the enemies' juices of life over the steel face mask, an organ still sticking down the sword's blade and there you spy in the middle of the tramped down grass lost paddock a lovely girl who with a lot of effort washed her hair and made them in to soft curls exceeding the shoulders by 2 inches.*
> *- I have to stop dreaming.*

- Wake up you fuckwit! Your hatred boss has left, your office chair has seen better days and so will you soon!
- I at least get that you are a lost princess in midst of fresh carcasses of fallen warriors. Shit, how does a girl get to this destiny? Worse than looking at the bought by your IQ deprived idolizing puppets flowers slowly dyeing away while resting in your comfortable homely world.
- Are you listening, my depressed honey bear…!?!
- Yeah my nectar pollen drop of gorgeousness, just wanted to take a detour from a good fuck up!?!

The new employment contract deal is immediately signed; on a Friday just before 5pm. The drinks are nervously calling! Plus it is a great opportunity to make love before boarding the plane. His received itinerary is directing him to a flight crossing the Antarctica where he is wondering if Africa will greet him with a warm embracing smile so shiny like the snow reflecting the ultraviolet rays on to the window seated passengers or is the message directed towards chilling grimes containing cold trouble as thick as the ice below? Is the airline actually allowed to fly over this stretch of world at all? Also where are those icicle anal bead popping polar bears? And lastly, to what music do those happy feet dancing panda chooks* groove?

Day 1

Long are the days gone where the in Witwatersrand located airport decorated the name of Jan Smuts, but Francois adjusts himself to the new reality contradicting his family's continuous whinging about privilege losses. But his professional calling is still based on the old white evangelistic fun hating system defeating the rainbow nation's future cohesion idea. Gauteng describes now Johannesburg & Co. while the political elite added more funny fanny* tongue twisters like Tshwane, Ekurhuleni and freaking Emfuleni; all to a cost of tax payers. At least the Keg Pub remains true in retaining a normal name. "Well would anyone drink at an over priced shebang called Mambo Jambo!?" Albeit not of importance his guest is not fussed and would go to any beer serving den on his way through, no doubt of that! But due to his unfamiliarity of being paid by yet to be revealed person he would be wanting to get out quickly. The plan is to allow anarchy partake in eliminating undesirable algorithms of competing bounty hunters, but all matters need to be coordinated smartly. Francois is aware of his guest's knowledge beyond that of Bruce being that stupid stone stealing laboratory lavatory rat. He is even scared that his guest executes an irrational quick reaction by buzzing off to Cameroon craving for a bush meat diet of raging tough biting monkey stew. 'The bastard is even capable in flirting up a Lilliputian to be his standing blowjob toy and most likely would be with her small hands elegantly juggles his itchy and scratchy while sucking his albino cave dwelling butt plug!" From what he can gather the interests are not only of silly nature. The school years sitting in the back row's window seat did not impact on his grades and for an English speaker he picked up languages exceptionally well. Therefore, paranoia is justified. There is no reason he could not just fly off for some hedonistic rampaging damaging to places like Conakry, Lagos or Asmara as even there he would be able to farm a lass. However none of these places provided Francois any excitement. On second thought he might just be having another anxiety caused by the evil stubbornness.... It was a mistake to take the stone back home. Now he knew what caused his father's malaria illness to progress to his death. Southern Natal was free of the mosquitoes, but as luck would have it the old man was stroke shortly after losing the diamond in a poker game. When the family was grieving he wanted to get his hands on it badly as act of revenge to the fat old fart who won it. "I bet it did no good to him neither", was his thoughts of not being aware of CC's and Tom's final fate in Swaziland. Thereafter his mother developed surprisingly bi-polar disorder, including associated lows, for example where she publicly announced racial mixing disliking whereby she was destined as queen to govern lower human life forms, specifically African heritage maids, garden hands and chauffeurs, but also the Indians and Pakistanis who have raised in power through business empires to the degree that they commenced forming local activist cells, sometimes just to anger the Boers like the shurah council in Transvaal or copying previous bigot movements in terrorism like the PAGAD*. His brother too ended up in a depressed condition that he shot himself with the old man's rifle. His younger sister was fighting with eating disorders and that unexpectedly in her mid 30s. But not only did she stop opening her cake hole for tucker* loaders, from one day to another refused talking and no one knew why, not even her investment wasted psychologist. At least his employers, especially the main bread giver was generously paying above market wages, but he too was now a slave depending on their own moods, who were increasingly being agitated, even aggressive since his stint in Cairo where he failed to fulfill his duties by opting for a short cut by purely kidnapping the bloody stone. And now they are seemingly hinting something is wrong, or are these resurrecting anxieties…? Therefore the stone had to be hidden, which was done in a stunt where it was transported by a private bus company while he flew for business purposes including crafting a lie to get two mid week days off for this purpose. He got engaged by an airline trying to expand on the continent needing good marketing shots of proposed future destinations. Additionally his working arrangements were convenient towards investigating trade relations or rare stone mining… It shocked him that knowledge existed about a mysterious pain inflicting diamond and especially Asian expats were dismissing it all as childish dream time stories, similar to the belief that monsters live in the sewers patiently waiting to grab a crapping sprog*. In his world all has gotten out of control, privately, professionally and now seemingly shit is flying from left field towards him too. There must be a way to get lucky with that god damn piece of coal shit!! After finalizing his thoughts, he stands up, grabs the next by-passer's arm from behind and makes a stern cough.

> *- Hello Sir, you come with me, right now.*
> *- Oh rats bait!*
> *- Yes Sir, you have a gun pointed on your back. Walk slowly to the back of the restaurant, sit down calmly and then you can turn around…*
> *- ……? ……. :-S*
> *- Now you can turn. Be quite when talking to me or you will receive what you deserve. And it will not be your lucky second price draw which you managed to score on the due date post your shitty diamond acquisition attempt in Cairo to then just*

bang it through in some exotic crack whore dens. Or are you mapping out a route through and over some diseased back yard hooker mattresses left in the outside to protect their starving children in make shift tin sheds without caring that it might be the last supper of hot and sour soup spicing up a stomach spilling kiss of death!

- So now finally it is happening, the South African intelligence nailing me..!?! It is like a Shona tribesman meeting with his San and Zulu counterparts to discuss who is the strongest Shebang entertainer. The Shona boasts he once drank a foul gin, while the San answers that is nothing compared to getting a water thirsting bitch lick her lips after ass to mouth performed on her, while the Zulu took up his shield by highlighting that his war craftsmen ship assembles the color of space docking* to a jong vrou*. So who do you think wins the competition?*

- En jy 'n gesonde...?*

- So what? A decaffeinated Tupac Shakur zombie or a little wanna be aristocrat Snow White hoping not to choke on all 7 dwarf dicks!

- Shut the....

- OK, OK, the mirror of boredom is showing your rort crook mirage acknowledging that you have survived life's first horror, your mother's blue waffle*!*

- You potbellied herpes sore! What tells me that the pimple on your face is not syphilis, you sick sewer rat!!

- He, he, he but still fucking you Hurenseun! Must admit my stupidity to come here; should have known it would be a trap. Bloody greed, curiosity; and unexpected good offer. Should also have known that some countries don't give a fuck to their citizens, may the Bali 9 bogans be noted as betrayed merchants. Fucking elected dictatorships! Bloody penny pinchers compared to what a jungle juice rodeo rider on a General Motors trash can spends his suburban Saturday night out with Wheel of Gooner*,*

burning out tires shitless and having girls do the spit in footy
boys locker rooms!*
*- Yes my dabbler, you are at the moment mine. Let us head out
for a game of golf where we can discuss some further details
later.*

On their trip to the Waterkloof Golf Club, Francois cannot not hold
off with rubbing another annoyance in to Shoetef's wound, the Voortrekker
Monument commemorating the Dutch settlers and their struggles not only
against the local ghams*, but more importantly the heart aching defeats by
the poms. At least it seemed that the executive capital remains theirs where
jacaranda trees unknowing to the history still blossom in purple, lila, dark wine
red colors covering the city in a surreal elevated hay fever causing carpet each
May, June and a few dry beskuit farts. That thought is making Shoetef thirsty
and unsurprisingly somehow a bottle of Stellenbosch emerges when wandering
down the Cenotaph hall towards the eternal flame. One sip for each flag. Then
comes one where Shoetef nudges Francois playing stupid when asked why did
his ancestors mingle with fishermen of the Comoros or were those poor souls
too tortured by force feeding chakalaka soaked boerie rolls laid with bush ivy
tasting pork sausages? Not nice to do that to innocent Muslims… Francois racist
heart was close to directing his fist, but strength is lacking.

Day 2

A new day for torture; a freaking museum with a bible collection!
Shoetef's sanity is definitely taking a beating. Yesterday's unexpected flogging
of Francois on a game of 9 holes, purely due to drinking more minus points
together, made them both lose appetite to hit any local nightlife. In all honesty
Pretoria is as lively as the Sudan's Khartoum, which is annoying Shoetef, but
suits Francois due to his diminishing noetic capabilities slowly attacking his
physical health. His skin is unnaturally dry, his kidneys are hurting like a blade
rammed in to his side, however his Lord Evil plan had to include means to

manage the guests' enormous energetic levels. Getting as much alcohol in to his blood stream is only partially succeeding; physically exhausting him might be advantageous. Thus the day starts early with arranging a fat dripping breakfast of fried liver, bacon and a pancake tower. Just keeping it unhealthy with enough sugar to ensure swift kick starting. It is deemed as too risky keeping Shoetef in Pretoria's city center as post the crocodile episode his abilities to fearless mingle in with locals is not forgotten. Preventing sexual desires is also a good strategy in maintaining concentration towards the proposed mission.

Shoetef himself is not happy to leave the small room at the Victoria, but obeys in awareness of modern slavery rules. So long he can maintain his cognition under control and ensuring his anus remains virgin territory, she'll be alright. But status quo is under threat as immediately after leaving Pretoria the greasy tucker* commences to make his intestine's as stable as a Pentecost church priest banning gospel singing. It's making him remember the enduring last day's of a previous escape from the prawn conquered lands of the Vryheid Volksstaat. But Francois is prepared and passes him dry baked potato cake. Vodka is definitely the more favorable desert! After two short toilet breaks they take a cable car up a smaller sized mountain north of the Hartbeesport dam, followed by a trek over a steep declining zigzagging path cutting through the hill's bush land. The coffee had to be left out as Francois eludes to digestive damage potentials, but in reality it is his own body lacking TLC*. The drive over the westerly located bridge connecting poorly replicating dam embankments is a waste of sightseeing time as a late morning nap is being done to the annoyance of the host. But at the next stop immediate curiosity awakens. A small safari a walk with giraffes is scheduled, followed by some side line staff promoting the cuddling of lion cubs. It makes Shoetef think about Bruce's gay attempt in convincing to accompany him to Sun City, which could be a good opportunity to investigate the host's liking to the place. But, but first, "dehydration is a serious matter!?" It is of high level of disinterest that the nearby water is sourced for millions. The real catastrophic event is the lack of cold beer in his hands; a reason for treason! And like a small kid he starts to scream, "I want to go where there is a water fun park with slides and all the kaboodle! Daddy please?!?" As a swift answer Shoetef is tackled to the ground, damn rugby boofheads. But, promises are harvested! Shag-a-luya, piss daarom daher*! A trip to the local disney land for adults? The first request is

met with a visit to Lesedi cultural village where Amstel is served while muggie*
snitches are keeping eye on valuables, followed by a dancing session where very
much to the guest's liking black booty goes hot in action. "Defo* baby!". The
African bokkie teasers know their trade! The show is providing Shoetef comfort
that he is not a stuffed mamparra* nor a melk terting moffie*!

Day 3

Francois manages to do an early sprint from the hotel to the neighboring
hospital for a check while Shoetef is remaining out off his socks thanks to a lion
kill* dinner with two bottles of Paarl* as wash down, meaning Francois' plan
is progressing well without any moer-toes*. On return the whinging kiddo
forwards the demand for real fun. "There must be some kind of gurdi gurdi gurdi
in Warmbaths; oh excuse another place which got renamed, in to dwankie* Bela-
bela. May the poor children who had to continuously eat bland millipap for tea*
lacking any accomplishing sauce have mercy for the leading deroes*! Likely those
greedy guts having thousands jumping up and down in trance at a chrisco*."
Francois is actually more surprised that no questions regarding the diamond are
asked. In return no interrogations are done regarding Shoetef's previous lucky
African escapade from the cheating Danish mob who provided national news
a highly satisfying story about the bad colonists; pure ammunition to feed the
anti krem kops* attitude by left wing politicians and their militant youth leaders.
While deep ion thoughts he misses Shoetef's returns to his room.

By afternoon the worn out guest re-emerges with forwarding a new
wish: Sitting in a hot pool. Fuck the wave pool or water slides, a spa is better to
jerk off. But opportunity is taken by Francois to describe his story incorporating
his new found foe, Juan Armada, el adicto loco. For his opinion South American
true evil breed. And as expected a hypercritical Catholic one too. A malice
knowing how to navigate between drug lords, European financiers and rubber
neck communists who secretly turn sides to satisfy their personnel greed with
liking of expensive scotches and Languedoc wines, African animals as pets and
Asian ladies to please them with food and tight pussies. All unlike his godly

seen father, who seemingly got hold of the diamond to an unbeatable price from a clerical guy. Both escaped Katanga in the same plane. The guy was seeking a few days break from a bad mentally torturous run, but it was a jubilant moment where his usually grumpy dad exercised good spirits. Most of the party involved guests believed it was an overpriced piece of glass, but the seller mentioned that it was possessed by a poltergeist, which he thought was ridiculous, however he was additionally eluded to that previous exchanges resulted in skirmishes with god making it revengeful on anyone it found disliking to. It acted like an old Egyptian priest confined to a cat's body wanting to be released from the holder's grip. Francois further mentions that is was perceived as all fluffy talk because as being a Lutheran the old dictator did not give two hoots about some ungodly stories of religious bastards and thus took it back home to Richards Bay where it could easily be hidden from attention and thus questioning. Until soon thereafter his judgment calls rapidly deteriorated and when his psychological state was weak he unfortunately lost all marbles; except the perceived priced big and ugly one. The crook was in his action merciless. He knew that it was impossible to survive on a South African pension while any inheritance hopes dissolved themselves like farts being neutralized by air. When observing the guest's repellent air bubbles a new hate speech against communists is released including the social-democratic-autocratic entities who engage him sporadically. Those Marxists are like chameleons in changing color from Cuba to China, via the Sahrawi Arab Democratic Republic and then off to rectum sniffing European butts to gain more cashed up allies, acknowledging disappointingly that liberalism is the real income generator and thus still happy to annoy a Portugal defending off big brother Brussels' eyes as it knows of its own continuous misleading, just like all the other wogs*! This is also the chaos religious institutions love as they can redraw their own evil master plan. A good example of rubbernecking is Spanish speaking dominant-party state Equatorial Guinea joining the Comunidade Lusófona. Poor human rights versa oil money; who wins!? Further coalitions are being bred whereby India is losing grounds and thus is seeking more trade with former strongholds like Kwa-Zulu Natal. As a summary western interests are at stake, the Anglo-saxon sphere is open for business, "so tripe face my conclusion is that the diamond needs to be retrieved from its hidden resting place…"

Shoetef's hang over quickly vanishes. As response he forwards the request to steal the nearby kid's floating mattress for a surf attempt at the wave pool. The answering "what the fuck" comes too late and is not noticed. Off he goes. Soon a child's crying is heard... Warmbaths Forever Resort staff are on their way to pick up the broken glass while its most mental fragile customer receives the next inner voice demand to party hard. It is also Francois' first time in life where visiting a shebang is desired. Later and scrubbed clean the two enter a messy tavern on the town's eastern outskirts; located between small illegal fish odor releasing shacks. A local dive with a stage, shabby music system blurring low frequency tunes pushing the speakers' capability towards full disability through slow deep skin attacking decibels while housing a small plethora of drunkenoids waiting for the chicken Maryland cuts to first accumulate a healthy portion of protein surplus in form of flies. While the afternoon is bubbling peacefully along the smells of local visitors are disturbing Francois' inner relaxation. Combined with the unappetizing views a fountain of brown spew appears glamorously. The spray shoots out like a wide ranging anti-clockwise rotating sprinkler directed towards a group of four men. Two normal sized, fairly skinny guys in their mid 20s are ignorant to the impacting. They are flying sky high off their heads thanks to rocket fuel sniffing from the nearby servo* where one remarkably tall skinny guy is decorating backwards rolled eyes while enjoying the day's last train to trancentral. All three of them sitting with their legs crossed wearing ripped white turned gray sneakers and blue worker's pants. But then the splashing fun escapes the bun towards an older man, dressed in a brown white collared Sunday church shirt. For Shoetef's perception the black label infused molasses quite well-match the bald head's tan of the by others respected gentleman. As a result on his left ear a snot string of former stomach jam is hanging down trying to cling on to his clean shaven cheek, seemingly trying to avoid any contribution towards ass browning the white shirt... An angry roar from the inflected and the good vibes cease. Immediate quietness. The two start quickly running from a machete retrieving bunch. Lucky that the main road is nearby and an Afrikaner with his buckie* shows up unaware of the situation's dire scale. The next stop is agreed home ground. One would think that sports advantage could calm the situation, but Murphy's Law is here to stay a bit longer. At least until Francois continues to repeat stories of white farmers' bad luck which has to be cushioned off with plenty of psychological barrier building Jaegermeister bombs. At once there is a smell. Oh great, Francois has crapped in his jocks*! At least the action is relieving them from local girl advances who would only win a beauty pageant carnival if it would relate to crowning the planet's ugliest rhinoceros!

Day 4

Francois is doing again a runner to the hospital. His skin color and health replicates a rotten avocado. He is slowly believing that Shoetef knows more than he is telling. Earlier just before knocking on the door, sounds from the room indicated that Shoetef is still embracing a late night oyster kebab. The receptionist eludes him that the guest did a late night venturing out along the Voortrekker Road east wards. It seemed that Bela-Bela albeit being low on visitors did contain a local population keen to party. But Shoetef's thoughts are traveling along an alternative tangent. Not often does a person have a nightmare later in the morning post the deep sleep, but his head is spinning around Francois' condition and intentions. Why the fuck would he steel the diamond, then hide it, but still be sick as a dog and why didn't he learn from all the previous bad? But there is another nightmare called "I am a precious lady and will not anymore tolerate your inner organic fouling releases underneath the sheets", "Oh baby, then all good and for free?"… "Right, no!" followed by a knuckle duster on his cheek indicating him time to sing his mourning kaddish… Even more after she gets him on the jaw where no jiu-jitsu wrestling move can anymore be performed towards taming this fan mail reading female carnivore.

To Francois' satisfaction it is taking longer than anticipated to get on track and even better his guest is not in a hurry neither. While sitting in the bubbling hotel spa digesting lunch with more chirpy bubbles, he returns to mentioning the socialist elements keen on overtaking the world and that Juan Armada Cortez is in town trying to gain knowledge of their whereabouts. And he is not alone. A small entourage from seemingly Angola's para-state run oil, gas and diamond companies are attached. Who knows where they are lodging and for sure they are aware that the nights are not spent in solitary confinement.

Not even the dirtiest porn in a cybersex suit comprising a cock milking device which stops at 60 liters will contain Shoetef. Therefore, Francois suggests that it would be wise to stay on hold within the complex and head towards north the followed day. He offers to drive to nearby Polokwane for the purpose making Shoetef feel like a pair of stitched up bum cheeks holding back the Pieter's brown shit as his thrown has been dismantled. He turns his sore neck to Francois and promises to stick to the deal to lower the poor soul's agitation. The intention is to relocate the precious stone, but South Africa is out of question. The government is too corrupt and is busily doing its own ethical cleansing efforts as distracting measure from economic failures. His perceived safe haven are the mountains of Lesotho. As if they are much better than the rest…?!

The night ends in unexpected tranquility, peace and dreams of an amiable future; just the early starting cards are this time swapped!

Day 5

This is the first and last time taking a night bus in Africa! Ending up in midst of muggers paradise squeezed between Newtown, Park and Doornfontein. No chance getting up close to Hillbrow tower. He is following the warning of other passengers; caring old birds who have wrapped up their big booties cozily in towels. But neither is the early arrival at Oliver Tambo international airport carrying fruits of success in scoring a cheap onward ticket. Plan B of arranging a rental vehicle is costly as the bank hobos at home prove themselves once again incapable; his credit card cannot be accepted as deposit. After haggling between several breakfast beers at the Keg paying and being flogged with a high price he is venturing towards Soweto. But misfortune continues: Junk heaven China Mall. Not even a decent eatery... Next comes a detour through the car park of the abandoned Gold Reef city which at least offers a skyscraper scenic drive over the M2 freeway. But no mull to honor! Shoetef is feeling like Van de Merwe exposed to prawns! Just there the Nigerians had drugs! Damn, in that case next action to conquer boredom. However the 100 Rand costing game of golf on Ohenimuri's neglected gopher pit further south is a treat with some action of police chasing some thieves along the 7th hole before the easy doable par 3 closes the session. All very nice thanks to a half loaded owner who spares a few tinnies* of Castle Lager to ease the swinging of clubs and as hors-d'oevre for the for further wash downs Walkerville tavern's beer garden full of complaining Boers. Like slipping from one side of the razor's edge to the other concluding it is time to depart from the blessing deprived white supremacist unicorns! With one detail, it can get worse by navigating past peasants in front of the local KFC.

Day 6

After a treacherous early morning drive through R82's peak hour traffic, followed by full scale road shut downs at the Germiston and R24 intersections, nearly missing the flight with some tongue twisting yodeling music accompanying taxiing, a new city is awaiting Shoetef. And a new level of traffic jams. Place of origin is literally a crashed UFO; how else would have Jomo Kenyatta made it as an ablution block?! Just waiting patiently in desire for a mercy gun shot to its metal head, which actually did then happen when a fire ravaged. Sadly zombies exist in Africa. The 10 odd kilometers in to the city is taking the entire afternoon where walking would have been a feasible option; that is if there are no domestic ethic, religious with Al Shabab and urban animal poaching crime existing. At least day light suffices for a quick trip up to the Uhura Park view point to take the one and only worthy picture of this metropolitan dump before descending down to its real face of street gangsters trying in gain access to the passenger side of the privately leased vehicle! Luckily the awareness of the driver is top notch and so are his car windows withholding a minor pebble storm. At the next light the Ring Road continues honoring the locals nick name, Nairobbery where from the passing poisonous stream crossing rabid eye twisting drug addicts follow the final hope that there is someone more bereft of their brains. After a smooth check in at the La Jardin hotel thanks to accompanying Tusker Lagers Shoetef decides to venture out to the bar across the road. Two girls enjoying a khat great him with relaxed smiles. It shall be a night of resilience. No eating and sleeping, but instead drinking and bonking! The hotel bed is massive and the naughty girls are enjoying themselves beyond his imagination; while still sucking him off like having their first lolly pop. It is enjoyable albeit there is some worries existing that lack of nutrition could become a problem desiring a bite of forbidden fruit, but on the contrary they are eating up his blow like the sweetest whipped cream. When the early morning phone call is finally received, the three feel depressed like a wheel chair users trying to access a rest room facility at Jomo Kenyatta airport, just hopeless lost in life's translation of purpose… A kiss on the cheeks of the girls while realizing that they are not necessarily the savanna's majestic cats, however their smiles and attitudes are worth a big miauw. Kenyan ladies are rightly not seen as Africa's pride. At least they are not outer suburban fat goofsters with nationalistic stickers on their lame instruments of movement while striving an anti-social codex of I'm rolling' they hatin'…

Day 7

It is a Sunday morning arrival in Lilongwe and on reaching the city center limits it is clear that the locals prefer lingering around at church rather roam the streets. At the first main shopping center the entire well sized car park is empty. Absolutely nothing, dead boring, not even an exchange agent eager for business, nor an Indian business man selling over priced biltong and cans of soft drink to wash down. Same at the bus station; nada. In summary there is fuck all and fuck nothing to Malawi's capital. Thanks to oh Lord Almighty at least the ATMs are working to retrieve cash for a taxi ride far out alright!

Day 8

After a tedious previous day which concluded in a nightly hurdle marathon searching a secluded accommodation on the foreshore where gentle lake waves crush over Nkhata Bay's rocks. Lucky the previous day's kapuku* kebab is not causing stomach pain. To his galactic surprise when exiting the room he spots an old foe and former friend: Francois's enemy number 1, bloody loco Juan aka I will never see you again in this life. "What a fucking coincidental freak show!" Any escape is now deemed as a waste as el amigo is standing stern on the entrance steps like a general observing a marching parade.

- Hola amigo! Nice to see you! What are lovely day eh?
- Need first a beer.
- Aaahhh, your liver seems to have readopted to your deviant
life stile?
- Stronzo! Darn ojetelito*!*

As they walked along the foreshore to a local shebang where smoke emerged from the glass deprived windows of the hop and malt worshiping place...

- Ahora querido amigo. Tranquilo con tuya idioma phrases. It*
is me, Juan your friend, always been your friend! What are you
doing here?
- Well guessing same same but not same....?
- No, no, impossible! I came from Mozambique for the purpose
of Mozambique only.
- Well really? Don't mierda de vaca me.*
- Tensions are growing and the rebels have been again
actively trying to reestablish themselves in the Tete region and
beyond to the north, which historically was mostly isolated
from Portuguese influence and hence representing favorable
recruiting conditions for rebels.
- So we are back to commies versa imperialists?
- Well, aaahhmmm, OK both party's did get a bad wrap in
naming. Just do not forget that Ulyanov's and Dzhugashvili's
grand-grand-children saved your life.
- Really? Or was it pure luck that you found a medium to
pursue me in to political counter active dreams to gain hold of a
vindictive minded diamond?

*- Bychit!**

- And now you are…

*- Ty che suka blyad!**

- I always knew…

- Zatknis! Believe me, I do not give a rat's ass on that piece of malicious crust of constipation nuked carbonized crap! I came yesterday in with the Ilha ferry with aim to maintain low profile. The upcoming elections will be like dogs on rabies feasting on habanero chillies before raping milking cats! Even with the cold war over, this continent is still in midst of it…*

- But according to Francois you are Lucifer's drug killing Marburg hemorrhagic fever infected breed coming from a goose's junk hole!

- Ha! But amigo, has he really helped you to date, huh?

- Hmmmmnnn, one nil to you. Carlsberg please!

Day 9

Juan's story is perplexing Shoetef. Might as well make those death plans as early as possible by taking the burrito deepthroater to a night dive. While he is now waiting at 2am in the morning on the nearby cliff's edge, there is no sign of Juan. "Bloody hell, not again the Egyptian games!" It seems that neither Francois is correct, nor Juan is undergoing spy agency vaccinating Valium treatment. To his surprise all changes at return post his solely executed cavity exploration a few kilometers along the cliff face south to a big lodge. When entering the accommodation lounge, Juan ungraciously bumps in to him. Immediately Shoetef moves his right arm to him, offering the in tarp wrapped diamond he retrieved from its burial site. But to no availing success. Juan denies interest while reiterating his planned path towards Lusaka as mean to remain incognito. Still not believing the plot and trying to not to rebuff the rebuff, he repeats a far flung promise. He hands over the phone number of Princella, may the crazy gods look after her…

After a breakfast pizza on the bay's tourists inundated opposite side seeking refuge away from local poverty and a good early siesta, a new place for quite drinkies is chosen located at the bay's far end shores on a terrace overlooking the vast stretches of this aquarium harvesting pool with the sky above embedding a flock of fish eagles. Unlike chip hunting annoying sea gulls, the birds are in tune with their surrounding by purely minding their own business. Peace, tranquility…until:

> *- Hello muthafucka!!*
> *- You deluging swamp mogwai*! My pint glass replicating crystal ball recalls nightmares of seeing you in London, Hong Kong and Buenes fucking Aires. So who ran out of nose boogie retrieving chop sticks?*
> *- You have not changed. It just clocked over in to afternoon and you are already in full swing. By the way nice spot too!*
> *- So be a proper mean behaving coolie. After you have gotten off your high flying qiongqi*, would you burn some money through for me too,!?!*
> *- Absolutely!! Malawi is great when you get past those watery curry frappe makers in Blablablant*.*
> *- I guess you want to first check in?*
> *- Have already done. There is seemingly a small bed and breakfast, just without the latter containing only two rooms and the owner's description somehow matched very nicely to your characteristics…*
> *- No! (sounding just like Homer Simpson) Stupid stone must have taken some ghost dancers with it!!*
> *- Stone…?*
> *- Ah fuck it. Carlsberg please!*

As the afternoon ensures the rivers of hop juice do not dry out disrespecting the blood thirst from the Mulanje Opapa Mugazi* where the taming of dehydration slowly opens a story book's first page, a story well known by the local children.

- Good money can be made with gem stones; a more adventurous than accounting like bunging jumping tide to Australian plastic money. All you need is to get a license for a meager 14 US. Then buy a mine close to a respected town relying on a rodent diet…

- Have you thought that they might be eating mice because they ate their crops?

- Well last resort of faith is good olle local bribing to avoid high interest from the national geology office plus international contacts to keep your back free from all sorts of evil parasites like this do gooders in Mzuzu with pharmacy background now believing he can run a non-profit association to allow the fei mossheads wealth, which they will not know how to manage as evolution has gone past their bush nut huts as fast as the cyclones Diego Garcia and Kamisy did…. And when caught up in the winds, they fly as light light paper weight leaves…*

- Aaaahhhh and I thought my demon is a harsh poem's narrative. Lets slowly get back to the old roots of not giving a fuck, however I do have two African stories for you.

- Since when can golliwogs exceed mongoloids in making up stories? Look at them, all ape jawed!

- You are a fucking drunk racist yellow faced gook! Listen, it's African karma. You and your business partners are like Spitfootsi and the toe nail chewing squirrels. You both go often hunting, but your partners are in silence hard working while greed is making you transforming previous sarcasm towards aggressive ridicule. When Spitfootsi kills an animal he shouts out "I have killed"! so that the nearby survivors can take note of his strength and appreciate that they are still alive. Also his town folk then knew that they had food to look forwards to. However one day a squirrel kills a human and says very quietly "I have killed". When the town folk realize what has happened,

Day 10

Shoetef is worrying that he will end up as the hunters trapped lion, proud as usually being the only animal of the savanna that cannot be caught, but like the stone's awakening a new soul deflating morning dawn is awaiting him by a Chinese medicine man playing herbalist with plenty of weed in a boredom drowning theatrical piece, but after days of begging to be freed is then so hungry it needs some munchies. The desire for sugary and salty delights will start gnawing on hands until the black stallion of a waiter serves him another cold beer with some sweetish tasting pap and spiced relish. The vibe is going down a steep descend where at its bottom the afternoon passing by NGOs are seeking to join the fun. But as per Malawian fairy tale, they did not notice the dire condition of the lion and told the herbalist it is up to him, up to him to tell more about his business. Their interest was purely for their own fruit harvesting. It is developing to the point where Shoetef is considering doing a runner. But the waiter returns demanding that both take another Carlsberg and another and another one as you should not leave your socializing savior behind to die alone. It now seems that with each smoked cone the stallion is drumming the medicine man towards a coalition. Never forget the trade of the far eastern shamans; skinning animals, cutting furry penises off and inserting precious deemed healing body parts up your rectum. Until tiredness takes place...

Day 11

"Oh holy fuck! Aaaahhh 2am. Damn sneaking out on squaaabubbly feet." After a tedious walk in the dark Shoetef puts on again flippers containing holes larger than 50 cent coins plus a regulator which requires one hand to cover a hole preventing accelerated air loss. It is the second jump in to the bilharzia breading pot, but this time to return the stupid piece of sparkling blood in vomit and shit quartz imitation. Back to its bed in the Rift Valley bum crack!

The group from last day is still up and about, humorously not trying to fly down the foreshore rocks while holding on to the never ending drops of local moon shine. They are nicely distracted in their own world not much beyond the tip of their noses ensuring Shoetef can blend in before day light emerges without causing any eye brow raising. When Chongstar's eyes are ready to accept day light, the adrenaline rush from the previous day takes a low batting swing. There is even a shy excuse coming from the previously generously greased monkey lips. The primate struggling with being able to stand up right, but is back on deck for more piss. Shoetef decides to make a game He requests the bar tender to mix cocktails for all others while he is enjoying refreshing juicy kick starting mocktail. The weed is maintaining happy high flying altitudes and avoiding suspicions of cheating. By late afternoon the NGOs actually manage to charter a shared taxi for safe home passage; wherever they are bogged down in some small village environment where cockroach arm pit hairs are used as tooth brushes. But Chongstar seems not to bother and his sleeping port of call announcement is done well before the sun sets. The final straw of pain is Shoetef carrying the obnoxious in former ancestry glory embracing friend turned foe to his bed, a gurgle about a mysterious big shining star is about the last whisper coming from the rice noddle chop stick juggler. During his mission he observes a young, beautiful girl who seemingly just finished her shift at the neighboring bar and sitting on its floor pad edge looking bored.

Day 12

A pre-sun-downer doobstar followed by a few cold beers with a few shots to finalize the lazy attitude creeping courtship ritual post the sleep depriving night runs. She is sporting marvelous well rounded breasts with finely hard peeking perking nipples. Her thighs are slim and where they finish a big bush embraces the jewel cave which itself has a flow of bodily juices sticking to the guarding hairs like lost spaghetti surrounding a longish vongole where red with an orange relishing mussel meat is in hiding while swimming in a small sea of squid ink infused sauce with white strains indicating the cheese spread. Or is the plate just in a darker color making the spider web of extremely thin and silky cavatappi* strings shine? However the most interesting sensual feature is her smell coming from wood burning shebangs giving her skin a taste of smoked pine to a teasing crest where it smells like a tropical tree exposed to harsh burning. She especially is enjoying the ride on top of him followed by gentle cuddles where he lays down behind her in a spooning nestling position. It is a night where her smile conquers all other odors, continuing all the way in to early morning when they leave the place quietly for a bus to Mzuzu and beyond. The beyond is a task on itself as the bus refuses to leave before 10am, meaning they are needing to hide in the back of the maxi taxi, which as such is a delightful short sleep worth as already a confused angry Chongstar is roaming the town square in search for his lost companion; and in search for some answers.

Day 13

Greed rots the soul of those out seeking it and may they be hauntingly hunted down in their pool of new found richness; as too ignorant laziness is a recipe for total loss of a person's value where some will seek disposal of contamination far away.

Day 14

As the morning sun is rising over Lake Malawi a special affair is crackling along in the air below the increasingly higher hills reaching the sky at the northern end of the African plateau splitting water feature where the sand of its shores are as gold-brownish like her fake and cheap jewelry. The two new found love birds are spending time in isolation. It is an opportunity to relax, play, be dumb and feast on barbecued chichlids. With the slackness of the days, the mull ration s depleting through smoke and her demands for flashy items from the western expat accommodating supermarket is increasingly driving the expedition to regain momentum as a one man show. The town is not offering much more than a cultural center promoting some caught out on the wrong foot dinosaurs. Admitting the skeletal remains are worth a remembrance picture or two, but the Ngonde pottery is not enticing her ancestral curiosity. It is unlikely that a savanna gerbil muncher invented the wheel of democracy. Although his Nubian butterfly is eluding him to the successes of the impoverished country's struggles which in his mind would be consistently undermined by guys like, "or shall ask who not...?

After a final good bye hug and a final Kwacha drip feed, the warm heart of Africa is swapped with the crazy attitudes of Tanzania. The welcoming party is an 8 hour wait for pick up by a local bus and there are plenty beer shacks up to the road from Songwe River to Itungi Port's turn off. There is nothing more relaxing to do other than watching witch craft addicted locals spewing burning fire water in to the spirit's fulfilled air followed by tag teaming with cooling down beers. But the annoyance too floats in the air; the continuous reference as Muzungu combined with the urge to touch white flesh. The top hill tin roofed bench offers last refuge. It is accommodating border traders who momentarily ditch their exploiting business relations with a foreign tourists for a MacDopey happy meal. Party everywhere. To the back below men are dancing in the street. When a honking is heard the boozing peers lift Shoetef gently up on to the bus where he receives the honor of sitting next to the driver on the vehicle's elevated floor platform. All strength is needed to operate the sand debris inundated cranky gear box.

Day 15 and 16

A hard weekending in a den unworthy of being a dog's kennel. No proper walls, no functioning sanitary; and the big bucket if water has been subject to some fermented brown colored gut brew. Nice, there goes the morning shower, although…. in all reality as a Westerner on a public bus in Africa you are often the only deodorant wearing guest, so for today it may as well be the flagrant of Jungle Jim. And to make the matter worse, the greasy breakfast burger's sauce being consumed at the bus station covering the undefined mashed up animal is running down his clothes making him look worse than the attire worn by the begging children eagerly observing his ignorant culinary laboring masquerading replicating a pig on caffeine overdose. Again a horn rings, a quick run for the runners on a squirt dunny*, followed by swallowing half a dozen of Chinese produced aspirins. It is a bitch of a day where further dehydration and Muzungu vocal annoyances embossing on his overall attitude. "Is this place full of colons bigger than Ngozi Crater?" Slowly with the kink of stink more respect is being developed with aim to access to the lake view point without bribing. Making the right friends at the right place and time can be an economic measure of success; in this case avoiding fees while feeling peckish in imitating Hitler's voice as communication approach incorporating loud complaining of their failure in providing a panoramic view sharing shebang all while to add to the insult the wild growing bananas are not used for distilling purpose, and thus retrieving the guide's bush knife to cut a 1200mm long thick tree branch and carve an amateur artist's impression of multiple headed snake on top to then run a scare campaign at the liquor store behind the bus stop embracing number one as name. Next he smears some left over greenish grated with water mixed plant paste on to his coupon. The birth of a new found shaman! May his twisting of eyes, uncontrollable movements of tongue and the shouting of some silly curses relating to stolen gold help defeat the existing vicious local curses given for some jihad trained penguin monkeys while the horn bills' loud warning cries shall dysfunction the protection giving spirits of sodomized witch craft ghost warriors who now thanks to his royalty have awakened their interest in retaliating ancestral decayed flesh on bones walking evasion in to the surrounding towns whereby only generous sacrifices of cigarettes and baptizing efforts of Konyagi sachets can provide mercy acceptance! Further he needs to drink the holy burnt waters, then strip off his shirt and pants, starting a rain dance to promote any forgotten gods towards compassion, kindliness, warmheartedness and hell yeah what about some psychedelic acid rain! On a positive note the town's albino are allowed in partaking rather as savior from their alternative fate of brutal amputations by the over zealous animist followers! Back home in Teletubbies consuming Caucasian households people are dealing with post stress traumatic disorders coming from actors marketing grave health and safety concerns while sucking ones mental life blood out to nourish their hypercritical evil souls. Like not wearing steel cap boots means the boot is on you; OUT! And those who lead the sheep actually do not give two hoots about any rules as fear seeding can be elegantly done through techniques like terrorizing subordinates with subjective performance reviews based on self defined meaningless key performance targets!

Day 17

It is a fresh morning up in the southern highlands where an exotic smell of freshly baked rye bread fulfills the roaming fog escaping the town site. The fluid Kilimanjaro Lager breakfast on hill's top post bottom up relates nicely to the girl's arriving from below via the high school path. The previous day's calm overland travel and meeting King Roy is shaping in to a new bush man state of affair. Last night's beer garden was a jolly where a session gremlin met warmhearted waitresses, or was that because of their big ears? With the blessing of Safari Lager in form of spillage on dry grass land the gods are content. The overnight camp is in breaking up mood. The ladies are departing on foot to return to family and their tit sucking critters. Matching to the surrounding's vibe Chief Muzungu spits in to his hand palm and sweeps his hair to the side and announces, "time to bock'n'brawl!"

Firstly thirstily shopping. Iringa is decorating its Sunday dress as esky*, masala chips and beer can be bought in one sweep. The shop is also selling mannequins! And as a good luck feed nyama choma, grilled meat with chutney and oil dripping plantains. It seems all is in cruise control until, yep the first police control makes its deep fried attitude appearance. And it is a big lady. A big angry lady. She is smelling the brewery on wheels and reaches out, further out, smack! King Roy cops not only a beating but also a hefty fine for speeding! Her next move is to halt travel plans, which is now making the white shaman stepping out of the car, grabbing his new found love and starting to dance a protesting anti-rain tango. All with some verbal tossing of angry Celtic sounding words with a touch of Hitler's replicating high pitched voice. And again it is doing magic! With a friendly smile fulfilled with amusement of the exercised show she does a waver. Misuse of superstitious combined with acting like a monkey can be useful beyond a Mad magazine subscription. After 200 meters it is a celebration time, crack'a'decka stubbie* bubblydooooo!!! After an entertaining 2 hour drive of gibberish vocabulary lessons the port of call surfaces; one of Africa's largest national park and a forgotten safari gem, Ruaha. The first stop represents also the first piss up session, which they choose to shindig themselves under the signage post stating Crocodile Pool, all while playing around with skulls and running in to the nearby bush to just be chased away by angry hippopotamuses. As if apocalypse is imminent these bull mongrels are freaking fast while huffing and puffing out of their wet nostrils! The attempt to poke them closely fails, whereby King Roy is struggling to crank the bloody car quickly enough in to motion avoiding getting fatefully bogged. He maneuvers on to a mound with both wheels flying high in the air. The plain stupidity of needing rescue by lesser friendly bird life, that is two female rangers is not brushing any egos. Plus the ladies are misusing the rare opportunity for lecturing about left overs can become delicious hyena kebabs where no amount of Safari Lager drinking under a boab tree will deter them. It is just not King Roy's lucky inauguration day, neither is it fortunate for the Hilltop Lodge bar having all its secrets exposed to a safari grogstar in need for private protecting night guards who sit the entire in front of his bungalow; thus the mission of destroying all amber is crowned by the bar staff carrying both pickled cucumber to their night quarters.

Day 18

After a zoological night dreams containing Shoetef being mauled by a pack of lions to only be saved by Sekhmet* which in return for showing the place of never ending amber falls regain the promise of having her lion's kill share replaced with a life long supply of dog-rat-vulture friendly addictive antelope biltong sourced from some placenta excreting rock to then emerge out of a star gazing Miombo woodlands back in to the essence of life still remaining post that carnivore galore annoying mental dimensions. The unconscious is playing cocky and too the hurting kidneys are reflecting a mood of uncaring tiredness. The awakening however comes quick when the two roam out with a bottle of Konyagi and the mannequin as lucky charm, who disappoints throughout the morning full scale. Zero animals. As the morning is slowly being given up, out of nowhere a sharp tongued civet wearing a head scarf emerges, who in her anger of seeing the two of her plans disrupting souls playing with a doll commences unexpectedly with harsh swearing. But it is of such inglorious format from a north English sharped shaped tongue that the nearby lions start crying. As a result the doll is set on fire accompanied with a verbal note that in the Islamic world women should be at home with their men and in her culture she has no rights to fuck around with the tribal souls of the bush, rather it is her duty to look after her own to the pleasure of her husband. "You are a hypercritical bitch and a stupid one believing that the tribal souls will accept your western driven emancipation towards a non gender equal religion while feeling you can still follow world views beyond the 5 walls which are destined for you eyes, the 4 in the kitchen and the bedroom ceiling!" The disgusted shouts of the idiot is heard for still too long. Chief Muzungu decides on retrieving back to the lodge to mentally gain again strength in ensuring the authority of commands remain in his mental favor. Unsurprisingly, but still disappointingly the surroundings are not used to hurry things up; rather lost translation of basic safari conditions. "Come on, you should know that afternoons are too freaking hot for even the hottest Hottentot!" The bar is sadly dry! The excuse is guards are needed for the one Qatari news network working gripe. It seems the Arab men are too evolving to gender neutral invertebrates like many of their European counterparts. The only viable mentally rehabilitating and thirst quenching option is to visit the park's head quarters. After a few drinks news is spreading that party time is on. The dropping of shillings on the bar's counter making melodic cha-ching tunes is heard beyond the screams of the raging civet. The holy capitalists' bling bling attitude invites the gardeners and maintenance workers to an afternoon beer pong game within the light deprived ranger's leisure congregation hall, out of trouble's sight but exposed to the courted doll's painted eyes.

Day 19

The morning is greeted by the lazily lounging of lizards baking in the sun taking up the balcony's view over a herd of elephants enjoying a far too early bath while a frightened looking guard is throwing in a reminder of a nearby lion pride on the hill side, just a few hundred meters away. "So what? Ah, yes this is Africa", while looking towards the car where a shit frightened King Roy is hiding crapping the only pair of jeans he owns! The animals are clearly in control; lucky them that Chief Muzungu is concentrating himself away from stealing a guard's gun to show who is master of the food chain towards a desire to track down yesterday's hijab jihadi media starlet as she seemed to have luck with finding the safari treats. A few minutes in to the drive her car is parked in front of a leap of leopards! Her mood goes in pendulum swinging after having to acknowledge the fast approaching dark clouds. She is not in to sharing. "Does she get away with men like that to?" In her rage towards the guys who by now are well enjoying their sugar fix providing Safari Lagers she manages to scare off the animals. "Well done girl, we know you are a grown up jelly bean!". A missed opportunity to show empathy towards King Roy, as next he is subject to being a new social media star through test eating giraffe shit! The poo is so dry that it is not even leaving any stains. The rear entry colonnade anti-lemonade juices have well beforehand evaporated, meaning lucky guy can swiftly relieve himself with digger champagne. To his surprise it seems not as half baked bad and et voila as the French say, born is a new media messiah! But to Murphy's annoying Law she surfaces back in to the movie makers scene with a new swath of screaming and swearing against Crusaders that can be heard over far flung away mountains scaring off any remaining high on rabbit food forest tree bonking gorillas. Shoetef moves on, "girl it is not the religious brothers who provide financial relief like the far reaching devastating Indus valley flooding in 2010. Thus the West is not always concentrating itself on wanking to porn but your brothers are continuously keen on building mosques and religious institutions, well guess what holy books are basis for poor social behaviors based on arrogance instead of providing real help. So get back in to your husbands' house, you cervical pea sized hyper-hyper-critteroo!".

The afternoon commences with a small surprise. The mentally unsettled reporter's private driver joins in for a royal savanna shindig* honoring mother earth for all the good stuff contained in a buckets serve of illegal brew and the master of disaster, Bad Uncle Konyagi! The new drinking friend deems it is necessary to follow a tangent by spewing the home made liquor or more resembling myth-y-lated mentholated spirit in to the air, lighting it to burn like somebody standing on an elevated chair with his ass high in the air while releasing a diarrhea shower of nutrients back to nature. In Swahili he is praying for liberation from his cruel and highly stingy female scrooge. Lastly, the gorillas far away on the opposite side of the Rift Valley are again foregoing their daily life in more relaxed nostril gold digging atmosphere.

Day 20

With an early morning effort to capture the beauty of snort facing warthogs at the swaps near Jongomeru and a two hour attempt of Chief Muzungu to convince King Roy to attempt wrestling either a baby hippo or a small sized crocodile a final Acanthosis Nigricans* bottle is tackled before leaving. Soon thereafter King Roy misses an impala and smashes the car in to a palm tree. "The sucked out ligneous plant might be above the 100 year flood level, but for fuck sake chopping it in a protected area, great work!" One light gone. One side panel gone. Tree slowly, slowly falling,....and gone. A two hours car retrieving exercise is not counting as a dream safari outing, especially in place with no mobile phone connection as the nearby lions tend to lick their balls instead! The decision is made to leave and head back to Iringa where when driving in to town towards an elevated roof top bar King Roy notices his loss of mobile phone all together! The final straw to wreck the poor guy is executed in emperor's of all sillynillywilly tribes best hospitality manner with a bottle of Makutupora wine aiming to invigorate a final blotto* duet. The late afternoon ending comes from a witch doctor's mouth, a mumbling that there is a curse, there is a curse existing, a curse that will attack the purse.

Day 21

It is 5.30am at the bus station. Time to embark on a bus. First customer of the day too, nice. He finds a nice cushioned double bench seat towards the back. The previous evening was mostly a repeat at the beer garden, just one of the waitresses went from kind to keen; gives him a soft kiss on the forehead and leaves. Exhaustion is needing a quick nap. An hour later a soft awakening with the first shines of day while being shaken like a baby, just on a slow motion driving rustic bus. But a bump or two he moves his upper body back straight and realizes that an immense amount of piled up third party luggage is resting on the middle aisle's entire length. Ah well, his stuff is surely safely lying on the pile's bottom. All good, just relax and enjoy the ride until a major stop happens, which after several hours is reality; just as reality of grim loss starts kicking post everyone disembarking. All lost with exception for some dirty clothes and some cash in his pocket. Plus an outdated Maestro card, which banking institutes are not accepting. Great… No fuck, fuck, fuck! In his mind dancing green faced umpa lumpa midgets surface and wiggling to the depressing tunes of welcoming him to the jungle of lost idiots in deepest East Africa!

- Welcome to the Australian embassy. How did you manage to find us?

Money is running out quickly. But still even where the rich live the maids and garden boys require cheap public transport, or at least something that can rattle from A to B on wheels. And back home unions are fighting for Neapolitan ice cream to be served every day at mining camps.

- Bonjour a la ambassade de Suisse. Nous sommes fermer. Normalement c'est nest pas possible de faire entre en apres-midi.*

- Pardon monsieur, mais ici on parler anglais! Alors bien, I shall now officially resort to the actions taken beforehand by Julian Assange and Edward Snowden. Thus, je refuse de departer!

- Ok, ok, firstly my name is Monsieur Epiney. I am the ambassador personally. Let us discuss in a calm, logical approach. A drink?

- What do you have?

- Well I just received a carton of imported apple cider. As being from the Romandie it is not my, well usual gusto, but it is a hot, humid day, made in England which is for this purpose tres bon and you look like in need for some bonheur...*

- Oui mon ami, la vie est dure sans confiture!*

As the afternoon is a marathon against time; and so does the neighboring Standbic Bank approach 5pm closing time. With sweat cider taste in his mouth a surprisingly quick transfer via a 24/7 call center in Manila is conducted. After confirmation a courier fetches the money. "This is not yet over!", as Epiney dials a call to a Libyan business man. How trustworthy! But like a space ship on warp speed he negotiates a rental deal for $5 a day plus some minor costs to accommodate an obligate house maid.

Day 22

Albeit saved from cuddling a road side kerb stone, the night remained sleepless. Just after 5am the decision is done to visit the nearby Barclays Bank hoping that at least the Brits can accept the remaining bank card. No money, no honey can be dire reality for a loser; literally. But to get there he needs to navigate past hundreds of sleeping people, all lying on the street of broken hopes. He realizes it as good timing in avoiding protection taxes, but during the day the street gang will be up on an androgenic hormone pumping run! But now they are sleeping in dirty clothes on make shift beds. Streets of Dar el-Salaam are the last full moon party place a Westerner wants to conclude. The dispensed cash is hungrily grabbed ion a similar manner as Homer Simpson throttles Bart. Next is buying a toothbrush, deodorant, well maybe not and instead breakfast beers to bribe the mobsters! It is already mid morning when returning to the small, dirty apartment where the maid is waiting to be let in. Shoetef is biting in his lips to not request any extra services with a currently unaffordable price tag. Plus the entire situation remains too stressful to allow any fun.

The long walk to the National Police head quarters to report the theft accompanied is tag teamed with a dismal 3 hour wait. Just before shut down an officer makes himself available who in all kindness is showing interest. Or is he smelling a bribe too? Both take a mini van to the long distance bus station; the officer mainly to score a free feed to accommodate his efforts in writing up a two liner statement, which will take three days including expectations of Shoetef conducting further harmony promoting investigation update visits in an old school building now used as police national head quarters' bunker. In one room are a half a dozen of typewriters, most likely an entire nation's judiciary paperwork goes though those ink strained mills! When realizing that no further bribes could be siphoned, the Africa's Sherlock Holmes summarizes the incident as a non local matter far away from Godzilla's breath, which to all of Swiss cheese holes lining up also writes a statement that no connection could be done out in to the bush due communication loss caused by maintenance works… "Maintenance works…!?! This is Africa, you must be joking…!" Before making a real premature ejaculation stating the reliability of the former colonial masters' glorious opera play. In case of Tanzania the Mangiacrauti as the Mussolini's cuzzies* say. They are still today in the country respected as efficient, fair, hard working; contradicting not only some travel lazy protesting lefties but also the new master's bureaucrats surfing on a nepotism loaded gravy train. And albeit promoting a gun fire spitting dinosaur of yesterday, the old tyrants did save the odd off person a lot of mental hassle when stuck in a lesser pleasurable situation similarly to free silly willy wobbling sperm trying to find the nilly uterus in a throat! Africa has bigger problems than the West's political correctness.

Day 23

- Bonjour monsieur Epiney…?
- Bonjour. How are you going?
- Looks like I am able to get some small amount of cash together every morning.
- Good. I have done some inquiries…
- OK, ok, I guess…
- Yes. Morning… aaahhh not even going to say it! Compared to drunken Schwobe, hand swiveling Cinques* and never ending chatting French, we Swiss like to keep things logical, short and sharp. And by saying that, I am not even a Calvinist! In two days at 11am sharp a taxi will pick you up. Have some passport pictures ready.*
*- I also learned some Swahili… Tomba! Kuma mbuziko!**
- Pumbafu…! Faire lentement.* And kumamayo!**

Day 24

"Sleepless nights in Dar are my bread and butter. Fortunately the muezzin from the nearby mosque is calling out to his followers of the world's second largest religion to the 5am prayers. Lights are on and my fan is continuing buzzing quickly in circles. On the first two night loosing my passports, cash and so on sleep was absolutely non-existent. Thoughts of managing the situation and writing daily pendency lists are continuous. The daily run is limited to a few hours. At 7am phone calls are received by my helping hand from the Traveler Cheque company followed by me processing through their complex identity verification process. The ads of 24 hours receiving lost or stolen cheques is a myth. As next a run to see if the ATM can help and if so, then a chicken run past the alley gangsters is on the program. Obtaining documentary requirements for postal forwarding to the embassy in Kenya fill out the morning. Police reporting and "investigation" assistance in the afternoon. If time allows other duties like visiting the further abroad behind the large port located Immigration office for guidance without being arrested for illegal immigration, how to make a runner out of this place and dealing with a retarded bank home to get extra funds sent through Western Union. At 4pm a visit to the nearby internet cafe is done to check on any news from American Express and more importantly to find help by any family remnants or friends, but the response is over zealous letters of concerns, purely subjective crap rather than objective views to assist. By 6pm the daily affordable food ration of two bananas and two samosas is ticked off. The day concludes with two final beers with a lovely, highly intelligent, black humor and sarcasm loaded old gentlemen at the Protein Pub, one of the very few juice hawkers 'in the city center from Kisutu mi want to boozoo!'. May the dust settle again in Dar es Salaam."

Day 25

The morning is feeling like Christmas, birthday and Easter all emptied in to a bucket bong! Cash from the ATM and a first pay out from Western Union allowing for plenty of change to pay off the telephone bills which the extraordinary angel of a maid allows the use of her device as means to devour some adultery to brighten the else wise depressed day; plus it is reducing the anxiety engulfed customer as therapeutic happy chappy healing. The left over coins provide the taxi driver some hope to earn an extra buck, especially today when knocking on the door early at 11am for a drive to Old Boma where a welcoming reception is prepared on the more secluded roof top by Epiney and a friend who after conquering the flight of stairs greets him with "may god be with you". His short answer "salaam" is met with a set of peculiar wondering eyes, but luckily instead of having to do a walk-about through the museum beers emerge from an esky*. "Nice move." As next discussions start involving a travel agency and a clothes shop; both open for a subsequent scheduled visit. All is going delightfully efficient and soon thereafter the afternoon discloses itself with a late lengthy lunch session at the Breakpoint Pub harboring a large green court yard decorated with cheap red plastic tables. The food is served piping hot from the barbecue whereby the day's menu comprises of fish with daal, roti and pickled coleslaw. Shukran* to the Sultan of Muscat for the good food! The speedy fuel tanking service is done by gorgeous girls making not only the punters sky high cheerful, but Shoetef wonders if they possibly carrying Reichsblut* remnants. Happy days where even the taxi driver is invited! And does he dig in, so that it is a guess work of errors regarding who drives who home!

Day 26

Finally a good night's sleep is nicely inherited by the taxi driver handing over a passport of which an average serve of worm food* would never ever dare to dream off to acquire. A free entry ticket to each and every country with one exception, South Sudan. Shoetef thoughts are, "thug kings border corruption?" The deal is one use only to get out and then a quick return. But not all gates are open yet, the Immigration office is waiting for its share, which to his astonishment is batting efficiently well compared to a recently experienced developed country's red tape and rotten attitude assistance hindrance. The return drive is a celebratory affair of Konyagi bag bashing whereby also a reserved suit is collected.

6pm, the bridge is passed and the two are now cruising through double gates up the small hill behind towards a private villa. The function incorporates not only influential business men, but also national ministers being exposed to the first time in their lives to weird Swiss delicacies like Ticinesi salami, celery root salad canapes and grated potato mini tarts called Roeshti, which are over baked with granny knickers smelling Paraclete cheese. The picked onion on top of one is stolen via an incognito modus operandi. Would have been good to fish and chips! The choice of wash down is a Fendant white wine; appreciated above milk, but the sour taste has a hint of nasty hang over. The wines back home tend to be made of sweeter grapes than sour fruits exposed to some ear drum raping yodeling tunes. The progress towards drunkenstein zombie is slow, actually full scale floating down a chilled river of slow flowing transmutation promoting waters.

Day 27

It is early morning. Still dark. Suit in the spare arm. Good bye kiss to the blond girl from Munich. A better desert than last night's served chestnut tasting astronaut food designed as worms hugging crisp marshmallows which lacked any chewiness. Compared to the old continent Africa still gives plenty lee way for adventurers beyond the clogging up of historical city centers where people are fighting for every square inch. Hoot, hoot, no time to think of how this toad pole came out of a frog's vagina! The taxi driver who slept through the night in his dark blue aged Mercedes while being harassed by a local street gang is naturally also keen as mustard to hit the decks. Back to the apartment to grab the few remaining smelly socks and then a sprint towards the Azam Marine ferry booking office. Until... "Damn, forgot the stupid letter! What now? Discuss at the Flamingo Bar? Or shall I just give you some shillings for retrieving the piece of vital paper?"

Tired he walks up the stairs, pushes the lubrication deprived entry door, where to no surprise the second guy from the roof top esky* shindig* is in full swing concentrating himself on shots. This time he is wearing a catholic priest's gown ensemble, meaning legitimate enough to share some fluid breakfast love, making it also a good opportunity to not hammer the final nail in to Dar's visitation coffin. The current excitement is directed towards the taxi driver to take it easy when passing by the bandits, while hearing him saying in a desperate tone that no actions to be undertaken outside the bar, just drink, be mellow, wait... and lastly a small spill of how his son deserves some funding for school matters. It seems to be a day with heavy traffic from heaven to hall and back while time is playing a gracious game by getting the catholic priest sedated. "Two bottles of Konyagi please. And here is some extra change for a bottle of extra lemony atomized cleansing product to sweep up any gut caused crucifixion."

It is later afternoon when the ferry arrives Stone Town. First bottle of take-away Konyagi is drowned and thrown in to the ocean. "Shit, forgot to write a letter to put in; ah fuck it!" A room is within minutes booked. Too drunk, too lazy, too happy being able to leave Dar. The basic hotel is located near the Anglican Church where an expedient visit to the slave chambers is taken. Zanzibar has not only been historically challenged, but still offers pain for any alcoholic during

Ramadan. Thanks to a second bottle of Konyagi the sunset views are performing in a colorful stile. The chosen place to sit is on the sea wall fronting the sultan's palace Beit-el-Sahel. The grog is pleasing him towards a peaceful memorizing close out of a marathon through a wild country. Or it is because of wonderfully pleasing odors coming from the nearby Forodhani Gardens where food stall commenced grilling their in tropical spices marinated seafood. With darkness the people are emerging from the narrow white walled cobbled lanes seeking enjoyment, may the cool breezes fare-well another hot day. The final task post the final sip is navigating through Stone Town's labyrinth past small shops selling exotic goods; all while getting lost is charming, until realizing the need for a taxi around midnight.

Day 28

Sitting in the last row, middle seat, no leg space and no reclining option. A night flight replicating rather a bob sleigh ride down the Celerina track. A push comes from the neighbor in the aisle seat every time somebody squeezes past to gain lavatory access which is preventing even more any sleep. The service is substandard as if the entire airline company is doing a comfort break. During the landing phase in to Bole International his window seat occupying neighbor starts engaging in small talk. Seems he is curious if somebody is up for an early beer pong session. He needs to bridge his multi hour stop over time and that preferably not alone. "Well it would be rude to not do so after the dry run on the sand bank!" making the day's first real action in getting to know St George's holy drops at 4am!

With a drunken stumbling past a few unclean shacks selling themselves glamorously as flash packer's aiming at spoiled youngsters who have to let go of their ego serving attitudes quickly as a harsh reality of poor little African babies having a tough life is widely being promoted. "The socialist heart must bleed for sympathy. But mine is drunk, so fuck off! Do these people ever forget to smile on the selfies? Bloody social media starlets who use parental paid notes to show off!" But those worldly hitchhiking celebration moments go swiftly astray when suddenly the biggest and wettest fanny fart is released! That happens to those forgetting the ideals of praising beer with more hallelujahs than a pope cheering success over his Easter week's long constipation!

But first the bags are dropped off, followed by a big leap towards the opposite pizza bar, all while in launching phase the nun converted to hotel manager shouts a last call; "be careful my son to not get buncoed!" First beer down, second beer ordered. Impressed by his performance two rasta dudes invite him over to join them. Nobody can refuse the dream of any fat white kid, free pizza! The three remain seated for hours well in to the afternoon where as a good Westerner Shoetef pays a few rounds. The two locals forward an invitation to their homes for a mull roallie desert and as opportunity to receive a traditional Ethiopian coffee inauguration. The house is sandwiched in an older city area, open plan white walls. When the appreciative stoner feeling kicks in the talkative gathering is moved from the back hidden dark man cave bed room to the common kitchen area. The visitor is greeted by a dozen of larger sized ladies, cuddled, touched, kissed and escorted with singing praise to the prime cushioned seat on the floor covered with a carpet of dried grass. At least feeling like dissolved in smoke and nobody capable of speaking a complex English vocabulary Shoetef just sits and lets the ladies explain in Amharic the procedure of roasting, grinding the coffee, boiling it in a fancy with flowers decorated pottery named Jabena and finally serving it with a high slow flowing cascade without a break between the individual small espresso sized glass cups. First shot is the welcoming drink, second shot for ritual blessings from the almighty and third shot for Shoetef to commit making love with all the ladies! Gangbang stile! "Taxi!" Albeit having more laughs and explaining that Australian snakes prefer Milton mangoes* over bush chooks* or the made up story of an Ethiopian lion released in Gippsland to ensure inter-sexual soy latte boys are confined to snub slums of Melbourne or drop bears representing mean gone flesh eating Koalas prey on humans by learning to imitate African animals flight skills over jungle trees, just only to fall on to heads and attempting to crack them open like raw eggs, suck the gray jelly out and let the cadaver back for the in hiding waiting rabid sable toothed possums, the party's momentum is slowly transitioning towards a relocation and the two rastafarians light up another herbal carrot to explain that the next port of call is a girls quarter behind a college. And they too there are eager to eat a white man alive! And you can only squeeze a certain amount of juice from a dry lemon. And more importantly bang someone who is not their mother!

The 30 year old yellow Soviet Union manufactured Lada taxi is winding down another steep hill of Addis Ababa towards another bridge crossing a mountain stream in to a secluded property adjacent to a small forest. The two pot heads are scoring the liberty of having a quick refreshing nap. This is giving the astute viking the chance to hand over some of his limited small domination dollar notes as gratitude and promises the driver a healthy loyalty award. But absolute loyalty is requested. As additional trust builder he briefly mentions his accommodation's location followed by specific instruction to wait patiently around the corner while maintaining view of the entrance. First day in Addis flying like an American missile up to Pluto, but it could be a tarnished North Korean rocket ready for a nose dive. On arrival a good hand shake and a happy grin from the gate keeper is gallantly responded by the rastas. The party can start.

Within the compound the three are greeted by two big fat gun wielding muscle monkeys where as next move they are escorted in to the main building. A beer is grabbed while in the lounge a pimp is sitting on a cloth covered couch. "Is it to prevent stains from sexual acts...?" In usually reserved for Nigerians show off as serious business man gangster style he stands up, jiggling the false gold chain around his polony sausage in looks imitating neck and wrists as big as an ostrich egg all while smiling with a big grin. He welcomes the guests with a greeting from some kind of outdated west coast booty bounce yo man yo bro yo cuz me cool man gibber rap accolade. "OK mate, nice joint! But didn't come to party between painted art starving white walls as clinical clean as my mother's vagina when she was a virgin!" The short, sharp, easy understandable and blunt reaction impresses the acting patriarch who in reality is bold headed chimp. At least the first round of beers are offered on the house making it a good opportunity to give the impressive made earth bongs in the garden a try. At least they seemingly do know some trade, which normally would make his eye brows raise, but in the momentarily overly cool mind of Shoetef the day is evolving towards paradise, a rare one in midst of an African city. Second beer is drowned and Adam's Eves starting to make appearance. All extremely skin, pretty, beautiful white teeth shining through milk chocolate skin with an odd off one being of Nubian decent who immediately catches the guest's interest. Music is cranked up, the cork of the first French champagne bottle pops open and some intimate dancing starts developing between the two. Soon a second bottle of Chambord is ordered and a follow up too! With time and spliff or two more most girls are retrieving back to no mans land while showing arrogant disinterest. The two weirdly enough remain dancing for another two hours; romantic teasing in front of the boys. When the pimp moves his hand showing them to buzz out of his sight she takes Shoetef to her private resting place; a small tinned roof house with open walls like a Samoan fala, but with fence mesh around and hard wooden storage surfaces representing beds where dirty mattresses are put on. Convenient for daddy as he can lock the girls up. All two dozen of them sleep on two stories squeezed together in this dismal health hazardous rooster den. Unsurprisingly after some interrogation, all of them are sick and diseased. None are at university as previously promised; no this is a place where modern slaves are held.

In the meantime five bottles have accumulated on the bill and obviously ch'afi* wants to slowly see some of it settled. His setis* are having a too good time where booze is consumed conjointly with bong smoking. He orders his guests in to his office: The house's main bath room! "Damn, he literally craps in front of his business partners!" The bath tub is filled with mud and a psychedelic mushroom garden made of dildos whereby the biggest is cut in half and put together as cross to imitate a scarecrow. The sight immediately increases Shoetef's awareness that there are some real mentally screwed up people in the world and they also exist in Africa!! However the sight is also stimulating Shoetef of seeing purple painted lesbians grazing in the mud to then do a soaping show under the adjacent shower cubicle. Him sitting with a pile of Birr note splashing in to the bath tub for the girls to fight for. The exposing view starts eluding him towards the need for an evacuation plan; something where he can fall on to hard rock as smooth as possible. And the rock will be hard, as his pockets are only containing 3 US dollars, well short of the hand written invoice of $4,000!! As like the usual birth of a war verbal accusations start flying around of who actually ordered the booze and what was offered for free. The dunny* money retrieving monster firstly explains that foreign goods are subject to high import taxes to which no white person can dismiss the fact of French alcohol being expensive. So there goes the yaddi, yaddi, yaddi* until the in poison soaked knot opens. The agreement is beers are on house, plus one bottle of Chambord, which still makes an outstanding $2,800 or actually $2,797. Albeit having two AK47s kissing his forehead Shoetef explains as calm and steadily possible that capital punishment will not assist in getting cash flowing back in to the cat houses' till. The suggested deal is use his taxi driver, one girl, one bouncer and one rasta. The suggestion is founded on the idea to approach down town smartly and to prevent any authoritarian interests. As typical people with more muscle than brains the gangsters are continuing trying to flex their arms; this time the choice is releasing a round load of ammunition in to the back yard's bush scaring the girls in to premature mass menstruation screams whereby they turn to crying uncontrollably. They can smell that not only the guests are in trouble, but for them too due to their greed for the pickled fruit juice. Except for that one Nubian girl.

When approaching the hospice Shoetef orders the taxi driver to stop a few hundred meters beforehand at a bakery. After such a long afternoon the dread and his companion the dead lock crownie* must be eager for munchies, which represents a convenient distraction opportunity to gain some breathing space. As agreed the girl follows suit up the hill where he then commands her to wait at the pizza bar where at least he shows gentlemen attitude by ordering a glass of Cellar Cask sweet red for her. Followed by passing through the guarded gates he immediately is approaching some of the former nuns. The head nurse is refusing to show any emotions and like professional gangster herself reverts to raising the idea of wrapping up a few small domination US dollar notes with three and a half corn kernel's worthy 1 Birr notes to create a large looking pile of dosh*. Then he wraps it up in a tight plastic bag, but still sufficiently attractive and easy for the girl to pinch a share.

Less than an hour later the taxi driver arrives, attempts without a second thought to pursue his way in to the compound, requesting for his share. Shoetef hands over $50US in a straight, clean and without a fuss manner. You have to honor your word. During the transaction the driver provides an update, "the girl jumped out of the car at the final intersection and with exception of some white shitty value Birr notes blown in to the wind behind her, the stoned sleepy weed mongoose had no chance in running as quickly behind her losing all traces and thus is now temporarily retracting to arrange for rescue troops to free his left back friend who is now used as a pawn deposit, plus as a warning big daddy's army is heading towards this as deemed breeding nest of supremacist evilness in full steaming hate of being outsmarted, meaning blood will flow!"

An hour has passed. The rastafari mob is knocking on the steel gates with loud shouting demands for a lynching opportunity to only then chased in to hiding with gun shots from the slave trading gorillas, who thanks to lack of intelligence repeat the same stupid demands. The guards are feeling safe enough and release a round of bullets themselves. It seems here are three different clans at work, but no idea who is who? "OK, time to decipher, all are Christian, so that excludes Somalis. The women are very conservative, so Amharic The gangster seem to sit on a lot of shit, so Oromo? The dope heads somehow are intermingling through the big groups, so Tigray, nah too big, thin and black so Nilotics from Gambela? Ah who gives a…!" More shots are released, but this time from an arriving fourth party; the police progressing through the street ignorant to the injured and half dead bodies lying on the street. A human life's worth here is like that of an ant, plus it makes their own professional work easier when the gangsters get rid of each other. The pennies are for the morgue! And neither does an ambulance make an appearance at any time during the night. May the stars shine away the traces.

Day 29

"Good afternoon! Hope you have a good book to read as you are going no where over the upcoming days. Your head is wanted and you should be keen to defer any new particularization of ugly African slaughter scenes."

Day 30

- Hi, here is some money for yesterday's chiko and ful* dinner.*
Now I understand the pics of under nourished big belly kids!
Not much vitamins, but with tea it was god's send. Also sincerely

sorry for the mishap and would like to offer getting a baker to do a chocolate cake, just for you.

- Dear sewi mogesi for me ts'omi* has begun. Do not worry about us. If you want some injera with meat stew tonight, give us a small donation and the guard will arrange at shift's ends. Good timing to get us all locked up!*

- You all are true angels, saints, souls of love. By the way what is the place's history. The hall way is wide, dark, the rooms spacious with very large open bath enclosures?

- Yes, you are a guest of Ethiopians first hospital and people often avoid us as it had some mental patients, who well, what can I say where a hindrance for not so dadi-adori ba'idi. Us being dressed as nursing nuns does not necessarily make it feel like a home from home, but a crazy old ladies congregation #giggle#*

Day 31

- How's your book entertaining you?

- Holy goose snorting gravy lard!

**slap* on the face.*

- You are lucky that there is an international convention of the African Union happening right here, right now. So I come here with the aim to swap domestic black man abusive kindergarten games in exchange for a junket only to read a newspaper article of the world's probably most angry, but accommodating world class stupidity and general loser of a rastafarian publicly venting! But the idiot mentions ham and pineapple pizza disrespecting not only unwritten fundamental Italian dietary laws but also dismembering his fellowship to the divine smashed corn, carrot and pea meal manifestation of Lord Jah. The ultimate litmus test of getting hands on to drugs with a retarded justification! But most people remain blissfully ignorant. But one soul on this

freaking planet has to get curious and, hey what do I read in one subtitle: The Birr Starving White Man. Well, well, if that did not ring my bells in my upstairs dome about a potential swamp mutants serving crook chef with humiliating recipe called McAnus!

- Oh yeah baby and was there a mentioning of my special sauce…?!

**slap* on the face.*

- Ouch! Damn!

- What ouch, you cheating fucktard!

- Now hold it. I am still a virgin here.

**slap* on the face.*

- Bush drums are not silent. I know you have been devouring Neapolitan ice cream; your vanilla cock stuck scooping chocolate before dipping in to the runny strawberry sold flavor.

- Fuck sheila! Are you purely here to give me not only physical abuse but also an ear bashing?

- I, I, I, somehow love you. By the way compared to many girls in this part of the world I am not interested in mutilating your genitals! Unfortunately the classy bad guys, like the real mafiosi are rare. And ironically the good men are too! And some carry this nutter element of where radical meets radical...

- Well let's strip off and get my honey shooter going!

- No. Not sexy.

- Yeah right as if we haven't done it in worse places like on the river side in Swaziland where the hippos could see my hairy ass shining out in to the night over your tender young beef colored Anus freckle burgers?!!? Did you know flashing the clacker cracker is called a mooner and when you get the entire rosehip flower to blossom it is a full moon and two together, well maybe a drunken blue moon!

- ??

- Your welcome for today's free Ozlyngish lesson…

- Good try hobo, I said no!*

Day 32

It is very convenient that both, the international business guests and the embassy are using the Hilton Hotel as their bunker. However as a volatile war truce is still in place, the plan of attack is requiring extra attention. The decided approach is giving some spare cash to get the bullet holes on the walls fixed and ensuring sternly that post fasting all the lovely ladies get a big chocolate with coffee from only the best roasted beans. Then two cars drive in to the compound, the Mercedes escorting Natalie alone out and an old Lada lady decorating a cheaply made Amharic Mass Media Agency sticker on it with some camera gear looking replicas as means to reduce the risk of attention. Shoetef's part of the evacuation is being squashed in the back of the cardboard wheeley bin.

When arriving at a fanny ticklish enticing sparkling clean secluded reserve containing in midst of the flower garden a luxurious tower with romantic water features, the bush pig is released to happily grunt around #oink, oink, oink# up and down the cobbled foot paths along garden scenery offering pavilions, followed by venturing the under cover light bright corridors and up the stairs to the apartment occupied by the embassy. The secretary is not amused at her emerging sight and starts with prejudiced frowning. Typical bogan attitude, comes to visit this governmental head quarters freshly from the property's swimming pool. Further adding to her mental challenge is the knowledge that hotel's outside is pool designed in accordance to the Ethiopian cross, seeing him as a reflection of a demon entering the opposition's turf while still wet, which is a lesser nuisance than the from sex deprived boner! It is even weirder of him exposing himself to and with a female conference delegate, a rather athletic ebony amazonian beauty, but who is surprisingly dressed up conservatively in a red wine colored aligning dress, proper stiletto shoes and black silken jacket, visually stylish representing a political campaigning women's rights activist who likely could keep an obnoxious playing up black fellow well at bay by calling him out on any kind of attire mistake these gentlemen tended to do too. Yes she is not dressed in chaotic colored fabric hiding a rhinoceros bum depriving grand customer potentials for Enterprise Scotty as their beaming chauffeurs to reallocate lovers from one cheek to the other while shouting for the ghetto gangsters respect. To compliment her surprise she is friendly, humble and exercises zero ghetto grace princess language. This lady is a gazelle, and the black elements in her suit gifted her with a statue of a smart, and elegant raven. It now came to her mind that the day before she observed her at the pool below where elegantly a bikini tight enough, but not as she it any potential pierced belly buttons, the big round cherry tips of her breasts and of course her accompanying mongrel's mouth watering whisker less camel toe. And what did her politeness neglecting extrovert counterpart do...? Cheeky bastard slapped her on the bum and said "miiiiaaaauw"! She had to finally admit that sometimes good girls need bad boys...

Days 33 - 37

Shoetef's #don't give a fuck# attitude is slowly requiring attention from Natalie. She is aware of the problem's answer, but remains adamant wanting to torture him just a touch more. So long she is in control of his life her right of buffer exists. In retrospective each day has been fulfilled by convincing the embassy to handle matters urgently. The actual frustration is the time consuming bureaucracy including the meticulous attention to irrelevant details. Does this country really use the data collected or is it just copying third world attitudes because it can afford it? Her phone rings. Flowers and chocolates are delivered by the receptionist. Shoetef is at least here doing a lovely job. Plus little gifts don't attract as male chauvinists tend to be blind on small female heart warming delights. The following cognitive frequencies tell her to stop whinging like a rich girl being beaten up by tragic first world problems while feeling more precious than reality. Somehow nice that Africa does highlight the fact you are only another quite dust fart rather than a pooping pop star; especially considering the atrocious, human life fiery wars raging over parts like the Congo whereby the average Western World resident did not give a moth balling sperm stain interest on the atrocities. Nothing has changed, only the slaughtering is for the West now more political correct as done by the locals. But if there a kid ends up being paraplegic because of a drink driver all hell brakes lose in suburban media. The West remain oblivious, arrogant and narrow minded! The society needs to concentrate in hating white middle aged men while ripping them off to finance stale arrogant bitching white wine barfing Miss Floppins!

Was the chicken before the egg is irrelevant with humans as the first known monkey was Lucy, whereby she all be respected as human race's mother's where without her caring nature we might have existed. These thoughts are gifting Shoetef a small soft touch of romanticism by subsequently inviting Natalie to the Holy Trinity Cathedral where he crafts finely the suave impression that one day she will have a faithful husband. The real heart melting movement is before entering the building where at a toilet break he buys her a presents to then softly unwrapping it on her return exposing a delicate silken imitating head scarf and places it gently over her partially straightened shoulder long hair, just enough to touch the upper echelon of her shoulder. To enhance the princess feelings the next visit is the Ethnological Museum, former Emperor Haile Selassie's palace. While walking through his old chambers they are admiring the eye catching medieval luxuries. The final affection move follows at the newly established botanical gardens where an ancient designed looking pebble road is leading them to a heart bonding view over pine trees down in to the Abyssinian city cauldron. And among them are mountain wag tails singing in accord with the odd grouch sounding crow. Dream on Romeo as all work is going to be ruined just around the corner. Yes, the stupid desire to also venture in to the Red Terror Martyrs' Memorial Museum kills all off, just as if ice cold water is thrown on to her steaming body. Not only is this episode of dumbness reinvigorating her past being ruled by a communist party with back land insertions of opposing right wing guerrillas. Both armies fighting for diamond extraction rights, where she lost her peasant father and made her mother a slave to a main local commander who then ultimately got executed under the abhorrent justification of diesel theft. It was a stupid internal fight leading to a bush court session. However somehow luck knocked on the door as the communist commander from India who albeit Catholic was a stern believer in freedom fighting, took up the liking of revitalizing her mother and to the nurturing of her daughter. He just had married a politicians' daughter who could not have children opening the path of mutual benefits, on her side limited love, education and a good protected life in a mansion decorating a pool with ocean views towards Ilha do Desterro. However, the sugar coated life ate within her the values she wanted to believed in. As young sweat looking kid she was advertised his including snowed under with useless presents all while her real blood worked as a poor maid sleeping in the kitchen pantry, hiding safe from any master hidings! Further the hypercritical patriarch society of pigs exercised typical fraternity characteristics like bribing and promising talk, but the real plan of full scale general population neglect remained, which until this day prevails. Sadly the increase of women in governance and business has neither produced a more motherly approach to those in need. The depressing reality is a struggle of not giving up hope towards a free, democratic, universally social bonding Africa where residents can and will act beyond their own interests. A liberal flourishing market to enhance wealth should too be envisaged, all just like… yes the west, the west which sadly has its fingers in the entire mess and but their eyes, like messing up seeds laid in a birds house which the critters have crapped in. Her adoptive father regularly departed in to the interior for some kind of business purpose while her mother began partaking in his wife's drinking and when one day all messages ceased, the old girl artistically designed a wooden pad, managed to drill holes and apply bolts to the equipment proposed, invented a simple level force system and bang, there it went, a shiny piece of metal, 122 destructive grains at 710 meters per second blasting the entire brain out of the skull. Remnants of the visage hanging down like a ripped out carpet taking what ever managed to stick to it exposing the naked structure behind, her mushy brain. To her surprise hardly any blood came flowing out to at least cover the gray goo mass. But the unfortunate tale of tragedy only ended when the passiveness exercising wife was accused of murder; and ultimately hanged...

Finally they left the place of her regained traumas, just to walk straight in to the next one: The rastafarians! A hoard of them occupying the Meskel Square and when being noticed the mob changes peaceful attitudes quickly by a second taking only reaction from observing, understanding to running towards them in rage. No time to laugh at physical engaging pot heads, that is beyond rolling up the next herbal fag! And as of course the taxi driver is having a nap the small marathon turns in to a cardio vascular viscous sprint gulping thin and polluted highland air while sprinting down the road to Dembel City Center where albeit offering physical and mental safety the ordered Yehemia ketfo lunch is not calming Natalie down. They are sitting on the floor in a wooden shack comprising little booths like private rooms in a strip club or karaoke bar, where just like a naughty working girl post spitting blow job glue, she too is still grasping for air long. Natalie is battered like fried chicken and is angry like a zinger* burger. Shoetef has returned being oblivious of her cognitive health by wanting to feast not only on cottage cheese, spinach berbere and a carton of Harar beer, but also greedily shoving the raw mince meat down his gob imitating a barbarous war lord celebrating his victory over the enemy by inhumanly beheading them and barbecuing their fresh flesh with blood covered intestines over hot charcoal to feed his thousand under ground dwelling hungry red eyed pet cockroaches eagerly awaiting the festive treat by releasing all simultaneously in tact bone chomping gnawing cries.

She is in need of a break! But she is also desiring to know the whereabouts of the hard precious shining goolie*. And that preferably quick, not only for her own interest, but also to promote this visit as a success. Catch 22, damn!

Day 38

Natalie is needing to increasingly concentrate on the conference as discussions are heading towards conclusion, what ever this may mean for Africa! Her hopes riding high towards a continent free of weapons. Additionally the past days did not help in maintaining close contact with institutions representing lesser influential demographics. Previous competition was limited to a similar multi faceted movements with varying institutional foundations limiting movements to specific catchments. And then there is the English versa French and Portuguese interests with indications of an emerging eastern partner. However, in Shoetef's unproductive opinion, hope in Africa is even lost in a church, as their ideals are happily mingling with egocentric agendas whereby many older wankers still rather pray to Lolo Ferrari* pictures.

Before lunch time Natalie hassles Shoetef to visit the national airline's office, which is conveniently located in the hotel too. Before departing for another scheduled talk fest she leaves a few travel brochures back. May they stimulate! The passport services is still in need for a few days and then there is the residual risk existing that the local mob find out their hide-away. A visit from them would be catastrophic. Black fellas are well known to lose patients quicker than grease drying up on freshly fried chicken which would make her entire house of cards full apart as nasty as Rwanda's genocide.

To lift her spirit she is adamant that the late lunch containing wat meat stew and spicy greens served over the sourish tasting soggy injera bread qualifies as a celebrating event. Ethiopian cooking variety is scrumptious and so is a groomed Shoetef looking deeply in to her eyes. She is melting to the pleasant smells. Even the herbal honey tasting tej* is charming towards an inner orgasm, just the way women love "love". The ultimate kick is Shoetef flashing the airline tickets after making compliments to her looking. It makes her promise him pick up service on return. And having sex. But like many of her sex peers, she is now taking a step too far by exercising her inquisitive urge by forwarding the question of Morning Glory's whereabouts. The short response comes sharp, "the piece of shit is drowning in its mother's hindquarters!" #Damn!# She struggles holding back her disappointment, while trying hard to imagine the whereabouts of that rotten surrogate's womb. In contrary his mind drifts away to the plan of continuous refusal in telling the tale of the ass freckle's harbor without being let in to the desired port of call.

Day 39

Gondar is a boring place lacking any decent restaurants or night life. The accommodation is located in the town center touted by men eagerly selling "traditional" Ethiopian nights to wormwood* stalks. Although Shoetef is keen to do an easy ride, which ultimately will still cost above an individual venturing out, but at least he has the budget hotel manager's brother as drinking buddy for the beer served on ice. Fridges are rare in the Semien mountains unlike liquor marinated chooks roasting themselves in Africa's Camelot. Yes, delightful weed is on offer and smoked within the castle; two dopey knights in shorts. The following 2 hour walk-a-bout is past the rampart's dark niches, secluded rooms decorating wall carpets, which if regularly cleaned would make an old girl's panty go wetter and tastier than a rich flavored cuppa of Darjeeling* at high noon tea! The day concludes with a final sunset smoke of the local bushie* near the inlet tower of Lake Angereb to the joyous splashing of fielding birds and escaping fish.

Day 40

It seems that visiting Lake Tana comes with a cost and Shoetef is slowly getting annoyed of his laziness costing him, "European dumb fucks, heh mate and now you are here considering begging for dosh* from Natalie? Fuck!". Although a true believer in equal rights, having her funding this outing is not necessarily building up self-esteem, plus the relationship with his new friend is deteriorating. The mini bus ride to the former capital of Gorgora is financially steep, even for a white man's wallet. The subsequent ferry ride is neither offering the sugar cane sweetness of fairy floss. The heavy wind is promoting nausea. The arrival to the monastery island does neither conclude in a happily ever after married scene as the abbot refuses the visitor hospitality due to concerns that he possesses a deviant spirit. His lack of action helping to fend off the soul munching demons combined with screaming towards others to run away as quick as possible from the diseased is a joke of a son left behind from the Solomonic dynasty where seemingly all he could do is moan the groan of late Emperor Tewodros II. It is slowly shimmering in Shoetef's mind that in the poor guys upstairs loft he too is plagued by touting religious brain washers on amphetamines, but obvious oblivious to independent thought patterns. The big cross around the neck is neither much help in fending off evil. Nor does minuse minuse necessarily give plus or Jason Voorhees' meeting with Freddy

Krueger would have transformed poltergeist to a sprogs' afternoon show free of malfunctioning weirdos.

Day 42 to 43

While climbing several times a day four flights of hotel stairs is strenuously foolish the attempt to climb Ethiopia's highest peak is failing miserably. Staying two nights in the sand storm exposed Debark between even more aggressive touts is making the proposal a full scale of time waste. A side effect of being stranded in this fun castrated joint are his more active hiking thoughts of wondering if Natalie is really awaiting him.

Day 44

It is nearing weekend and Natalie's previous expressed expectations joining in for a spiritual sharing is slowly biting him like a bone gnawing hyena. At least it cannot be much worse than living isolated in an Abyssinian highland village. Her hormones might be slowly juicing her mood uphill like a horny bunny outrunning blender impellers and thus the mind is saying that it might be advantageous to ensure some female attention again. Not that Ethiopian ladies lack of being cute, but outside of Addis Ababa they are undeniable religious fruit loops*, inexperienced in emancipation and low in self-confidence towards playing a white man's flute. With these thoughts the hypothesis theory swings towards needing an ego satisfying bachelor party. Or else wanking.

On return to Gondar a local tuk-tuk driver introduces him to a cheaper and more modern hotel. And it has hot water! Plus he indicates that a soul rewarding retreat is hiding in the nearby deep mountains; a brewery comprising a large outdoor beer garden. The definition of now takes a turn to boulder dash run to Dashen Bank ATM followed by the diesel run reindeer sledge to warp speed him up the twisting mountain pass road to the, yes (!) Dashen Brewery for happy dasheholic days honoring hoppy fruity fusions with dashy fashy friendly Dashinien tribes seeking pilgrimage dashabrations where big towers of golden waters mingle with frozen pint glasses beating any royal wedding! Not only are specials offered, but he is also partaking a private tour with some tasting and a drinking competition with the known strongest dashendabadoos. The party hits past 11pm where everybody is chased out. Luckily his sleigh arrives on time, "rickshaw dashing through the snow on an open dashenroo, jungle hells, jungles hells, rummy bungle bells, bla, bla, bla, bla…" Only with the luck of the insane the down hill is free of accidents, albeit one swerving out making an ending down the steep slippery slope a potential misfortune. The luck of the insane persists as at the hill's bottom a cautious road guarding police officer maintains vigilance against dangers; where safety can be bought as policemen here pray! Also his chosen location redeems any hope of road death reduction, "but hey that is not the point, is it!" Swiftly more counter arguments eluding the benefits of avoiding bureaucratic processes are forwarded fulfilling the purpose of scaring the hard bluffing governmental moralist preacher as evil's offspring comes tax free! And he does not care if it reaches wife and children as it is well known that African men do not excel in romanticism or else they all would be rastabaristas served on flower bouquets!

Day 45

Miraculously the Ethiopian Airline plane lands on time to pick up the few travelers on its way to the famous city of churches, Lalibela. Of a lesser miracle is getting to sit next to Natalie, subject to looking a bit sick while fighting off a small cough. It is a rainy day, and cold, which contributes to a panoramic highlands scenery of lush light green flat sloped grass fields floating above clouds of mist with deep canyons sharply cutting through the terrain and rugged, brown somewhat water deprived mountains in the background. While visibility issues are existing at take off the flight itself is exposed to strong winds shooting like cannon balls down the upper altitudes of the valleys. Unfortunately a bit too strong to consume a coffee on board, but phew, lucky wise the air hostesses are not opposed in serving a St George for breakfast!

Post arriving at the accommodation the two are finally passionately engaging. Natalie declared forfeit to his desires. The early detected traps luring in the back ground helped as in the kitchens, behind pepper bushes and lush back yards assisted… While looking for a place to have lunch a cheeky local girl is already intrusively intensively attempting to gain interest on the set target and even gave him a small woven friendship wrist band before she dashed away from her desired dashen-master for relieving deep breaths. Albeit admitting being crook she is taking all efforts in cleansing her teeth properly, having a shower and allowing her lover to get his adventure pack of 6. The move is giving her a rational sense of aching bones alleviation and dampening resurrecting head aches. It was a tedious week in midst of bad behaving male politicians; all of them avoiding any female the right to talk or allow tantamount eye to eye negotiations. For her pigs, but now she is sharing herself with a slice of bacon. A last wave of frustration emerges with thinking about the fact that the few attending females are representing countries of non relevance. And now she is enjoying sex with a rude burping white male exponent, but it eludes to her that his rough edges are not directed to her; and never were. It is like he is acting in a testosterone infused defense mechanism of what ever perturbations existed at home. Without a second thought he most likely grabbed the opportunity to engulf a big sip from the anti-venom containing chalice to defend his society's given deprivation back home. When they made love he shows the right level of heart melting affection. His hedonism batteries seem to exceed the capability of the ones stuck up bunnies' asses. When they are engaging in synchronizing movements he holds her hands sternly while passionately thrusting but consciously knowing to keep well under any pain emanating limits while still being able to maximize the tingling feeling on the tickling nerves ensuring a joyous over drive. He made her perspire hard and his bodily droplets are emanating a smell of honey smelling Indian Pale Ale similar to her experience in South Africa while being the bitch of those two old perverts roaming the prairie between lions and corrugated iron shacks of the poor along Krueger National Park's fence line; land protecting the racist blacks from the misfortune human tragedies coming from the east. Finally she is lying side wards with him embracing her from behind, with one of her delicately brown silk skinned legs resting on top of his hip, the other softly under him in the gap below his rib cage; all locked in to a slow developing powerful climax. When she is able to rest and sleep, she starts cursing her inner self beyond feeling unwell, meaning questioning getting over the bull shit from the continent's leaders' unwillingness to enlighten towards a defining a peace strategy, agreeing on freedom developing tactics and operational execution to better serve the people. The Nigerians showed how to sell themselves as serious business spoofs, the Arabs did not give a wet fart about the Sub-Saharan countries, with exception of Libya which however is demonstrating Utopian aggressive influencing expansions and a large mob continuously reverting back to the colonists as main source of problems. Her last thoughts before siesta takes hold is, "at least I had a nice fuck".

Day 46

Shoetef sat the entire night next to her. He is worried. No sleeping. He dodges the desire for local food by having take away pizzas and minestrone soup delivered to comfort her. After midnight well in to madrugada she manages to eat a bite of the Italy cooking delights of which its former colony admiringly does a very formidable effort. The little bite of nourishment is immensely appreciated. The commonly applied clarified ginger butter and spice blends are for her stomach's liking a touch too exotic; African ladies are generally not keen on culinary adventures. Out of her sight he miraculously scores a bucket of home brew also known as tella to calm his own nerves. When then seeing it she is too weak to ask or be angry of him of making a shopping runner to a local lady; his hacky sacks should anyway still be sufficiently drained. Her stamina is too weak to push any alert buttons; and wait, there is actually a man caring of her!

As next he goes out to secure two local priced entry tickets to the nearby wonders. Yes, again the multiple language including Me'en speaking girl is glued to his hip and her help is paid off by her receiving life's first delighting tongue touching kiss education. Smart cookie, shows first off her half open wide smile while holding up a tooth brush! Additionally her tongue had its own remarkable competency of knocking on her mouth walls making the famous clicking while talking. It is giving Shoetef the opportunity to brighten up his own day by imitating and making a fool of himself which is well results in a mix of laughter but also feeling shocked by him stealing one of her few rare traits. Natalie is kept at ignorance length; but she too is soon ready for her own treat; an invitation to partake in an unethical an unorthodox operation. May her inner opposing hymen be cracked! Up on entry she is playing as per master plan by verbally plucking down the restaurant lady's drafted words. Some say white men cannot jump; in Africa it is no passing without bribing.

Albeit having a bad conscious in breach with her values, she appreciatively is embraced in one arms of her lover standing high above on the rocky cliff overlooking the stunningly brown three high raised chipped out crosses of the St George church. His other arm is occupied in drip feeding him with celebration purposefully smuggled beer. She feels they have finally found the holy lands' nucleus which exceeds when entering the churches, including one smaller than Aladdin's carpet. And Shoetef's? They remain Neanderthalic around the lack of drainage and questioning where are the naked genies serving him camel shish kebabs or have they gotten lazy making any oil lamp wanking tedious as they are too fat to exit! The women are wearing white robes while the men retreat to the front of the wall painted saints in brown, red, dark blue gowns with heads down exposing their curly hair as potential radio receivers to prayers of mercy to appease the volcanic farts coming from the Rift Valley's bum crack.

Day 47

The flight to Aksum is uneventful and spending an entire day in this northern remote outpost is a stretch on any tourists' itinerary, but it is enabling the two time to bond, fondle to rediscover each other, share smiles, gain mutual loving confidence and to keep him happy with her sweet scents merging with that slight touch of an African girl smell of ammonia-nitrate infused bitter onion. Her mild body odor is attractive, but too much can make a hyena go vegan! Natalie is feeling recuperated, refreshed, hungry like a lioness on fresh kill while taking an Egyptian queen like horizontal position in bed with a big smile going from one ear lobe to the other under the imaginary gazing eyes of King Ezana's stela reaching in to the sky like a battery deprived vibrator, which with the stern grabbing of her hand while with restless commitment being penetrated by her lover is catalyzing her emotions towards an electrolytic reaction beyond a nuclear plant blasting. And for him; the town's obelisks look like a fanfare of gay dicks reaching out in to the dry desert seeking a date palm to plant the seeds, but to no avail as while the sky indicates a sand storm; an indication of an emerging shit storm, "I am not as sick anymore baby and one last affection will fully cure me; so tell me where is the stone!?"

Day 48

In the afternoon after returning from yet another church, this time St Mary, Shoetef is annoyed and bored. He turns to fluid rehabilitation through consumption of alcoholic concoctions while she is engaging in mobile phone games. The magical transformation juices make him surrender the diamond's hell tell tale of being on its way from Malawi to Beijing by some weird Chinese guy. However lies can be convenient so long they can be purposefully explained when the female habit of scrutinizing emerges. He is slowly feeling that time is ripe to move onward on departing paths and that far away from the hassles of Africa. His thoughts are directing, "who gives a damn when I am gone. And Natalie? Well she might buzz and bust her ass off in Nairobery in midst of Chinese expats competing with the Indian business men sitting on some edge of a Cryptosporidium infected resort pools while basking views of the city's ghettos while with ravenously forging upcoming white supremacy inheriting economic dependency creating colonialism plans."

Day 49

Natalie gives a last kiss on his cheek with a reminder that he is still being stubbornly hunted by others. She looks again in to his eyes and they seem to confirm his desire to leave the continent on the first possible flight. She eludes him again not to trust that his enemies are contained, however at least Francois should be decaying away at some dung bug cave incapacitating him from venturing out. For Shoetef the reverse racists too adore a feeding containing mentally fried spoken sweat and sour saucy words covering rotten perspectives.

As Natalie leaves as cunningly like a second hand car sales man disposing his grandmother to an organ dealer, Shoetef decides to ask for a smoke at his arriving bar which usually greets travelers to the hot pot of mankind's cradle. But first he eagerly opens a fresh stubbie* of St George. A refreshing gulp of the amber wonder and…, "for epidemic sake of a parasite gangbang affair why is Juan roaming this damn airport?" It only takes a few seconds for the sneaky Latino to glide in his ugly white sports shoes over.

- Buenes amigo!
- Hi, can't a man start his day rather with tits on toast?*
- Hola, good to see party boy here. Lets leave for a better venue than Bole International.
- No way Jose! Addis also accommodates an entry gate to Dante's inferno. Is the stone still hiding in the world's largest cichlid's spa?
- Who is still on the chase? Where is Natalie?
- She is gone; just like Francois sent on a deviating bush man's track!
- He, he, he nice. Lets go to a nearby hotel. Entertainment thirsting needs our attention! Go shoulder shaking ladies, go!

The dark void squeezed between unpainted concrete walls has seen better days, although still would please any horny grease bag gobbling a big bucket of popcorn. Girls with massive asses are chasing customers around the bar, while the biggest whaling gnu plays up like a Vietcong hero in full metal jacket and loses her bra. To the amusement of the two she sports a red colored cheek tan on her already ebony skin pale shading where minor pimples became clearly evident, making the guys question if she qualifies as anal bleaching peach beached babe? Later towards evening a change occurs. Slim Habesha girls surface who compared to their rounder, forward grown jawed African counterparts embrace distinctive inter racial contributed narrow formed face contours. Juan the old picador concludes the clock is striking to apply some hands on tactics whereby acting as a true matador commences inviting ladies to their table. The drinks are not cheap, but luckily it seems that most ladies are as arrogant as their boozed up sugar daddies. Juan is feeling delighted in midst of his gathered group of very dark skinned Sudanese beauties. Shoetef plays uninterested. Then a third party joins in; annoying local men exercising passive aggressive moves by denouncing the two as Ku-Klux-Klan followers followed by ridiculous cock blocking. Not only does money talk, but Juan does neither like sharing the alpha male rank. Thus a second later the man on top of the food chain pulls out a gun and chases them off like an outside open air market vendor ridding off flies from the fresh butchered meat. The event comes to no surprise, the hang out's sales pitch of being a luxury mansion is merely a thin cushioned seats' equipped stable with table's containing carved initials and music droning from a crushing cheap stereo system. Imagine a halogen light pushing out its last energy as strobe waves in the waste storage of a Walmart! Shoetef is over of the messy game. He is regretting not taking the flight and decides to do the next best by heading down the dark corridor to the lavatory. "Juan is defo* a suspect of killing Bruce! And for the script writings of the All-drunken Synod of Fools and Jesters*, I miss Natalie too. It is really time to fuck off from this crazy bowl comprising too many churches spiced up with copious amounts of alcohol, THC, khat and prostitution; at least it could be served on silver tablets..." While losing himself in mind numbing translation when departing the bath room he bumps in to one of those dark skinned girls, who introduces herself surprisingly in a very suave approach politely. She recommends him to leave for a more upmarket place. Further only low life wanders around the bars in lower Addis and why would such a rich man get interested in those AIDS infected bitches. And then her face turns in to a real sour lemon when noticing a mid sized group of Indian business men enter the bar. It seems in her belief the real rat pack has arrived! One guy even cheekily gives her a hard slap on the bum making her spit like a cobra defending itself from a Zar*. Shoetef takes action and grabs the guy at his throat telling him to behave or his last meal of bullets is imminent. No need to tell him that there is a trigger happy Juan inside as his face turns quickly in to showing a shock followed by uncontrollable head bobbling. The scared guy leaves without a pardoning. The girl whispers in to his ear that in future he is the only person allowed to do on her the act which later would be known as a Weinsteiner*. The two move themselves in to a private niche for a cigarette where she informs of her work in a nearby budget hotel. Her duty is holding the fort at night. The best she can score as dark skin is disadvantaged through the public perceiving her a lower social caste. However, she speaks superb English and next to her foreign national lingo Amharic is additionally capable to communicate in Italian making a paradox of many whites believing in a superior position, but in reality hardly any English or Americans can speak more than one language excluding their nuisance gibberish when overloaded on $CnH2n+1OH$*. Not only her statue of slim, tender hip curves, nice formed breasts with poking nipples through the silk thin bra, but also her thick hair weaved in 3 long pony tails nearly reaching her clack line* is gaining traction of love with Shoetef. Yes Ethiopian girls, no matter what money is available do adore looking after their hair and the rose water smelling lotion spreading amalgamating with her mild body odor from dancing is beyond any divinely created crème brulee; here cooked in slightly burnt ginger butter.

Day 50

After all is was a pleasant night where as a rarity for a decent Ethiopian girl who is content of this short term mingling arrangement while still doing her best in maintaining a decent standard above the gutter trash. At least in her thoughts the exotic seasoned pork chop is not only clear in communicating the situation, but he is giving her the feeling of being equal in reserving her the honor to have an orgasm. "Oh good lord, did anybody hear those thoughts and read that mind? Even the flying Spaghetti monster would have to clean his meat balls from bechamel!" The lonely girl from Finchawa was discouraged in having a relationship. Her current life's concentration is dealing with an impatient male boss demanding excessive hours. Early mornings after her work shifts she snuggles in to a ripped sleeping bag in a crevice behind the reception in midst of previous day's dirty bed sheets giving her some extra cushioning for the first hour before rudely being shoved away by the washing troopers. After having lunch at a nearby Korean restaurant, her first Asian taste bud adventure beyond stir fried rice the two cuddle up in a room of the airport hotel where in the final minute of their life path's crossing he gives her a departing good bye kiss. He miraculously has butterflies in his stomach making him wonder why his body is attracting a kaleidoscope of feelings giving him a mental boner. But at least now he can leave Ethiopia in peace. And he knows where bye bye drinks are awaiting! Albeit adoring the rare treat of being pampered by a gentlemen, or a pig who knows how to behave, she is appreciatively happy for this odd opportunity to dive on her own juices spoiled sheets. Disease free sheets… Well she is believing in it while understanding his meaning of danger is different; a hidden chest requiring a lot of time to unlock and retrieve the goods stored. Soon her heart retracts back to the scare of her social status which nags deep in to her. She questions what powers directed him in being consciously street smart and wise enough to make independent choices rather than taking the easy ride similar to his obnoxious behaving amigo playing below par with his ridiculous stories like influencing Congo rebels to play strip poker over slaughtering children or tickling bellies of the nearby resident gorillas as means to protect their habitat all while attempting to bully his words through the room's half-private en-suite like a stubborn rhino fondling with kittens who in reality are more like a monkey business foregoing baboon congress carrying the intelligence of troubled gold fish? Conclusively, she admits that exploration of a female's mind can get messy.

Day 51

"Chi, chi kati*, how are you Muzungu? Jendi?*" It is an unexpected friendly morning greeting, just with requirement to clarify that the "chief" is missing in his greeting. But on second look the butcher had in one hand a cow's eye and in the other a pipe of tripe hanging over his hand's edge, still fresh with bloody patches sticking to the rougher surfaces of the offal eluding him that the engagement tactics could do a positive refresher. The Kitoro market is well under way with children screening the new white face on the block who just poured a final drop of their Konyagi in to his glass as a mission catalyst to secure some healthy vitamin C accomplishment to breakfast. The in process of being cooked omelet will undoubtedly reset energy levels back in to kick ass party hard gear; even just the smell escaping the kitchen is providing him the calmness a general requires before the battle. Next move is crossing the dirt track to greet the friendly meat king with a hand shake, who most likely due to accessing plenty of iron in red meat is above average in muscle weight which will mean a tight grip on his knuckles, however the sun and flies surrounding him are feverish nagging on his curly hair not only weakening his physics but also resulting in growth of weird patches allowing deserted spots of shiny black skin. The cheeky joke of, "why did the monkey eat a banana, because it had to" appeal was responded with a warm laugh exposing white teeth from a dark background. And Shoetef continues with, "what do you call a monkey in a minefield, a babooooomn!". Again the joke is met with laughter; this time including the neighboring fruit seller. "Next joke, what does a monkey say when it has bananas stuffed in his ears. Nothing, he cannot hear and answer!" And then while desiring to purchase a mango he mentions, "if your ever wanted to catch a monkey, you climb a tree and act like a banana…" More laughs, and soon thereafter a few extra bananas exchange hands. On his return way back to the Glory Guesthouse, he makes one final remark while putting the bananas on his head and one arm under his opposite arm pit and saying, "monkeys see, monkeys do, monkey pee, monkeys poo!!" While these kind of attitudes may raise wanna be do gooders' anger levels to steaming, Africa has a richer heart than many know of and of those so called liberals the majority does not bother experiencing the real world while the minority which does so, does it via a mental condom packaged tour. And what Western media portrays as racial fighting of the under privileged; well it annoys many who the affirmative actions are targeted too. The same goes for feminism. Many Africans honestly do not give a shit of you spoiled retarded boredom; try to first fight for your food every day! And neither can people sustain themselves on bibles or other religious scripts! Before retreating from the sun Shoetef promises buying every morning fruits and asks the butcher to arrange some liver to accomplish his eggs tomorrow, although this does cringes in him as he never imagined in getting a desire for Safa* habits! But he is keen to support local communities rather than buying western food at expat operated restaurants. Many white tourists are double faced moralists telling people back home happy crappy stories through a flow of talkative diarrhea while truly acting like having constipation. As an example the UN does not have a good reputation in Uganda due poor handling of conflicts like those raping gun lords in the country's north. Neither did Israel's ass kicking Thunderbolt operation in 1976 gain much love as Palestinians were seen under a similar awful wrath as them under Idi Amin and that well beyond the treatment of dukawallas* post a Bollywood worthy beauty giving the butcher the excellence of bootie expulsion!

Day 52

The previous day did not only provide a welcoming break from all the hassles through hitting a few balls over Entebbe's golf course and a late afternoon live jazz concerto at the Outlaws beer hall, but also stroke through the intentions of visiting mountain gorillas. The horrendous asking price for an hour hiking in hot humid weather without a warranty in seeing the genetic cuzzies* is not worth the costs. And bribing attempts fail on deaf ears and blind eyes. For Shoetef's opinion only those with an IQ of a mountain goat would accept this Russian roulette ballad of choking on thin air in damp cold high altitude forests where the constant rain would make trees shed and drop some carking* insects targeting a person's skull to plant a deadly contagious virus.

After defending the golf balls from Vervet monkeys under the spying eyes of Colobus monkeys while trying to neither lose any balls in the adjacent rhinoceros enclosure, the afternoon's piss up in a tent full of jolly people going slowly bonkers awakens a returning urge to venture out at night past the pub and bank strip down to a few road side hawker stalls serving the common ugali dipping stew diet. Hope for some strolling through hilly terrain is developing...

Day 53

"Chi!, my darling." Reality is greeting. The last night ending in another beer garden where the only other early guest, a lovely local girl asked the visitor to sit next to her culminating in him being asked to slip his hand over her smooth legs uphill. All the way up the slippery slope, allowing entry under her skirt where as cream of the crop she avoided wearing private garments. Her slit was humid. He was asked to massage the surroundings while leaving the clit to burst in yet to be fulfilled attention; preferably like stroking a cat from the head downwards. It was a surprise encounter where with time jealous female bar staff commenced making advances which were responded by defensive cat claw strikes followed by Lugandan shrieking statements eluding that he is her trophy. The big surprise is her wig attached to the bed's malaria preventative curtain. She is dressing fading mascara where bruises slowly shine through the face powder. The response to his questioning reflects a punishment given by her boss and the associated omuyaaye* decision of her deserving a physical lecturing. She is in search for some comforting moments, which in her desperation are sought by a Caucasian man. Local men are only interested in a quick fix relief for themselves as a mean of putting some salt and pepper on to their life's bland food served by an angry, disappointed mother where while living a tin shack the alternative is vegetation in a dull environment. The few fortunate who have some pennies can afford a second hand motor cycle stolen from Europe whereby odds of themselves being relieved are high. The really jackpot crackers use these lemons to earn a few Shillings, however the earned temporary good times have to be shared with friends. Well, the other option are listening to constant demands from the family for their stock of fortune. And girls? Maintenance costs often do not provide investment returns on never ending female melancholia.

She is not very amused of the served breakfast containing pineapple and kidney pate instead of the ordered liver. Hell no, I am a lady and do not eat that. Shoetef is not in the mood to fight and caves in like a spineless brute by promising her pizza later… And to cheer her further up, Shoetef is happy to arrange manicure as he is slowly understanding that many operate as semi professionals where men are subject to inheritance from the previous short term friend. And who does not prefer well presented charcuterie* as appetizer!? Just like a nicely wrapped up gift with a decorating laurel wreath. At least he only has to contribute to a nail decorating kit. The afternoon's plan is a suburban visit to Entebbe's outskirts where on arrival he is in need of a piss. She refers him to a shared ablution block lacking a throne; just a hole housing plenty of flies, mosquitoes and a 5 eyed sludge critter feeling cozy. The block contains 3 private en-suites devoid of any toilet paper. A simple tap and half meter long garden hose does the job including washing hands over an apron with restricted drainage. Yay to free party food for the insects! Albeit no soap it all seems to be flowing smooth down whereby not even a blessing of pink unicorns would disturb the ambience! At sun set one of her friends is desiring to move onward. It is a good opportunity to lure Shoetef away with a promising chuff*, but rapidly the heavens doors dislodge. The shouting of a high pitched voice destroying Saint Peters' ear drums comes tumbling down "oyo deemu alina embwa!", that girl is dirty and diseased, "get away, hands off!".

Day 54

The previous given promise to visit her family in Kampala ends quickly. Lucky, as it would have involved non-existing motivation, especially post yesterday's gangbusters with the druggie* lass with subsequent tedious lovey dovey verbal coryphee while fine dining at a steakhouse! She too is slowly recovering from all the hoo haa. With soberness emerging some rationality returns back in to her upstairs cupboard making unnecessary squeezing in to an overloaded matutu* navigating through a large sized chaotic African city known for traffic jams not her momentarily chosen leisure activity neither. Her scream under the cold water only shower is pleasurably swiftly answered with a naughty play on her fresh oyster. The landing air strip is fine kept and tickles the tongue. "Black men don't do that! It is nice darling." At the breakfast run the butcher informs about a road block post Entebbe and thus the place is currently isolated from the rest of the country. But with a smirk on his face, "but my meat is still crisp and juicy like morning dew!". While being served Uganda's finest breakfast, a heritage Bell marrying a special Nile the waiter transmits the newest news of several police officers being killed in an ultimately successful jail rescue attempt involving foreign mercenaries; in this case the grapevine stories are concentrated around bufferbreds* who are keen on depriving the government from its fair share, what ever that actually means in Africa (!). The authorities are reporting arrests of foreign business men angering influential expat communities. The result is a blame game needing white South African security personnel to deescalate the chaos, however ironically it seems only one foreigner could escape, a CEO from a small sized Hong Kong minerals corporation. And with him a horde of criminals imprisoned for terrorism and support of thereof. However the press is unreliable as the men could have well been harmless queers which the country's law stipulates fatal punishment as a viable and acceptable punishment. Shoetef slams down the beers quickly in hope not hear more of this chaotic crap with pejorative cake icing and orders an extra relieving finest quality local sorghum containing Eagle which is served with an old copy of a Red Pepper tabloid article; Gay Monster Raped Boys in School but Failed to Bonk Wife. He apologetically and positively acknowledges the waiter for his progressive views, but is keen to maintain some distance. Not because of sexual preferences, but foreign politics is none of his business. Without astonishment the television show is switched to the president addressing his country as part of the morning news demanding answers from several countries while demonstrating alpha male aptitudes worse than a spoon fed gorilla. Clearly he lacks empathy for any poor young souls who had to flea the dogmatism because of parents dying from AIDS. At least the elected dictator cuts short of blackmailing a threat of extortion. For Shoetef the first question is, "are Dollars, Euros, Rupies or Renminbis flowing?" Then secondly, "is this monkey show tailored to political face saving?" Thirdly, "all bets are on that in midst of the chaos local authorities having no fucking idea what really is going on!" For her this is nothing new, but she still has sufficient energy to release a verbal snarl highlighting disgust, anger and lost hopes that the continent will ever be free, fair and serendipitous towards any smart, compassionate, visionary leadership.

At mid day the two have calmed down and are on a boat visiting some of Lake Victoria's islands. One the first they lay on a jetty surrounded by reed. It is a romantic scenery where both are holding a glass of chilled white wine in their hands while conceiving the barbecue smells of over charcoal grilling tilapia fish. After a two glasses she eludes him of her encounter with a mad Chinese guy full of himself, extremely arrogant, harsh towards locals and constantly placing prerogative comments about his races' evolutionary superiority. Sadly he was protected by everybody, from tribal leaders still being a ruling power in Uganda to who ever, what ever, it did not matter if they had blue skin color, two noses underneath their arm pits all while sniffing infectious boogy snooze droppings from a hyenas' ass. A real foul smelling omuyaaya* where not even a cockchafer carcass devouring cockroach close to death by starvation would dare to steal a bite.

On return the sun is setting and darkness befalling the town. The two return to the guesthouse, where she in a pace faster than sound heads for a cold shower, which in sync to the environment is missing the head. Shoetef moves to the bar to order a gin tonic as means to keep the risk of malaria infection low. He remains in good spirits albeit having endured a rather boring visit to a chimpanzee sanctuary. His desire of a real spiritual methanol induced awakening gets interrupted just after the first sip. A taxi driver pops out of no where and delivers a telex; a freaking telex in these modern days..?!?!

The note: "Get out! Trouble. Diamond left Nairobi. Miss you."

Shoetef's plan of planting the seed of chaos has succeeded, however it is back firing on him! "Why is Natalie helping me? She now knows the deviation and must surely be close to exploding!? This means only one thing; she too is a suspect of killing Bruce!" Shoetef's conclusive thought of the day will he ever declare a girl sincere mwagala…!?! Will there ever be anyone who deserves honest admiring love, everlasting bonding or bluntly said beating the attraction of beer and accompanying salt nuts, which only a true goddess can achieve as further it would mean longing for her in every aspect including cutting off the ears to allow them being all hers without any distraction? A content relationship slave until death whereby his hardened piss weasel is stuck in her for all eternity…!?! And is it possible that one black sheep is capable in being a true maverick? The answer discounts any influencers leading low esteem influencibiles replicating a rigorous reality of unaware retards lucky enough to have arms for swimming in a pool of ego brushing genes of mostly drowning spineless morons! "Gee Sir, the moon shine is thundering its blizzards strikingly…"

Day 55

Never the less the received message is not making sense which leads to the paranoia founded asking if something happened to the evil piece in the geological riffraff aquarium pool. He is quite sure that nobody knows the detailed location, except, on second thought possibly a bored to hell observant fucking dive master! Did he possibly…? If yes, then Chongstar, Francois, Juan or anybody else could manage to bribe their way to its surrounding, but would have had to exercise super powers of patients in trying to retrieve the damn thing! Or is an angry Natalie playing games? "How the fuck does she know I'm here anyway? Ah right, Vikings tend to shit stir and the news here could have legs all the way to Le Tampon in Reunion!" The assistance offered by his returning back to sweat heart playing and in her conscious slowly protruding soon to be ex-girlfriend is warmly being welcomed. Her suggestions are escaping via the back land ferry to Lulongo or using a dodgy dinghy over the lake to Rwanda; but considering that his travel insurance is not anymore valid the idea is neither frolicking. His value proposition is to first go hard at Four Turkeys. "Let us conquer a cranky cranberry bush!" And all her friends are invited, "death shall reserve a peaceful departure!" And so did the shack rock its wall affixed aluminum memorabilia to rare sightings of Sodom and Gomorrah girls dancing and rubbing each others honey pots. To satisfy her social inclining position desire the night is containing a generous showering of fluid wealth.

Day 56

A final shit, shave, shag and Shoetef is walking on the tarmac towards the British Airways plane. However those last scheduled minutes in Africa suddenly evolve in to a hiding game; Francois is disembarking from a small neighboring plane! As Shoetef is hell keen to make this day his final continental episode his physical motions are aiming the prevention of collecting undesirable memento. He is wanting to return back home and reset life's clock of being again a professionally embodied ant. A stern good bye to the kingdoms of Ankole, Buganda, Bunyoro, Busoga, Rwenzoro and Toro; but a loving silent adieu to all cocoa chocolaty smooth smothered velvet padded muffs! The double faced, bull shit talk about caring, rubber necking pecking but back stabbing to save their own bacon soulless West is waiting; most likely impatiently like a brat thirsting to clip off happy high flying wings of innocent birds. He is ready for first world crises' cries! He is ready for exaggerations given by brain washing lawyers, politicians, industrial leaders and private television stations. Many of those reality detached souls have created circles of control and means to fully remove liberties through infantiling an entire society through the forwarding soul deep protruding help screams! The growth of a new generation crying on media about all sorts of unfairness but still keeping a tight grip on comforting commodities incapable in understanding that their wealth is only guaranteed so long there is a third world manufacturing cheap products. And the buck does not stop here. While depriving Africa in gaining traction of closing the gap, it is only getting bigger through drying up of international aid, all while crying foul play to the Chinese filling up created gaps. While mentioning cinnamon burners, on his way to the airplane a very pretty, eye catching matured bronzed lady with short hair approaches him while continuously concentrating on her mobile phone. With her a one arm guardian. Both have freshly disembarked a Kenyan Airways plane and are playing oblivious to their surroundings. When passing he bumps in to her. They stop for a second and mutually simultaneously grasp a deep breath of the by asphalt heated air. Not yet understanding why. Not yet realizing whom. Never the less they take a second to look in to each others eyes. Several hours later the penny drops; it was not the first collision of their life's paths. Who you are does not matter, be a beauty queen or a Quasimodo creep or right now an intriguingly with disgust soul penetrated reader of this story; turd cakes do not discriminate in their stink!! However of importance is to detect the oven smell and else if shit is thrown at you, pick it up, hide a stone in the molasses and throw it back to return an escalation of pain to the aggressor. Sadly and truly some only learn the hard way; sometimes even nicer when the pain spreads more globally....

11 RELIGIOUS UNDOINGS

The Birth's first Week post violent Baby Screams

Chongstar's dad awakened this morning feeling a bit nauseous. His anxiety was pushing the need to quickly check on Morning Glory. His conscious demands confidence that he remained in possession of his ticket out of the Congo. As the Angolans noticed yesterday the bad behaviors of him and his Asian counterpart, a reminder of the dangers reappeared lively in Lalaland*. Or could it have been that the stone was excitingly looking forward to a return to its grave through sending unknown transmission waves which were perceived by him timely reminder to save his own bacon? While physical health returned and body covering scratched up mosquito bites were healing, his mental health went backwards. Also the local army chief was slowly expecting some form of payment, but this was a hard thing to do while being captured in a padded den in midst of hell. It was hard to digest the shear amount of poverty, cruelty and medical ill people ending up in this port city hoping for treatment by the white man, but it was just freaking 20 years' too late for this sort of hope. Weren't they able to communicate this through the forests with their bush drums?!? Maybe not as any postal transport by train was slow. According to his calculations the embassy should have received notice at least a few weeks' ago. A month long wait was bit of a stretch. And the money request via a telex message home was a done deal, however it still had to make its way past the Belgians followed by satisfying the hotel owner's expenses, local authorities protecting him plus the immigration office to allow the illegal bacchanal life stile. But debts were heading upwards. Not only the femme élégante was increasingly charging, but also the more economic pygmy cock sucker was aware of her rising market value. In summary any highly appreciated cash inflow ended up in third party's pockets due an unsustainable life stile and concluding that the fortune believing performance enhancing machinery greasing was more like a small drop of oil on to unwashed salad, dearly limiting purchase power. However his Indian counter part as poor as he seemed to be, finances were not running dry, why…?!?

The first Month and while awaiting Baptism the Decision is made to spew up some juicy Disappointments

Taoism is not necessarily a religion rather its bedrock is laid on the philosophy of being aligned with the surroundings, the environment, the nurturing of mother earth and its designated already written, but to humans unknown bigger picture of a greater plan, meaning a person shall follow the principles of wu wei, that of non action allowing history to be created as per nature's desire. The family's turbulent history was already heavily muddled up in religious waters; some deep affectionate roots still existed, just they were not capable to free themselves from the self brewed toxins making the good and strong rot similarly to wood exposed to wet and dry cycles. Matadi; a great place to degrade back towards being part of the earth crust at an accelerated speed. His stomach was slowly churning painful pushing against other organs increasing existence fears and nightmares of being chased by a furious metallic carapace canines commanded by three ghosts decorating body shapes from rising smoke, where the male replicating cloud had a frozen face of ash with eyes lacking pupils, the female decorating a charcoal black visage like an asphalt lake on fire with long upstanding flaming hair and the third a cluster of scales of which a clay formed dragon head containing sharp teeth of broken glass making the dreamer wonder if it was a product of a bad acting kid desiring to shape an innocent looking artifact in to hidden evil; it was like a foreign intrusion mocking him with his departing Tao traits of genuineness, searching for refinement as stepping stone to be one with the cosmos, the hedonism removing his spontaneity of moving forwards and away from the continent's dire living standards, pursuing him to accept and liken his loss of any hope to transform towards a healthier being, especially mentally. His initial recovery was back on track towards decomposing. Combined with his betrayal to the global ecosystem all hope for smooth running longevity was cognitively accepted as lost. His soul was possessed by a torturing bitch capable of outstanding outer sphere power heating up the barbecue in hell for him, his sprogs* and eagerly awaiting to devour his ancestor's reputation by slowly roasting his pungent smelling flesh. And the remaining chi flowing through the veins was just enough fuel to keep the fire underneath burning! As a last continuously reoccurring reminder being delivered by glowing unidentifiable contour missing surrounding accommodating clouds like cheerleaders supporting their team, was that the universe will only return to harmony when his physical being incorporating forbidden knowledge was fully wiped out while his entire family is swallowed by Lucifer's rejected spiritual clouds simulating the eating act of whale sharks with wide open mouths engulfing innocent small breads to ultimately defecate the nuisance and have the matter nuked by intergalactic radiation in to Te's* final heart beat ending this one wasteful chapter of Pu's* story. The final straw of horror was received when he woke up seeing a cat chasing, capturing and killing a snake on his first level window ledge. The supernatural, cunning sign of power being subdued by an evil spirit. In desperation of recommencing the day on a better foot and desiring some fresh air he hastily leaves the room, rushes down the stairs where he sees the grin of his escapee friend offering him with a big morning smile to join in for breakfast. Immediately after taking seat a plate of rotten smelling discolored eggs emerge, causing the man from the middle kingdom to scream as loud like an excited crow feasting on a fresh carcass, "gun dan*, huai hun dan*, I'm not going to be anymore a ben dan*!!" Two days later his passport papers finally arrive; just a pity the diao si* was already traveling a rusty blue colored train in reverse direction. They passed each other at Mbanza-Ngungu station as blind like the myriad barbs in the nearby caves. Both trains standing next to each other in the dead end station were picking up passengers lining up in front of the long stretching servicing hall where the original white colored walls were accumulating a yellowish covering mold along the two decorations, a portrait of an African despot wearing wild animal fur and a sign proclaiming the colonial's township name of Thysville. It was definitely not the right timing to consider a few days resting in the struggling resort town.

As to the stone's liking and selfish hope, the transaction between the former keeper and the new owners, who thanks to a national defector conducting and facilitating the brokerage went seamlessly and so did their plan of escaping over the river at Port Marechal during bright day light and distracting any nosy authorities by separating themselves first to later at dusk conjoin at an airstrip further north where river rapids made it impossible for any authorities to pass. It was also impossible to allow anybody encapsulation by closing in through a clothoid loop approach. The night skies were favorable as was their landing an hour later at Loubomo, a low key airport sufficiently distanced, reducing the risk of unwanted visiting aggressors. If it wasn't for some hiding Cabinda fighters keeping a low profile from the opposing MPLA who were being sick of their mountainous jungle camp desiring cigarettes and cash who were congregating in neighboring Belize town, the plan would have been perfect. Luckily the soldiers were so tired that without their weight loaded guns their meager starved bodies would have been blown away in to the bush with the smallest possible coughing wind withholding the mentioning if the weather would sneeze. The guests offered some can food and immediately thereafter assimilated towards Africa's deeper equatorial heart. But in making the most, the new owners of Lord Hard Rock's evilness beyond a genetic mutation pool containing elements of some perverted 70s rock legend riding in front of innocent children a satanic Wolpertinger masturbation machine were finding themselves slowly becoming addicted to authoritarian abuse behaviors. They waved their few dollar notes in front of the mercenaries while promising more was on offer. It was executed in white man's stile of attitude in seeing themselves on mountain's peak of the evolutionary chain as rich Indian too are known for similar chauvinistic approaches. They were careless minded towards being in midst of unfriendly territory where a loyal fellowship to the quasi religious Matswanism movement was just waiting for revenge opportunities to any intruders.

Albeit a preference existing of entering Pointe Noire, the option was dismissed due to the Angolan border vicinity while the northwards route was disliked due to the risk of road controls by governmental forces who were locally deployed to break down protests of a rogue unionized mob, making a quick muster* pointless and risking any fast pozzy* gains. The party of two went onward, but little did they know that a rat race commenced when leaving the dry grass lands of the Niari Valley department. Rain was awaiting as uninvited accomplice on the rugged road to Sibiti hindering a timely departure. The following days were spent in a hotel on the main street. It was a dirt track designated as the district's future administration boulevard, cutting through lovely large sized green gardens containing a decoration of flowers in tarnishing French colonial buildings prone to slow asset life cycle expiration by time tag teaming with its surrounding jungle environment. However as a somewhat rarity in this neck of the woods the foreign architectural creations were remarkably withstanding well the unfavorable conditions. Only the agricultural school seemed to fade away behind the long sharp grass emerging from the surrounding mud puddles. Behind the facade it was occupied by a lively bunch of protesters defeating not only hunger, but trying to gather in starvation the strength to oppose their new African rulers who were basically controlled puppets by the former colonial masters. Effectively the place was a breeding ground of mistrust towards the exotic convoy party where even the Cabinda rebels became suspicious of potential black magic playing an untypical African chorus. When the singing stopped, the two lone warriors ripped away from rest of the world, the sons of the fortune goddess Lakshmi were being subject of reprimanding by her jealous elder sister Jayeshtha. Just like lost and left over lesbians fighting in a watery pool of mud, with the elder sister still feeling challenged post being spat out by Shiva as venom. At least telex messages could be sent and the relos* were on their way. However a day later death visited. The rain was beating the unpaved road harder than an Arabian whip handler laying his hands on a virgin for outer marriage adultery. The slope was not steep. Rivers of red-brown fluid were turbulently flowing down the clay ground. The hired worn out Peugeot D3 seemed to be drifting on brown crème de brulee. The driver fighting to keep consciousness. The vehicle hit an odd off stone, like some hateful mongrel dissatisfied with its blood taste lacking can food. The tire tried succeed and failed. The original white, now multi colored decorated mini van gives up and slides firstly slowly, but then declaring victory over itself by descending at an accelerated speed downhill towards the bush, braking through the low leaf hanging foliage and nearly coming to a halt in a tree before the a doing a final fall in to a creek bed containing flood waters. The big ditch would have finalized everyone's fate, but the stone had other plans. There was zero interest in any fast deaths. They had to hang in there while getting soaked by rain. When the driver awakens he ventures out hunting bush meat. A day later he return with a small decapitated monkey which had to be cooked in shelter. As wood was too wet for cooking purpose fuel was extracted from the vehicle. The animal's hairy skin was set alight and roasted within the car resulting in one of the Indian escapee refusing to partake in any nourishing. He was feeling like passing away squeezed between contaminated seats. Needless to mention that through the meal preparation the back seats hit damage levels beyond any possible redemption. On day three there was only one human breathing in regular, non erratic patterns… The consumed meat showing signs of partaking in the revenge plot. When late in the afternoon at dusk the rain cleared, a beer transporter attempted to find passage in good knowledge, low faith that it was containing safe to transport goods and in no favor of offering a ride to any potential thieves. However it was worse. The driver stopped to satisfy curiosity. He looked at the three guys of whom two were subject to cold shakes, red eyes, muscle pain preventing them to even sit for more than a few minutes. Their light brown colored army pants were soiled with blood stains from juices shooting out of their sphincter portal. Nope, those two are not going anywhere any time soon. And no time to waste as no daring to risk the precious load neither!

As last measure the keys were in an unfriendly rough manner grabbed of the weakened public transporter owner to assist as deposit for the most likely survivor to gain incognito passage in to Brazzaville; past the troops still dealing with the aftermath of a recent coup d'etat. The driver is seems to on his way out from the living as his face gave a half sided ecliptic smile as if a spirit exercised a comforting trance over his cellular dismantling bodily assemblage. It looked like he was envisaging an acceptance of seeing all through him cheated wives throwing to his feet his unwanted and mentally discarded children while enjoying being double and triple penetrated by testosterone drooling warthogs!

The hopeful Chinese guy desiring being one day a famous mining magnet, received a late better than never warm welcoming from a country man who on invitation saw his rat plagued den, giving the feeling of guilt and thus awarding a cleaner quarter. And he received relief through a payroll admittance with official presidential endorsement! Zaire seemed to be pro-western, but its stability was founded on the usual dictatorial political basis. Albeit retrieving well through rest, the nights prevented quicker health as they were not at all low key. The Congolese were known to shake their booty under the sky to rumba, especially to classics from Wendo Kolosoy. After a few nights even the two Mandarin speaking guys knew the lyrics of Marie-Louise and attempted to participate in the soukous concert body bumping, beating their hair deprived chests to the hot pot tunes of happy passionate Cuban ritmo, cha cha cha, creole biguine, the slower waltz and as sugar on the icing the sad notes of tango. The newer artists were expressing themselves by singing deeper African soul music like Franco et le T.P. OK Jazz, speeding up the pace of booties bumping in to each other. In reality Kinshasa as being the world's second largest French speaking city had else wise other than mziki ezelaki eleng ndeko* nothing to offer with exception of cheap beers like Skol or Primus which could be consumed with pleasing river views whereby on a clear day the sun would set nicely behind the hydrogen surface saying Au-revoir and hello to more shakey shakey, bakey baby! One day down on the shore of the mighty jungle cutting river while having fried cassava and banana chips with a big dollop of beloved mayonnaise the repatriated soul vaguely saw the loading of a privately chartered yacht followed by the boarding of darker skinned people, possibly Indians…? Was the corrupted Naxalite also part? The sugar spiked diesel resulted in a rescue mission of not so missionary rescuers, whereby the treasure hunters missed the already departed precious load resulting in a disliking attitude towards fondling with ferrous remains making their nerves as stable as francium. Lucky the armory had long range capacity. The river waters started crying red leaving a new converted post-traumatic stress disordered captain to keep on moving upstream with the two surviving passengers of which one had a gun shot wound digging through his leg.

The first Year; Time to shit beyond Spew limiting Diapers

It was just pure luck that all parties met at this one table in the middle of this capital city harboring not much more than dirt roads and rifle wielding paratroops; paradise for sable skinned locals and sun burnt Europeans. The one and only rapacious Emperor Jean-Bédel Bokassa who crowned himself lavishly in front of starvation plagued servants, followed by killing hundreds of youngster who refused or could not afford the forced school clothing provided by his wife's owned company was just recently overthrown by the party's fund raiser. While the Marseillaise vinyl seemed to have a big enough chip in it to halt the licorice pizza's circum navigating, the inheriting tunes came from Lumingu Zorro's Mosese album's chasing percussion beats with jamming guitars and uprising promoting horns ending the race at this seldom so highly attention receiving isolated dust town in the middle of no-where. It completed the Ubangi River's chapter of challenging safe navigation without being murdered by some jungle rebels turned pirates who were continuously hiding behind the shore's rain forests which was slowly opening to swampy grass lands accommodating less sheltering options and hence driving an even more tiresome competitive chase aiming at the luxury of possessing the cursed jewel. Diamonds were rarely held back by authorities as smuggling was lucrative due to the border guards being outnumbered by a crass* factor and having to chase the snitches beyond a black stump's* stretch of nearly 6,000 kilometers with maybe 1 or in maximum 2 functioning vehicles; that is if the wheels were not removed for what ever purpose an inventive thief had. With all eyes on Lord Arduous, the negotiations were led by a French speaking diplomat chosen by both party's due to a perceived neutral back ground. Both being Asian, both somewhat being bound to Buddhist founded doctrines of Dukha and Trishna, meaning suffering belongs to life and it has a reason, which made the church a good harbor representing diverging path of self fulfillment. The mediator was a smart, elegantly dressed man in white, a bit too light colored for the happening taking place in the city's 1930 constructed red bricked cathedral. The accompanying arch bishop arranged the removal of several rows, placed the missionaries main table in its midst and post delivery of spicy barbecued chicken, baguette and home made pickled croutons the dealings were made behind locked doors and guarded by the foreign legion. Albeit the outside troubles including the ravaging famine and under guard of the French authorities, the Catholic institution was accepted as a trustworthy negotiation facilitator and received through mutual agreement the stone's guardianship! The applied tactics were simple; either you stay and get buried before Christmas or you leave where with luck you might end up more favorable than an angry bored garlic farting Parisian on isolated Saint Helena island defending himself of not being a midget, nor gay, nor had only one functioning arm. However, soon thereafter on a missionary visit of the bishop in to the Muslim majority region his temporary installed "religious" serving quarters were raided by locals. As the area between the varying National Parks of Bamingui Bangaran, Saint Flora and especially Andre Felix was serving as an open door shopping market for illegal wildlife poaching the competition became fierce to gain financial advantage. And the activity only increased when international efforts towards banning of ivory intensified, which worsened with the nearby South Sudanese crisis. However the desired escape route was towards north as the by rebel fraction supported hunters had their safe return path, still largely uncut but with exposure risk to disorganized fund thirsting freedom fighting movements. It was messy. And the mess continued. The mess entertained. The stone adored the mess. However the last Central African written episode was that assistance from the French government was needed to calm down the trade negotiator resulting in him being side lined to a new diplomatic mission in Djibouti where the Red Sea was becoming less secure. The ultimate win was achieved by retaining justification towards maintaining the almighty status of the French while the holy sea's representative's life was secured from any negative public attention. While his pilgrim ended, he kept to a secret oath ensuring survival as a smiling regent for another 20 years plus…

A sleeping Decade produces foul Breath

Over the upcoming years the diamond was used as passage payment between the various fractions invading each other slaughtering play ground; in many cases by the West disinterested human abattoirs. The Sahel was continuously being subject of invading northerly located para military groups. The trade offs included cotton from at gun point held farmers, luck deprived mining operators needing to purchase oil from governmental rogues to human smuggling Chadian Tuareg caravans exchanging camels as dowry gifts. In the late 1980s troops from Libya occupied the Aouzou Strip and ventured beyond the rugged Tibesti mountains where once again the stone was handed over between chaotic desert roaming fractions. The times were for the darn thing enjoyable vacation, a smashing party usually only celebrated when someone is 18 or 21 where unlimited flows of alcohol are allowed to be legally consumed; just in this case simulating a vampire's blood bath inauguration. One day in the turmoils a group of disadvantaged dwellers were in search of rare water access opportunities. They lost direction resulting in being black mailed for a deposit by a smarter, more modern guy who found pleasure in stuffing his disco stick* up exhaustion pipes of jeeps instead of the raw deal of using goats. So the light ray smashing spirit hiding geode swapped hands; another change that entertains. The new owner belonged to a family of former shepherds who not only kept their hairy meat puppets* away from the butcher, but also their knowledge close to heart to dodge Qaddafi's troops. Strong minds ensured survival surpassing lives through directing caravans of smuggled goods undetected while sober attitudes guaranteed safe voyage through the rugged terrain containing towering sand stone formations. At least until one day where rogue officers from N'Djamena took him hostage, strip searched and when finding the stone conclusively made the usually for god reserved right of to end the captives' life by tying rope around his wrists and legs while lying with the other caught out people on a sandy patch in a circle unable to move. They left all back in the secluded surrounding of thorn bushes the pebble stoned wadi where the new found friend ensured the ordain of Murphy's Law; a flash flooding event making the entire tribe drown the middle of the Sahara!

As per the chronology of another Toyota war story tale the stone's ride with the Chadian National Armed Forces was not only bumpy, but also without cushions getting thrown around in the glove compartment. Subsequently it continued havoc culminating to houses being burnt down by directed angry starving residents who in the same momentum enabled dismissal of the nation's ruling generals. During the uprising the stone maintained its malicious influence. When approaching the country's border an angry elephant bull took up chasing the jeep and after unsuccessfully driving a few kilometers in return gear managed to catch up on it and mount it! However the stone still had safe passage unlike the driver who post the elephant's coitus was trampled down in to lifeless molasses while fronting sun bathing lions wearing 3D specs munching on crunchy dried antelope skin. Even when the wildest psychedelic dreams turned in to radio-active waste, flamboyant narratives were still communicated back to the modern palace in Djambal Bahr overlooking the Chari River merging waters with the Logone River where as rare as the stone's travel itinerary disinterest was shown by marshal law executing kahunas. For once there seemed to be a lesser greedy African ruler existing. Yeah right! The new guy in charge was too much concentrated in gaining the knowledge where long term sustainable fortunes could be sourced and oblivious to the obviousness of laziness or not even giving a lick on his maiden's tit for a piece of glitzy debris. The satisfaction of joining the inner alpha male circle playing geopolitical roulette was enticing him towards leading a grand entourage respecting him like no one ever before and that combined with a level of awareness to curtail prestige as it only bought bad luck to his predecessor, who 3 decades later was charged for breaching international law, becoming the first head of state convicted by a foreign country's court for crimes against humanity! This wise decision allowed him to view Africa's Pinochet's trial sitting in front of the biggest home television the nation ever witnessed, plus a big bucket of chilled champagne gifted by French "bon amies"*. He perceived the received education at Muammar Qaddafi's World Revolutionary Center made him capable to join the African leadership honorable ranks of undisputed reigning longevity. With his correct instinct of money where some spare change could be made available beyond the corrupt pockets as investment towards a grand boulevard originating at the palace, following past the national square with an unfashionable end between a back yard mosque and a disease ridden lake; a convenient place to lay off any enemies.

While one of the previous adventurers regained the strength of a blossoming desert flower in his chosen exile the latter replicated an inventive approach to confine his monkey roots in thick mist. It took both a few tears of the sun to drown down the inner rebelling Shaka Zulu king playing a director's forgotten role as ghosts in the darkness. In 1990 the world was slowly changing with new potential game players commencing to venture out their feelers resulting in men behind the scenes now directing national interests as low key meant out of site, out of mind, out of trouble. Some lower key ministers scheduled visits to Yaounde and Douala under the now more left, socialist leaning governmental joint venture umbrella of new economic development which was initiated by the Minister of State for External Affairs. But the Asian community pulling some of the strings in the back ground were also keen in capitalizing financial benefits; and just like their African corrupt brothers on loose loathing, they too were hungry for private financial gains beyond the safe confines of Ile de Maurice. But to achieve their dreams local knowledge had to be sourced all while many Indians were in fear from the previous experiences, most notably the darkest and last King of Scotland. Additionally the dodgy mission through the Congo ending up half of the family killed still sat in their bones. However, greed is strong and can supersede disliking to a political traitor who once again marketed himself as a vital enterprising partner. Conclusively the two politically diverging allies made a reunion. The revolutionist's task was developing stakeholder relations to curtail every man and his dog's money hunger similar to the cravings of American police men for donuts, while the engaged business man's job role was securing port and air transport facilities without causing too much international attention. As both of them were confined to a small, heavy guarded inner city lodge, leisure time became a real rat race to escape away from the confines. Gyms were rare as a tame T-Rex. The nights became ongoing hedonism exacerbation in the bars along the Boulevard de la Liberté. Like others before they too started a liking to French cuisine delights of sole meunière, pate de canard, fromage campagne resulting that both developed unusual Asian self esteem towards seditious pleasures; and playing them as a choreographed tag team. Over time ritual weekend outings to nearby Limbe's beaches commenced with evolving themselves increasingly in to luxurious life of bumming around, especially that the nearby port offered eye protective business opportunities. And thanks to this African Riviera's English heritage, fish and chips serving were not only big and fattening, the feed opened the doors to go beyond the devouring of marine originating seafood. And when the first major pay out for timber extraction came in, followed swiftly by securing a good earning through receiving land percentages for a gas refinery a big party was held at the most expensive hotel located at the port's east, nicely viewing the bay with admirable the sun set views. It was not only deemed appropriate to arrange bucket loads of champagne, but their extravagant moral philosophy reached the sky's top by even engaging foreigners to properly groom the local girls and have them specifically nicely dressed up in bikinis who were like a load of expensive cargo softly dropped off standing within the town's only available loader's bucket, nice peacefully slow with an operator capable of conducting heavy machinery artistic motions accompanied by two old gentlemen dressed in old German garments blowing saluting brasses. Old stile of which Africa can open its doors to welcome associated crazy attitudes. With money any service can be bought. It was an egoism feeding theater which felt like demoting Greek gods congregating around Zeus to crying in the back row. As it was not high season; only a few third party guests were enjoying the pool garden setting. They were without hesitation invited. The two insisted that they were first to be greeted with a standing ovation as official party commencement declaration. The loader's bucket was thereafter used to serve raw fish fillets and chilled South African white wine, albeit this racial segregation paradise being largely boycotted by the continent. The conservative puritan released from his island's confinement was feeling like a happy little devil while the equal rights fending Naxalite was already a pure rubber neck making both prone to a magnet pulling them towards one particular new born party animal dressed in Arabian clothing who represented imaginary remainders of their corrupt Mughal heritage. And so did the shindig continue beyond the weekend until the early morning hours of the following Thursday where this intoxicated third wheel attempted to gurgle the last drops of booze, but instead slipped out a secret…

The two guys could not believe their luck nor were capable to memorize their previous roller coaster rides including the wanting to logically add one plus one of reviving their deepest jungle fears. It was good timing to finish the party properly by serving themselves each an antique from the previous colonial masters left behind liter stein with any remaining grog, growling "we are wild men in Bubblywood" speeches when lifting the glasses to motivate the Chadian gem keeper to continue his journey of losing his consciousness; and while doing so the other two poured their drinks in to the nearby flower pots whereby after one of the cheers both threw the entire glass in to the pool. Finally came the opportunity to carry the passed away victim to his room past his remaining two friends who were sleeping off their own deliriums in with each breath creaky sounding woven wooden chairs aligning the marble hall way. Slowly they went up the steps, unlocked his door and gently laid the guy on to his bed. It was disgusting as not only in the process he passed water under his white gown, but also the alcohol marinated the else wise shower shy body which was slowly taking on a smell of Korean kimchi dipped in to melted Roquefort. Without distracting the lively bedside table light kissing mosquitoes they found the stone; in all laziness left in the top wooden drawer of the old Romance antique armor. While the devil's turd ball rested in the hands of the communist ideology traitor, he unassumingly walks backwards towards the door and with one quick bang, a bullet blows his brain away splattering over the floor. An event ignorant in his wife's boiling kettle pot, however making a far away poverty escaped girl a return back to survival hardship and future fending for herself as a disrespected adoptive daughter of a subversive defector whose last remaining fresh drops of life were engulfed in the crying mouth of his fellow culprit holding him and preventing a total collapse on to the floor. His feelings were drifting towards being part of the nearly forgotten and by many authorities banned movie: Cannibal Holocaust. 21 grams of soul wandering off to view antediluvian hunters roasting a fresh piece of human corpse while enjoying homo sapiens sushi as dinner's prelude. The soberness seeking eyes tried to avoid the previous day's happy memories of boozy girls gone wild and spotted the intruder standing in front of them; a Chinese man full of angry flames burning in his eyes, spitting fire out of his nostril like a chili corn dog choking dragon, "Why so surprised you rotten dahl japa!?! You seriously didn't think that you can get away with such a crazy adultery ritual!?! The piece of rotten greed bag in front of you won't get any attention from the disgusted church neither, as you know what, they not only know what messy masala you have been up to, but the even the best curry spice mixer will have to defecate in his own gravy when trying to deep fry my rock in to a samosa. You all shall be baked as roti in hell! Yeah, first you by swallowing this non halal meat, yeah yeah go, go, likey, likey the taste of this morning's ruining moment, yeah you too have tasted the red blood drops belonging to today's breakfast, yeah you will likey likey motherfucker!?!" Two more sudden gun shots are released. A few hours later the reject's trustee wakes up, not understanding why the party was not anymore smashing out of all coconut shells, to just be angrily greeted by the party's ultimate surviving alcoholomaniac. He seals the poor man's coffin lid by hand cuffing him to the jeep's railing for several days; alone in deepest jungle. Thereafter time repossesses the world to hand back the anger rights to the coastline overarching mountain of greatness, Mongo ma Ndemi or also known as one of Africa's most prominent volcanoes, Mount Cameroon.

Cockroach tears flowing like thundering waterfalls

Three years have passed. Diplomatic delegations in Rwanda are reporting human abusing tumultuous events occurring in neighboring Burundi. The news attracts not only the media rats, but also third parties not interested in soul porn. At the same time behind closed doors a conference of bishops announces that foreigners are seeding racial hate in a deeply divided society by supporting stray governmental officials representing the mistreating minority race. The circulating gossip is that some officials are keen on receiving a debriefing regarding rogue Chinese elements marketing themselves as model leaders who are referring the dismantling of unruly public on Tienanmen Square as success. The events attract a merciless forest dwelling brigadier to gather his troops in Bujumbura's nearby hills. The open jungle botany meets the purpose of team building nicely. The troops set up a bonfire where on top of the wood pile enemies are subject to bush law founded punishments. He is keen to feed their ethnic patriotism with fear that the tide could change if not pursuing racial cleansing. And yes also the wood of the society's tree is dry enough to carry its destructive ashes beyond the mountain ridge guarding the Rift Valley. As not many dared to venture out in this deep nest of historical conflicts, one Chinese importer is well known for his crude, rude, sarcastic jokes against anybody lacking far eastern roots. He is known to subsidize terrorizing gangs to his advantage and his quick rise to fame is being disliked by many. Unfortunately he is coloring off his bad attitudes to his young son. However, when the fire of pogrom is lit the sparks spread rapidly, quickly promoting the rising of brutal egoistic survival need. Crime is ascending faster than a rocket to the moon.

In all that time a new tourism opportunity seeking business man is making his way in search of options to satisfy European clientele. He just opened a hotel on the beach at a safer island with good flight connections to Paris and London, but due to continental related isolation and previous wild life extinction actions, the lack of safari options is rated as unfavorable and thus not a feasible option to hold back the avalanche of hate. And while the big 5 game was not an option there are still mountain gorillas existing, but off economic limits. He is also plagued by the stolen opportunity and is well aware that following destruction there will be again a path towards eternal soul nourishing richness; and that of his pockets too! His initial investigations were directed towards Algeria where a socialist regime was playing the bad loser against an Islamic opposing party who won the first free elections, which when deprived of its victorious rights transformed itself in to a viscous cancerous cell. For thew time being corruption is ripe as a fruit fly devoured apricot representing a dangerous situation lacking money splashing big daddies all while the developing civil war is more suiting guys believing martyr death with ultimate relieve from due date expired one-eyed yogurt slinging hamstrung clumps swimming chin deep under their skin and having wet dreams of hairy fairy virgin armadildos.

The events in Burundi are escalating towards a mob chasing the business strings pulling foreigners; away from the military governing marionettes. It is in the very early hours where news is provided by a fleeing soldier unable to continue protecting the family's warehouse. In a rush bags are packed and they hastily leave for Bukavu. The father still knows a few friends on the other side of Lake Tanganyika, but crossing its waters in this dire situation is deemed as suicide. The vehicle chosen is a rusty, when ignited pulling itself upwards in to moving gear mode old Citroen. Brown like average poo in color to not draw attention. But the plan eventuates as a failure. Soon after leaving the city limits, they are caught off by opposing guerrilla forces from the north before being able to cross the Rusizi River. Dawn is emerging and hospitality is granted by allowing the family to consume breakfast, mince pork porridge. While the family is eating others are igniting heated discussions. One assigned leader provides approval for all to leave, except the father. The scene leads in to the tragic tale of last sights; the little boy while observing the final episode played with atrocity screeching violins is trying not cough up the freshly swallowed chili flakes. The revenge taker goes a step back to theatrically play the destined execution serenade. In all motion he shouts loudly out like a barbarian forced watching a play directed for an audience comprising children, starts moving erratically as if a voltage load took temporary control, then releases the bullet. But it bores through the leg instead!! The surrounding spectators are slowly showing puzzled faces, actually there is a round of hard guys being gob smacked of the unfolding stupidity until one of them grabs the injured wanting to finish off the job on the for mercy fledgling deviled egg. In the final moment of desperation he retrieves the diamond and stretches it out as life's last loan attempt. Far away his young son hears the shot and observes the tears representing his mother's pain, while on the other river side his father is shedding tears replicating physical pain. The day's irony is him being delivered to a local Christian missionary operated hospital where before night fall he falls asleep to the sight of a warm smiling middle aged fair skinned man wished him a good night. The receiving of last rites enables a departure in mercy. May heaven show leniency and open the doors to its floating clouds or at least to some smelly bean curd fed chicken feet carrying clouds of his ancestor's farts.

After the chaos in Bangui and following damning exile stint in midst of the social incoherence between the Afar and Issa while deprived the luxury of drinking wine, the reuniting is received with mixed feelings. The interests of the regained owner are founded on new knowledge gained associating with troubles only a muddy jungle river can carry. But the diamond too is aware that local resistance groups are keen for favors coming from former colonial masters; even wittingly knows that they sought negotiations on eye for eye parity. Angola like its neighbors continues exercising reservation towards democracy, but the elite afforded itself a glitzy life stile allowing strong international influencing, while the majority remain a poverty stricken mess. On some occasions the Catholic church is appreciated, not only because its own democracy diverging practices, but also its potential to act as a third party in closing any war lord money loss making rifts which could swiftly open like a trench created by an earthquake. And like everywhere else, there are elements following their own agenda while the silent preach noting commander wanted to now return the hard bastard to its origin. To any price albeit it would make a nice decoration underneath a cathedral's dome bearing his name. His sleek diplomacy skills became once again a great tool of negotiation by calming the unitary militia slipping away towards heterogeneous behaviors with risk of losing position of being the new owner against equal wealth distribution talking guerrilla elements, while when it came to the walking par some pockets remained deeper than others. His was to allow the church regain historical importance through acting as trusting guardian, hidden guardian in name of his diplomatic passport of another nation known for its liking to anything luxurious. First action is to have the jewel confined in a locked and secured room. The gem gets embedded in an openly visible display case to allow for everybody's comfort. The agreement contains a daily check and chat ritual until a final decision is conducted with aim to mutually benefit both a strategic minded leader trying to find a tactic of solitary possession gain while nervously scratching his lose curly hair patches under his old war wounds hiding beret and the suspicious fellowship mainly comprising of peasants barred from their lands. The first ritual already requires some soothing efforts which unintentionally are aligned to French aristocratic codes like keeping calm and you will be marching with swords of gold through triumphal arches as the stone will provide the stepping stone for the founding of a new modern French African bourgeoisie expanding all the way up to Timbuktu! "The entire Gold Coast, the Kingdom of Mali and a reunited French Equatorial Guinea will knee down to you, so go out tonight and raise your glasses for the scheduled victory march on the Boulevard du1er Novembre, vive les saints! And may the Boulevard in front of the French embassy be renamed as the Grand Avenue de l'Empire d'Afrique Societe Unifie. Allez allez vive la vivir, nous demarrons spectaculaire!!*" The following party accelerates quicker than a tsunami wave ever can to a scene of gun carrying premature males merging their rogue bachelor's celebrations towards a forced spinsters' mass wedding night; raging bulls seeking old cows on an ever green paddock. As expected the screamsters are going beyond pulling off a ripper. Some girls are subject to spastic eagle* partaking. The event speed accelerates to out of control. Brutal practices emerge. Some are using guns as sex toys culminating of one girl being shot length wise with the bullet exiting her head blasting her inner organs in to mash and her breast nipples being ripped off by the force up to dislodging her neck as if a fruit was picked off its tree. Led by an invisible force the tortured population's temper turns 180 degrees in to the aggressors. Women are retrieving crockery as weapons of choice to eradicate the evil acting spirits. One person even manages to fatally stab a soldier with a miniature sized fourchette d'escargot*! Another guy gets grabbed by a dozen of older, fat women who hold him in to a standing strangled position with torn down pants, his junk put on to a steel table where a flat pan is taken to make puree of his testicles. The guy next to him is nailed to the table through his bush whacking tool, which is as next finely sliced like a Soppressata salami. One unlucky idiocracy fueled chimp face receives a quick and nasty fate of choking to death by his cut off roe paste grenade! However, in all the chaos nobody keeps the gravy train* rider at station allowing him to grab a long stretching Tarzan rope and swing his tinned ass* over the Tanganyika billabong* to a, "Auf nimmer Wiedersehen* you reeking retardigrades*!"

Unknowingly of the previous event, and himself in dire need to have a drink to digest the just seen heinousness mentally merging with the heard cries of molested women resulting in a quick stumble on Lubumbashi's airport tarmac exposing the stone to a crying little fat Hokkien noodle. The on foot approaching flight is registered as a charter service for the first post Apartheid white South African business exploration group. The stone's trip to daylight attracts a mining entrepreneur, who releases a small flow of saliva, spilling out of his biscuit crumble covered mouth corner; the juice fleeing from its bad breath emanating tooth brush deprived containment. The man's mischievous intentions were avoiding the smell of the poor by neglecting his own odors. But to make things gross, there are maggots hiding between his unshaven facial wrinkles! A man from the rainbow nation shadowing all possible pale bleak colors aligning to his mood not giving a fuck about any colorful shining arcs, even if one would have shone out of a hot water enema douched out ass hiding a chest of gold. "Bon voyage and for sure au-revoir you death stalker!".

12 CONFESSION BOXING

- Buongiorno, siete de onorevole anti revolucionista Cinqueli Francisco de Moderna gran Amici leccare de Gelati con Frutta Salsa de Papelito's Culo?!!... 2019 and when receiving advice to finally open the letter from Dar I was gobsmacked to read that you knew that we all will be in the shit several years later! And you bugger had even bought that freaking airline ticket on the same day you handed me that secret Santa declared present! Fuck me…?!*

- Preferably not. Gifting me the mannequin was embarrassing enough! By the way, where is the passport? By coming here you breached our agreement.

- You are worse than Rabisu! But what if I had not breached? You'd be sitting now alone!*

- Yes, never forget that most myths have a grain of truth. And a smart farmer like the Roman Catholic church knows how to seed and redeem. When Christianity conquered the world, the pagan beliefs were seen as a threat and opportunity; meaning while we denounced the practices wide scale including applying rigorous death penalties for the unruly, we still very keenly harvested knowledge from Greek oracles, Egyptian prophets, Iberian astrologers who by the way learned their trade from the Moors, gypsy crystal gazers, Brezhoneg druids, hell even some of the temple eunuchs were clairvoyants while must admit cannot recall that the church got much from any Wetterschmöcker; and hence they were left alone, most probably to fuck those holes in the local cheese. Anyway...*

- Hokey pokey to you!

- Thanks. Wait. I smell... Oh no, no, no, you are not seriously…!?!

- Well what does it look like? I entered the citadel as a citizen!

- Lucky there is no jus soli here.*

- Well for forbidden knowledge sake, I might be partaking a leading role in a new play written by your sick master brain desiring relief through some kind of anserine behavior. Shall we call it the Misadventures of Anciblotto?! Oh lord of the religious frowned upon lotto loser making a sacred crucifix pledging to be dechristianised by running away from the darker than their never found g-spot destiny proposed for the king's mother, sisters and that horny dirty minded midwife! Yes, the one who thought the snake's message was to shove an apple up the back end instead; and then pleasurably turning it around in the gravy pot before spouting it out!*

- Wake up grasshopper, we are not peeling an onion in the dark web selling dirty fantasy island wank material dreams through job advertising of dildotronic operator's with stale fuck rod greasing through passion loving medieval freaks of nature resulting in mental pain screams replacing wolf whistling night plays, nor in a flagrant fulfilled Arabian tent containing toga dressed floozies* serving your grapes and dates. Nope you are back here on planet reality which has so kindly offered you a seldom luxury of being allowed to pee on an open street's verge in midst of suburban mayhem!*

- Alright, one nil to you. But my savior should highly appreciate that the pigeons domesticating this below of us weirdly round place being named after a square cannot pass stories down the generations and speak beyond consciousness of their daily dried white bread crumb chase.

- OK, let us start in peace, amen. I might enjoy the breeze through the wall too in hope I forget any ridiculous yarning quickly. So crank up the baggy given to shaggy for a scoobie of doobie*!!!*

- Thanks for agreeing that there are no loose roos hopping merely around in my top paddock! This morning I was even*

deprived of a hang over nuking fry up brekkie plus the ridgy didgy advertised affagulo coffee was a bit fishy tasting!*

- Sounds like a worse destiny than being home with Hubert, the Missus and other hope stealing thieves, heh?

- Stop and stay right there in your cubby house!? Do not spit the poisonous saliva of interbred Hobbits, Orcs and Gollums! Now I would even bet on Madam Gustika of the Duckbill tribe's grave that you most likely know more of those left back home tantrums than me!

- As paragraphing your attitude, a few cabsavs' and SSBs'* go a long way to loosen up the tighs* for some lip servicing stories! Purple circles intruding in to a castrated fairy tale corporate hero's game plans, heh…?!*

- Aaaahhhh, now you managed to touch my weak point. Never thought that you guys could adapt to this crap called affirmative action while in reality it is discrimination against the middle aged Caucasian man. It is like a car's reverse gears being modified to allow for overtaking speeds above those forwards driving. It is a bloody copying of the racial aphotic NSDAP's approach whereby again a dumb minority gets hijacked; this time with soul porn rather than racial supremacy, but both grow on anxiety and mirror progressive outer retinal necrosis! Positive discrimination is still discrimination, period. I mean political correctness has developed itself like a point system where brain washed European ancestor mutated cyborg order cheers up on anything non standard making an albino Aboriginal midget female with one arm, say let wiggle along with the length of a t-rex limb who to top it off does rug munching and can only say the c-word*!*

- I hear, I hear, that is why they got your missus in to a higher position…?

- Yeah, right straight after she came out of the loony bin! These puppets believed the entire thing of her being subject to mental

tormenting; in the front row cyborg Hubert who then hushed all those special children together for a picture, like a farmer showing off his gold plated Simmentalers and Holsteiners close having their udders explode! And then this squashed frog brain acts further like freshly shucked out of Goering's dead rear by gathering all others who cheer him up for a sadly not fake smiling a memorable ego pleasing vista capturing with a meaningless promotional banner in the background. Now, one would think that those who the measure is enacted against would do it for fear as we all know jobs are getting rarer as the government produced unemployment figures are as true as sugarless caramel fudge. As already mentioned, just like Hitler's youth they believe in this crap! It astonishes me how easy it is for a modern day Romulus to create a coalition of the over credulous!

- Can you pass the smoke through, I need a puff myself to calibrate with your communications frequency band width. Thanks. By the way, how did you get it pass the guards? The passport would have catapulted you behind an Italian steel curtain.

- I am aware that I do look like a stoner and wearing this bright blue shining hoodie with some octopus tentacles hanging from the hood downwards does not necessarily make me look like a serious sugar babe bonking business man... But I am sure there are bigger dip sticks around more capable to cause havoc around this secretive chamber harbor and the below catacombs which are most likely full of bones from innocent victims knowing too much. In summary master in disguise ready to go down to those catacombs to sort shit out by removing gold teeth from false apostolates, Opus Dei rings, stone ring cock piercings of gay cardinals! Might even find some tabernacle acolyte deprived goiter carrying bald headed hunch back wanking dufus* down there!*

- You are shocking!

- Yeah my fan mail is not for the fainthearted! And subscription costs need to not only pay for quality sarcasm but make horny chicks go in to meltdown! But for you it is free, just keep the touching to yourself.

- You are a cum gun.

- Yep, did you know my sexcalibur changes with every meter a degree Fahrenheit and covers temperatures from those on Australia's highest mountain Mawson Peak to those beyond its hottest detonation shack in Oodnadatta!

- Ah god, size ain't power!

- No, I would be so humble to appreciate a love rod which with every meter changes color covering only those of a rainbow. And hey mate, you too must admit that I do not act like a dingo eating baby nappies!

- Well hopefully it won't be in your way while defending the heinous. As you are well aware Lucifer's worst and upmost vicious siblings act like wolfs hiding in sheep skin. And yes I personally agree that religious institutions have been continuously being engaging themselves to the disgust of dear Maria in the board game where the ladders were reserved for clerics doing well in hiding their forehead horns, and during past modernity sometimes in no faith except the epiphany behind their pants' zipper. Immorality went well with the invention of money, which by the way was not done by a religious push, while the down winding snakes were a wonderful slippery lubricated water slide to ensure a commonly open path for those opposing the main stream. The gay. The non believers. Or in short the black sheep, just like you!

- And so, where is today's difference? You, nor society or the almighty of this cranberry sauce coated deep fried cheese cake have undergone an evolution so quickly that they are bathing in a blow load of the holiest principles of a bell on a pole bursting ejaculation!?! We might be in the days where it is less likely of gruesome punishments publicly done, although some sand

apes still like this stuff, but the theology still largely remains and is gathering mind fucking strength. An example is the newly discovered potential of artificial intelligence. While some countries have officially introduced it as a mean of protection, like middle earth on its western fringes vegetating desert foragers who used to proudly sit on powerful horses while sporting sharp eyed falcons, but are now up for total racial destruction. The West is screaming foul play while promoting nefarious souls like Hubert to market CCTV, biological identification prints or selling health initiatives with hidden agendas for the purpose of common health; just not yours! We will soon have everybody wrapped up in nano technology control equipped full body condoms. His newest Nero imitating glorious idea is trying to force his minions to adapt to car driving behaviorism apps with the distracting selling tactics of lovey dovey social corporation cares about you all while drooling like a fat kid in a candy store to gain data which can be used to mentally torment the proletariat, or pursuing a futuristic goal which in plain Latin said is, "Consente erga obedio et propinquos meos aut futue te ipsi!" And my dear friend while adhering sneakingly outsmarting the bible, you surely know that the age of Pisces is being replaced by Aquarius; the first step of your religious brotherhood's extinction! Just wait until artificial intelligence will allow people to communicate with the dead reporting back what a congested dump heaven is! Earthly traffic jams are nothing in comparison of all those historical passed away souls continuously fighting for real estate on the clouds above.*

- Yes and no. The universe has bigger plans. Unlike Moses kicking the bulls' ass out of an age old worn out paddock away from his Israelite community as creation of a new breeding and feeding ground honoring a single god, we will be smarter in creating future mass beliefs.

- We...?

- Finish off your whinging and whining grief. Start listening. I am here to guide you out of the deeper ultimately meaningless soul grabbing vortex which the left and right tearing apart forces are justifying existence through a mutually benefiting love hate war with clear aim to ridicule anything originating from moderates, animists and true liberal democrats. And the sheep are loving the crunching through this packet of Cheesoes*. They are unaware animals being fattened up before finding themselves in the abattoir. The middle path is not as smoothly direct, it goes on a knife's edge while balancing both sides. The system is eradicating any consciousnesses capable of identifying road bumps. However, there is a pro and con to everything, a theory which might be of help!

- Yeah, hope is for the church!

- Well, hello....?

- Alright, I have trusted you previously, you have helped me out there in the wild man's land and I guess you will not ask me to find a singing couscous pearl.

- Oh no, Evil Lord Semolina! I am more the warning host trying to give you the throat smoothing mint tea to defend the ever growing numbers chili con burn to hell aggressors!

- Well it is just that we are in this religious heart beating artery, just behind one of the organ's main flaps which contributed heavily to what ever and where we are...

- Don't let my past deceive you. By the way, I gave you are warning long before we officially met. And that was in a church! You were on you own unholy accords sitting in that church... So let us prevent burning down bridges to those who play and not act as being our friends!

- Two nil for you.

- Wrong three nil you druggie.

- Well thanks to mind altering substances I could mindfully jump the raw tomato serving of the Westminster system while others believed it was a bottle of environmental friendly *produced democracy sauce. Put lip stick on a pig, it remains a pig! Bloody animal farm too retarded to see that common law is masquerading elected communism. One person does something stupid and the system enacts corporal punishment by changing processes rather than just telling that fucktard the truth about his limited intelligence sub par to a brick stone. Oh no, special kid is getting a slap on the wrist and will now be for the rest of its life a mental case, dole* bludging society for money and empathy brownie points! Hurry up old sock, time to return my fattoush kebab!*

- Wow, blunt or arrogant...?

- Neither, just feel like a misunderstood chest nut running away from a lose bunch of psyche numbing areca nuts!

- Hmmmnnn, like you are told when being a child to ask questions and there is no thing like dumb ones; but now when you get older you shall not be a sticky beak?

- For an athletic swimmer seeking water in Lake Chad I shall rephrase the wording; it is like a mother walk back from the market with her son telling him to be grateful that he didn't get traded off for a goat!

- And are you going to drink on that?! Luckily this sea you are swimming in can show compassion by transforming itself from a desert in to a barbaric hunter and gatherer satisfying ocean containing beer!

- You are defo getting in to the good memoirs of mine! Want one?*

- Hallelujah!

- May it rain over the dry barley fields!

- But never the less you do not yet see the ultimate goal. In the end we all will be dust. Thus, as short answer who gives a fuck what you are doing here and now! Religion was made to make people feel comfortable with death. And by the way we Catholics....

- We?

- Yes, but don't get too excited, you will soon lose interest in trying to trace your family tree, as it too will become dust. Never the less, while most humans are purely created to breed, some of us can shape future generations of this animal farm like the African led mob at the beginning of this age.

- Heh? Africa...? Aaahhh penny has dropped. Italy does not lie on the European continental plate or...?

- Now grass hopper please close your shlucking hole while I attempt to elude you to the real purpose of humanity!! And of course the story of monogamous evolution from the sun worshipers to a bunch of misanthropist protectorate assemblage who seemingly also allowed their self acclaimed leaders to not only isolate the by leprosy disfigured poor souls to the more efficient starvation solution, burn mentally challenged women under the omen of being wart infested witches which were more likely shaving equipment avoiding ugly scare crows or do shashlik out of religious diverts as a masquerade called the crusade. The good big caring brothers in robes and gowns dressed, honorable as cattle ticks* they were, actively promoted sexuality exposing carnival, barbaric concluding booze sessions and all forms of soap operas like the Winchester Geese*! In today's contemporary, but highly temporary spinning social media times this role has nicely been inherited by big business by not only offering people cheap targeted advertising of sour pokey porcupine milk or humanity do gooders selling packaged holiday on beaches surrounded by poverty gutted and diseased baby whores while moving towards asking the first world to protect themselves with all sorts of vaccinations, but back to the point also the opportunity to have their life's stories printed for eternal access to be shown, marveled at by future movement restricted generations, that is if those virtual world junkies are interested which is unlikely and made available to be jacked over with lousy jealousy cream. For the never tired dooms day warning over zealous moralists a nice byproduct proving*

their mental partaking in kinky sex with what ever humanly unnatural are killfies. But then again, they all will be as pure as a bleached ass berry as they too are drowning in low self-esteem; just with added chlorination. Again, lets get away from the narrow minded fluff of the white sheep and back to the Real McCoy. The truth is that one day there will be no life on Earth. Zero. And nobody will come to save us, meaning neither will your mother, nor your lying grand father or any other Neanderthal DNA sharing ancestor coming from the past or the future to make a soul frolicking stunt like trying to squeeze an adult in to the home fridge, get a market stall owner to sell you a single grape, an afternoon long attempting to balance a light switch between on and off, trying to lick off your own elbow, typing on your mobile phone with your nose backwards elsupercalifragilisticexpialidocious, trying to get a fish and chips shop fry up a bag of gummi bears, use your tablets as Star Wars light sabers or sharpen tooth picks as medieval hobbit feet hair grooming swords, swipe on Tinder together and make fun of the others or discuss the rational explanation why the word Cucumber does not start with a "Q"! Therefore the context of your mission is to retrieve the only independently dynamic universally operating non organic thing human kind to date has been exposed to. It might have the key for at least saving the future destiny of ultimate dead souls. It is also the only hope beyond life as we know it and will ever do so.*

- What, you mean no aliens around?

- Well bluntly said there is absolutely no form of any extra terrestrial life existing or to kerbside the narrow alley of consciousness is interested in us and honestly you could not blame them for any sort of disinterest.

- But in all those movies they love crashing in to the US…!?

- Stop it, they most probably would prefer a wild night out in Mogadishu!

- Guessing they would not have the time and patients wanting to deal with dills like bloated racists who crave for intellectual destructive fast and furious flicks, or having to engage in political talk with flat breasted feminists fighting against a fast food franchise outlet where on an unlucky odd of chance a fried wing looks like a cranny axe, Hindu sects joining forces with vegans for the purpose to reduce their perceived likelihood of being reborn as dogs, but unknowingly increasing their odds ending up as dim-witted donkeys, greed bags chasing the young in to debt, anxiety, dull jelly beans screaming of their nutter when served their life's first beer in a pub or as climax calming down a potbellied abdominatrix monster shortly after being refused chicken nuggets! Further some might be physically bound to a wheel chair but mentally healthy enough to act as mean evil middle aged white men lurking you in the dark web to reflect in their own failure of believing some kind of super power will catapult them in to leading this rotating kindergarten play ground! So what exactly cuts here the mustard?*

- Ha! Chaos has some benefits.

- I have a quick question, when did I hit the nuclear explosion triggering radar button?

- At an unfortunate colonist's auberge. I met you in action wrestling with your inner tranny who seemingly still is in possession of a selfpoking sebastianic sword seeking painfully to cut out the unsatisfying knowledge that epicureanism remains shackled towards justifying boundless self-indulgence. Yes, mental does not always mean mental. Then the story diverts to an invitation where words were harder to digest than brick shitting constipation. I still cannot believe that the theatrical signs of the Kissi tribal shaman oracle with heritage links to the Krio, who like his ancestors survived several tragedies originating from external forces, in his case Ebola, civil war, diamond poachers and the anglicizing of his children while playing with some weirdly shaped soap stones; there was one*

looking like a bag consisting of multiply row covering sow's tits, a fish tail and a cat fish face which when thrown they came to a halt looking in to the eyes of a carved frog body with chameleon eyes aligning above a mosquito nozzle and while this all was happening a bottle of local Star Lager fell and broke itself. He said that there is a guardian roaming places unworthy for the preaching mob and seeks the thrills beyond that of those comfortable in maintaining their status quo of ignorance. And to date with exception of ass licking third world diplomats, second world glorifying spies under control of middle earth and first world supervising secretive deals of the illuminates, who can blame the playground locked out kids for seeing themselves as leading a big donut dough intelligence equipped bunch of gronks; hence making you the only one coming to mind... One question if I may, do you have a bucket list without risking drowning in bong water?*

- Yes, yes, yes, my dear carnivorous anima mea betraying vegetarian! Over all these years I have always wanted to meet somebody with 6 digits on one hand, but never had the luck. Got close to one guy with 6 toes, but that is because he lost four of them, but I swear to Maria's virgin vagina he still could walk in thongs with only that one big toe on!*

- Interesting and a good yarn to a can of cold azzurro. Allow me one more; did you tell those naive, bull shit talking caring homotronic mob to get their off pushed buttons while walking out?

- Oh yes, but they already knew that the kettle well exceeded its boiling temperature... It is so unbelievably mind striking, having to regulate Venturi tubes when seeing those numb skulls actually believing in their country's great care for the common!?! It will haunt them one day.

- Good man. I cannot believe that there is a kind soul desiring for you when taking in to consideration your dogs ball stand out suitability, just worse than Stevey Irwin trying to stick his

dick in to that sting ray's poop hole while unknowingly being taped in a David Attenborough's documentary movie as an outback "drinking with the flies" dugong yobbo*... Lucky the secret services finished not only their break of eating a humble microwaved sausage rolls, drowning in some cheap home brand barbecue sauce, but were also allowed to rest from helping repressive chum buddies chasing democracy promoters piss takers like those black and white painting university students with Chinese origins or outer suburban refugees who escaped atrocities from their home land to just promote that crap in the West. So no wonder in midst of this social septic sump the authorities ruthless deliver the Bali 9 to their deaths! Worse than the medieval inquisition! But I guess they are all still biting on our churches' pedophilia stuff, which for your info is a very convenient distraction from our real tactics, he, he, he....*

- You mean the entire virgin mega store is involved? And even you must agree that the kids don't like playing with all kinds of twigs and berries, as some might be poisonous, or even venomous...!?! Taking it to a metaphorical perversion it is like anime fairy tale telling trees with bold crowns seeking alliance with their rooting stem closer to the under scrub bold bushes!

- No, no, no, firstly I am like a complex carbohydrate, just with an extra over load of fiber for this molestation center, which itself has hugely limited knowledge of this conversation, but many of those kiddy fiddler do follow separate agendas to please the higher orders of what ever they are. Let me drop the verbal dime that a priest or cardinal has a white clear shining halo above their heads like a skin color barren medieval tannery slave escaped gong farmer! For my opinion you can sacrifice them as belated Crusader reconciliation gifts to preteen jihadi brides as middle eastern cooking school education; sizzling them to juicy shish kebabs for each and every hungry desert sand hiding barbarian graboids fart! Even better if it would be in some public viewing format as the small minded would*

adore to watch it; the narrow minded are entertained by small stupidities like a honey suckling bird slowly fattening itself on the same boring pod of flowers, rather than ordering a senses animating supersize meal of lilies, gladiolas, carnations, orchids, chrysanthemums! Unlike flowers being of temporary in nature, good stories tend to prevail, but are rare. It is more common to polish the imperfect ones up to the degree that the a crude oil made product is seen as a natural blossom! Even with a fresher smell to enhance your shnozzle filled nozzle pleasure! So behold, when something is not understood by the dim witted, the cerebrum's containing miniature railway will commence going away from the regular choo choo train steam releases through the sapiosexuality confirming path and will start whipping up his mother land's stale crotch droppings in hope that the old bird might find the secret recipe to re-ignite her social homogeneous striving nationalistic mega tits to lactate!*

- Wow, wow, wow, cuzzy, you are kidnapping my brain away from ancestral dreamland. Woop woop to a spaceship crew getting sober through warp speed travel where all to control center beamed up sergeants conduct a ritual exodus in to mass ceremonial screaming of which its tunes circulate the sterile cabin as shrewd like the visual mouth deformation on Edward Munch's picture, highlighting my discomfort that there is nothing anymore available to skull down in this claustrophobic enviro...?*

- Ran out of booze...?

- Yeah... at least I am not so fucked up like an animal exposed to bestiality!

- Ooooohhhh, holy Maria Magdalena on a dating site choosing between stale gone fruit cakes and nutribulletted raw veggie shakes! You plane is leaving in less than in two hours time! And then there is Rome's traffic...! Time to stop this back door trotting philosophy; here is your ticket, hotel address, some extra play money... and I bet you need these...?!*

- Cholera cocktail and malaria tablets…?

*- Yep, no time for the other stuff or better said I don't trust you handling with needles! Just bad this is all confident, urgent and shall leave you to follow your instincts towards adoring the guys on Lemon Party while figuring out how to make the tub girl thing work without partaking in the innocence breaking two girls and a cup affair. OK, Allez, allez, vite, vite, just take and get your pissbum out! Bon voyage. Run Forrest, run!**

- And what about condoms…?

*- Himmel, Arsch und Zwirn!!**

13 SHALL THEY BE FRIED, BOILED, POACHED OR SCRAMBLED? NUKE THEM; AND DO THE SAME WITH THE CHOOK!

Here is the captain of Flight AZ866, we are bringing a lost Son of Africa back Home

After a hectic drive to Fuimicino with a taxi driver aggravatingly irritatingly waving his hands through the car's interior with excursions beyond the window limits, while continuous attempting to talk about his pain of living with his parents and excusing his laziness, incompetence to leave Hotel Mama by sweet talking her gratitude beyond views captured by the Hubble telescope of Jupiter's gas clouds, which most likely emanated similar pungent waves of odor like his arm pits, the flight luckily left late and gave Shoetef a quick break until… it takes time for the plane to taxi to the bloody run way! "Far out, Italians know how play on a person's patients."

Day 1

As Shoetef passes through the Tunisian custom gates, his day dreaming mind takes a break as his visual deflectors observe a leaning sign on the column bearing his name. Before making a notion that he might be held to ransom on a packaged stay, a voice knocks on mind's portal.

- Hello! Hello! Helloooo dear…!!
- Yes and where is the welcoming marching band lining up a red carpet decorating corridor doing an alley?
- They are too good for a cheating hyena like you. Only one here who used to appreciate crunching on your bone!
- He, he, he, Natalie, you dirty minded bitch in sheep skin!! Good to know you are ready to release your crunchy crutch lose on to my skeleton!
- Woah, woah, woah, still as romantic like a polished turd!
- How about I have reduced my drinking…!
- Really!?!… Honey, that is great news!
- Ha! Not! You silly noodle soup broth.
- Well guess what, I shall get smarter whereby reading is a leisure activity which one does alone!
- Oh, oh, oh, I deeply regret hearing that the agent got her knickers twisted…
- You are booked in to the Grand Hotel de France.
- Wow, sounds surprisingly nice.
- Yes the house kindly reminds you to respect their Muslim traditions by avoiding female visitors! Wish you a wonderful solitary mediation!

Day 2

The day commences with an uneventful late night ending. The sparse nightlife seems to concentrate around the live music shack named overly elegantly Strasbourg, where local songs comprise a chain smoker coughing up tunes defying depression while squeakily squeezing out vocals like a spinto soprano singer going on a countertenor coloratura adventure similar to the

Marlboro man riding an Apollo space ship. The place is jammed with drunken men competing in hand gesticulation dances and beating those from the Italian taxi driver. It is worse than a congress of jobless ventriloquists seeking urgent toilet breaks. By the time all brain fogging smoke managed to disappear, a friendly, dressed in a 70s brown colored suit, clean shaven and spiced perfumed chin stinking older man approaches Shoetef and hands a note over, "There is a reserved car awaiting you at Avenue Habib Bourguiba, which if treated well could direct you to a spicy adventure beyond the tastes of a vindaloo! Search and find the local curry mastery".

Just stupid that he does not have an international drivers license on him. To avoid an early bad book entry the decision is done to flag down a taxi where the first stop is buying some weed on the freeway crossing from a homeless man to develop some food adoring munchie feelings. The second stop is at an empty Indian restaurant where the view of Lake Tunis covers taste bud disappointing palak paneer served with mountain of stale gone shaved lamb. After a spoon full he gets the driver to chauffeur him to a nearby Salon de The for a more hangover pleasing lablabi followed be locking in a shisha smoking session, which ends abruptly albeit politely asking if some mull can be added. The owner calls the police, who are fast. "No donuts?" He is cornered, receives a few cane strikes, gets hands cuffed followed by having to take the authorities back to his room where a detailed search through all belongings is conducted. "But hey, good hiding without a hiding Eustache Dauger*!" Although not the ark of the Covenant the exercise does result in an extra score; a free ride back muting consciousness from any cops forwarded words, "I do not understand Arabian or French!" And the taxi driver; well that reverse gone drag queen set him up. May bad luck accompany All-bin-yadumb-snatch!

It takes a sobering up to resurface in the afternoon. Luckily there are plenty of bars along Avenue Habib Bourguiba, some nicely arranged where ladies drink, but real interest is to no avail. The sad story continues with a so called new found friend keen in drowning beers at a centrally located sausage sizzle* until his advances in smoking through all the cigarettes increases a desire to leave before a wrong turn is taken. Night befalls in a shoddy, old alcoholics' oasis located on Rue de Serbie. All chilled slurping and burping until a drunken

English speaking history lecturer gets the better of himself by performing a verbal Swan River ballet over an intoxicated brew smelling pool. After two words he retreats to singing some love songs until the bar tender grabs him by the shirt and literally kicks him out of the Maghreb shebang. The last attempt to follow the morning's lead results in a night visit to the Bombay Fast Food cafe, where to no surprise more shaved lamb is offered… Wishes of receiving dragon drilling* are nagging.

Day 3

The previous day's conclusion is avoid any bars as even the modern places are as boring like myotis punicus* shit waiting for dung beetles as relief from its stinking meager existence. Thus, the real game is just to accept the boring local life of drinking a strong short espresso and smoking cigarettes. However before any pleasure can take place a new note is shoved under the room door; well after a cheeky early 6am knocking spree, "post for rajul aemaa*" resulting in a response of, "Tozz feek, kol khara ya ibn el sharmouta*!", which is then answered by, "telhas teeze*!". The positive is, "Conservatism is here out of the door too; so bring in the whores!"

The message asks for attention as far East can go. The morning is young, still fresh, the dew rising as steam towards the sun all while the market towards the city is already loudly pumping out its sales pitching noises. Everyone is very busy even on the tram to Tunis Marine business being attempted to be done, followed by similar chaos on the ride towards La Goulette where the train is in tune puffing its last breaths while crossing the big lake past fisher men trying their luck in the dirty waters. Shoetef decides to get physical and starts roaming Carthage, which is not only famous for its Roman ruins, but also as affluent suburb. Who knows he might get lucky to some cardamon scents eluding to companion opportunity. Horny bastards third leg is slowly growing itchy feet on its one eyes stump! From hill side ruins to amphitheaters, the aqueduct and its nearby cisterns, Antoine baths which would have and could still accommodate naughty pleasures and pass the by tourist inundated cathedral.

All is actually happening pleasantly mellow until from nowhere vendors surface like Frank Herbert's sand worms lurking the old aged Contiki customers with free samples of Saharan crystal; likely harvested from some addax bocked up bonking sand pit with more stones than fur hairs. It turns out to be a tedious navigating past for relief at the rather mind numbing than shocking children graves. The next episode of stress awaits under the palace's extensive line of national flags next to banners depicting the president copying the devious smile of his Anatolian counterpart. The scenery too is similar to the Bosporus overlooking Topkapi including the police presence where the guys from previous day's exercise take up a fondling of shouting towards him like banana allergic gorillas injecting additive loaded powder milk shakes making them go in to mental overdrive, "yalla, yalla, yalla*!!" Like in the third war Romans destroying the city from the children of the Phoenicians, so is Shoetef's desire wanting to commence a ninth crusade against the Umayyad ancestry donkey dick sucking derogates.

Day 4

Oh heaven forbid, especially after the final cry of trying to get lucky. Visiting the blubber through the skin pores dripping love handle's of Impasse Sidi Abdallah Gueche where even Goliath would have difficulties to swallow those fried shanks is still shaking Shoetef's body all the way in to the deepest bone marrow crevices. The dead end of hell bitches behind Bab Bhar shall remain well hidden and out of sight. Also still no sign of Natalie, except the usual stupid notes shoved under the door at some ungodly early morning timing, "You were close, but failed like a European army trying to invade Russia, I mean does one really believe those modern metrosexualights* would ever be able to tame addicts who have opiates for breakfast with 90% vodka as wash down?!" #smirk#

Albeit disappearing motivation and somehow the place slowly showing its Dullsville* face while asking the puzzling question what attracts Libyans here, the day's search directs itself towards the suburban railway line heading southerly along the beach to where Hammam-Lif is providing a relaxing lunch, followed by swimming in penis shriveling cold waters. The afternoon tea, nutty sweets and shisha smoking is taken at the popular white walled cavern golden pictures frame the below red plush cushioned seating decorated Cafe Sour, with hilarious views of silly sandals wearing tourists doing their best in navigating through the city market's labyrinth past zealous vendors who can corrupt the hemisphere's hovering strongest Greek god in to a headless winged vertebrate, flapping around like a sparrow being eaten by a bored castrated house cat! Maybe the secret lies with visiting a shopping mall where possibly an Indian themed shop exists? But first smoke or sleep...? Yeah both do good after a serve of fresh pressed pomegranate juice.

Day 5

A banging on the door, louder, louder, louder... And an angry women's voice! "Natalie!?" The vocal chords are striking as zealous impulsively fiery like Mount Nyamuragiraa spewing its volcanic gases due to being deprived from drinking the cooling waters of nearby Lake Kivu...

- Aaahhhh, aaalll right! Good morning!?
- Right?! I ain't got no time for that!
- Ha! Must say even when you are angry, you look prettier than the common camel head served at the local restaurants!
- Don't you dare!... Aaahhh, am I missing out on something?
- What? The great nightlife of shy whores sipping coffee; and when you approach them they are just as like the so called progressive Middle Eastern Christian chicks, expecting you to buy them on the spot not only a BMW, a house and a life insurance for the ckickpea dip and goat lard stuffed avoirdupussies...*
- Oh, you poor boy. Tough life, heh?..... Wait, I hear..... What?!?!
- Ooooopsi pooooopsi, forgot to direct Marish to remain in the bath. You don't do Arabian saddle and alternatives to French is non existent here.*

- I cannot believe the Vatican switched on for your snow globes* to shine!

- Never thought Moroccan girls are too progressive for the Pandatheistic Randomism prehistorian pee-historics like representing a harissa spiced scrambled eggs foundation. And my gracious fuming oryx, just leaving bland messages, even lacking with a smiley will never get those nargberries to blossom!

- What about your commitment to the mission..?! Already given it up for, for, for...?

- What? A rip snorter?* Or because of not bothering with glassy classy fish skinning? Tell me, what makes this little sexy angry soul of yours happy?

- No visit to the supermarket? No visit to any of the Indian restaurants..!?! I did all the walking...

- Well you could have shared time with me and then... By the way where are you residing? Some 5 Star Hotel? Most likely next to an Indian Restaurant where you could already spy days ahead...!?!

- Hey! It is not easy to venture out in the wee hours from Marsa Beach...

- What!?! Beach!?! Without me! Marish, mon gracieux flacon d'eau de rosehumain, attendris avec une douche tes jarrets juteux, en ayant lentement faim de chorba de poisson et de felfel mahchi...*

- And me?

- Well you go back to your luxury pad. Afternoon tea is awaiting Agent 99* as power up for some donkey dicking investigations!

- Come on!! Kick her out!

- Well she... she... she was nice last night. Was even able to introduce this daughter of a Tuareg rebel the protective benefits of Saharan goggles*!

- Right my chauvinistic stoned pony*! Where did you get her? And how? Too hot for the red light district, those in the cafe strip *would refuse any cheap desert crystal exchange and neither black enough for you…*

- For this discussion, I ain't got no time!! Ooooh no, you are now smiling…?!?! And it is not even fake one imitating those incapable, unsuccessful buffet slayers hunting a wealth generating perceived belly dancing career!

- Well my smootchie muuush muuush…

- Ok, let's walk, sprint, allez allez!! Au-revoir Marisha!

- You don't have anything that is precious…? She will take it!

- Nothing you guys would not reimburse me for! I have got news for you, that is if you don't hit your nose on the stair's edge as clumsy way as a cherry drinking grandmother descending in to Dante's hell.

- Keep running or you end up in the circles of doom.

- I didn't offer you a cucumber sandwich did I? I think Algeria holds the key!

- Ok, firstly not talking about stalking the posh tower of bland food thing, you mashed cervical pussinimal! Why now Algeria..?! What next? Sao Rico, San Theodoros or Syldavia…? By the way I saw Sanji!*

- Nice try with Tintin fictional countries. Reporting in hope that dumb dumb here is uneducated, which to your bad luck the kid in the last back row on the window seat got taught by day dreaming light waves while watching swooping birds terrorizing some fucktards like "remote controlled wish mops" and their cretinous with angst full packed crying mothers, "oh my child is going to lose an eye and half of its brain" of which the latter has already occurred thanks to Australia's love to flavored milk, showing a hypothesis relevance between diminutive flyspeck farts and convict genes! By the way my favorite destination is Babar's Kingdom*. Less translation lost in evolution than what many wombat bashers can take, as they go soft on proper booze beyond colored cans of light weight grog!!*

- Plan is you are going to talk to Sanji!

- Algeria tells me that there are hidden caves in mountains which offer seclusive security; both in the north thanks to the local Berbers' disliking the elites and the south where religious extremists fondly enjoy praying for the odd day in a century of bless giving snow falls where they possibly believe to be freed of sins against shitting on thorny desert scrub, and....

- Did you hear what I said!?!

- Me dumb dumb...!?

- You are going in to the restaurant and exercise your so adorable smart casual Giovanni Jacopo Casanova de Seingalt magic!

- Must say, must acknowledge, must devour this; you are evolving in to a sarcastic black mamba! She nearly ended up being my wife and...

- And what? Hey old love does not rust, not even for a swines!

- Might as well kill of my charcuterie potential by asking you this one question, do you know what are the two most important holes a women has?

- Aaahhhrrrggg, I smell bacon!!

- Wrong, wrong, wait, wait with your dirty mind!!

- Damn you over stuffed rotten pineapple juice glazed pork roast, what?

- He, he, he, her nostrils of course!! What did you think.

- Huh? What? Steering away from a female vortex?

- Nearly! It is because without them she cannot breath.... While sucking!

All the hurry is a waste. She is keeping calm like dark clouds in the sky holding off the lightening strike. The restaurant is not opening before night fall. Plan B drops down cold as fresh death by the hands of John Allen Muhammad and his sniper son as Natalie refuses to lift her accommodation veil resulting in a flood of swearing and the decision to walk towards the train station to jump in one of the old barren shacks on wheels serving

Tunis Marine. But he passes a clothing boutique where his eye sockets nearly explode.

- No ways, you saali kuttayi chutia*!!
- Hello my former heart melting honey pot.
- You were the highlight in my life, the good, the bad and the hairy...
- The hard rock has gone somewhere else with playing its satanic rhymes, right?
- Tell me who is here the bhoot-ne-kaa*!?!
- Oh my tantalizing deep sea conquering gem; you are as vicious in attitude like a mosquito being refused of sucking blood and now is spitting its malaria infected saliva on to you!
- You are a jaan-var tatti licking haraami*…
- Stop the Bollywood drama! I know I am not a majestic Indian peafowl, nor popular like a baya weaver, but sun birds are beautifully colored too, just stiff bikkies they fly away to the next nectar pod.
- Theek*! I have an article from a Moroccan left wing newspaper executing schadenfreude in all its glory by describing ardent flames in Jewish jewelers' eyes before literally sacking in dead like a choking fatwa where instead of the matzo ball being dropped in to the chicken soup it is a pair of false teeth! Further explanation is the occurrence after being exposed to the "Revengeful Soulika Hajouel Agunah" referring to a sucrose gorgeous local girl who fought for religious choice to overcome prohibition to divorce from historical strings where she...
- Thus, in return is on a revenge spree!! You are a hero, love you!!
- No you don't, you bahen-ke-land*. I'll only give you the article if you promise to stay away from my businesses, especially Lagos!
- Bet you mad-oh*! How is actually Aadarsh doing?
- He lost his arm… And Prafula was eaten up from within by a tumor!

Day 6

- Salaam wa sabaah al-khayr, may I offer you a surprise? Instead of sitting at the back row smelling the ablution smells of pleasure, what about getting pro-active in to the grime time by accepting an invitation to the mile high club?*
- Damn, how did you...?
- Loved your note, but do not under estimate me! Racy saying, "catch me if your camel toe runs fast; to a place of greed and ban", nearly got me thinking of Cairo, but we both know the associated toxic obnoxiousness there; so next best guess matching was a touristic place in Morocco! And as a cheap scat you are I had a look at airline schedules. You nearly got me with a stop over in Algiers, but getting a visa is too tedious. Thus, next best port must be a busy tawook shack.
- Damn, you might be smart, but not in maths! You forgot the description of variance potentials plus a real genius would have said 1.99999999999....
- Ya shar mu taigh, you only get this one offer, take it or tarajueh*...*

While the air hostesses are busily serving meals, the two finally manage to re-ignite their simmering coal back in to a flame. As space is rare, a stolen airplane blanket from a previous flight is laid out on the floor, where she is laying with her head down as avoidance measure bringing attention through banging her knobstuckling* on the door, him kneeling on the fragile toilet lid whereby dropping down his erected trajectile similarly dipping a fork in to cheese fondue. It all goes quick, dirty, sticky; but efficient and it is giving her relief too. The involved pain relating to her positioning evaporates smoothly due to concentrating on maintaining moaning levels low. And it is an encounter which she is telling her mind to savor for a longer stint, as the budget hotels nearby Casablanca Port train station refuse unmarried couple to share rooms; even those located in the seedier end town of an else wise low key nightlife comprised city where it is even more exciting to find the Key of Perihelion in Isaac Asimov's

Robot City. Not even any half way romantic cardiac tickling remains of the classical movie are existing as not even the beach front offers anything to trigger involuntary dystonia reversing twitching!

The visit to Alpha 55 shopping center is a waste. Disinterested jewelers in a play ground filled with indifferent rich bitch towelettes sporting arrogance as far the sight can take a person's eye over the ocean's horizon. The subsequent pit stop in the old city is more accommodating where when at sun's descending a rather unusual loquacious rabbi crosses paths. While the Medina walls are cooling his tongue is warming up. He eludes that a Spanish speaking slime dribbling worm offered total vanishing of Lord Evil in the desert; and that for eternity.

The surprise news is calling for a digestion. The choice is venturing by foot past Africa's largest mosque down Boulevard de la Corniche, then the shut down clubs of Ain Diab beach including surprisingly the shisha advertising Las Vegas bar. Shoetef is keen on keeping pace, ignoring the soccer playing beach boys, navigating all the way to a small rock crop island linked by a bridge accommodating Sidi Abderahmane's tomb. A halt is needed for a knackered Natalie, "is this man riding an asteroid while being sick?" But the albtraum* is only starting! The group in front of them on the rock outcrop's ledge is conducting an animal sacrificing ritual whereby post slitting up the beasts' throat a quick cut through the stomach is done followed by the chunk of a butcher slitting up the carcass in length. Within minutes her mind spins between the unlucky dead ready to serve as nourishing roast for the survivors and the fact that Lucifer's hard blood drop has not shown any merciful interest or sympathy towards earthy creatures. "Why is compassion following an unkempt path?" No answer from Shoetef as the scene is providing a nice excuse for a later venturing out solo in to bars subject to typical local cock blocking efforts. Sometimes this is still better than being misused as a psychologist. "And beer must surely be cold served in the uneventful nightlife hot spots of Les Ambassadeurs, La Bodega, the overpriced La Bavaroise or the final night's death breath; the two bars below the Imperial Hotel!?" Both somehow feel like desiring to participate in the artificial squeezed out laughs of a Trinity Channel show where miraculous can annoy. Hardcore religious people don't get in to heaven because they are useless to serve

Peter as wing men when stalking angels. So hell? Nope; ice age is of no use there. May the decomposers celebrate reincarnation!

As a final note, Casablanca offers high quality restaurants, examples being those on the round-about south of the Imperial where marvelous food is served with local wines. However, distrust Moroccans telling you how great their hookers are. The bad stay in the mountains, the worse in city dens while the honey flows far away. Choose your sizzling maqlooba wisely or instead of a wiggling belly dancer you get belly up drifting fat raft!

Day 7

The flight to Marrakesh is surpassing the initial hills post the coast line with slightly higher chain of peaks in front while Shoetef is antagonizing the fact that only a cup of water is being served. This sight rather justifies a Rif Mountain parsnip! Maybe the stinky toes of the Middle Atlas do not justify a mighty herbal blessing. With diving in to the international airport, where to their surprise large quantities of European carriers are congesting all possible the traffic realization kicks in that the place's earlier days of tranquility are more of historical note. To the hordes of frightened and anxious tourists scrambling in clogged up lines at all the stores including currency exchange are as scary as the local taxi drivers eagerly mouth drooling to eat as many of those poor schnitzels alive! Poor little European vegimites deprived of any tourist information. But of course at the far end there is a bus to the city; a nice move for Shoetef to go Dutch*. Natalie is aligning with the creamy homo stupidibitchus stampede; playing up a round of "I'm too good for this" aligning to the common arriving passenger's mental illness of desiring wet wipes users whereby being carriers of a vicious contagious virus and its liking to attack Western men resulting in them going in to defense mode of transforming in to spineless non-queer non-porn-consuming gaytipedes. Of course many unaware of wearing culturally seen shameful clothing while spouting out first world societal garbage in midst of people who cannot afford pain killers; they will rather have to blow up their ear drums!

Away from the storm, on the bus, hidden quite piece of paradise; until Menara Garden where warm afternoon's weathered souls of obese pork guzzlers join. But the olive grove and a decaying over sized reservoir don't make a slim built porn starlet gusher take up on head wind neither! Although her juices could give a good deserved flush out of the mosquito infested irrigation. Soon thereafter Marrakesh's charms of orange-pink colored buildings with the surrounding oasis and mountainous horizon surfaces whereby positively worth mentioning is the architectural design of merging new town with the Medina quarters. However, Shoetef learns when taking the bus it does a long enduring circle around the old city's walls before returning through Gueliz where the patients ends at the La Grande Poste square. He first needs a cigarette and a black coffee with view of the plaza before tackling the final meters towards the train station where he finds a suitable hotel comprising of a fronting cafe. And more, a mosque within the compound behind, meaning conservative enough to keep Natalie bay! Most boys back home are such cock blocking imbeciles deprived of this luxury! May the muezzin's prayers guard. The lovely smells coming from the neighboring clay pots sizzling along slowly are making him addictive to lamb tajine just like an opium junkie desiring to smoke heroin at Menara Gardens and buzz his brain cells off under a shade giving tree.

Shoetef has no clue of where to go and decides to follow a passing stream of sandals wearing European tourists. No real Australian wears archaic foot. The Emperor Tiberius sports arena times are over, although feeding the lions might be enticing! Most likely also a bit action than sitting in Stadium full of soccer shirt wearing Shwaboe-shnaboes*. When reaching the city's main mosque Shoetef takes a turn to, damn there is no escaping the crowds here! However for the body and soul it is never wrong to follow green open public spaces. On the small foot path linking the city bus terminal with Jemaa el-Fna Square along a back drop of aligning full blossoming jacarandas bushes providing a sweet smell of blossom bosom corona sweat intermingling with seasoning counterparts a he receives an ozy* of pure delicious violet crumble* on steroids offer at a price of 500 Dirhams. "He, he, he, yeah right, what about 200 Dirhams to meet the correct demand versa supply line of pricing practices!" Not that the two are out and about seeking to engage themselves in cutting up their wrist and forming blood brotherhood; but trust and patients tends to result in redemption. Plus an opportunity for an amusing chat with nearby observers. They too need attention or sweet redemption goes sour. One older guy is serving hot tea, the other is polishing shoes! But with delivery investigations are swiftly put on hold. Shoetef politely excuses himself without mentioning that his score needs to celebrated through drowning a few Casablanca stubbies on a nearby roof top bar with views over the orange-pink buildings, well in to the night. There he is again lured in to visiting these so called cool clubs containing oceans of lusting whores for big waves of dicks to smash them on the shores of eternal pleasuring. Yeah right, Morocco is full of smoke, just like Shoetef's hotel room on top level right in the far corner; a room which the owner purely reserves for his visiting special stoner monkey. The room next door is reserved for the poorest guest, usually a foreigner on some religious pilgrimage.

Day 8

An early morning start, no messages under the door, cruise control wandering through the Medina, all the way to a freely accessible viewing platform where the next harassing local is awaiting; again eager to make a small fortune from the early morning visitor. This time it is the store owner below the tannery overlooking the real workers exercising hard labor in harsh conditions. He feels the tense vibes, but is surprised on the relaxing acting relationship medium with them. The guest's red colored eyes are focused in finding something beyond the commonly sold leather, silver jewelry and other mass produced souvenir crap. After a lengthy discussion about the details of trade, they venture out to a hidden cafe for a strong brew to mutual kick start luck on more fortunate paths. The new found friend takes him towards the Al Azama synagogue where he gets introduced to a rabbi who informs that the boulder is on its way to the mighty sand dunes, whereby Ouarzazate is the final refueling stop before its last journey to an isolated and lonely death, hopefully also deprived of any refreshing cold winds coming from the High Atlas crossing through the Erg. Yes, deep in to the Reg this menace shall rest, sucked dry from its own horrific mischief.

After sorting out a bus ticket, the day is spent with tag teaming between dope smoking, coffees at the cafe and venturing back in to town, where at night circles of musicians are providing surreal mystique scenes of long ago times in far away dimensions. Hammering drum beats, singing, accompanying instruments all the way through the Jemaa el-Fna past the overly aggressive open air eatery waiters in sync of the overwhelming experience for foreigners; great for lurking silly first dayers, but else business as unusual for spacing out zombie hippo happy hippies! The continuous annoying approaches reflect the average scum bag behavior of the local vendors. Needless to mention the oblivious exercised ignorance to a cloud floater "leave me in peace you hill top hood dero*, I am above and too high for your rip off". However when the night slowly finalizes itself, a small square shaped bar attracts the munchie voices in his mind. The place is eagerly serving snails to local Amazighens*, who in scooping rhyming rhythm slurp the sluggard broth; like a cult ceremony of followers around a white gown wearing cooking master directing the enthusiastic mass towards ecstasy with a silver spoon. It would have been no wonder if they had a shrine installed highlighting Slurm McKenzie's mum's butt magic!

Day 9

With a hash brown Moroccan stile brekkie roll full of fresh pressed goodness from the Rif mountains containing a colorful taste spectrum as exotic as the blue city walls of Chefchaouen a hastily run to the bus station is done; past already awakened beggars trying to convince that global life's luck will begin right now and today, but for that to occur a few hundred spare Dirhams are naturally required. Just bad luck trying to tell that to an atmospheric wave riding keen in catching the next smoking hovercraft well before being taken on a radiant leaving the oasis along a wadi creek in canyons where on the wetter weather exposed slopes pine trees grow versa an opposing valley side of erosion resisting rock crops with spots harboring just enough fertile soil for small scale farming. Sporadic basic clay huts accommodate the tough alpine souls full of boofhead power, leathery endurance and strength to beat the hardships where the desert meets snow and where possibly some goats get fucked by alien DNA carriers! A rough place where traditional parents are at high risk of losing pretty daughters to the seedy glamour of Tunis! Or as private belly dancers for some rich dude in Tripoli. Next best bet is street hooker in Rome. Then German swinger clubs are continuously on the look for modern sex slaves. All better places for an Atlas beauties than getting her first deflorating body tequila from Epiney in one of world's ugliest dungeon, the Schmitte Grill and Bar in Wil, Hellvetia. To redirect focus and as honor for the majestic mountain peaks a fresh scoobiedoobie is rolled on arrival at Col de Tizi-n-Tichka, with 2260 meters above sea level the highest mountain pass of North Africa. And a second one is smoked at the first coffee stop where a brew is served underneath a roaring posture of the last in wild known living Barbary lion!

The first positive impressions of Ouarzazate is obtained before a dealer can annoy. This time Shoetef leaves the bus station in a less attraction causing direction where one street behind an impressive masonry built large white stoned plaza with red rectangular perimeter aligning plates exists, plus Hotel Bab Sahara. He chooses room 217 with views over the entire length of Place al Mouahidine, past the outdoor seating offering restaurants to the right and commercial businesses to the left which during late afternoons hide behind street stalls. On arrival however the hot desert sun is striking its power harshly keeping everyone in the shade, far away from the open sizzling plaza. A great scenery, romantic, lonely sitting on the balcony, with a fine dining reefer beefer! But, but, a second look, an extra second to mentally digest, isn't that…!?!?

> *- Hola, got ya!*
> *- "Oh mia madre gran puta*, ¿Cómo me encontraste*? ¡Los tentáculos del diablo son de largo alcance*!*
> *- Now, now, be nice to me!*
> *- I actually first thought it was you when walking towards the postal office. You were sitting there on the balcony, not!?!*
> *- Hmmmnnn…*
> *- Y puta*, you know what, I thought no way that you burro* are still kicking!!*

- Ah yeah, and I thought that such a sleek snake like you would never end up having his head bandaged. Looks funny to see a pure devious hydra being wrapped up like an over sized knob.

- Sneaky? Well while you were following me with the taxi up the hill slope to this rarity of a hotel bar, I did manage to ask myself one question: Heracles was sent by Eurytheus, but who is the real Myceneaean stronghold or are there two others competing?

- What?

- Do you still see Natalie…?

- And? You don't mean she is the king of Argolite?

- No, but maybe the queen!

- La hostia esquinera! Pero, porque? How does jodeterino* know?*

- Me cago en todo lo que se menea, especially if they are Safasinos!!*

- Damn, how did their paths cross?!?

- No se amigo!*

- Ok amigo, lets forget the past for a moment until well I guess with a few accompanying coldies and talk shit about the old days and…

- Don't make this in to a history lesson! And if you desire, then let us first have a smoke, look at this baby, it is so oily you can rub it in to small sausages and lay on top of el tabaco… Because creo que the guys have guns and funny enough I would have given that evil pebble to anyone who'd just nicely asked! Be aware amigo, greed has decomposed their souls in to stinking fly feces strewn rot which has incubated them with an illness which transforms these infected dung choking maggots in to rabies steroid pumped up Gollums!*

- Well, that sounds like a Pulitzer price winning novel! Never thought that dodgeroos like you could show fantasy; except maybe in hiding a dead body!

- No amigo, believe it or not, have never ever killed a person. You guys were close, but would have thought that my professional code is better known to you after all our...

- No history lessons amigo!! By the way, can you get your hands on some guns?

- Tsss... ask Natalie!

- For effin' sake what has she to do with this?

- She always had those determined eyes, and by my mother's grave she ain't far away, yo se yo se**

- Just..... now look at that baby as sexy as a quaffing Thai badgie...*

- You have one?

- Tranquilo, let us hide...

The new guest arrives with perspiration dribbling down his developing baldness which is partially covered with thin strings of black hair combed from the left to the right, stretching any definition of acceptable norm. Good look for dealing with ruthless operating commie skippers who successfully in alignment to their own political bankruptcy make foot soldiers live in fear that failure can be punished by death; and unlike their Siberian Stalinist brothers the Maoists get away still being accepted as partners of the West. A society exposed to a propaganda machinery fogging democracy with society's desire of egoism driven greed and linking its political disinterest of individual freedom towards global welfare creation. In midst of this momentum a man with blood stained brown khaki pants emerges. The sight is giving the injured short raging buzz attacks. Shoetef needs to pin him down behind the nearby dark green leather couch like a jiu jitsu wrestler with one hand covering the antagonizing moaning mouth while suave whispering "just shut the fuck up you agitating toddler, are we acting as hung like a light switch?". The exhausted arrival decides to first hit the comforting bar. Southern Comfort to be exact. Not really the drink he would share with business partners due to potential stigmatization through being perceived as a weak fruit loop* juice slasher. The move is giving the other two plenty of time to reverse, leave and walk to the nearby creek containing a viewing platform over a small valley overlooking the old city wall with at its toe palm trees offering welcoming shade for a spliff, or six. When happy delirium days kick in they move onward to a rare cold wash serving bar in the Ksar Lina building.

Shoetef's intuition and learning from Malawi, Chongstar's health of thirst has become astronomic making him now rather an exoplanet exchanging his previous role as a shining star in the dragon constellation. When entering the hotel corridors, turning to the right towards the rest room facilities, just around the corner, *strike*; not even a gurgling is heard from chopped suey.

Day 10

- Damn Juan, just a moment too early and could have gotten the details of the stone's travel itinerary! Instead thanks to your inner loco locomotive we have to not only carry this fat fuck up the stairs and depart without suspicion, but also need to rearrange ourselves. Tomorrow morning you get guns, while I have to smoke all this hashish before where who knows we are off too afterwards; and damn have to now deal with two gangsta clowns!
- Vete a la mierda coño!* *You might have a few more stinkpusses to deal with!*
- Oh no, that's what you meant with Safasino?

After 3 cones the day's start is a pleasant ride to welcome dawn. The destination is a major regional tourist attraction: Kasbah Ait Ben Haddou, a famous town built of dried crap? Finding a half dead Safa would have been easier if the chartered driver is not laziness in perfection. He is even too lazy to sit under a date tree, observe the traffic over the river bed while letting the fruits fall in to his counter productive busy mouth. Nope, it is too much to ask for. Thanks to poor planning not even a pair of binoculars are obtainable to accommodate any alternative strategies like sitting on the town's hill above its 4 families who are well accustomed to tourists and even more to their wallets. Post charging town fees they lure visitors to a house and charge them to enter a pile of rotten structurally unsound crumbling dung! As the sun is rising the impossibility of identifying and following any professional photograph takers is frustratingly acknowledged. Inauspicious flocks of sandal wearers, but not nomads are preventing a day's starting orb event. And due to fear of authoritative road blocks, the herbal breakfast is being delayed impacting on his calmness. The on activity gaining mind wanders of too, "by gosh what a new born porn Moroccan film shot containing virtual fata morgana where arriving caravans are given with their fouled months welcoming fellatios as means to protect their virginity whereby the lack of cock is mentally drugging them towards sexual deprived spinster stupidity of believing this attitude will make them angels! Fucking sun is getting on my tits!". At 10am the exercise is declared abandoned.

After a few spliffs back in the plaza overlooking hotel room the decision is done to return to the seedy bar containing lodge where unsurprisingly the clerk informed the departure of his guest, but oddly as anti-anti-climaxe did not officially checked out. "Is he designing a false path of indicating an escape, but is not? And is night really a better timing choice to leave? Thus what is this broiled chook noodle soup up to? Bingo! Might have to be nice to the taxi driver and pay him generously for some investigation work!"

- How did, could you, find me? I left the hotel and said was going to the hospital with not being sure regarding return. This Latino friend of yours is up to no good!
- Welcome to the world you boiled bat testicle soup eating deep fried fortune cookie! And stop acting like a female reproductive system powered by a turbocharger! Who is your helper?
- Jian nue ren!*
- Are we still playing alcohol infused bian tai girlie games? Thought that was more in the realm of the japs!? I bet you too are asking where your paei mae pii* is?*
- So it was the taxi driver, huh? You can never trust these male xiao jies!*
- Yeah I first did wonder why the heck does a morally rotten egg like you visit Ouarzawood, the place of biblical movies! But

after buying the tickets and in need for a smoke, bang, of course it is not because you want to eat bland silken tofu neither! The bloody bar is part of your tactic...?

- Yeah, you saw me taking picture of actresses while you did a Darius on Cleopatra's litter! All history. So, yes I thought the best is to get this done over a beer and over another one just like in good old days!*

- He, he, he, but you will still end up as ugly pulp beyond a racial laji mixture of choubaguai* combined with Anne of Cleaves marriage luck and the intelligence contained in Aqua Teen Hunger Force's milk shake's straw!*

- I wish you death in searching the precious. As you by now know, I was not your fried scavenger's unfriendly guest!

Day 11

The tedious afternoon bus trip is taking its stoned passenger over the Anti Atlas and along a fertile valley cutting its flowing path through the vast terrain of the reg dessert sands. Shoetef is following information given by old silver jeweler who described himself as the desert's oracle beyond the smells of camel farts. Still better than ending up as a lone wanderer in the hands of ruthless tour operators dishing out two hour historical lessons of surreal twin peaks and the Almoravids' conquer chapters. But ultimately the town's best offering is its euphoric blazing hammam defeating collapse through heat exposure and preventing being an exuberant Pedro Almodovar movie scene with 1001 genders going in to competition. Thus, for a rational mind it seems better that the structure's non existent mental health receives a splash serving of sex deprived boners rubbed by the local sponging masseuse Bob the Knob. But during the cleaning process evil thoughts capture him: Natalie pleasing him while whispering in to his ear, "go to the desert baby!" triggering a fast over a rainbow excitingly flying response, "hey girl, I saw that Tombouctou 52 days away mural, so no thanks!" But the voice persists by recommending to tackle the search from the south via the nearest capital city as to his astonishment the voice agreed that the desert crossing caravan has already disappeared in to the desert and chasing it on a camel's back might not be wise for his family jewels. "You naughty black magic embracing darling!". Additionally the baths offer as much travel accompanying rubber duckies like the country's flooding of whores…

Day 12

Who would have thought that flying in to Nouakchott could be done so smoothly including having the opportunity to flirt! The young lady is dressed in a modern pastel yellow and blue colored dress with a matching turquoise-greenish silken head scarf, but to his surprise leads the conversation by asking which normal person would ever think of visiting her home country as it is a large vastly open chamber of evil men purely interested in maintaining archaic traditions including slavery and mistreating women to banditry. The custom officers are keen following meticulously their bureaucratic process, which whereby can be fast tracked by offering the confiscation of a bottle of single malt. As next further proof of diverging values is obtained when hitching a ride in to the city; a car where every objective thinking person would award the technical ingenuity art of squeezing not only the fruit but the entire skin of a lemon out!

Day 13

Lodging at the Wissal Hotel, the unofficial national palace where politicians meet all sorts of interests groups within an atmosphere weirder than camels sucking off each other's baby hump. All this love is shown on the impressive tiled picture above the pool, which can cool nicely down over excited men. The setting is better than double charging foreigners with force, that is a gun held to their heads! And this in 2019!

After an uneventful plate of Lebanese bean stew and a shisha for desert a taxi takes Shoetef to the town's most famous site, a harbor lacking of any sun downer options, not even offering a fish restaurant! During the boredom killing discussions the driver indicates that there is a remotely located mosque to the north where Bidhans, white Moors meet. Their origins coming from the northerly located Adrar and Tiris Zemmour regions align with the disputed territory home to the Sawahris, who trying to defeat Morocco's colonization frontier. They could well represent his searching touching point. They drive there to meet and greet. After pouring a warm welcoming tea the Bidhans eagerly commence marketing the benefits of meeting their leader who can be found at nearby Bahamas Beach. Of course he owns the restaurant, offers tame camels as children rides and harbors odd off illegal parties to entertain depressed NGO workers; well aware that the right customers can channel the money from iron roof gutters in to golden gushing rivers, even in midst of the desert!

Day 14

Nouakchott is bluntly described a dirt pit hidden in sand dunes where not even a stray dog would leave his crap alone back! No booze, no weed and still having to deal with continuous aggressive vendors aligning the unofficial grand boulevard. A country that still punishes atheism by death! Time is surpassed with visiting the national library. Unsurprisingly he is the only interested guest and that in a country with a rich bibliographic history. Followed by hanging around smoking shisha pipes and drinking coffee. Boredom until at night he joins Senegalese expats at their local shack celebrating some gray tones. But, even in midst of the dark ages there is a rainbow shining. The portiere knows a southern Wilaya girl who is keen on earning some Ougiyas through massages! The lack of asking for approval seems needless as do his expectations for a financial rewarding! He is the man which has to be relied on for a 3am wake up call and helping the desert departing party exit safely. The man keeps to his promises, with exception that the slim advertised girl is only skinny in an African male's eyes; or a piggery butcher's! When getting down closer he observes her mutilated clit between the unkindheartedly half removed outer lips!! For her sake he stops and settles in for a blow job, "still not bad for being in an Islamic Republic!"

Day 15

Sun rise tea in the kitchen of Restaurant Tani, Akjouit followed by driving past a weird pink with white striped decorated auberge which itself is picturesque like a deserted knock shop located in a bum fucking outback town at the turn of the previous century where women wore knickers longer than kangaroo tails!

Day 16

Stock up in Atar and continue the good run until…

Day 17

Morning blessings have taken a wrong turn. A gun is pointed between his dear binoculars and an excitingly jumping around Tuareg is adamant showing off his catch of the day. What a freaking disaster and humiliation. Just keep smiling and if they start Osama binning lard games; then attempt to die honorable.

Day 18

"Alright, it seems the interest is directed towards securing a financial deal. As a small win hands are not anymore tied behind my back. The winds over the dunes seem to cover the tents with sand making the owners regularly brushing the sheets. Good distraction."

Day 19

Watching young girls getting force fed and seeing them gathering all their strengths to endure the pain of couscous loathing, followed by sloth behaviors making their fathers double happy. Fattening geese for butchering through marriage.

Day 20

"Al-Foeck yeah, sand storm and we are yalla yalla yalla* out of here!"

Day 21

Fuck no, water has run out.

Day 22

Natalie!

Day 23

On a freight train rumbling through no mans land…

Day 24

- Good morning or good afternoon, you are now safe.

- Good, yes, what ever. Where is the black gazelle?

- We don't know? You got dropped off here on the other side of the border and we picked you up as the item you have been searching has caused some annoyance to say the least with our freedom fighters.

- Huh?

- You are by tomorrow out of this mess, so be appreciative and thankful that somebody has an interest in stupid shit stirrers like you. Your friend is still somewhere out there.

- My friend?

- Yes, a soul or spirit is still creating a path of destructive havoc. It emerged to set fire on a larger diesel storage facility, followed by men dying from fevers. Additionally our animals are producing sour-bitter greenish colored milk; and don't laugh, this is literally happening! But for now relax. Enjoy the views over the ship cemetery; we believe in providing our guests finest hospitality. You are already on your journey out of our own beloved barren world's rectum cavity!

Day 25

Flight to Gran Canaria…? On an empty airplane belonging to Mauretania's national airline. "Possibly the easiest way to ship drugs to Europe unrecognized as the boulevardiering spornosexuals* of Paris, Berlin and London who happily also spend their money on vogue designer shoes, multi colored socks and summer wear declared pink pajamas? All glazed with help of an evolution bypassed society surrendering a good party night's ingredient to a bum scratching bunch of Neanderthal brotherhood!"

Day 26

If Nelson Mandela knew how much the taxi drivers at his name carrying airport are ripping off arriving passengers; he would turn over in his grave!

Day 27

- Not even 12 hours in Cabo Verde and already stoned!
- Huuuhhh, yeah man, thanks for the rescue. Didn't even know you could live upstairs of a secret service bunker. Well, didn't even know that outside of South Africa any explicit further secret services existed, especially not in such a small island nation...
- What's the John Dory for the mull?*
- Damn, you are surely not a few stubbies short of a sixer! Well 50 escudos is a fair suck for a fair crack of the whip!
- Pipe me down! You can sometimes be a few sandwiches short of a picnic!*
- Put a sock in it, you ocker* trainee!*
- Your Buckley's chance has not only shaken the rocks in your head, but you are physically as strong like an emu to fly over a galah's fart.*

- Well to let you know, I was frothing, so don't think that I tried to 'do the Harry'*! I'm not here to tell spiders how to catch flies!... You,... you flaming galah*....*

- Still, your IQ is replicating idiosularmaticism!*

- Don't talk garbo or I'll crack the shits, carrying on like a pork chop* goosing around has at least resulted in sussing out the block party including old chums; it is like a school re-union after the headmasters office has been burnt down!*

- Strewth! Time for an Accadecca work out... The army is teaming up for a BCF*, and believe me we will avoid you being shark bikkies*!*

- How long did it take you to learn talking Gibberish?

Day 28

Sitting for hours on a rattling freight train would have sufficed!

Day 29

If there was a paradise existing then Bar Techa in Cuidad Velha would fulfill this role nicely thanks t abundant sun kissing days. A sweet smell of the bougainvillea flowers playing a melange symbiosis with the salty fishy air carrying fine droplet molecules from the nearby beach crushing waves, all intertwined with the acidic smell of stale beer evaporating of a middy* placed on a heated terrace's stone formation used as table. And there she sits, waiting for her love to emerge from the canyon in to the first European settlement of the tropics or may he even descend from the curvy trail below Fortaleza Real de Sao Filipe and sneak behind the derelict cathedral on a hidden stone masonry created path to heavenly give her a welcoming touch from behind; his strong arms embracing just under the breast line, a peckish move towards full loving explosion. Mauritania sparked a renewed love. The mind asking, "why in all Almighty's script book can I be such a fool!?" But the heart is attempting to win the war in a godly versus evil created theatrical play containing a chauvinist plot between a man desiring being a lady's best friend who is an atrocious bitch readily happily executing inhumane doings, worse than any African dictator would ever be capable to do; and that would be a major effort investing exploit! Sickening thoughts of possessed lust. She had a message to convey to her recipient beyond her consideration of declaring or re-declaring her heart's emotional hijacking. Yes, her consciousness is continuously increasingly wondering off to him, especially over the past three weeks when receiving orders from a Vatican influenced executor to stay away from him as women generally represent trouble. "Hey, but he was trouble!" The guy was cheeky enough to ask her to name a movie with a vice-versa plot where a girl rescues the man! Further to the insult he demanded if she had ever seen Knight Rider saving a dude!? But somehow she felt like a failure as she was good enough to be sent in to an Islamic shit hole, and that as a female alone! "Men are bastards!" To add it was painful retrieving the soul of her dreams in the eye socket of the Richat, where the desert sands cover the lost city of Atlantis. Instead of glory it is a vastly uninteresting place. Similar to having sex with air, meaning fucking nothing. And fuck all represented her frustrating mood. And so she sits acting calmly, drinking a coffee followed by a glass of cold dry Vinho Verde wine, which gives her a tingle of sexiness and watching the sun set over the ocean feeling the deprivation of romanticism only making her disappointment grow steadily with the lowering of candela units per steradian lumen intensity being released from the lighting beams vanishing over the horizon of blue sea and pink turning in to purple sky. Back to rational reasoning; she has news. An old foe was seen in Marrakesh. It was a week after the scenic flight to the city of souks and its merchants trading rugs, leather goods and silverware. Here she bought a present for her lose moose wanderer of whom she now felt again attracted to, but in all chaos on the iron ore train from Zoueret where she arranged two tarps to lay on the barren red-hot steel surface as buffer for her half dead baggage until the ride ended in a beach shack! The feeling looking after her love were her first ever feelings of motherly nature; all while he most likely is dreaming of something stupid like a zombie apocalypse being bitten by the infected and participated in a brain munching orgy only to be saved by a bullet through his head! Even that thought is making her heart take over emotions resulting in the emergence of feeling like an elegant zebra falling in love with a wildebeest and damn, once again her desire is denied by the undoings of some higher priestly influencing powers! And while she missed the last common transport option to Praia due to this newly discovered nipple erection causing also a twisting in her panties, she somehow regains consciousness back to her man of love who in her last night's dream rushes from the overland bus on to the Casablanca airport train mentioning that the desert is a lost case where no sand is needed to cover any succumbing illusions! She is in need for another glass of wine; something sweeter this time like, "oh nice, they even have Moscatel de Setúbal!" And so turns the only functioning light on town elevated abandoned cathedral. One thing was marrying, but the other more important life changing question is can somebody eat an entire plate full of spaghetti and look sexy? "Damn Shoetef, you had your chance today!" But had she ever ask herself if she wanted children? Was she ever asked to have someone's child? Would she be able to offer a child a life in a safe environment? Would a child have a bright future in Luanda? Would she easily forfeit the for African circumstances extremely rare given roaming freedom? And having a child, is there currently a method available to guarantee that her partner is fully committed? Is this big question of life worth denying another glass of Moscatel de Setúbal?

Not far away from this Home and Away* scene the new neighborhood quaker shaker is watching the sun go down, sitting all alone at a table, too on a hill top, but overlooking the bay of Quebra Canela and drinking a few too many mojitos made of local rum, which is making him wonder if his sight soaking is not misleading…

- Got you!
- Amigo, amigo, please let me…
Smack
- Just to get things clear, you betrayed me, the Mao's butt face
betrayed me; and then there is this bosbefok brak on the lose*
betraying all of us!

- Tsss, let those mongrels be for themselves! And you weak cunt hitting an injured man!

- Ahora, bien, disculpe. Pero estais un perro*!*

- Wow! Amigo, honestly I do not want any dealings with that. Even the cocaine pushers are a more enjoyable company! We are soul mates with maybe a touch too much pepper...

- What, believe exactly in what! You left me out there alone!

- Yes, my freaking arm got infected, look at the bandages! You left me back to die! So I rushed back to safer heavens. Lucky I didn't get sepsis!! That messes you up....

- Hey bro, your cerebro is already basura*, basuranda, basurinha, basurpanorama!!*

- And you are not docto loco or shall I say docto lactoso* loco? You do like... by the way, why do you look so rough?*

- You wouldn't believe it, and most probably blowing up in my junk inbox here too, but for the past two days I got sent to a boot camp somewhere in the hills of Sao Domingo with expectation that you fend for yourself and traverse a plain towards a canyon where they pick you at a castle, or ruin somewhere past a few stupid palm trees lining up a wadi alike. While the army guys concentrated themselves packing up sleeping gear, clothes and reading maps, I only grabbed a can of macerated dolphin baloney pony, and did a runner. Bloody buggers first save me to throw me back to exposure of rogue elements... Fazer sexo* sounds nicer than what it sometimes is!*

– So you are someone's bitch!?

- Compadre, all I say is it took my battered body only a few hours to conquer the concur. Thought it would be smart to avoid the open terrain and crossed an additional chain of hills and another one. Walked through the night too. Valhalla can fucking wait! When finding Sao Joao Batista church I found the local priest sleeping against the holy place's wall; seemingly overcoming a heavy piss up exercise as digested juices were

splattered all over him. He looked like a stage scene of Peter Jackson's Bad Taste spooning out the alien brain sequence half of the wobbly gobbly running down his shirt. Anyway, got me in for a quick nap.

- Must acknowledge you are good sport when it comes to drinking stories! Do you need any cash? I pay for the beer. Feel honored, you are my first guest that receives no curse for smacking me!

- Thanks amigo, not stupid, managed to hide my credit card, he he he…

- Alright you come to my place for a shower. I have some baggy clothes. Then think about arranging your passport. I am soon departing to a crazy place, it is right up your alley! Enjoy the unusual African calmness here.

Day 30

- I cannot believe it! You ring the hell out of here in expectation that the door gets opened, drunk like a skunk, with a girl in your arms…?

- Please let me in. We both are tired and…

- Rarasa respect! Fucked up body still performing like an ace! And you managed to get Natalie seeing in to you as a dag* again…*

- Please, not in front of… ah well… all good she doesn't seem to understand any English at all, so you can continue smiling and I'll have a juicy smirk or tow upstairs.

- You don't think that the nation's blue healer's kennel is the right place for…*

- The buzz killers are all asleep aren't they…?! And the girl is OK, so all set, ready, go for newly found miknot* shindig* times!*

The sun rises in an uneventful manner. Just the same as the day before. She leaves like she has done with previous romances. In sync she misses the sun downer at the Alkimist where the vibes are slowly tendering some juicy rumps!! Shoetef's visit to Aqva is a total waste of paying entry as adding herbs to the shisha results in being unfriendly booted out. It all seems to be a waste. He decides to visit the police head quarters' neighboring hotel bar, where to his astonishment the local blue berries are smashing a party including an unusual chirpy, forgiving lieutenant dancing to the horrendous live music performance and offering free shouts!! And with time Shoetef is not only getting introduced to daughters of the raw lobsters*, which due to religious conservative cock blocking attitudes adds to a morale's waste bucket contents, but a Berliner nerdy guy in his 50s tackles the isolated soul. He too is seeking to break out of isolation like Tom Hanks in Castaway, just instead of a foot ball to grind on, something more organic whereby synchronicity torso moving princess would be nice. It seems that the next stage of hell has to be experienced in some Achada de Santo Antonio located dead beat clubs where melancholic fado music merges with drowning of spoken words from this socialist messed up "NGO wanna be" which all culminates in him perceiving a higher social codex right, albeit the taxi drivers proving him twice wrong. The nerves are now at boiling point, time to direct this menace towards the Real McCoy*. Next stop is the dancing tempo-drone of Club Zero where hot female bodies are soaking up the beats and boys; but local boys only!?! Not one of the cream cutters has the chance to slice off a piece of truffle!! They are all standing around on the top level floor drowning their beers down hoping every drop might be able to relinquish a heart's fire. In the momentum of turning around from the bar with a Cristal stubbie glued to his left hand she stands in front of him; last night's girl smiling with upmost gorgeous lips desiring to be kissed. They move slowly and eagerly towards each other, just right and ready for to be affixed with "A mão livre mimada procurando"*… He feels a grab. Is it a jealous cock blocking from behind…? But nobody here? Is Juan playing games? Or did Natalie procure a pestering guardian ghost?

Day 31

It is a wonderful day where the fish lucky of escaping any fishermen enjoy being alive to swim happily over shallow rocks, flapping without care their fins as they cannot masturbate in ignorance of the happening above them. The sky is holding back on any crying and is offering mellow temperate conditions inviting the city's pot smokers to the beach. For munchies pizza is ordered, followed by bumming around at the girl's house while the local drug mule is carrying water up the stairs. The broken house plumbing allows him to earn a free smoke. The final streaky violin sounds are played at midnight where Shoetef departs from beloved comfort embracing shoulders where as last act they mutual shed a tear on each others…

Day 32

- Bom Dia senhores! The two of you come with me. Juan, you know the ritual, so just adhere and get to the Ceiba bunker. Your amigos are waiting there and el luggage will be looked after as we all know; only special people visit this special slice of tropical thunder!
- Sir but I'm a NGO official accredited by the faith defending Queen with political support from the United States of America. I am here on invitation of your president. May god be with you all by aiding us in bringing hope through defeating malnutrition, giving education and sanitation to your all nation's people.

- Sir, 180 US dollares.

- That is not the visa price!

- True, I shall reflect... 280 US dollares as an eye for eye measure relating to refunding me what your friends on the other side of the Atlantic charged me for a day out in Disney Land. Your multiple day pass to Ebola's adventure park should be honored as a grateful steal!

- I can demand improved customer services...

- Goofy, your privilege is like mine, pay it or leave it, just the latter will be exchanged with the N removed from G.O; aka go to jail as first world reflecting abstinence enjoyment ride! And as the cheery on the pie, I am the refuge's owner! So would you now shut up the fuck up and suck those eggs hard!

- I will report back... I'll be going directly to a westerner representation like the US embassy!

- He, he, he, you are a middle aged Jersey shore survivor with a mind of a sprog!*

- What!?! Don't bull shit me. Your balls will get a beating one day. Every country except for maybe Iran and North Korea has US presence!!

- Oooohh, aaahhh scary, scary, hell has opened its portal making me nearly shitting me Scotsmen skirt full of hemorrhoid juices. Hah! Just nearly. Nope no US embassy here neither.... oooohhhh wow, what is that...?!?! Cuddly koala key rings for my children!?!? Please Sir be my guest, you are free to enter!! And gift some bears to the guys outside, they appreciate cadeaux' too!*

It is still dark; a nice timing to stack up the Royal Maroc plane with "virtual" guests. While Osvaldo Vieira is rewarding its drug trafficking potentials a lone taxi is waiting outside of the terminal. Shoetef jumps in. Soon after departure the vehicle turns left where an unseemly dead straight road requires driving skills beyond an outback dirt track; and it is not even monsoon!! The bumpy ride through the back roads of a neglected capital city ends the central paragem* which for 5am is unexpectedly loud, busy, pumping the stink out in midst of people covering all the national demographics where Shoetef learns to partake in a common ritual; pissing on the mini bus van wheels for good luck!

While a person can be forgiven for believing that a trip to Sao Domingos in the northern districts is a torture, the 35 mile ride to the coast beats that ravisher. The bus is squeezed to its limits with wedding guests. And albeit being a Muslim country the women dress up in erotically crafted long dresses, to the degree that Shoetef is painfully holding himself not only back off on any flirtatious advancements, but also covering his ram rod while observing the young slim dark skinned hotties who are taking a decade to eat through either boiled egg or canned sardine baguettes. Instead he attracts a fat bird who eludes him that fruit and vegetables are as beloved like a demon possessed soul lusting for a crucifix dipped in holy water and stuck up its anus! On a positive note, she also directs him to a few bungalows accommodating the town's only bar, which lacks of customers as a bag of weed costs the same as a pint of piss. However there is one guy who occupies the bar fridge to his benefit and is keeping a few coldies happily fresh...

Day 33

Imagine a several kilometer long beach, no plastic and not even an animal's foot print; welcome to Praia da Varela. A slice of paradise well hidden away from mainstream. However derelict buildings, former hotels robbed of their glory and an army fort crumbling in to the ocean tell tales that historically high life existed here, where most likely rich chicks from Lisbon appreciated the Atlantic ocean waves kissing them here. Sadly the coast line has gradually shifted the boundary in favor of Moby Dick's octopus' kingdom and is as such happily partaking in diminishing the African jungle while unintentionally supporting the Sahel's hunger of expansion.

Due to lack of English speaking company, boredom is kicking in quickly. The decision is done to walk a few kilometers north exposing himself to the mid day hot sun, but with expectation to meet in Niquim a crazy Spanish backpacker who has erected his tent there. Like plenty of his imbecile European counterparts, he too took the liking of traveling the world with a bicycle. Just swapped any painful outback extravaganza with riding through Polisario's grass lacking front lawn. The real bright side is the abundance of not only fish, but also weed which quality wise is described by him as medicine the town folks use to get their cows lactose. It relaxes. "But why then setting up an egg plant farm?"

Day 34

- My dear friend, if it was not for you I would not have come all the way to this god forsaken isolated place...
- Juan, don't tell porkies, you most likely have a ship waiting and causing you headaches.
- OK amigo. Two purposes here; the Spanish guy is seemingly the only person of trust when it comes to the border area, meaning he knows what boats are passing...
- Yes, good for el caballo, n'est ce pas*?*
- Hold your French for when in need! The world here is a bit more adventurous in attitudes. Guinea-Bissau has its political turmoils, adding that the territory north of the Cacheu River can already be perceived as part of the Casamance. And I know that you will soon meet this world's heart more intimately.
- What? You will need a good reason for me to take the tedious bus trip back to the border town lacking of anything and everything. Not interested in having my bum amputated through a raping ridgydidgy nutcracker ride on a civil war highway track.
- My friend, firstly plans change. Then after 4am you are here generally stuck for the day. And next comes the red sock. As you know this place is competitive in keeping its reputation of a secluded business hub, meaning there is always somebody pissed*

off in Bissau. In this case I believe the airport's immigration generality; the honored decision maker of allowing traffic in and out. But sometimes he is overruled by opposing fractions. Initially I thought there would be some French guys luring in Club Med 20 clicks north of here, but our buddy in Niquim informed that there is no such activity currently occurring. Doing mathematics, Portugal is not interested as it is very happy to have a rogue state to restrain any emancipation of Cabo Verde by influencing behind the brotherhood backs. Both original regimes are crafted by the same political party and thus the main reason of my visitation. Then you have some day dreaming opposition sitting in Dakar who historically has shown dissatisfaction, but only at times of soberness and honestly is probably annoyed having to deal with any shit further south but then they too earn money from their controlled coastal strip; so when 1 plus on 1 does not add up to two, then there must be 3… Just some conglomerates end up too greedy to operate on 2.99 marketing specials, even those delving in mind fog!

Day 35

It is a delayed 6am departure. The motor bike is not road worthy. The stupid chain decides to break during the night all while the owner most likely is fumigating his brains to puree with low quality bhang. As a positive Shoetef too receives a final opportunity to numb any concerns before relying on safe passage over foot wide paths traversing a mine field before arriving at a ferry port on the border lacking any buildings. However, a pirogue captain soon spies an income opportunity; a customer who is also going to fund transportation of school children, a dozen of women and a few tied together chickens. Unlike busier crossings the nearby Senegalese army is not showing any interest towards formalizing documents allowing legal entry, thus making it possible to continue the trip by flagging down the only potentially available car, parked in front of the local mosque. The driver chucks a few newly purchased chickens on to the back seat, while Shoetef locates his backpack on his knees for the few kilometers in to Kabrousse. As per territorial ancestry rights, a new guy is needed for further transport to Cap Skirring; a total different world full of loud and never ending talkative froggies. Here the wait for a bus takes over an hour. Les 'conducteurs' are first storing weapons and ammunition in the double floor constructed chassis. Most passengers are using the freed up time to merrily drink tea and smoke cigarettes, plus looking at half naked hairy Gaulistanies* flaneuring*. One exception is a women strapping her chickens on to the mini van's roof while hysterically crying around as if those Red Roosters* will grow brains making them smart enough to jump in to the fryer instead!

All goes well with trespassing another savanna where a mid day vehicle transition is scheduled at Zuingchor's chaotic bus terminal. The squeezing in to a sept-place is promoting a hunger games attack. While sitting on the middle seat a boiled egg from a sales empress is handed through. "Any salt?" As response she hands over a brown package. No shaker? "Relax Chief Muzungu". He starts unpacking where surprisingly a gram of mull eventuates. The fat bird sitting besides him observes his bewildering complexion, starts laughing and adamantly demands, "manger*, manger, manger!!" A few seconds later the three hour journey to the border is passe! Here the formalities commence in the spirit of Commonwealth brotherhood and associated opening up of arms, only to be then interrupted by an over zealously circling vulturous taxi driver. The cheeky bugger has even the guts to play hard in haggling offering an exorbitant fare to the nearby town a few kilometers down the road, resulting in an officer's awakening and subsequent revisiting of the entry requirements. "For fuckin' sake you scum bag!"

The Gambian formalities continue in their tedious form. Just in another building, whereby soon two ladies join. The next move is the three arguing the price including share of bribe. Soma border crossing clearly misses attention of travelers. Senegalese buses cruise ignorantly through the dust pit; then over the bridge and quickly out again. Just leaving behind the air fulfilled with a diesel smelling cloud containing dried particles of all sorts; shit stirring literally! A long hour passes. One of the female officers approaches him with the question if he knows a place to stay, followed by giving further advise regarding eating options which is immensely limited compared to the competing exchange offices. She points her finger downwards towards her love handles or more like truck tires while raising a climaxing interrogative query, "Do you know what is best for this lady?". Shoetef answers, "The Australian government recommends you the daily intake of two serves of fruit and five of vegetables!".

Day 36

The day starts with an undesirable delay. Accommodation lacking Soma seems to represent a great place for customs officers to hook up with white meat. However, not without some hurdles to jump over. At least she had fulfilled the religious and society's codex by first marrying and having children before divorcing and declaring game on! The two keep hiding in the government's hostel until the major ranking officers leave. The wait is a tiny winy bit too much for the girls who cannot bear their bladders and commence a champagne shower session turning the room in to a make shift kinky dunny*! Astonishingly this country was recently run by a conservative dictator! But the Benny Hill show has not yet finished. Shoetef is deliberately being prevented boarding the upriver moving bus at its designated stop east of the petrol station due to the possible views of those higher in the army's food chain… So here he goes walking 2 kilometers out of town under the watchful eyes of Big Booty Sister who is stuffing some sugary loaf loaded with jam and peanut butter in to herself while riding a struggling moped. She ain't gonna bust her chops today! The result is a 2 hour delay. Buses in Africa tend to leave only when full, which around lunch time is low as passenger traffic halts, plus taking in to consideration that the continent's time continuity aligns more to that of a piece of coal transforming itself in to a diamond rather than a Japanese Shinkansen train. With the good 4 hour rickety slow ride the day continues being a bitch. The next inconvenience is the bus stopping at a branching jungle path demanding its passengers to descend from the vehicle. It is already dusk. Unsurprisingly no further transport options are awaiting customers. It takes a good kilometer of walking and listening to an accompanying older gentlemen exercising his English; like many Gambians not being capable to fluently talk the language of their former masters whereby in comparison to former French and Portuguese strongholds the locals master the European tongues perfectly. Gambia just seems as weird as its country's geographical shape of being a long sleeve stretching in to another regent's territory. The next obstacle is trying to find accommodation. The bush camp dump site is experiencing an unexpected large visitor influx. The choice is either an overpriced, airy, rats and cockroach infested room at the Annex Hotel or seek refuge on the northern side looking over the river where prices match the heights of the ancient Babylon Towers. Plus this decision comes with ferry costs capable of making a nuclear plant go in to melt down. West Africa; you can get any service done, but at a cost. Therefore, many of the private posh car drivers are parking their vehicles nicely along the main central business district strip comprising of jungle shacks whereby the chauffeurs are fighting against any early nodding off to avoid shame to their employers; the seemingly refreshingly equality promoting national government…!

- You?!?! I was expecting so see the white skinned story telling turd here!?!
- Yeah, he cheated on me too. Was hoping to find him here too. A large crowd, and I'm sleeping in a taxi with the dlivel. So solly, no diamond.
- What happened? Gotten back to being to commie comrade?
- Fuck off, this silly game, I had it..
- Really, you seemed to have a laugh with the locals while waiting for the president's arrival…
- Yes, but Flancois should have handed my shale over and instead got his Islamic fliends flom Maulitania to hold me and cut half tongue out! Only Chinese used to do this!!
- So keep it short, he has obviously got his fingers in this president's campaign.
- We should have met in Dakal, but he convinced me to come to a beach south of thell…
- And then OK, you got another serving of fisting love… So the bugger is somewhere between here and Dakar. You have a

*taxi, I have a bed, hmmmnnn that is going to be a nightmare!
But they serve booze at the Road Side just a few meters from
the ferry terminal. Locals told me that the president is arriving
soon, but time is not money in Africa, so basically lets get drunk
as there is nothing else to do!! Looks like you need anti septic
medication anyway.*

Day 37

As the sun greets a new day over the Gambia River; Shoetef extinguishes his last joint. It was the last crumble of local bush he'd manage to get hold off a local youngster lingering in front of the town's shop. He is not only keen on selling, but also on munchies and having a sarcastic yarn*. It seems that albeit Gambia having strict rules, they are null even on a full authority occupied McCarthy island including a non visible president… #Bang!# Within a heart beat he realizes that everybody is wearing a white tee* with already fading black print except himself!! "Was up all night and guess all up in smoke!?" Even Planet Snorrstar comes walking down the old cobble stone made up alley wearing one defying any sun damaging exposure. He passes the open space where police are attempting to clear the path of vehicles which are hindering access for and to the government operated ferry jetty in midst of curious folk excitingly anticipating to obtain more gifts from their reborn Mansa Musa*. All in view of Georgetown's river fronting former export warehouse decorating a large wall mural of its sad history as a place of torturing where slaves were kept in water inundated cells; lucky when only their feet were wet, unlucky during the rain session where they basically had to piss and shit in the brew they were living in!

News emerges that the president stayed for the night at a lodge on its northern shores instead of making an appearance. "But hey you still got those free shirts!" After a few trips using a second ferry the journey finally continues. A visit to Kuntaur is scheduled, but still no sign of the countries' master and his South African marketing mischief. The perplexed party decides to make a breakfast break at the Senegambian stone circles. The menu is limited to tailored cigarettes. At some places anything is sold, here at the circles the dire sales pitch is limited to an odd off lost gone European tourist with high chance of being again some bike riding albino cave dweller from Paris or Barcelona with ornithology enthusiasm while wearing khaki pants over Jesus sandals. But in all the unfortunate developments the place still easily beats its European counterpart, Stonehenge. On return the streets of Kuntaur remain deserted. Some locals direct them to continue their search further west, where in Nyanga Bantang a music band is playing in front of a cheering group of where one character shines; an old guy dressed like Uncle Sam in Gambian colors with more stars and stripes than a red neck can count! But still no president. The party moves onward to Ker Samba Sowe which to continues with the lack of luck in finding any national leader's shmusing liking. They remain a mystery, even for the local witch doctor fortune tellers.

After crossing the river at Farafeni, Soma awaits again. "No man-eaters please!" West of the town site Shoetef decides to do a sprint following a bus heading towards Banjul. However baggage is holding him up; still hearing Chongstar's aching breaths. But he is having a gut full of this shit. Before final arrival in to Banjul he hastily jumps off, grabs a taxi behind the busy Westfield junction while ignoring the screams of his Chinese friend and foe sitting further back in the bus squeezed between two big black men. Chongstar's plans are herewith thrown out of the window; all newly crafted hopes are instantly crushed! For Shoetef he is just a waste of resources. The real remaining question is, will somebody miss an opportunity to finally get rid of Francois or is he the man who can enable safe sailing with unharmed departure of the country through pitching his negotiation skills full of sugar bush burping, protea perfume farting and warthog mud wanking fairy tales?

Angrily having to pay above the market price, but grateful for the quick delving in to the local shanty town area with its associated complex laid out dirt track system, the escaping party's final destination is a well known African hell hole: Senegambia Beach. The shiny side of the coin is it takes less than a minute to buy weed from a wheel chair bound beggar, followed by meeting a half way decent bumster named Solomon and getting conveniently girls asking to be friends on the 200 meter stretch to his new hide out, the Princess Apartments. Wally, the smart host containing a delightful mix of temperamental and chilled

Lebanese blood invites him for a coffee, cigarette and to harvest any other wishes. All in a calm, large, well decorated yard comprising high reaching frangipani, oleander, jacaranda and bougainvillea scrubs while sitting below an old native, thick trunk tree. The two men resting in cozy rattan chairs with views of the building's approaching white marble stair case widening itself as radiant towards the garden as if it is desiring to hug all surrounding vegetation as if a Greek god had built a Mesopotamian garden in western Africa's jungle.

Day 38

Wally reports that people are searching for a person describing him, however he has defended any sneaky beaks. Further he forwards the acknowledgment of Shoetef doing a wise move by inviting a bumster to a few beers, gifting local girls koala key rings, having a coffee at the road's end barber shop plus buying goods from its neighboring shack and showing appreciation in form of a few Dilasis to the roaming homeless guys, "Level of hassles should be low now."

As even on a sleepy day a sun set happens, so does a re-energized Shoetef receive itchy feet. First he passes the whinging and whining Nzérékoréan forest dwellers who attempt again to drag him inside their shack, but his deed of purchasing is done. Although there is an enticing delicious smell coming from their grill; just who knows how fresh the chicken really is before its final char coaling chapter. The next pestering smorgasbord comes from Solomon, but nothing which a healthy ration of ganja cannot solve! After a few beers and buying his bumster gang 4 baguettes for dinner he turns his attention back to himself and only himself. Next stop is a late night flirting with two ladies, one drunk and ugly, the other the most hottest girl Conakry has managed to let go. Like a good unmarried Muslim girl she elegantly defends his advances with a gorgeous, but polite smile while still excitingly waving her partially straightened curly hair over a pastel orange colored dress covering the knees, but leaving her arms to a joyous eye soaking view. She is maintaining toughly her ground while providing educated small talk beyond what many girls at home are capable off. Towards midnight Solomon catches him out on the lose again and reattempts to eat him alive. The bumster's efforts however are coming to fruition. Bluntly said Shoetef is as horny as flies searching for dung. He funds Solomon the GT Bar entry fee. While paying at the door a cheeky lady buzzes around his head like a bee in search for a sweet corolla. She is keen to continue exploring him over a beer. There she continuous her endeavor of interest by shoving her hand under his lose shorts, slowly moves up the leg and starts caressing his tool while both anonymously sit on the bar chairs with their back to the plebs.

Day 39 – The Story of Glorious Aisha

And there she awakens naked in bed while smelling the sweet smoke of a hot and horny white traveler and looking at his naked thin figure, a pleasant chest hair decoration blowing out the fumes of joy through the small bed room window with views to the garden workers' shed; a young African guy with minor mental disorder, gentle giant in nature. It is her first extra marital intercourse. To his delight she even delicately, meticulously shaves her fanny before moving towards petting. Not an easy task for the first time neither; she is sweating over the water bucket to ensure no cuts are done. The procedure represented a conclusion of her tedious journey which commenced in Zaria, a city half way between the flashing Neo-modern structures of Abuja and the nearest Islamic center of gravity, Kano. Her life was dominated by the traditions associated by the Grand Sultan and his minion Emirs' guided autocratic regimes' associated attitudes which were dominant well in to the 21st century. They were closely directing the daily lives of the Hausa-Fulani people for centuries. This feudal, patriarch favoring orientated social system made her leave her own kids behind; technically at time of departure only one, but both indefinitely lost. Albeit the daily phone calls to her mother and receiving much grateful heart warming mental support from home she is caught up in a vicious cul-de-sac. Her husband's sister, a hoofed greedy rhino knuckle sold her fair skinned daughter to people smugglers employed by a brothel in Gidy* to offer banditry low lives fresh high grade purity yansh*. She noticed the kidnapping too late. When crying, screaming, complaining, the family set a fatwa on her, increasing her pain wrestling as if acupuncture needles were exchanged with railway track nails, being deeply hammered through the flesh to be stuck in the heart. One night she fled to the local Catholic priests' mission. A charming Swiss reverend who provided a handful Nairas as assistance to reach Niamey. She avoided contact throughout, even when offered an escorting opportunity with a rich NGO employee. She smartly knows that some represent safety threats on legs. She avoided eating pizzas or burgers; it was too foreign for her and added to her anxiety, being scared in a world outside comfort of where she was born and bread. And bread too, "what the heck is a baguette..?!?"

It took her 8 days. Sleeping on dirt roads, crossing borders illegally as passports are of luxury, bribing Islamists in Mali, getting thorn bushes biting her on the walk through the Senegalese steppe as path to avoid rogue police officers and hiding in the open sewers of Tambacounda. When finally reaching her west end destination she found an apartment lacking a kitchen, but with dirty shared bathroom facilities and had to purchase a mattress from another Nigerian girl, soaked up with body juices and urine. Only then she allowed exhaustion to take over by dropping half dead down in to a 2 month malaria stint… A tough soul does not give up easily. What does not kill you makes you stronger! And only the toughest survive the jungle!

Her tragic story continued through the lack of any compassion by her new surrounding of fake perceived smiling locals, eager to do a buck on her back, while still being consumed by utmost poverty, hunger and disease. The result is a loud final releasing cry of finding love, even if it had to be of temporary nature. Her adventure is educational Nollywood material, however questionable if a male dominant society would allow the tale telling. Standing in her partner's bath room while listening to Yemi Alade's song Issokay is providing relief while she too knows that the fridge contains sweet fruit; an uncommon delicacy in the lands of her ancestors, but importantly life in Gambia is on the mend...

Day 40

Her hair is scratching hard on the scalp and Shoetef is desiring physically distracting activity without the hedonism stamp. Her mathematics add 1 plus 1 faster than David's stone with more accuracy than taking out Goliath: "Shopping!" The two venture out to the Serrakunda markets. Beauty for her, information for him. "Is no news from Wally good news?" While making their way through the make shift stores' created zigzagging path, he loses concentration allowing her to happily fill up bags. The vibes are good, so good that he even allows locals to take pictures with him. The long hair and beard do stand out. After she gets a new wig fitted, they with sharing smiles happily conclude the outing with a surf and turf aka reefer'n'breezer at the Baobab Beach bar. The sun sets over the vast stretching ocean behind a magical pure white fine sand beach to the rhythms of local djembe players and two girls who are taken liking of performing some casual dances.

Day 41

A telex message from Natalie; received from a coast guard…? "Police Activity in Banjul", but, "are you legitimate?". Wally confirms that nothing is spreading beyond the city's limits confined to an island, "most probably some dug up peanuts over cooking their groundnut brains…"

Day 42

The previous night's dream did not bring any new learning. He is already aware that his quest needs to continue. Natalie's spiritual presence is felt. It is making the physical touching, caressing and smelling of his new girl friend even more ecstatic! The mind is lecturing him that everything will slot in with the time... The morning is booked with final arrangements for Glory to have in her room a small kitchen containing two gas burners installed. Even before buying the bloody things she is adamantly keen on cranking up with boiling her adoring cow knuckle pepper soup! And the accompanying starch, grounded and pounded cassava known as fufu. "Fufuluya!" A dish most Westerners would avoid albeit open to consuming pork knuckle and sauerkraut in a beer garden accepting too the awful accompanying polka music. For Shoetef the affectionate feelings are flying beyond the entertaining stomach's butterflies. Thus, the day is first spent with assembling, then buying bulk rice, followed by searching for a Nigerian butcher where as expected the large slaughter house has blood streams flowing down the tiled walls and animal feces on the floor. Albeit lacking disposed organs it is still stinking beyond Lucifer's tolerance level; no wonder that the poor creatures in life's last moment release their bowels. The halal throat slitting cut must be a relief! And party time for the flies. Shoetef realizes that the real wicked District 9 fried prawns are not those competing against the Cosa Nostra in Palermo or the Straight of Messina oppose roaming Calabresi Ndrangheta. The sons from the unification fighting fathers who defeated the Biafran freedom movement with mass murdering Efiks in Calabra, finalizing the death of the theocratic Kingdom of Nri and its associated 6 taboo codes are enjoying here the freedom of brutally killing animals under the influence of hemp, pills and passing ships' offloaded cocaine.

Day 43

The morning starts early with a walk along the beach before any bumsters get the opportunity to annoy. Shoetef has already received the dubious honor of visiting the gardens behind the Baobab Beach Bar where after a so called informal tour the begging for funding for overpriced fertilizers eventuated, which could only be ceased through an economical bribe. The rastafaris are as true green, yellow and red like a pedophile priest desiring a snow leopard*! And here they are too; in adoration mingling closely with athletic built toy boys whereby their parasitic story of being a proud local and honorable member of society flies rapidly out of the door like a gravity defeating cuckoo bird after being kicked out of the nest by its real owner. The pristine beach combined with the rare tranquil ambient is mirthfully impacting on the two's mood to walk all the way to Cape Point. A loving bond is in its wonderful creation phase continuously growing all the way to the Kachikally crocodile pool. The heart throbbing culminates with the freeing of shock cries when her love decides to uptake some wrestling on a Nile River saurian. Needless to mention that the park officials are not delighted neither. However, the day has already reached temperatures too hot for a fuss. Plus "behold", it is proving that Shoetef has gained full throttle bottle strength back and is ready to tackle his future path. Not only beer, boobs and bongs, but also diesel, dust and a diamond!

The day ends in a repeated peaceful setting where as cream on the cake Glory is for once again feeling really happy in her life. She knows that the kick in her life's gut is slowly evaporating and thus decides to participate in sharing the engagement of burning destruction of the last remaining green resin crumbles. Due to the treacherous tiring night life contain an overload of sentimental playing mood crippling vultures the love birds stay in. To her pleasure Shoetef is cooking spicy vegetarian noodles with holding back his carne for desert. She is enjoying this new world as if a fantasy has come true. She is eagerly desiring to taste, both the food and his salty foreskin. It is the right timing to make romance go wild. He even lights up candles! The first man ever doing this for her. The exotic event offers further soul nourishment via him opening a bottle of South African red wine. Another new discovery for her which is delivering previously never imaginable sensual pleasures; she is ready to gladly lose her virginity towards Western cuisine! May the future contain happy cheeseburger eating KFC birds flapping their gravy dunked wings around her! With the last berry drops they share a shower together including slow and gentle soaping. Then she is carried to bed where he places his tongue in to the hidden sensitive crevices beyond her imagination. With the event also the absolute last portion of dope is going up in smoke resulting in accelerating their shared arousal; him having a continuous stiff ding dong Mcdork and she experiencing intensification of blood flow all the way down to her tingling lady lips, giving her feelings beyond a harp orchestra played by angels in the clouds. And wooooohoooo her vulva area needs inflammation titillation. Now! Both are laying in bed, him spooning from behind, covering her back with kisses while stroking the side below her erogenous arm pits and leading the rhythm of two body's synchronicity with mission to fulfill expectations of exciting long holding pleasure via penetrating her slowly from behind, first just the tip of his penis followed by moving his hands towards her nipples to fine tune the horizontal sexual audacity. He manages to make her scream and forward returning demands to not dare stopping this special moment. For the first time in her life she feels like a real beloved person. She is alive and if this is hell as described by religious authorities back home; well then bring it on and turn up the heat!

Day 44

The choice of ride is for once stylish. He flags down a taxi in front of the lodge, taking the two over the Denton bridge, past the empty ranks of the Independence parade seating behind Arch 22 and in to the very sleepy Gambian capital. Wally was right, things are eerily quite, but possibly it is because they somehow found a recipe in dealing with the nowadays regularly emerging Chinese power play annoyance; Kung Po in popo and off the rot may go! While peace and tranquility is maintained the day's first ferry ride event vanishes quickly when docking at Barra, where the two will forever say good bye to each other while trying not to drown in a river of tears. Even for Shoetef, the past days are too nice to leave, but the urge to move onward is nagging hard. The momentum temporarily halts when being unfriendly pushed at the Senegalese border post where he responds with head butting a rude scavenger. The queue is shocked, "hey you red phone booths on stilts, you are constantly mashing up your green peas!". The Senegalese border force remove him for extra paperwork bureaucracy exposure with associated hopes to score an extra buck from another safari drooling British tourist impatiently waiting for his promised package trip in to the nearby overfilled Fathala park.

The menace is dealt as efficiently like floaties on speed, just with the toughness of a steel boat ramming heads made of wood which are first hard, then with tag teaming of words and thoughts go soggy. His French knowledge is good enough to even pursue a free lift to Karang's bus port where for a belated breakfast he buys a coffee and two packets of biscuits from an overly attentive lady carrying the goods on her head and kettle of hot water in her non money pocketing hand.

It is a hot afternoon where the great Saloum Delta is being kissed by the upcoming season's first Harmattan winds. The motorbike taxi drops its sweat dripping customer in front of the Kerry Saloum resort, who soaks up any fresh air on offer appreciatively. It was a tedious journey in a rolling human sardine can. However, his stay at the lodge is of short. The reception is busily keen finding means for a theatrically play instead of serving. The attitude is pure ignorance. While waiting in the office Shoetef observes a faded, slowly dislodging piece of paper with prices designated to satisfy authorities. He reads it. Looks up. Another staff passes by without bothering saying a greeting! "Fuck that shit you arrogant turds!", and leaves to find comfort with the souvenir shop owner opposite the entry gates. There is nothing that cannot be healed with a herbal paper bag of fun from Amadou!! A smoke for the nerves, a smoke for the mind, a smoke for the body to kick again and one to inquire the neighbor about a room. Check in done and phone connected to the Wifi where soon thereafter the devices rattles like an angry Rocky mountain snake missing its hibernation timing while getting snow fall dropping on its numb skull. Somehow one of the social media bastards sent a picture of Glory to Cape Verde, Tunis and Natalie!

A rational person could perceive that a few more joints with Amadou on the river's edge would help, but rather the opposite is happening. Two of the girls are forwarding rigorous text messages, while he as the only guest of Les Coquillages unsuccessfully tries to avoid making the manager on duty aware of the mess. But she does have an absolute cute gap in her upper front tooth row. Her seldom laughs look impressively sexy like sweet tea with a hint of spice. The appetite is boosting for some sweet cherry pepper all while she is dampening any hope cool. But the smile is as rare as a Senegalese snow avalanche. It comes to Shoetef's mind that Amadou has never had the honor to smoke an ice bong!

Day 45

It seems Marisha is accepting her fate of being one of his historical repeats, but never the less she keeps shouting and exceeding already ear drum exploding decibels of Strasbourg Restaurant's favorite Arabian wedding musician's love songs electrifying male chest hairs. And back hairs!

Amadou is sitting in front of his store with two town bikes; both knowing and showing interest towards the new meandering soul… As per African hospitality all affairs initially commence without exchange of money, but still conducted with eager eyes badly hiding the common opinions towards the white man being a walking wallet. The best to do option is milk it, make them curious and tease them as girls especially in their younger years often play snubbing bitches. Shoetef starts his tour past other stores awaiting a good sales pitch, but although the continent offers refuge to many artistic craftsmen finding a special artifact is often challenging. The doors of a chance open when forwarding a requests for specialist service. He desires to have the shell of a deadly cone snail attached to a hand made leather necklace by an artist marketing himself capable of intertwining a fragile amulet with a string of rough durable whip cracker. After brokering the deal Shoetef accompanies Amadou to visiting a local couple's place for lunch containing a big shared plate of fish head thieboudienne and bissap juice as wash down followed by passing the hot afternoon with smoking pot, relaxing at the hotel pool and drinking beer at its bar; all with the complexity of arranging now peace with the Cape Verdean girl, who too now slowly realizes that her chances of eternal twosome bliss is fading away like the blown out fumes of la mauvaise herbe*. And mauvaise is also the bar manager's face signals, even before the phone starts sending more messages, this time from Natalie… "Ah, merde*!"

A break is desired. Amadou charters from a local fisherman a pirogue and stocks it up with plenty of supply. As next they are speed floating their way to a sun downer session under a big tree known for some bats shit crazy stories, where behind it a natural terrace overlooks the wide river. A nice chilled place to capture the first purple and orange sun rays foretelling the imminent arrival of dusk. Pleasuring thoughts and silly ideas conclude that a full stoned modus operandi could sweeten things up. In the next moment they are circulating a bird infested mangrove island five times while disrupting Kerry Saloum's customers of their previous solitary scenery of anti-climaxing perving of warm blooded aves vertebrates. Lucky the binoculars are lacking a conscious. A few good laughs, followed by a massive scoobie doobie* are creating an enjoyable return where the boys decide to grab a few coldies at La Mangrove before crashing at Amadou's shack. A female friend decides to join and sternly attempts to pursue Shoetef's liking; disinterested in taking note that his sexual fantasies are more directed towards the girl with the tooth gap. A few surf and turfs later Amadou fetches chop chop. She grabs the bull at his horn and attempts to give Shoetef a blowjob. But the silly man defends! The arousal which rastafaris get from larger boned chicks is not shared, especially when some start acting like ostriches chasing you through the shrubs! He quickly changes plans to an alternative by swiftly dropping some sleeping pills in to her drink and on Amadou's homecoming excuses her for excessive beer consumption!

Day 46

Appreciatively Natalie's rage remains limited to the previous night. Her change of tactic by questioning his whereabouts is enacting the gray tubes towards sending an odd off sober pulse transmission, but all is still cool enough to avoid tripping any circuit breakers. In the morning he receives a new message from her. Luckily nothing which gets him gobsmacked as there are worse rowdies doing their undoing. His chosen travel direction seems to be correct, although being unsure regarding time constraints and its temporary nature representing an unprepared haute cuisine objection challenging an esurient dénoyauter caillasseur*… Soon after reading the note he switches on the television. The head line consists of major internal disruptions along the northern river border. The report accuses rogue elements of the Africa Liberation Forces of Mauritania of illegally entering the country.

While initially it is amusing to have local girls following him to La Mangrove, all keen desiring an innocent date comprising of a can of coke to flirt over, one of his eyes is liberating away from the current partaking zebra circus show to a left behind airline magazine describing increased interest by Asians to film movie scenes around Cap-Vert including the nearby islands. "What is so special here?" He knows that the resurrected Manchu Empire is now conquering Africa, but compared to the more equal rights and fraternity matured old masters the new players are recovering the racist cards secretly, polishing them first before using them as liberating jokers in a late night poker game. Keep the locals out as ultimately their cultural curiosity is limited to dried carnivore penises of endangered species. Just like the West no interest beyond their own dick's length!

Now the penny drops. But considering the value of African timing, there is surely still plenty of time available to eat scale free fish mafe. And today's girl is only desiring one can of coke. Subsequently the next move of offering her bed to him follows quickly. The lovely soul and what a rarity too as she is cool and trusting enough to allow her chosen man to first take time out for horny making pot smoking! She is one of those women who senses his need for pre-work hormone tickling. She truly believes in giving him some extra space will boost his sexual stamina beyond Super Mario's adventurous 12 level run through Sarasaland with ultimate orgasmic saving of Princess Daisy. May the beers make him grow bigger than jumping on those moving magical mushrooms, may the cones blossom his manhood in too shooting similarly to the game's offered flower power all the way to her castle of pleasure! Before mayhem receives an invitation, he stops short of promising to exterminate Tatanga's spaceship and free her for ever.

Smoking dope and talking shit does does promote forgetting time and of course he departs late from Amadou's cave to navigate towards the next one room home lacking toilet facilities. His princess is all cuddled up, arduously holding back her lady juices reserving any premature excitement feelings for the scheduled horizontal adventure. She stands up and opens the door wearing a fine piece of lingerie. Her former husband had an above average African gentlemen affection taste. However for Shoetef her beauty is unfortunately not providing the sought stimulation to maximize his libido potential. Additionally the late night chop chop is making him thirsty and her shack lacks not only of running water, but no kettle is to avail neither. "Does she drink anything at home? Her own urine?" He wants to first pleasure his thirsting taste buds at Les Coquillages where when entering with Amadou the bar all new others, new arrivals leave the scene. That Swedes are uneducated in dope control is unsurprising, "but no girl for Mista Rasta???" Blond babes from the north do tend to feel magnetic fields pulling them towards well built black men, but it seems the group's mood is as cold as summer in the Artic or maybe as naturally blond girl like skiing octopuses? Nowadays real blonds only live in Walhalla! The two grab a beer. And a second thirst quencher. But Shoetef is now giving Amadou signs of fatigue, receiving in return an outspoken lecturing that his guest needs to return to the lady; "do not break a promise, it is an honor to have a girl waiting back and if you fail she will be in rage tomorrow!!" However, Shoetef's mood for her is on a steep decline and when indicating to go back to his bungalow at 1am, a protesting Amadou departs. The observant bar manager acts quickly, "hey you are smiling…?" and offers her guest a beer on the house. As next she sends the two remaining drunk Gambian tour guides back to their rooms. She herself opens a large Gazelle; with her teeth. A quick but long sip followed by rolling out a basic futon while releasing a sigh that she had to rent out her own room to those two men as all new arrivals filled up the rooms. The survival struggling hotel needs to attract as many customers, taking and enacting on all possible open means. And while a prospector keeps a gold mines' blood line secret, their found nuggets of kisses are an obvious path shown by a convey of empty beer bottles all the way to his bungalow with a final lucky stubbie* hiding underneath the bed sheet.

Day 47

8am and "au-revoir amour". Early traveling has its charms beyond a refreshing breakfast beer with coffee powder mixed in to it. In the first city a local guides him to an ATM and is too reimbursed by beer, but this time with cocoa powder stirred in. A fume feliz at a quite market's corner makes Shoetef all ready for an energizing sleep. The nation's chaotic capital is awaiting, including the associated vultures offering private transfers. Sitting there the entire day with blood dripping from their beaks for that one carcass alive enough to count as fresh meat, but too dead to defend off the ripping apart from its carrying bones.

Day 48

Finding a place to eat Yolof at Yoff Beach is a small challenge in its own while venturing out towards the city center a task similar to Cheech and Chong staying smoke free beyond a few seconds. Albeit feeling fresh again, the scale of the place is just too overwhelming and refuge options are therefore first sought in the Les Almadies quarter, whereby Shoetef also attempts a detour visiting the most eastern point of Africa. To his disappointment not even a designated path exist. The guarding of derelict and dangerous neighboring site promotes corruption annoying corruption attempts by security services. The justification is so shit poor that they have to bribe with tea! Else the summary is a shit sight near a shit bunker with shit dudes to lazy to clean the shit of their asses hoping for a shit paper payoff while exercising pure laziness; an attitude shared by many shit politicians who seem oblivious of the marketing potential of the eroded stretch of shit shit shit!! However a nearby beer bar fan mile serves fresh seafood to employees of the nearby embassies. The small talk is not going anywhere. It seems nobody is capable to share any details of potential previous horrendous ending events. And looking further abroad in Ngor, Mamells and the Medina everything seems to be eerily quite. Dakar is busy, people are friendly; but as a capital there is a reservation existing towards inquisitive foreigners. The investigation work's scope is reduced to a fat cone containing crumbles from Amadou. A nice mellow wave of light psyche arousing emerges. A visitor riding a dream-creamy-exclave-enclave intercity serving mini bus, sitting between swaying psychedelic purple colored egg plants on a green background of smiling hemp leaves covering a visual radiant of blue, orange and yellow shining sparkles being released at Niquim Beach whereby as next floating in to the imaginary scenery is an Indian buffet where Sanji is serving Chinese men who are tightly holding on to chains with African slaves on their short ends and behind all of them stands le fou grenouille puffing out charas fumes of wisdom forming clouds of short words. "Be aware." "Visual signs can mislead." "Let me tell you something." "What? Actually don't worry. Keep the colors coming in. The stupid bus is too noisy while good old stonehanger here is struggling to move his mouth for any palavering and cannot afford a translator neither, nor a boxing ring cheerleader holding up the signs with paraphrased bubbles you are desiring to communicate me! Bubble, bubble, bubble, cannot read this stuff and have to now avoid drowning." The ultimate decision is to wake up and arrange the next splifferoo.

Day 49

- *Psssst, you have run out off weed, haven't you?!*
- *Damn, you?! Any?!*
- *What?! I can offer you more than that…!*
- *I know my love. And…*
- *Nope, you won't get your dirty mind satisfied! You left me alone. I am angry. I waited for freaking days on this hell hole island of aggressive vendors; lucky I am black and can say, va te faire foutre*!*
- *But what about my thunder sword?!*
- *Well now I see it more like a mushroom head!*
- *Aaahhh, salope*! You women never know what you want. One day it is spicy fat dripping sausage, the next day laxative dried prunes…*
- *Blame me, huh?! I saw you leaving the boat, directly walking to the first crook selling your desired crap and did you do? Only a clown buys one cas cas on its own!*
- *Hey the guy seemed legitimate; on Youtube known as Salliou!*
- *Here is the second one. My gift to you.*
- *So you also followed me through the narrow streets?*
- *Yes, kept an eye open when you bought over priced weed for $10k cefas*; and then went smoking for two hours somewhere behind the fort walls…*
- *He, he, he, smoked 8 joints with that fisherman!*
- *Shocking! However admit it makes a person invisible to the aggressive vendors, except…*

- Yeah right, the mama at the small courtyard on the first incline, then the artist on the following path along thousands of those beautiful paintings with the mighty baobab trees aligning the back ground, followed by...

- Yes by allowing a very pretty lady lure you from her store to her literally constructed perfect man cave for more smokes and maybe something more? Now you have finally ascended to the islands' top hill, stoned, in lose moose lovey dovey mood, most probably asking if you have enough money to afford the boat trip back. May the souls of the dead slaves turn in their grave!

- So what now? There have been grape vine stories...

- Oh, you mean the 2.99 story from Juan?

- Yes...?

- Ha! He is trying to fuck up your mind. Ask yourself; who is in the game?

- It looks like there is some kind of commander in control of seemingly hard piece of extraterrestrial powered inorganic compost which everyone is chasing. Which would make it 3 if we exclude Juan, but...?

- So in summary hasn't everyone telling you that they had enough of the beatings...!?! So think who has not...?

- Africa's woebegone odd ball still exercising a high-spirited effervescent vivacious behavior in the dejected sands where even camels feel disconsolate!

- Maybe he too had enough of being tormented in his own misery and is pursuing a different agenda, which would then make...?

- Me...? Or is us more political correct? But that still does not answer the 2.99!!

- Oh you poor josher*, don't commence playing a downcast.

- Hey, you are the one who does not want to be cocked down*!

- Go and choke the chicken*.

- Just don't be surprised if I declare you as my side bitch...

Albeit not getting lucky, at least funds are still sufficiently available for a lunch and beers at the ferry jetty; plus a smoke with a rastafari while watching his boat dock to Ile de Goree's wharf; and one when departing! It is already dark when navigating back to the beach through the centrally located dump serving as a market. Cash is dispensed by an ATM under observing eyes protruding from the dark before another smoke helps hitch hiking an overloaded bus to Parcelles Assainies; 2 hours in standing and dreaming. The final walk towards Yoff Plage against the wind is strenuous making him before arrival drop half dead in Sunset Hotel's lost gone glorious lounge's couch. Another wrecked place in Africa, however beer shouts are taken care by two caressing attention seeking girls; big girl, but not overly fat decorating long Caucasian stile waved hair and a sexy slim girl with a straight hair strings equipped wig sown in to her natural hair. It is a pleasure containing an invitation for dinner; a big pan loaded with pasta and meat with ultimate sweat plant burning fumes for desert to enchant all his bodily molecules towards being keen on dislodging themselves from their atomic gluing forces and amalgamating with the exquisite, relaxing surroundings… The clock is ticking towards suave action!

Day 50

"Damn, merde*, encule la chatte!* Pourquoi tu ne m'as pas réveillé?*". It is a harsh awakening up. But he has to do this 4am marathon back to his hostel dump which is not allowing guests inviting visitors. Some form of sophisticated European sanctuary for 50 years old sausage chokers. The owners are strict in ensuring guests maintain low decibels while they enjoy partying on as long as they like. On the previous night some kind of ave maria kiddie diddly bukkake party takes place well past midnight… But for now he is again in trouble by trying to obtain entry all while already the ordered cab driver is standing next to him, "relax Mischief Muzungu, time does not matter in Africa!" There is no time for a shower, nor powdering the nose or brushing the biters. The scheduled plane departure is 7am and the new airport is somewhere out far in bum fuck. In the old days, it would have been a minute cab ride around the corner, however Senegal decided to go big with Blaise Diagne International and locate it at a place where even the rats go suicidal from boredom. Unsurprisingly the newly established national airline fails time performance; and customer service. The buggers are forcing him to wait for enduring 9 hours! Without any delay reimbursement. It is a day being subject to a consistent chase by security guards and when falling to the 57.24[th] time asleep, a revived nudge is received with associated reprimanding from the mentally wrong wired sadists.

It is after 8pm when the plane kisses the tarmac of Aéroport International Félix Houphouët Boigny, one hour short of the time his visitor is expecting him; at a place 250 kilometers up the road! After negotiating with several taxi drivers and realizing that in a country exposed to curfews, seemingly with an extra alert level of security concerns relating to foreigners desiring overland travel at night. After a while wondering around like a head less chook while being hassled by mobile phone vendors a lady from the help desk shows some mercy and offers a free lift to her house at the end of the prostitution ridden Rue de Cana. Her husband is in full swing arranging a friend to visit them for negotiations!? As per custom special services come to a certain price. The haggling is testing Shoetef's patients as it eventuates him alone against a group of close friends on enemy territory. He is praying for some green to smoke! Slowly but surely his future business partner is grinning, the dark complex coupon is brightening up and the price is curtailed to level where both can agree too. It is now 10pm and time is running out. Damage is done, there is no reason to go retard when dealing with this business matter! Inpatients can be left to those trying to enforce their cultural values to only harvest a good healthy serving of frustration back. The slow progress continues with the driver's obvious need wanting a security guard engaged; an old chumster who would crumble to an ocean breeze. Next stop is to fill up fuel. Shoetef's is defending drunk-bots surfacing from all possible dark corners and all desiring a free ride. As it seems that also Murphy's Law takes the liberty of joining the merry round contributing to the vehicle breaking down on the auto route 3. And they have not left the city limits! With times comes increased aggressiveness from the locals. A crowd gathers and chants for free booze, loud and obnoxiously, until time arrives to punch one of those muthafuckers! It shocks them. Bus does the job as even those equipped with machetes are moving away while digesting the puzzling outcome. The entire scenery reminds Shoetef of the Walking Dead series before the bat shit boring season 3 kicks in! Lucky he bought at the last servo* black coffee and a packet of cigarettes. Time is now passed more pleasantly, nearly as up in smoke. Soon the car is repaired. The driver shifts his concentration now towards moving as slowly as possible allowing his so called security Mobuto plenty of opportunities to praise their service excellence! Luckily all in French giving Shoetef a reason to ignore and mentally prepare for the fact that on arrival finding the desired destiny will be a new exercise subject to the two's reinvigorated hijacking efforts, although the dismal back road street lighted is sufficiently enough to find whoring GILFs*. The further away they are venturing from the main road, any urban related quality standards go quickly downhill, increasing the likelihood of flies, bees and rats hiding in gray curly pubic hair as shaving these would have mean losing fucking, sucking and drinking time! Cote d'Ivoir dots plenty maquises harboring a happy chappies covering all sorts of pissed up attitudes. Compared to other countries Cote d'Ivoir's drinking habit does clearly show a living standard, even if it is plagued with political uncertainties merging with former statesmen constructing silly personal glorifying projects like designing this new pseudo capital in midst of the jungle! For Shoetef Yamoussoukro is pure monkey mania built by apes for drunk baboons; with the spiritual approval of the world's religious alpha male capuchin. However before any Westerners start to laugh, Australia too had a bunch of money wasting platypus tail hunters who envied the wombat excrement gatherers resulting in the bunch of single-celled microorganism yeast extracting brains building concrete chambers for kangaroos to marvel at! The Ivorian comparison has at least a decent nightlife stretching in to the early morning hours where rich bitches love themselves a bit too much by dancing in front of a large mirror in Hotel President's basement. May they bend down post farting and smell roses! This behavior is not exotic here as it is neither uncommon to politicians, especially some of those nationalism advocating hillybillies! But unlike wearing cowboy hats, traditional polka garments or biting on television in to a raw onion to demonstrate Volksnaehe*; these girls do represent true beauty by pumping up their booties with copious amounts of palm oil fried plantain aka alloco, piled up dishes of riz graz and cow feat to piecemeal all together with from Indian girls' harvested wigs plus a bulk loading of bleach spreading over their curves. Don't we all suffer!

Day 51

- Ah bonjour monsieur! I never doubted your deviant attitude in disrespecting the privacy by those who reside on the property of the world's largest church.
- Which is a vanity project on the backs of the poor!
- That is still not a free ticket to sleep for an hour on a back bench, followed by finding another imbecile to muck around in front of a television crew while replicating scenes from The Exorcist where you even attempted to fly above ground like that possessed white gown wearing jail bait spewing out some left overs from Lucifer's blow!
- Free ride?!? Mate, I paid entry, so does not seem that you guys are part of team Shoetef?! I even bypassed the port known for the world's hottest baked tarts, Monrovia! You spoiled my intentions to find a real female challenge!
- Oh sacrebleu! My ears are on flame by the ungratefulness and greed in search of beyond a monogamous harmony with an already found partner, who deeply loves you, but has an aching heart and mind; and that sadly not to her fault!*
- Alrighty, please excuse for roaming tangent wise on a motorized Luftmatratz through Dante's worlds while maintaining a radiant steer towards the ultimate goal of pleasuring a circle of female cult followers! And neither beyond this occultism sought confirmation rite shall you consider giving me an anointing of the sick. I am sane, at least enough to venture out where most Westerners crap their skirts while nervously trying to comply with other average vegetative cells in seeking their own rotating*

cog in the human herd machinery. By the way please excuse for missing yesterday's catch up.

- Ha! African timing is sometimes not very vivid. You might ask why here…?

- Not really. The only annoyance was not being allowed to take a stubby with on to the dance floor.*

- Anyway, there is an odd off Cape Verdian who is known to accept bribes for opening door to foreign brain washed intelligence zombies on psychedelic paranoia, causing steroids bugging up places worse than a horde of cockroaches hunting down fried chicken scraps. Thus, the entire idea is to prevent conversation tracing! Stir in some dynamics and it messes them all up; both the religious do gooders as well as the alcoholic investigative socialite. My first suggestion was the Residence Berah bar club, but when investigating and grabbing an ice cream from the side shop my mind did not only get beyond fairy floss tasting brain freeze, but a hellish decibel regurgitating sound system commenced its nightly terror reign. I'm too old for this shit. Conclusively, this place here too has its stories of smoke trying to vanish through fresh air; just with the potential of a civil war between religions as if the star of Bethlehem tagged off its duties with the birth of our savior. And who knows, maybe this age is seeking an early passing too. So take this envelope, read it and follow the instructions. By the way I would avoid walking all the way back, as you might get a bit unwell due to eating at a gare routiere garba barba shack. Locals avoid it, thus you might have gotten an unhealthy serve of stale fish. Plus add fried cassava in stale oil and your internal organs might be looking forward to an anguishing dunny dropping assemblage. Ah, also the coconut juice seller in front of the gates is neither known for godly comforting hygiene!! He even gave our Polish headmaster diarrhea and that at the building's inauguration! The world's largest cathedral should have a diaper put on!*

- Ha, blasphemy at its heart! I guess evil has many faces at many places, but some cannot be healed with a cold beer!

Day 52

The by the gut made prediction of foreseen guttingly gutted gutteroo becomes reality on return exposing the hotel pool filter to an unplanned performance testing. An added wet and it goes in to overdrive screaming inertly for more chlorine to nuke the vicious foreign rectum nutribulleting* additives. 12 hours later at 5am the bodily treatment scheme has recovered allowing Shoetef an early departure before the godforsaken carnage is detected as special service comes to a special price, even for special children. "Is that the pool still crying?" While his walking strength remains limited, the happy days mood is shared with the taxi driver who he gifts a few more cheap ass koala key rings. As it eventuates the driver is Muslim who just finished morning prayers concluding there is desire existing to do something good to the first person he meets and with a white man there comes the expedient excuse for a thé au citron and brioche au chocolat invitation. Avec un drôle ami* to share it all, even better! It is not only a relieving a battered stomach, but provides an already needed break from the pushing and shoving goods madness in the busy bus port where personal items wrapped up in plastic bags including wallets go lost. One event takes place all the within the yellow painted, two sides open concrete coffin representing the waiting lounge. Finally dawn receives the opportunity to greet a new day through the morning haze surrounding this surreal city with its massive empty presidential palace on the northern side of the dammed valley behind the crocodile spa where the Ross River virus gets its tan. Somewhere behind the mist is also the Basilique de *Notre-Dame de la Paix serving* unpaved road containing *pot holes larger than school buses! On a positive note the long distance bus is clean, but nobody adheres to the seat numbers as written on the tickets. The journey is mastered on a bench stool. "Darn, looks like you cannot always win on real estate." To his surprise the distance back is done in less than half the time the taxi had, concluding it was wise to not hand those two old cheats any tips,*

Navigating public transport through Abidjan represents a nice occupational therapy opportunity where the hot and humid of the tropics mingle with the queues of cars all the way from northern urban sprawling cluster Adjame past the estuary to the Akwaba statue where plenty of time is given to ask what actually that white stone thing should actually represent. But there he scores a surprisingly delicious tuna baguette! The local ladies surely exercise sandwich making artistry surpassing those young snots working for that American fast food footing conglomerate where pungent smelling bread is layered with nutrition removed soggy salad over low quality meat cuts or chemically modified veggie patties and sugary sauces tasting worse than the sweat dripping out of a toothless drooling drug addiction engulfed homeless person's arm pits! For Shoetef, if you eat fast food, do it properly whereby exercising character over excuses! The final stretch to Grand Bassam is a breeze as is checking in to Le Koral Beach resort. After inspecting the yet to be tidied up room a relaxing drink is taken next door where a new rastafari makes his appearance. He is offering an envelope full of welcoming weed to pass the day on the breezy beach. Just stupid that the breeze is a bit too strong for the jujitsu rolley master. However thanks to the laziness of staff the beach is full of trash, sadly permitting a potentially beautiful stretch of coast line to vegetate as a feculance ejecta gunkland. Luckily the pool side of Le Koral has a relaxing setting for pot smoking

The town has its nice side with all the deteriorated buildings; dooms day movie makers would have their pleasure, no doubt! Towards late afternoon the beer gardens along the lagoon side is welcomed by several locals inviting the seemingly rare foreign visitor to free beers. Southern Côte d'Ivoire comprises an African soul's attitude to just enjoy life. This gets even more evident when venturing out to meet local ebony delights at the Epilogue; a starting point for some cocktail to thereafter kidnap any sexy physics to the Ibiza nightclub for some public genitalia rubbing before fucking a loaded giggling corpse back at the hotel where the American owner is maintaining all night awareness. She is worried due to her guest's herbal diet is resulting in snacking on black chocolate.

Plus she fondles to the liking in finding means to swearing at her useless employees. To avoid any foul rape allegations as sometimes done by stupid white women post satisfying their cock cravings when the moral hangover cranks and to be assured that all takes place in a clean, safe environment he first chucks his babe under the cold shower! She shouts a short awakening scream to which he answers, "L'eau chaude, n'est pas on offerte dans ta patrie*!"

Day 53

It is an early morning taxi escape. His present donation to the pricey shit shack which is purely relying its survival on a nice garden containing a well maintained lawn, sky high palm trees and wooden artwork hide any crumbling supporting beams which are as brittle like biting in to a dried out Crunchie chocolate bar is done by throwing the female shaped booze barrel in to the pool. Her demands to get paid did not go down well. He gave her a risk free night's rest, saving her from ending up in a beer shack gangbang exercise while additionally ensuring she does not spit life's dummy. On the home run stretch to the airport next event unpleasant bakshish* episode is in writing, just the involved secreting epithelial duct changes from cervical venom release to seminal bullshitting. The airport gate police are standing with determined empty open hands all aware that their near to bursting red blood vessels of the eyes are intimidating. However when showing his boarding pass, the officials immediately show respect; "Vous flying with Egyptair, vous exempt…?!"

No alcohol service, stale cookies, seat recliner broken and late departure making the last possible opportunity to polish up this Maghreb state's reputation flow down like wasted water of the Nile released in to the Mediterranean for some horny spider crabs to jerk over. Funnily the delay is appreciated as waiting for the transfer flight at Kotoka International is rather tedious as any leisure can only be done in the over priced lounge which itself bathing in mold makes even the wildest wildebeest hunting carnivore pull its tail between the legs and leave saddened.

Day 54

- Now that is a surprise!

- Hi you yarpie barbie male doll!*

- I've heard some stories from ChongiBongi about his bad luck in bumping in to you with a regularity beyond his comfort; worse than being an Uighur exposed to a Xinjiang re-education camp where everyone is transformed in to halcyon, golden sweet but not sour fried meat balls. And now you are here for the ultimate prize!?!

- Well would anybody with some sanity make their way to this Harmattan plagued dust pan which is romanticized as the crossing of three trade routes and the largest city of the Kingdom of Dagbon, which seemingly in itself is still a volatile ground of competing and killing chiefs!

- But as it looks like, you have found me out here in the forest of…

- Of strewn plastic bags! I am actually quite surprised that after escaping from several druggies at the Aboabo market and walking like a remote control golem this exchange dude far away from any border crossing tried his best to reel me on board as a new anthropomorphic customer, showing early his frustration of screaming to me about my desires. And it worked, didn't it!? In zero hope I unassumingly answered him with Mary J. Subsequently he nicely offered a ride on his motor bike, back through the over crowded CBD, past some outskirt beer shacks, a school next to the city's rubbish dump, over a few of those hills and in to the woods along who knows what kind of paths to this make shift thatched roof stand where to my grateful eyes see this huge mountain of weed piled up with 10 local guys sitting behind smoking it while sieving though the harvest to increase quality output to their customers, nice!*

- Well look here, that guy just has thrown the wastage seeds and leaves. It won't take 5 minutes until a poor desperate soul will

pass by, pick up those remnants together and take it for a smoke in solitary.

- The grape vine oracle told me you two gained access to a lavish party arranged by the governmental official representing the Republic of India in Senegal and then disturbed it badly with iniquitous behaviors...?

- Ha! Wishful thinking of those being roasted be hell's fire. My dear friend, you are invited here, so grab some of the goodies and start rolling! These men here are very honorable, unlike what you have been dealing so far, so please do not disappoint them in their hospitality as you will see albeit them not being rastafaris the smoke here is free. You will be then also safely escorted back to your hotel, believe me, believe them and now be nice!

- So this is all legal?

- No man. Ghana is as strict as the morale upcoming police in the Sudan, so keep flying low, but smoking high!

- Thanks for handing around the doobie...?!?*

- Ah yeah, passing the dutchie around is not common. So roll up what you manage to smoke and let it do the treatment alright.*

- So, tell me in all honesty, as I don't want to and wont chase your cockroach ridden by maggots eaten body around the continent again, but need to know; why did you kill Bruce?

- Let me clarify. You had the opportunity to punish that culprit on several occasions recently!

- Juan?

- Yes, it could have been him. But your guess makes me think that I still need to roll up my hand and go over my nose to highlight the lecture I got from you of, fuck knows...!

- So, Natalie?

- Oh now you are truly a stubborn born Siamese twin of a bock hoof and a ram's head! But yes, she is for sure still somehow in the game. But do you remember who told me all about you?

Well yes we were at this rare Indian wedding event, where an entrepreneur found it sexy to fly a Bollywood statistic belly ass wiggling dancer in and while I was engaged talking to a friend of hers who was investigating means to gain influence in Nollywood I fell unconscious. The hundan fetched the round of drinks and went off to dance as only a silly drunk Chinese man can do when approaching the level of full scale retarded; then these guys think they cannot sing enough karaoke love songs... Ended up in an ambulance and needless to say that my hotel room was not neatly cleaned that night neither...*

- And where, what, the stone...?

- Ultimately I have had enough of it, but my aim is to destroy it. I believe my health can be regained by this action. My initial feeling told me that it was taken to Mali. My religious friends indicated easier border crossing formalities and where any bandits fall happily asleep after assaulting a brother. Too scared for the real game. Both air and land options are wide open thanks to the simple exercised level of corruption. The intention was to retrieve the extraterrestrial constipation and then transport it north for eternal forgetfulness, all while it painfully smothers, smolders, inertly screams its inner crystals to shatters under the Erg's thick layer; capable of torturing the evil, solid, adamantine believing piece of unforgiving geological roguery. However, as Bamako has extensive international operations accommodating quality services for expats, including Asians, it was very soon clear that newspapers were not reporting on any havoc while the militant Islamists where unexpectedly quite for a lengthy time nor was there any diseases spreading out like kraken tentacles wiping people dead with Ebola, nor any signs of misbehaving slit eyes; therefore it became clear that Johni Chongi jumped on a different flight out of Dakar and the only simultaneously departing alternative was Air Burkina to Ouagadougou which is so bored that any foreigner interference is quickly known.

- So again failure? And I guess lost of ideas too? Stranded in heavily French influenced area, which would also challenge our Mandarin slurping and burping chop stick panda belly ninja! Plus as the cherry on the Black Forrest cake, no friends, although you mentioned religious affiliates…?

- Ha! Hope you dropkick are enjoying your smoke as just wait another few minutes and your world will start to spin around! By the way our Sino chubby is not stupid. He speaks French better than a Spanish cow makes Asturian mantequilla*!*

- So what and how from here. We both have aligning plans, just…

- Yes, what does that just mean? I know that you are not a fortuitously piss farting shackle dragger, although you would just piss bolt off to the next pub without any inheritable reason, but since our last mingle through those lethal drankhuisen* of Bela-Bela I know that you can be cunning as a shit house rat! Until some form of news surfaces I am not going anywhere, this place is chilled, low key, ideal to pass time with smoking and can draft a new news article about the local artist scene. Hey you need to go and visit the local artisan village behind the alley where the banks are. Plus my good friend, I believe there is plenty of time for you to venture out in to a nearby national park depending on which route you desire taking out while I nicely keep track on local news. We both know that shit will sooner or later hit the fan! What about a suggestion? Let us do a strategy. It is likely that the diamond will end up in Accra. As being English speaking it is removed from any hidden France's colonialism agendas and comprises good international connections.*

- What about Lagos?

- Nigeria is too rough for that twat-bot, plus there is the risk of crossing even more borders which would the increase likelihood of customs finding the precious gem stone. It is not like a piece of

jade, malachite, amethyst or any semi precious originating from a turd caught up in muscle spasm.

- So what does your voorhuid voorspel drup besmette stinkgat wart tell us?*

- There are a few main routes going north to south, which highly likely either will be stopping in Tamale or Kumasi, Ghana's real capital and culture hub. Both good places to not only stock up, but to hide as a tourist! I'll give you my email address and you can make your way towards Kumasi by heading off to the western corridor where there are some nice pools where hippos and other critters bubble bath. I would say the Sino macaca's movements will meet time continuum expectations in 4 to 5 days, so no hurry, just keep your eyes open while entertaining the eyes. Just like a female partner explaining the alignment of your zodiac signs while keeping the eyes on her boobs! By then Lord Evil will have stroked a devil's charming path of mischief. Then we meet to nail the deal and...

- And what then? Who gets the stone?

- Will you promise me to keep it far away from anyone?

- Hell yeah. Well...

- I know, I know, you are a muppet being played with intelligence equipped puppets!

*- Gaan pluk jou riem!**

- Ha! The donkie kont's Afrikaans knowledge is still draadtrecking* beyond a pay per view porn web page operator's dream!*

*- Jou hol naier bliksam, fok die kak, ek loop!**

*- Jou dom stuk kak von ya ouma se bloed poes!**

- OK, so what tells me that when your mother shoved that sperm donation past a lost umbilical cord she reversed her decision due to recognized urine soaked uterus by rather stuffing you up her ass and blending it with shit to allow for timing to consider if she should even gift you with a life!?

- What about I offer you to surrender the egregious hard solid non metallic mineral matter without any conditions, other than keeping it far away from me? Of course that is if you've finally accept the fact that on your eleventh birthday you will not receiving an invitation to the Hogwarts School of Witchcraft and Wizardry. Ultimately you must agree the best is to bury the damn thing away from anybody for all eternity! Look at me, happy as Larry as you say in Oz and grateful for living; even when burnt with smelly turd stains!

At 5pm exactly the call of the muezzin hollowly vibrates vocal chords through the woods from a far flung mosque. All guys including Francois stand up, knee down in an openly constructed prayer bay located right behind the thatched roof stand and commence following the religious calls. Shoetef remains seated. All alone while letting the drowsiness of the drugs press the play button. His strengths are now needed to avoid spinning out. He feels like a yo yo stiffly holding on to its string when flung around.

Day 55

As no damage potentials are perceived Shoetef jumps on the 6am bus to Larabanga. On arrival he is hustled to the local mosque, the country's most etiquette marketed place of worship. He captures the attention of the grounds keeper after eluding him to the devastation of a foreign mighty villain. The reward is allowance to enter the holy confinements; but then is asked to participate wailing, although this is not his first mosque visit. Usually non believers can just be rather than being subject to religious conversion. And to add complexity the bugger understands English! Shoetef stands up waiving his arms, "Good health to our guide. May the almighty provide this mission with a large serving of fortune cookies. And show the greedy their path to a water fall dropping ablution pit!" To all respect, but this place is just another well maintained drain siphoning off tourist money making which would make a crested porcupine poop mound cry!

A nice trap set up for the typical silly European tourists believing they are helping out a community, whereby the funds are invested in to bullying the surrounding towns by starving any signs of competition! However, Shoetef admits that the guys are acting professionally, especially the outstanding experience to be gained though a tour to their bush dwelling cousins where the only pleasure is tickling their freckles* with thorn bushes! The well organized town also offers a fairly luxurious taxi service to the government operated lodge which requires some haggling to achieve a reasonable price, "BI will only pay a third of your asking price; we are in the jungle where a virus beats an elephant sized hyena any day!" The ride is smooth and the driver is content, "hey man you don't get everyday to polish a leather seat for Chief Muzungu!". Before saying au-revoir he gives an indication that more services are required with one option being a budget lunch outing to town, possibly tomorrow. Two minutes later his mind pushes a nudge, the bloody dump lacked anything close to feeder breeder serving beer. Mmoasɛm sɛɛ nyee*!

The lodge eagerly welcomes its newest guests. Even the cook from Togo is on a happy days drifting lager slurping path while the lady assistance cook is all ready to set go with dishing up dinner including as desert special house baked mud cake. All in all, the friendliness extends all the way to the rangers eluding that cheap beer can be purchased at their camp before continuing to promise visitors elephant and crocodile hugging at the billabong* below the hill where the lodge panoramically overlooks the surrounding savanna. The Mole National Park Lodge is truly a picturesque place, until one realizes on the first walking safari that the general large animal population tends to be camera shy, "miau, where are those pussy cats?" The most exhilarating experience is fresh elephant crap in a dried up mud hole and that is it. And what did those guys in Tamale mention? The hippopotamuses of Wechiau on the Black Volta river...? Slowly those initial suspicions are arising again. Not only that the nearby Wa Na palace could be just another ludicrous overrated building, but "why would Chongstar travel on a road along a country's border where next to a dusty enduring road higher security is likely to be existing...?" In that moment the only other customers at the lodge, both from the Netherlands come over to his table to offer him a spliff! "Well thank you" sprints through his mind followed by "is there more?".

No answering is needed as he explains that today is their one off exercise. After two puffs, the more confident young NGOs hands him a half full bag of fuming pleasurable while wishing him well in being happily high for ever afterwards!

Day 56

Early smoke before an early safari drive. Shoetef reserves a jeep all for himself and has to defend his right against a bunch of decision lacking skilled penny pinchers! The rangers seemed to smell his fruity stale breath and while being very content to accept full vehicle payment, it is deemed that more could be earned by allowing an outside party to join; and have them pay the same price, meaning that a good wage is foreseeable! "Right there, some animals produce bigger foot prints, giving you better return, don't they? Well, gentlemen of dishonor, this ain't freaking Upper Volta's Centrelink* shop!" Shoetef is standing strong, barging hard while trying to do shlucken* hard breakfast until a third of the guest's payment flows in to his pockets; plus they have to sit on top of the roof! He is not keen in having any witnesses to his pot smoking. The imbeciles comply very happily. The revenge of cognitive laziness kicks in physically soon thereafter with the buffet opening to the mosquitoes. The drive in lengthy, mainly through thorn bushes; it just seems the locals here have eaten or traded all the valuable deemed savanna shitters. Even the ranger is admitting most fun is offered at the lodge with the roaming snorting warthogs and thieving baboons! Like a predicted deja vu when he is having the subsequent siesta one cheeky monkey is not giving two hoots of the indoor occupant and is attempting to wrestle the door down like Hulk Hogan, just to be defeated by German quality made doors. Lucky only rangers have guns or that zombie acting mammal would have its brains blown away!

The afternoon safari outing is limited to the pool overlooking for kilometers the Sahel vegetation. A nice terrace to pass the afternoon as the sole guest before evening brings in new arrivals competing for any rare scrub hidden gems. But for now this smokers lounge is pleasurably used as an ego sun-downer hot spot while observing the crocodiles in the small stale lake beneath who go diving when a thirsty mob of elephants appear. Finally some action! And even being stoned like a monkey high on fermented marula fruits, the animals are not transforming themselves nicely in to perplexing orange elements of the occurring sun setting and more smoke neither makes them turn in to green eatable gummy bears. Seems that something is bugging him. He is feeling like a father knowing his child is out somewhere, but not confident if it is safe. Stupid paranoia stuff which especially youngsters have when consuming too much weed, however it is also known that old hippies get them when driving a car fleeing a rabbit riding tortoise. The female cook now slowly realizes that her coquettish efforts are unlikely to result in her wet knickers getting attended to and makes a final desperate move by cracking the news that no lions live in the park and she is the only cat option far away from the port of potential call: Kwame Nkrumah circle, a place of real cunningly attractive dressed wild felines roam a strip full of horny dirty old dogs! Matthew 17:17 - And Jesus answered and said, "You unbelieving and perverted generation, how long shall I be with you? How long shall I put up with you? Bring him here to Me." At least she is not opposed to rolling up a smoke. A few minutes later the Togolese cook joins in at his first pufferoo break. Shoetef asks him about the north south corridors, to which he responds with that parts of his great country was historically occupied by the Teutons and a major road passes through it to the east of the country's hydro power station ocean of devastation, Lake Volta. Not really what a stoner's mind is after, but education is neither wrong. This world's largest man made reservoir is located where modern slavery still exists. Young boys are used for fishing with no reimbursement other than prevention of starvation. Their only luxury is trying to see beyond life's impoverishment through asking themselves silly questions like what do fish drink when they get thirsty. It cannot be lied that well in to the 21st century most Westerners are still fully ignorant to the lives of humanities' majority by preferring to chase down plastic toy specials at cheap discount shops or cry like babies when their soccer club loses or even worse, slit their wrists open as the word is football and not soccer! First world problems are definitely worse than any lush desiring vegetation providing food for millions, defeating the Sahel its bullying right to be the sole swallowing master.

Day 57

A final stumbling between the warthogs occupying the front lawn, followed by a quick departure and back to Tamale! The tourist guide of Larabanga is keeping to his word and even buys the bus ticket in advance allowing for a relaxed coffee and doughy meat pie at Damongo before being squeezed in to the bush taxi, which itself proves to be surprisingly effective by arriving Tamale before lunch. Shoetef has now plenty of time to inquire about Francois, but the low hanging fruit seems to have gone over ripe. Firstly, no white man anywhere. Secondly the exchange guy has vanished. Thirdly, being prey for fairly dumb born bumsters hanging around in search for free cigarettes and beer is a waste of time and thus decides to walk towards north until finding the Chucks Bar and Restaurant. With already the first sip of refreshing cold beer, a treat in any African dust pan, he hears South African expats talking about one of their sons falling violently ill just two days ago. Further to the chat chit is their surprise of him avoiding CHAG* operators and instead selecting a university medical facility or similar…

Day 58

Accra described in one word: Messy. Before jumping in to the chaos, a beer is enjoyed at the Chinese eatery in front of the domestic terminal while hunger is tamed with overpriced honey chicken, which is less ugly looking than the sweet and sour counterpart. This open area also represents a good opportunity to haggle down a reasonable taxi fare. A long affair until an an hour later the competing drivers start to slowly soften up as if Wheatbix has been swimming in milk for the entire time. Like their counterparts they too seem to lack of the city road system and finding a hotel near the beach is resulting in a circum vidi navigation effort where Shoetef decides to have a rest stop beer from all the bull shit to only receive a harsh demand for extra Cedis. The response is done in a lower voice than even grim creeper reaper would allow, "wɛ akɛn waa*". The taxi driver jumps at him wraps both hands around his necks, followed be receiving a responding blow to the side of his head between the right ear and his eye. A witness crosses the road, picks up the knocked out guy, swears at the visitor and adds to the insult that he should neither hijack any local girls as men are proud of their girl friends bodies, even if they are not together. The taxi driver sobers up to participate in the poetic contemptuous play by placing words like may his next girl be a gonorrhea infected poltergeist discharging her green-yellow body fluids over him or even worse a Liberian girl shall make chop chop stew from his testicles, bla, bla, bla all while his thoughts scream "wɛ akɛn waa*!" It is all getting too much and he leaves the scene of drama, hops on to a passing mini bus van for a few hundred meters where he jumps out at the intersection of Ring Road and Labadi Bypass. It is a lucky pick. To his relief a veterinarian is operating an illegal shack; and not only selling cold long necks of ABC Golden Lagers, but also offering pleasant captain's picks of long stretching mind aviation smokes. "Sweet sugar". The afternoon is now developing to his taste of devouring magical fruits in a hidden garden. The two are sitting behind the low frequented foot path whereby any chilled friends make an appearance to meet and greet; and go up in smoke! After a while a temper maintaining smiling girl joins in; thin, skinny, very polite, somewhat shy, but born and bred in Christiansborg. But she ups the self-esteem and makes the move to introduce Shoetef to Hotel de Zews; a hidden bunker in midst of the nearby residential area where the concierge sits behind a desk similar to a bank teller followed by a dark corridor along brown painted walls to the stairs which take them upstairs. A cheap place where the owners are not fussed of him taking her upstairs and to where she is happy to partake in an hours' rest with the odd off cuddle and laying her head on to his chest just below where his arm joins the shoulder blade. It gives her an opportunity to have her finger nails wander through his neatly grown chest hairs, which cover nicely in a curtailed fashion and are straight unlike to the patches decorating African lads. No sex. Her excuse is having lady days. Shoetef is anyway too stoned to be bothered. Towards evening he regains strength and motivation to take her out for fried chicken and chips. What a date meal! At Osu's KFC she eludes him that her only duty of life is maintaining the outside perimeter of the neighboring house to the back which is owned by a rich Gibraltareño business man. After dinner Shoetef invites her for a subsequent coffee, but she humbly thanks, there is even a small tear coming from her glossy eyes showing some momentum. He is not yet ready to understand shame. Her request to be allowed to leave is granted with a charming, disappointment hiding mile. She gives him a final small kiss before departing. On return to the hotel he is informed of her baggage: HIV. The disease taking slowly grip of her frail body stature extending all the way deep in to the soul, biting it and lingering there ready to accept the following social stigmatization branding, which is worse than words coming from breakfast television show clowns who often are as thick as two short planks. This is Africa, the bad and the beauty so close together, where life is harsh, but hearts remain warm; and where people still fear god through pray, honesty while maneuvering past over zealous hope marketing evangelist preachers who ultimately are only interested in relieving the poor souls of the little bit they earned hard.

Day 59

The first port of call to find Francois is the obvious choice, the University Hospital. He finds out that there are various buildings strewn over an area as big as a black mamas planetary sized booty with each cheek expanding the size of a nuclear radiation atomized water melon awaiting to be touched by a horny poke starving dickvapor. During the entire enduring process of navigating by foot in hot and humid conditions he even ventures off to a few private hospitals south to the nearby highway. When night's darkness arrives he continues his inquiries if the bugger was by any stupid chance dropped off by am ambulance at the Airport Women's Hospital. In modern days of 5 biological sexes and something like 56.87 binary defying gender specifications he could have been such a big pussy-wussy-fuzzy-bear that some dazed and confused transporter had to invent unhermaphraditing clitoral testicular mercy!

As therapy towards acceptance of luck impoverishment the around the corner located roof top Sky Bar 25 provides pleasant chilling city views, but as expected the prices for nature's natural fluid anti malaria prophylaxis, Gin and Tonic has a sour financial taste while below on the Accra Mall interchange the scenery is social demographically transforming. An influx of dressed up women are gathering for the purpose of seeking clients, and no they are not old socks knitting masters! The previous nights' experience is keeping Shoetef momentarily at bay. Preparing some joints for the upcoming night is deemed a better choice, as further efforts from passing hookers are going to be as likely disturbing as loud reggae tunes emerging from the passing cars. A smoke shall guide his way. The Honeysuckle Pub, home to old drunk British wankers watching the premier league well past and beyond their bed time represents neither the height of entertainment. However positively noted, beyond the lame games entertaining some fogged up island donkeys the Star Lager is served ice cold matching nicely the aperitif serving of hot chicken wings. Thereafter the visit to the Crossroads for a Gulder Lager wash down is topping the day's uneventful taste budding adventure before venturing out a little bit wobbly along Oxford Road past some willy wagtail attracting birds eager for bush nut poaching cockatoos. He takes a few deep inhalations through an empty drunk coke can made bong to accommodate the horny making scenery. A stifling grind house vibe kicks in his pants like not wanting to lose a leg but still keen for shooting. With a few Club Lagers at the outdoor seating equipped Container Pub he gets very politely and suavely asked if his current party could double in size.

Day 60 - Genevieve Rose Barclay

A living voodoo doll in perfection dressing physical and mental scars from Charles Taylor war machinery, which even scared Abonsam* back in to the ocean. While the family managed to escape the rogue soul draining bush terror machinery, her exhausted mother then succumbed to the bodily orifice drainage exercise known as Ebola. Her brother's fate was worse. First the army hacked off his arms in front of forced spectators including herself as a young girl, then he too was possessed by the virus which took time following its anguishing path of destruction like throwing a few unlucky coupling dice numbers at the casino determined selling its as Russian roulette free. She can still clearly see how the poor stumpy body is shakily winding itself in blood coming from the nose and ears merging with oral foam while the uncontrolled released watery excrement is being tenanted by the flies sending attracting messages to the gourmet devouring bugs to feed themselves on what ever they sufficiently deemed palatable of his body tissue. As soon as possible after death her father buried the body in to the muddy road base foundation as spare place on the capital's isthmus is rare. Monrovia has never and will never harbor any compassionate feelings towards the infected. The alternative option was her dad's ultimate grave; the malaria mosquito breeding sewer pit decorating swampy mangroves behind the else wise invitingly named Chocolate City. It was Charlie's terror factory of controlling the human entertainment and manuring potentials with help of spineless evil spirited lemmings. Just instead showing some culture by dancing, these ones limited entertainment to rounds coming out of rifles. Liberia is Africa's only colony built from returning American slaves, whereby after a visit here a person can show empathy to white skinned US civilians preferring to live in segregated suburbs. A person can protest as much as they desire, Liberia's sad homage is a good example of fertile grounds feeding denounced racists by those who have no fucking idea how bad most sub-Saharan failed countries really are. Lovey dovey socialists too scared or too protective to strike down an annoying fly. Liberia even inherited its US heritage in the national flag; but there former home land does not honor this. But Genevieve Rose Barclay was determined to be no failure. Albeit a broken soul she is a tough fighter, ready to take what was hers even when starting to fail on her monthly menstruation cycle story followed by challenging her new lover who when the blood flow made its hasty appearance failed neither with eating her out! She smiled through her upper teeth gap while basking to the feelings of his tongue teasing her outer lips with the odd off slithering over her little pleasure knob to then take upon this spot as center of his articulating organ's movements.

Day 61

Shoetef is exhausted, tired and morally broken. Luckily he is finding himself with a partner who is warmly embracing him from behind while the sun is shining through the window blades; an event deemed to not succeed in morale boosting with those brown painted walls. And the morning did not get much better as the visit to the nearby General medical center opposite of the first happy city sit in smokodelic session ends up in his solo accommodation defeat as she swiftly grabs her garments and moves in! Easy task as her entire possession collection comprises of no more than two mid sized plastic bags containing two dresses and some make-up. Although being a lone warrior the move is not opposed. He is content to help out finding her a more comfortable place post seeing the miserable living conditions of her neglected hotel room in a building re-functioned as a refugee center close to collapsing where three bold headed, obese mafia miscarriages under the guide of an Indian master are trying their best to milk any poor souls seeking affordable accommodation through imagination producing variations. True interbreeds of shmucks and douche bags. African cities are not necessarily cheap and safe hubs to grow roots in healthy soils, where due to general declining of average local living standards prices can quickly and heavily accelerate, especially for places meeting Westerners' expectations.

It is already afternoon where she is suggesting to find some endocrine promoting relief at a shabby back yard den behind a church on Labone's Olooti Street. First weed is bought from the priest supervising the scene from the opposite road side, followed by crack from the property owner, then a visit to the head honcho whose job is to prepare the pipe and joints with precise technician skills to transform the minimal quantity of crack in to the maximum amount of woopydoopyflyingloopy! The den is already providing refuge to two already zonked out girls, who most likely in exchange for a free puffing fix suck off crusted sausage filler. And there is no air conditioner or a window in the power connection deprived bunker. "Hell it is 35 outside, humid and not even a fan!" Boiled, broiled and deep fried! At least it is possible to take some remains back to the hotel room to have, well literally bloody sex. It feels like adrenaline shooting through the body faster than ejaculating, making it only comparable to a storm chasing a tornado and ending up lost in its eye, to just sit back, relax and drink a Coke Zero! Thus, the day concludes with a sun downer at the funny wise naming incorrectly but bullseye meaningfully place of purpose: The Rehab (Beach) Club.

Day 62

After fruitless attempts in not only inquiring at the Military Hospital but also lack of securing an apartment in the up market areas of Cantonment, Labone and Labadi it is a quick return to her joys. First a visit to the Makola market hell hole for lunch. The sticky slimy okra soup proves its revitalizing potentials as energy is gained to venture further out to the western suburbs beyond the Korle Lagoon estuary, where to his surprise the Teaching Hospital makes an appearance. But any visitation requires a permission incorporating an anally retentive procedure. African bureaucracy shining bright; all the way in to his wallet. And the approach is done with full laziness infused disrespect towards any stimulation unlike his new loves' drive to find a new unit which is this time around a new found drug den with similar operandi modi… At least traveling backwards through the tedious traffic jam will bring them back again to another already known happy back yard lane. But with even all post drug consuming mucking around at the Purple Bar they still need to visit Burma Hill in the Teshie area for more… As the time continuum dynamic flight path has already been hijacked all what those crystal healing powers are doing now is acting as transitional translators too the spirits, who then after enough stupid talk tell to go on a night long chronic colic shaggaholic gymnastic event, "scream baby scream, go hard in the yard!"

Day 63

Rose is a Liberian dream come true, rough around the edges but so sweet in so many aspects. Her body and soul intertwined miraculously well with the crazy mind, continuously seeking adventures like tripping out on psychedelic native plants in a mine field before luring soldiers in to traps as retaliation pay, then burying them alive in the woods where quicker was better to avoid attention from screams or shoving up odd off toys up her holes knowing if her Pentecostal church following mother would see her she would break the make shift coffin and rise from the dead for a vengeful aftermath rite and thus when she did insert a smaller diameter gadget the entire length up her ass the release of her devious endocrines culminated to a feeling replicating an animal indulging in its rabies infected blood flowing through the veins pumping an inner cell destructive carnivorous tickling. That would trigger her to twist eyes far back, get the tongue moving as quick as a snake's determined to capture scents of wounded animals. Her element is being a trance voyaging fucked up voodoo doll. She took to the liking of being excited also on small delicacies of life; but the morning serve of Teshie lab stretched crack just started kicking in mellowiiiieey giving cravings for an afternoon partying session at Labadi Beach.

It takes the two space cadets a few mini bus rides to reach the beach entry which is designed like a gate way to heaven with shops selling barbecued food and cocktails while behind the portal a looming army of rastafaris are marching along the small stretch of ocean ass kissing white sands in attitudes soldiers usually exercise post a victorious conquering of the enemy; and similarly they are preying on to torturing the defeated. Be warned, no white man can ever go to this place without being eaten alive. Not even a graceful dancing ebony princess pumping her juices to venom is capable chasing off these vultures. But just like the nearby fair skinned guests, with a few smokes not only the ears, but also any veins containing sympathy turn numb. The two first walk twice up and down the beach in search of a more chilled laid out area, followed by sitting it the center of a see consisting red and blue sun umbrellas while ordering over priced gin tonics which would even hurt a successful Wall Street broker's pocket! The music beats are slamming the boxes and thus soon a new voodoo spell takes control over her soft but battered body. A nearby sitting South African makes a move to Shoetef and sits next to him with rudely blowing cigarette smoke straight in to his face before introducing himself. As a white Boer working for their secret services his keenness on a few magic puffs is surprising Shoetef. But then sucks intensely on the McVegan Wrap making his fat soaked pores perspire a waterfall from his bald forehead, over the fat beer belly and backwards down his hairy back to where on completion of the destructive rude act his twists his eyes around, which is going beyond annoyance making him look like if he is on a suicidal mission to be locked up with a perverted theater full of gaystars who are eagerly queuing up to have their pubes set on fires to be relinquished by a shower of freshly squeezed jizz. Shoetef wants to throw up on these thoughts, or at least knock out that fat pig's pizza dish. Next the pork rolls younger African friend comes over, who is initially perceived educated. At least he introduces himself decently, a medical professional from the septic states* before showing his real nature; a psychopathic sleaze bag gone lose allowed to act like a sick scientist capable of separating corn from a bucket of turds to serve it afterwards to a poor soul as a hearty desert treat while patting down the person's hair with his unwashed hands. Without allowing for a breathing break he waffles on with explaining his cognition coming from Francois, moving to his psychological healing capabilities of Shoetef's acting mental disabilities which are sharing similarities to technetium, francium, astatine; all generally uninteresting unstable chemical elements. On the contrary Shoetef limits his thoughts to, "What an egocentric fag bag sharing similar attitudes to the local seaside hog faces who likely would eat seafood chowder and go down on a girl to throw it up in to her vagina!" But they are confirmed when he gets to know that one of the story tellers' girls was a basic, average strawberry milk shake drinking bitch but once sucked 10 cocks from guys with the same name and once twisted a lovers' dick before taking it up the grimy tube to conclude he knew a lady who started crying after getting prostatic fluid in her eyes but enjoyed it when he licked the mixture out of the socket. While maintaining posture of trying not to be offended he asks, if they do acts acts containing freezing bowel movements. And then recommends them to take the next step by visiting a cemetery, dig out a half rotten corpse of a witch while one would hold his mouth over her vagina and anus while the latter would jump from the gravestone like a Wrestlemania scene with flying elbow smashing in to the dead girl's stomach making the flesh bag a healthy juice booster going in to viral overdrive! "Thank god the music is taking now a break", Rose returns with the desire to be accompanied to the loo, where he could in a rare moment of tranquility roll up a new doobie*. While she is trickling tickling her praline he smokingly wanders back to the disgustingly acting Safa*, where he demands for a written accessing confirmation letter, to be immediately expedited plus requesting that the besmirched foul gowks* leave their table to allow for some privacy. The girl wants petting, shmusing, licking her toes uninterrupted and just enjoy the upcoming sun downer undisputed by attention seeking smudge fudgers*. But as true fat heads, they are avoiding the grease dissolving sour vinegar by funny wise appreciatively chasing the local scam artists around followed by going in to tribal beats pushing stumbling bodies around while simultaneously performing uncontrollable pirouettes, sweating out the consumed drugs which are running like sparkling crystal fountains down their faces while visually the show culminates in to an egoistic merrymaking act of zerophrenic consuming amoebias causing dodderiness resulting in the desire to dance with surrounding young teens. A solidified sloppy basketball player tank shirt wearing black gook decorating a scar on the right side of his bold head indicating that he literally once dodged a bullet and a weird mid 40s racist man bold head with odd off crisscrossing hair strains impressing hard their abnormality, to which the latter' culmination ends up in tossing a young boy in to the air. Now he has an angry mob circling him who wrestle him down, the boy's father kicking in to his abdomen while the uncle's fists are neatly placed on his head with some heavy motion while bystanders are shouting pedophilia accusations. Wright or wrongly, Shoetef's own frazzled cerebrum demands for a rest; and some pussy cat patting. He is desiring to hear some happy purring.

West Africa is a place where at night the ghettos are safer than the beaches; and so do the two soon conduct the decision towards another crack exhilarating night by firstly visiting their favorite den. The same guys are surrounding the miniature cave dug out in the former fort wall, where she goes inside to receive her fix with tag teaming the exchange of different drug containing smokes while he is outside happily mucking around with the two guardians. All is going well until up at the road a visual communication in local sign language for the deaf is given that authorities are preparing and moving in for a raid. Within less than a second he is shoved swiftly away by the newly met junkie friends who are uproariously telling him "run run run" through a vast network of mud trails cutting past make shift clay and tin huts with asbestos roofing until ending up thirsty at a local chibuku* shack, the Bamboo Spot. One of the guys is keen to take up a free beer offer, while the other is exhaustively showing signs of contentedness through his unexpected weed fueled adrenaline kick and amiably decides to recover Liberia's lost gone smackadelic daughter.

Day 64

- Hi Titkop, already knocking on the door to Dante's Inferno?*

- Hey man, this thing, this thing never, never lets go of you…

- What? You still have the strength to play captain dickie on your death bed? Look at you, an utter mess guided by children misconceived by their daring affirmative mothers!

- You know, but you don't.

- I admit that your traits are beyond a compulsive hee-hawing Highveld donkey fattening himself up at the Spurs, but still a hardegeit gomgat*. And now you look like a Hottentot goffel gooi* who in all mompie* jux* lost her holvlos* in life's vrot gracht*.

- It will get you too…

- You are talking like Sasol's glug-glug-glug, but while the car remains a dikbek* dwankie* gham*, its driver is now loskind* scrap.

- Have mercy.

- Of what in knowing that if I stay another second around your mompie* mob will donner* me in to droëwors*…?

- No! The white guy is actually an old family friend and priest of our local congregation!

- Really, a man serving god…?? Well I guess a bag of jellybeans has many colors aiming to please all consumers, thus nogal* maat*, your vrystaat vernier* attitude towards former friends makes you a not only look like gum disease where toothpaste is too late to treat the vrotbek*, but also it seems that choty goty* has had enough of veë jou gat aan dit af*. Where is Morning Glory?

- Gave it to Chongstar! And as one to add, I did not lie about it's itinerary! It is on its way to Lagos; this is an oath on my dying bed!

- May you find that hidden treasure of final luck as per the bible phase 9:43 from Mark mentions that if your hand causes you to stumble, then cut it off as it is better to enter heaven maimed than having both hands ready in hell. But maybe they taste eternally grilled better than an organically non-destructible beef patty between sugary buns with a potential life span of a thousand years.

Day 65.69

"Was this just a day dream or reality?", is Rose's way to say good day! Shoetef however is still feeling the slight edgy touches of previous night's adrenaline rush. Now combined with an itching scalp and being aware of her new lover's near departure, she believes that might as well go full scale crazy and retreats to a special wish of insisting Shoetef to shave her hair while she performs fellatio and blows of his load on to her fresh naked butternut pumpkin, just like adding creme to the donut! All to please Mama Mahu* in favoring and enabling a future reunion comprising her ultimate destiny of marriage with him. May one day the spirits make Broad Street her reserved party mile!

Day 66

With the past few interactions it is becoming soberly clear that the rat race is fought out more bitterly than a swarm of dormant tuberculosis coughing moribunds awaiting a caffeine kick. Measures resembling a milkmaid treating a small pox outbreak are needed. It seems that Accra attracts too much erratic behaving critters which is complicating a safer low key exit. The coastal highway attracts local gangs, the bus port too busy allowing low effort thieving while Kotoka represents a very easy spot to keep a watchful eye; all it needs is one agent sitting at the Chinese hawker store feeding his ugly beer belly with meat piled fried rice and cold stout. The precautions are promoting Plan C, that is hitching a bus ride a few kilometers out of the mud cake. Somewhat costly as one passenger will have to give up seat and others will observe the bribe too. But as Rose is still on his side, not missing the good bye kiss on his cheek opportunity, she can share the transport back with the person happy to offer time for money. The chosen destination are the hills surrounding Lake Volta where to his surprise eastwards operating transport options seem to not exist or very minimally. The well sealed lorry station of Ho is already heating up quickly. The driver of the only mini van servicing Togo gave up income deriving hope already early in the morning whereby handily easy shifting his concentration towards getting drunk. The few available customers are exercising astonishing patients. Two indicate that they have been sitting on the adjoining wooden bunks for over two days! Time definitely does not have a monetary meaning for many Africans, but for Shoetef it could be a decider of continuing being alive or else maggot food. Albeit a horde of self declared station masters taking comforting attempts by forwarding straight lies of a soon to arrive tsunami of customers. "Yes, I too believe there is a procrastinating magician capable to just pull out human breading rabbits from his hat, vaaaboom!" Thus, a quick deal is deemed as a high priority as it seems to be only a matter of minutes until the driver ends up as an island in himself surrounded by an ocean of booze. Luckily as the former colonial borders remain as major language barriers, the poor guy had nothing more to do than in solitary get drunk. Money out, seats bought, "allez allez allez, vite, vite, vite, fils de pute* lets go!" All is going smoothly until the Shia border post where except for Shoetef nobody really bothers about any passports! The border guards are acting like precious gem stones banned away from peers in midst of tropical Siberia; while the white man offers a few minutes of work, they surrender to the other passengers only after tedious hassling and lecturing. All efforts of invigorating authority is responded by sheer ignorance. Both parties know that their exit as illegals is preferred than welcoming them somewhere in the bush dehydrated. Ghana is trying to revive its branding as the region's new golden child, including having to behave, especially when a white man has situational visibility. But too throwing them in to jail makes neither sense as it adds fuel to a potentially wide scale destructive fire. Driving away from the customs office, the nice wide, good quality sealed road ends abruptly below at the gully. A new flag marks the change, same in color as the Ghanese counterpart just with a white instead of black star. May the heavily eroded bush track ride commence by winding its way through dense vegetation up the hill past a few by farmers occupied shacks to the opposing immigration office, where as confirmation to Shoetef's peace in mind the entry book notes only 3 arrivals the previous day and the one before a staggering of 4, no wonder the driver numbs off in Ho! While the formalities seem to be more of an annoying siesta break, some officers are keen to join the party. The initially in luck dwelling bus driver gets his dreams quickly shattered by receiving a hard landing. His calculations that his major customer's low level of local trade education would prevail gets a nose dive. The seats are bought by the white man, meaning any collected fees had go to him! "Bon chance, nice try and thanks for bringing in business!" The hassling with the determined extra buck hunting driver is slowly biting on his health; the lack of a nearby shack selling booze to relief the heat's pressure on his own meager dehydrated body. And the driver too is showing signs justifying a needed return to the basic of him being allowed to drink drive with non contradicting authorities! Well, their alternative is to stay up to a week in a low entertaining jungle sitting desperately for the opportunity to get their mobile phone accounts recharged. The back injury promoting second half of the journey is concluding peacefully in Kpalime where mouth watering smells of soups and cooked meat inherit the rancid odors of the ultimately fully occupied bus. It is early afternoon and Shoetef has earned a decent little wealth on Cefas*, which conveniently suffices for a spicy goat stew at the neighboring market and a hoppy tea juice to celebrate that he did a free ride which also subsidized a drink! While resting he observes a well visible roof advertisement on top of a small nearby hill. Hotel Djim does not only offer cool rooms, but also a great restaurant and a barren roof top hangout offering great views over the entire valley and its surrounding with forest covered hills, plus the lovely lady working as concierge offers him a 20% discount out of just pure African compassion, "did somebody whisper her sweet words in to last night's dreams?"

Not only the city's environment or the delightful hotel make Kpalime a great place for a short break, but it takes less than 30 minutes to secure 2 ounces of weed for less than $2US. And not to mention the beforehand stalking advances of two older mid-life crisis defying ladies. Although the first mentioned 5 children making him wonder if he had to finger her with both legs protruding her! The latter is an evergreen sexually crisp and pulchritudinous bar fly, operating a make shift bar near the a small stream destined as the local natural hang out. She shows him a nice spot for smoking and having a session of mutual caressing while being guarded and protected from the nearby cemetery spirits including her ancestors... Further the weird social codex extends itself towards disallowing women to venture out at night albeit Happy Life bar's live music is pumping loud beats out all over the valley. The night can be described as atmospheric virtual disinterest of any girls; a weird event for not only the usually cheerful West African standards, but also for a place decorating plenty of smiles during the day.

It is a pure BB Pils infused fete de saucisson where escaping the outdoor arena's testosterone madness is only possible in the early morning hours. Conclusively in the world of political correctness where the developed world exaggerates its first world problems to ensure that spin doctors can maintain their leadership of the ignorant and giving twisted minded girls the allowance to behave worse beyond a hypocrite wired feminists nightmare; poor young men here are deprived of female loving counterparts. For 90% of the world the "no money no honey" rule is well alive while equal love waffling mental fruit cakes in the West are angry that doors of chivalry are not only closing, but with messages added that they can stick flower bouquets up their rear. Sadly these hopeless cases do not realize that hijacking a man's spirit will not result in favorable treatment; actually even one second of such a thought drives these ego satisfying hate spreaders towards more aggression... So this bread of human harmony opposition justifies their existence by continuing to enforce modernized discrimination, banning anything that gives a male soul a drop of happiness and then full scale bullying, even to the losers who attempt to adjust. Well they do it anyway only in dire hope to get laid as ultimately bad acts against general population generates income; and only the strongest in nature survive. That is why both religious institutions fancying a gold rush and evangelists humbly equipped with children bashing canes harbor a haven for psychologists dreaming of to ejaculate on girls wearing reading glasses. Plus it keeps nut loafs of their back. It is a mutual happy salvation surrendering to NXIVM masters, Osho or Adnan Oktar; gurus calling themselves spiritual divine spirits who like everybody else don't give a shit about protecting the vulnerable.

Day 67

Definitely a break is needed from Xevioso's* stormy mental lightening strikes which are aimed at disabling the intellect and germinating the feeling of being a dismembered laboratory monkey head connected to a jungle of high voltage loaded electrodes. It is self inflicted pain as it is his demand to start the day at 5am! Sometimes self harm creates true relief, just do not mention this to a spoiled emotional special retard kid who would as a result cut his wrists open. Thus, the hike up Mount Agou represents an early morning marvel starting by gaining passage through strict police control posts, followed by a 6 kilometer climb to the peak past idyllic clay huts hugging the steep incline while tucked away between forests, coffee and cacao plantations. The towns themselves just commenced coming alive. Roosters and children are waiting for the sun to properly give them a good morning kiss before making noise. Unsurprisingly the top of the hill offers sweeping views to the ocean and deep in to the Ghana. Its strategic location is used as a militia camp with duty to guard the communications antenna and more importantly for the occupants provide an opportunity to harvest income through guiding an odd off foreign visitors around. It is not only deemed an absolute requirement to pay special passage rights to access the road leading up the mountain, but also to question how on hell was Paris and Berlin incapably towards setting the border stones on top of the ridge rather than placing the weathered out rock in some unmaintained lower lying field where the grass grew over the former colonial masters' pieces of primitive artwork. May the poor black fellow who was chosen by Legba* to carry the rock up to the Togolese Meiensäss* rest in peace. Else at least he is now belated commemorated with a grass grazer* friendly breakfast roll. The morning culminates to a treat, but not without another walk. This time several kilometers down to a waterfall where his feet can relax in cold waters. Marching efforts are for all Australian's tedious, especially when done aligning to the nations' culture where hiking boots are swapped thongs, back packs with a carton of piss and our compass goes as per the wet stains on the brought with stubbie holder.

Day 68

2 days and 2 ounces gone! And again an early awakening, but today is Monday. Sunday ended up in him and his bar fly sizzling their brains away with the odd of fire extinguishing beer. For her it is a relief away not only from the weekly bar duties but for once her Sunday is not reserved for cooking lunch while the rest of the family attended the church mess. She also enjoyed this

miniature break away from the local riff-raff*. On the contrary Chief Muzungu is for her so alien that with lying in his cottony fondling embraces took her in to a never experienced dream land realm where his unreal male softness and exotic approach of kind warmheartedness managed to blend with a flux of a strong flying spirit enough to defy natural physics with the ability in convincing others to meet his uncommon tangent swerving desires and somewhat atrocious demands through utilizing rational thought patterns as sharp as finely grinded, extensively polished metal edges while maintaining a poker face. His departure is not bothering her. She is rather feeling reborn like an eagle. Intensive cognition waves are protruding giving first a message that any status quo can change quickly. However, "hey this is one of Africa's sleepy hollow, so lets have a breakfast beer first!"

As expected by 8am the bus port is already busy. The buses are filling up quickly suffocating any competition driven fighting. At his turn Shoetef is shoved in to a five seat Citroën station wagon with 10 other passengers, plus a goat strapped on to the roof. The animal is continuously peeing down the sides on to the passengers. As promised an hour later the vehicle is down to conveying only 6 people, of which two are babies, however when approaching the capital, the driver insists that his earnings are below expectations and returns to picking up new passengers. Soon again he is transporting 10 people. As next he is navigating past the traffic directing police officer who decides to abruptly stop the vehicle for a lengthy wait while all passengers are watching the mess unfolding to a chaotic background of merging vehicles where the boulevard of 30 August merges with the quadruple lanes of a grand rue* named after the president; the son of the former president who represents an institutional leadership dynasty promoting democratic prosperity towards best possible national welfare interests since their coup d'état in 1967. In summary a true real African dream just like Lesbian feminists eagerly praying every night for a prince charming ready to obey their orders, written by arms decorating male instinct hungry for conquering making hairy pits! However, guys who are laughing to this, most of you are neither worth a beacon of bacon! The mid day sun is slowly biting on Shoetef's current content feelings. It is time to stand up and take negotiating matters in to own hands. The officer is gobsmacked when told that a white man sat in the cab for an hour without bothering. With a small nudge the taxi driver offers the offloading of half of his passengers before the next crossing. Lastly, the officer needs to save some face. He adamantly warns that wearing seat belts is law and as an honorable constable he has no bribing intentions, but serious safety concerns, albeit forgetting to consider that back seat passengers are all deprived of such luxury. 2000 Cefas* later and the itinerary is back on track until the next hectic crossing. This time the driver seems to have learned and asks his passengers except of one women with her infant to vacate the vehicle and walk. A good opportunity for Shoetef to have a piss in the green patch with views in to an opposite shanty town located in Ghana. On return he is keen to continue the voyage in to down town, but the idiot driver forgot to wear his seat belt!! "Enough!" Shoetef swaps mode of transport faster than a peregrine falcon after eating caffeine injected laboratory mice!

The day's last question is how fast can a Chinese walking beijiu bottle proceed overland without disrespecting any moonshine infused guanxi sessions? Or is there a super nova sexy bootie which can stop him?

Day 69

- Bonjour mon amour, ca va?*
- Hell, what now the Russians attacking us together with Teheran's mullahs and Rocket Man's drug dealing Stalinists!*
*- Alors, nous prenons des croissants et café du lait! Le pain ici est plus bien comme le moelleux à moitié cuit carton ghanéen!**
- Yes, please! At home they look at you with the stupidest faces one could imagine when you lovingly dip this buttered up pastry in to your freshly brewed warm milk suffocated bevie. Sweat, bon appetite.*
- My love, I forgot to give you a small present; one from our earlier days on the road…
- What the busted rubber dorito from White River?*
- Ha! … I am actually a bit speechless. Shall I be shocked or surprised that you still remember…!?! And looking at your

eyes, what does the below associated perverted mouth want to say?

- Oh la la, tiens! Tiens, tiens oh mon dieu, seulement si te ne le fais pas*….*

- I might need an odd off deep breath, but do you really think there is anything virgin on me that could not deal with any of your blows!

- OK, you just said it!

- Qu'est'ce que?*

- Well… I lost my virginity…

- No way?!?

- He, he, he, not the way you imagine. With you it was the first time seeing my white blow dripping out of a negrita's vagina!

- Sacre merde! You are sick.*

- Can I eat now my brekkie as planned and make a runner afterwards? Manger* before your tits freeze disgusted in to a 10,000 year long ice age!*

- Tiens-toi Monsieur Capitano Stabbin'! You have not stoned the crow yet! N'oublier par comme nous les deux sont dans le joux. Plus I am not your old age disposed 3 eyed Fuggler fucking cunnifungus! Why are you so mean to me? Did I say anything wrong?*

- Well…

- Common, do you really expect me to pat you like a pet and say "good boy" after your rubbed your quiver bone against my shin like a horny mutt? I love you! And we are not only in this together, we are soul mates representing a form of yin and yang. We represent in many aspects opposites while balancing the equation of forces, only….

- Only, that often educated women tend to verbally regurgitation excretion reminiscent of all froth no beer while exercising full ignorance. Which all goes well until that blue moon of getting caught strikes resulting in their Plan B execution of stupid excuses like shark feeding week. Want an example? Our upper

middle class bogans who after a dimwitted Bali vacation go to a hard ware store, buy a Buddha head and place it on the ground as decoration to their dog poo exposed artificial lawn of their tiny outer suburban back yard, all oblivious to the total disgust of rational thinking baptists while maintaining belief of right to drum up at their convenience spirituality misinterpreted mind raping ear bashing! So may I ask, do you believe you are better!?*

- Tais-toi!! Ferme la bouche, tout-de-suite! Your brain has not yet gone troppo. You are aware that a carnival corrupted Quaker is paying you! Plus thanks to him you are equipped with the eye of the Horus, meaning capable to see that your budgie smugglers* have skid marks too. Else why play a fizzing* lubra* duffing* duffer*! Think about what kind of affirmative social punishing life would you be at this moment subject to? One day all Australian males will be banned to modern donger* gulags and only released for either in-vitro purposes making hairy tree huggers happy or as a self serving chicks' toy. The male's sole existence justification will be the prevention of being called the spillover headsman of Foggystan. You won't even get the opportunity to cry like babies as that will be gone after the tasteless pissing protest when the all female world introduces for gutrot* a maximum alcohol level of 1.5%!*

- Now you are insulting me! I don't use lube.

- Oh my poor baby in pain…

- Now that is better! Fuck the gut rock part too!

- Is your Bad Milo refusing to retrieve back up your rear!

- Funny, sometimes men can smell that their partner has booked herself in to the Red Roof Inn! But believe me, I do not…*

- Arrête s'il-te-plait. I dearly love you and promise we will soon be together. Crois moi. My gift for you today is a necklace comprising a Saharan compass. May it help finding us together, may it help find…*

- Ha! Please don't tell me that this thing has any connections to a b-grade horror movie emulsified fluid rubbish vortex?!?

- No mon amour, I have the feeling you are near…

- Well I have elegant fingers with healing potential, but first…

- Stop. I promise you unconditional love for what ever you are now going to unshackle!

- Yeah, nah…, with women on the rags you are never going score any mates rates!!

- Regardes-la, un moment, moins une minute, et voila ma serviette hygiénique pour ta souvenir extraordinaire*!

- Woah… sales pute*! C'est épouvantable*!

- I am only learning from the Master.…

- Alright, respect. FYI*, before Francois carked it* he gave our price to Chongstar and told me it is heading towards a big city known as a hustlers' slog hole.

- And you really believe that the bulhond* was honorable enough to tell you this Cinderella spiced story? And how long was that ago?

- Yesterday…

- You liar! You fool! This is chowed up canine regurgitation! Let me tell you one thing: Chongstar speaks better French than a Parisian newspaper editor! We have lost a few days, but luckily Lome has an international airport with good connections, so I suggest we head there immediately.

- Paris? Romance?

- No, not know. And why visit the metro's piss stinking walls when there are plenty in Africa!? Let us brain storm your disintegrating hard wiring regarding alternative options other than Eko Akete*. My suggestion is one of us goes back to Abidjan due to its higher standards.

- Do that. I am not going to rely on visceral female irrationality and will be heading eastwards; and if that takes me to Timbuktu, then it will.

- Timbuktu is north-west from here.…

- Have you ever tried sucking peanut butter out of a colon?

- What does that mean, you snail paced treasure hunter? I am going to Abidjan. Rien d'autre? I believe you were there a few a days ago; il ya quoi que recommender?*

- You really think I was close to anything there…? But did go to the local Bunnings, avoided slipping on saw mill containing sausage roll escaping onions, got wood, built a bridge, got over it, saw that the grass was not greener on the other side, but before burning the sticks I shall answer your question aligning to your whacka whacka* approach: By firing away a fully sick cooee* you might get all go of an airy fairy taxi driver and if his pants can contain the dags*, you'll be apples*.*

- Your dick-brain mind is as mashed up like burnt caramel filling of a frost bite exposed toe grub in anxiety urinating egg tart pastry!

- Don't act like a raw prawn! You are giving me psychological trots! Yes, thank you for the present which in sight of your avoidance yesterday seems to be a bludging blunder*, or do you have next to squeezing the beetroot* a 5 o'clock shadow* on your twat?*

- If they'd have lab rats where instead of the ear a vagina is growing on to their backs the poor things would be subject to your a-rack attack!

- My mind is rapt of your insults, which in their origins are clear as mud similarly to beating around the bush like a stuck up reffo* bitch on heat!*

- Bien mon amour, prendre plaisir! I got told to patiently wait for the nearing end of your foul playing clapperhappy* ballet dancing. Néanmoins*, tu est plus beau que dix milliards couchers soleil*!*

- Wow mercy. Alors à bientôt; hopefully next time in your birthday suit!?

- Sadly you being mean is keeping me keen. You don't have any love?

Day 70

The big mistake has to be erased fast. Crossing the border to stay overnight in Grand-Popo Beach is as exciting as a fat chick digging in to a plate of raw vegetable sticks. The nearest cocktail bar is not only a tedious walk along a suicide straight stretch of road deprived of any street life, but the rastafarian owner played hard when a hearty smoke is requested. Aneho on the Togolese side seemed to contain more livelihood between its colonial buildings. But he admits too late. At least the beach is not too far off paradise's stamp.

The choice of transport is to share a taxi with two older ladies to Ouidah, where thanks to their motherly inputs the markets at their destination can be navigated peacefully past vendors and tourist guides eagerly advertising their products or services similarly to a fishing sportsman seeking to catch a prized marlin. He observes with a cunning smirk the randomly caught bait to lure in to the nearby main Votun temple; keen UN employed zit* faces being chartered in from the nearby capital keen to buy overpriced souvenirs while taking selfies in front of the plastic statues aligning the dismal sacred forest's foot path where each step can result in forwarded demands of a deity honoring donation. Even large weeds are sold as purity sacrificing anal flora whereby being promoted as untouched from outer realms making a potential customer believe that faithful virgins are acting in the girls gone wild series. The art of sad cat eyes is played to perfection with greased financial laurel singing mirror voices as it neither matters if any bank notes have been chewed by a Djiboutian smack head low on khat! Although Shoetef does acknowledge the statue with a devil horn wearing guy is respectively decorating an impressive phallus representing a naughty minded girl's wildest dream of riding a sickle pickle, thus making the exposed trouser snake a viable competitor to Prague's Wentzel statues' balls!

Never the less when walking along the mile to the Door of No Return Shoetef's exposure to road sitting elders gives him the anti grudging nudge to befriend some local spirits, not only the daring caring coming from a bottle. The soils of Benin contain the blood of many sad past historical events where at its destination on the ocean an arch reminds that albeit an import ban existed in the United States the flow of slaves continued another 50 years. Ruthless brothers still exist, just executing highly extroverted tactics towards earning a hyper ventilated buck on the backs of the reversed tortured!

It is later in a more secluded setting of Agobhe where the unusual sight of a long hair braided female shaman gracefully emerges. A witch doctor dressed in wood bark moving her thighs between the bushes elegantly. She immediately takes on the liking to her visitor, followed by gently offering refuge from the afternoon's heat. "She is a snake on some form of tranquilizer, no doubt." She invites Shoetef in to her estuary shore aligning sanctuary, in midst of mangroves refusing the ocean breeze to allow for cooling with back dropping tall jungle trees. Underneath them are already two chosen voodoo dolls sitting and waiting. Their specific purpose is initiation through the blood of fresh butchered animals whereby both have a secondary purpose of soul cleansing and carnivore nourishing. As a priestess and queen mother she instructs her husbands and lovers to commence playing drums while the children are dancing around a make shift fire slowly falling in to trance trough the green seaweed brew set aside for that purpose. With increasing pace eyes are turning exposing purely the white flesh with some red strains crossing the eye ball in ensuring all initial praises are directed towards Ogun. The god shall ensure strength to succeed in an upcoming scheduled feud, which is already smothering on a too small flame for one party member's liking. This universal's discarded compact gut bean is desiring another drop of fuel in hope to keep the fire going and to eliminate unwelcome game players, faster, if possible stimulating a wide spreading jerrycan explosion. The heat rising from the ashes indicates to femme fatale that the hostilities are transforming towards a war declaration against human society, but due to lack of flares properly engulfing the wood the readings conclude that the requisite actions are to be executed without conventional weaponry whereby targeting fake smiling poker players who replace their hand of hearts with other suits aka eleemosynary preachers following hidden agendas who are not interested in defending values of progressive liberalism tied to free speech promoting democratic values but rather promote repressive measures sold as benefiting the common good. Some of their desired strategies of war are isolation through media combined with education cuts while promoting artificial intelligence, implementation of nanny state controls and selling globalization as justification for national isolationism and societal protectionism. At the height of trance the priestess holds reaches out her hands in shaking movements, but grabs with a clear targeted adequacy a spit defending black cobra. With one swing she catapults the reptile against a tree mounted machete where during flight its head is smoothly cut off ending its devious nutter to make a final lapse over two small boys in to the fire! Hell no! L'enfer ouiiii*! Shoetef stands there motionless with his mouth wide open, holding the dark brown nearly black colored voodoo figure to his hip where as next the snake is squeezed out from the tail to the cut open neck. A gush of blood covers him. Damn! Stains! But nothing that a half cut coconut filled with fermented palm tree sap cannot heal. When the trance is slowing down the male partners retrieve exhaustively back to take place underneath the trees awaiting for the sun to finally set. A few minutes later chickens are brought in to the arena, but instead for a cock fight their struggle is to not regurgitate on the blood flowing out of their quickly, precisely sliced open neck veins before before alleviation through beheading. The elder followers start sucking out the headless flapping bird, spitting the fresh extracted blood over the white gris-gris* representing Erzulie; mother, peace, security, health and clean purity. With time the blood is drying on the orange colored sandy ground between the char coal remnants. The sorceress summarizes a new verdict that a third mojo is not required as the confluence of all evil has already progressed too well with its destructive agenda wondering if an ultimate forfeit is even achievable. Plus the white doll is equipped with sufficient rusty nails for protection against powers seeking harm while the dark counterpart's determination is directing emotions towards real global covering peace beyond worldly arrogance while perceiving their minor problems as being superior. The two represent a merging of extrovert behaviors requiring the rope handling of an introvert to maintain ever lasting congregating mutual love. No further colors are needed, as these are the distracting weapons of the weak explaining their meager existence of decision avoidance and low personal resilience! Or in other words folk with IQs of a Smartie. Only now he realizes that her face decorates two scars. She calmly eludes to her own initiation rite to thaumaturgy and soon thereafter concludes the official ceremony with forwarding the request of him to sustain from any women, nor exchange any goods or money until the following day. She is not stupid neither; thus to ensure success he shall lie next to her tonight to allow for the oracle's acceptance and its digestion that an unfamiliar convent participated, breaking the traditional worshiping circle seal. Plus in the morning hours to make a fertaholic bastardy conception endeavor!

Day 71

Sometimes sex can also be for a man painful. And it is not because of the lack of lube! A night long smell of smoked salmon on sweaty skin is only durable when there is no risk of kissing a tooth brush deprived mouth! It is an early start and weirdly enough no stomach problems are persisting. His concubine seems to soon after action regain her healthy sleep and her ability to not add weight on her bones defunct any form of snoring, albeit age usually promoting the habit. For him the story's real uncanny deal is his acceptance in the nest of female refuge only. When discharging himself from the short term prison term the men and young boys greet him. They are all awake sitting opposite to the entry portal. A big tree is giving shade to two wooden benches easing the guarding duties of the open space surrounding the visual protective bushes where the women reside. Anyway the moment is not appropriate for dwelling through any Sigmund Freud theories of anxiety towards the likelihood of developing a Bertha Pappenheimer neurotic paralysis. When reflecting of the ceremony's revealing of the influencing desire the pimped-up squatted particle had, time has arrived to concentrate on making Eros stronger than self-destructing Thatanos. Although some mental damage is obtained; from sucking on a pair of lactating tits hanging like chandeliers above the caves' entry which provided the moisture and heat seeking comfort of his venomous tamed throbbing python of love. Now he is choking by containing the fluid cough attack.

Post check in at a lonely standing lodge behind Cotonou's airport strip and realizing that the Fidjrosse neighborhood is rather bland the decision is made to venture swiftly out again. The choice is an afternoon boat trip to Ganvie. In his mind nothing all too exciting, but visiting a lovely settlement replicating West Africa's Venice on Lake Nokoue can surely have some charms. The private boat operators are haggling on the steeper side of pricing, but bartering can be made easier by patiently taking a seat at one of the plenty of little bars aligning the access road. After the trip over the lake Ganvie soon the red building of Chez Raphael is in sight, a pleasant place for sun downer beers. With the magic view over the lake time is going lost. After multifaceted drowning operations of Biere Beninois the privately chartered barge captain approaches him with a cheeky inquiry attempt. He is hoping to sneak off already assuming his guest is more than content to stay overnight in the swamps rather than in his urban ghetto hotel behind the railway line. However, before all goes in to typical African dysfunctional attitudes, veto is submitted. The place is not much more than as an open air shit house; just like what Venice is! "Bad luck buddy", the self declared guide and motorized gondolier is lost in sobering thoughts while drifting prematurely towards satisfaction his soft hour needs. The return trip is rescheduled in direction to the big squalor congregation of Cotonou. At arrival the place lacks any street lighting. Without any duty of care in mind Shoetef is left alone on crossing of rue 669 and 888; what a great land mark to find a way out of cabbage town! He is most likely the first white man to set foot in this part of the planet. When venturing a few meters further he hears a groaning... Its origin seems to be a nearby building where possibly not only fish processing is done; but also the dismantling of ingredients stuffed in a greasy McAsia!

Day 72

- What did you tell this girl? Look at her she is shocked, sitting here utterly in disbelief digesting your fairy tale of having the first cigarette and beer after a tour d'amour relais...!?!*

- Juan, let us rest the fudge sickle cream whipping for a short moment, as this sponge cake comprises of a few fruity layers where some of the frozen ingredients require heating, baking, maybe even nuking!
- Ha! Well done, eaten all candied monkey fodder*!
- Francois is dead. The five spiced crook roast is held hostage; tied nicely to a grid with his rotten attitude replacing a load of stinking fish!
- Be careful mate, this country has some nasty treasures!
- Tell me! Tonight's marvelous sexually spirited girl will never be forgotten. She was a Muslim chick from the north and could speak English! What do think, borderline Nigerian…? But admit it took a while to realize her linguistic artist characteristics after observing her wonderfully shaped c-cup sized breast nicely distracting from her fully white glowing eyes while acting like a springbok drinking its first drops from a trough filled with King Browns* whereby doing sexy tongue wiggling to indicate her fellatio skills, which seems ultimately giving her the strength to ride a giraffe like an African matador seeking for the ultimate strike! She possessed a kinky caliber by asking me to remove my finger ring due to discomfort; but it was my watch!
- Ha! Wishful thinking and a beer coaster like you is useless in sport. Benin's kings used to promise the heirs more land than they had, to then embrace slave trading as the next fortune making opportunity, followed by a Marxist-Leninist government leaning on Chinese Communist party rhetoric to then get totally robbed of any luck by a nepotism president enjoying being the female in his relationship with French politicians, mainly due of being incapable to shut the fuck up for 2 seconds.
- So you were in Addis for the Chinese?
- You left before all the good stuff came shaking in to town! We scored just that one harvest from the fields of South Sudan; a place where not even an inflow deprived shit farm would bother polishing a turd. Zero interest. It was beyond diarrhea as more

leaning towards full scale infectious social disease. When your main currency is cattle theft, the president palace receives as a morning greeting a spread splashing of AK47 bullets and your arch enemy shows as much interest like a house wife in the West to do anything beyond Netflix; then not even the most vicious antibiotics will seal the deal!

- So I guess back to South America?

*- Yes the life's eulogy of once you go black you never go back can be done there too, but the real attraction was Ethiopian Airline's inaugural flight to Sao Paulo, therefore opening a door for business, pero ya sabes…**

- Caballo antes de armas!*

- Y ya sabes como la mas oscura la chocolate, el mejor el gusto**

Day 73

- That was nasty. No fly-flaring ostrich riding through the Jonquet strip for me today!

*- We need to give him some of that weed tomorrow. Unbelievable, those guys were shitting in a bucket and holding his face in to it! Creo que…**

- Yes, he definitely has the stone.

- Give me another smoke! At least we have found a loud spot where the rich can mingle while getting the poor beach boys to do some running and enjoying the sun set over the beach!

- We shall starting the day in the expat hangout of the Livingstone Hotel might have called upon the wrong spirits! Talking about hidden interests, what was your involvement relating to Commies in the former fascistic Abyssinian wog fog joint?!?!

- To make it clear I represent the interests of oligarchic operating business partners and with them their political allies desiring

the creation of let us say idealistic pleasure utopias; and yes sometimes we also work with left wing governments like Cuba or Angola. But right now the Chinese are seemingly unknowingly having their fried rice burnt, the anglophoniacs are most likely following their modern buzz word of acting agile and nimble, which in reality means full scale knee jerk reacting headless chooks flying from the razor barb wire in to an electrically loaded fence while the Russians are influencing Natalie! And then there is you under the jurisdiction of Europe's only country with substantial and sustainable power, the Vatican! In some kind of an over fuel injecting session, my client's came to the conclusion that a vehicle's spare wheel could eventuate as the winner; which does somehow resemble the 2.99 theory we discussed a few weeks' ago. Hence, if you don't mind, I might grab the stone this time! In contrary you would be able to away with your client, as they tend to network with mine and as a team we could finally end our odyssey. I had enough of corrupt Tuareg in Mali, dodging the harsh winds in a waste land called Burkina Faso, where I was stupid enough to believe that the Land of the Honorable People would attract a chop stick freed stir fried pork dumpling albeit the horrendous visa costs. This was then followed by another unsuccessful detour through the lands of constant kidnapping fear of Niger where I actually believe that this isolated place would distract Chinese as it is somehow similarly set up like Xinjiang. Never the less my dreams were continuously directing me towards that deflated tire needing change, for the benefit of making mine a 2.99!

- We cannot just let them kill him! He does have a funny side when it gets to asphalt diving!*

- I said deflated tire, didn't I...? And anyway his fate is all at the mercy of the worldly as wrongly placed constipation like its inheriting prime evil devised plague-some stool defying hero from Vlakplaas, Eugene kack-no-poo Kockhead.

- OK, so what 's in for me?

- More fly-flaring ostriches?!

- Ha! Pueril como un infantiloide! It is actually a fun thing to try. Let me tell you it even makes her laugh, that is when getting the loving rhythm right, maintaining comfort of her lying down on the back, you on your knees and then when the meat racket is locked in you lift your arms and flap them, just like a retarded ostrich turbulently trying to fly but has its head buried in!*

Day 74

- I don't care how much overpriced the beers are here at this boring Jammin Bar, but today's outing was messy...

- Amigo, for that shit I want to hear your promise, oath, make a defection of Catholic faith through renunciation and if breached a holy commitment to get that piece of hard shit rammed up your ass, so that if you succeed all humans, saints and goofy dogs can worship me as their religious leader!

- What? Get back to Earth Pluto bub as Mars for you is limited to a chocolate bar!

- Well it was your plan to get guns at the low life pub on the other side of the bridge and then wade through the waters to the hell shack, while being bitten by leaches; most probably like the horny ones down south being inventive when there is no crab back to travel on.

- Toughen up princess or maybe it is time to go home my dear religious leader! I can hear your bacteria drooling heterotrophic decomposers' fellowship drumming with fungi stems to transmit organic rejuvenation praises.

j- Believe me, there are more souls in need for saving. I once saw an online video of Russians who are on this Krokodil stuff where one bloke had necrosis on his leg that only the bone kept the foot's flesh attached. As it was going stale they took out a saw, choppa-di-chop and ultimately he wheel chairs his was back to camp where the limb is cooked and the entire group of junkies relish on it!

- Please don't distract. Seeing those guys cooking up a soupe de bébé and then going cannibal on their half human lab rat!? This stuff is really malicious and needs to stop!

- And so may the Africans share the love of eating exotic goods with the Chinese; and if it had may they eat each other up too! Has nothing to do with me.

- Chingar! Chingado! Chingon! Is that how you finished off with Bruce!? Gun wielding panda bear pandillero* in front of others, but skittish when it comes to execution and ending up tail between the legs when la verdad coños* are on the soccer field!*

- Pendejo! Guardapolvo atonto es llamativo!* And it is football!*

- So it looks like we are two useless Japanese anime characters like plucky girl and the one believing in happy slavery! So amigo, to work towards the future, we need to understand the past. The rise of Eternal Zion needs a solid foundation!

- Yes, but outside of this cursed continent, a place where your assertiveness will flourish to build in my richness blossoming empire in a surrounding of a governing pistil containing a dedicated shining and protecting corona; the new-age cult temple of life and rebirth!

- Dreaming is nice, but today's legs are not that of a man's dream relating to an African queen's shanks, nicely formed thighs of dancing out in Luanda nor appetizing thin shins of the below Skeleton Coast!

- Amigo, my dad is scared about the stone and that says a lot for a caudillo.

- To be honest all oligarchic rancheros are paranoid.

- Verdad. His belief in disbelief towards the Chinese is built on the foundation that not only is the gem seeking something like a Pancha Mama, but it at its original site of finding in Angola

there was something like a Germanic "Das", a third wheel which does not represent a powerful pole, but rather a moderator role between. Hence 2.99! Imagine a beehive or if you'd prefer an ant hill where a powerful queen represents quality over the army of ants representing quantity and the moderator is responsible for the outer environment plus generational knowledge transfer; like yin and yang responsible for the physical species survival while the dotted eyes in the symbol ensures endurance beyond confinement limitations. This moderator can take the species beyond a defined geographical location. Some turn themselves inwards in being as-sexual like apodeictic priesthood celibacy while others venture out on a tangent as some eunuchs and lady boys do! Now I forward you the argument that the gem is the ultimate oracle artifact hiding behind a door with the key to open it, meaning seeking mastery with the wit to pass.

- Put on the breaks! The plan for tomorrow will be dementedly cemented enough by going straight to Dantokpa's Marché des féticheurs. You want to obtain the mankind "dissoluter", fine. But, I'll keep the gun. And stop looking at me like a dog fronting the master aware of its bad behavior!*

- Woof woof, open the door for me!

Day 75

"Ooohhh damn, they have now nicely widely opened hell's gates for you!! Might as well throw those taxidermist fetishes in to the corner. I guess you do not need to see the monkey shrink heads and dried porcupine bodies with the one eye the crows have not yet feasted out. Looks like they are mimicking a Zoroastrian funeral in using this decommissioned tin shed as the dokhma, the tower of silence which seemingly is needed as reaction to your annoying words, or premature screams of pain? Looks like they left everything at once all wide open for your bones to dry as future linkage chain to their ancestry ghosts. I wonder would they dress in black robes, tell me, ha, you cannot as they broke your jaw with a pear of anguish, meaning respect; you must have braved the torturing with some good foul words! If Juan would not have started playing ragtime girl by doing again a freaking runner, I would at least have somebody to relief you from the misery. Sorry, killing is not my thing. What about you…? Let me wrap up your Henkersmahlzeit*, a doobie* of which I shall blow the smoke in to your smashed pumpkin; it will be the best and most enjoyable event happening in the remainder of your dismal existence! As your good night story I shall tell you about the adventure of a greedy gonad face, who just like you wanted to steal what was not theirs, desiring something which belonged to the aristocracy and not the proletariat, enjoying getting drunk on power while never have learned values thanks to being born in to a social circle lost of humbleness. Yes, you knew another man bearing the exact same inscriptions and albeit knowing his history you did not change. Inhale my friend, inhale, you need it, as those who should be interested in you are not. Like dogs they vanished with the tail between their legs. These kids have won the lottery of evil, and hell they exercising coolness in dealing with the win! Inhale, inhale my friend, your story's ending might be of greater tragedy than the traitor's of Sodom and Gomorrah, but no violins will strike melancholic shrilling accolades for you! Your only hope is to pray for godly mercy, whereby you might want to start collecting compassion promoting discount coupons! Insh'allah, may your tourist guide through inferno's gates allow you have an ice cream, even if it is a stinking Durian fruit popsicle! Au-revoir and I shall now take what is not mine, neither yours and is a more to be respected deity for this cesspool."

And so Shoetef removes himself from standing over Chongstar to fetch the found crow bar left in the corner of the wooden shack. On return he locates himself behind the lost soul, looks down on to a nervous left eye seeking some holding hope to the dire situation. A hardened secretion filled flickering eye surrounded by ripped off body tissue observing Shoetef's investigations towards finding a suitable gap to stick the shorter snake tongue looking tool in an available crevice. Here he goes with a bone cracking sound merging in with a victim's thumping kick and a final thrush to dismantle the gem of the partially, but insufficiently broken skull socket where it was rammed above the nose bridge as a myth reproducing third eye.

Day 76

The luggage is quickly disposed in Residence Veronique Christine; located just 2 kilometers down the road of Léon-Mba International *Airport*. *A few minutes later Shoetef is sitting in a taxi eagerly for some late nightlife action and with a second beer in his hands donated by the lovely accommodation manager. He is less than being 30 minutes in the country and already paddling out to surf an urban barrel! The watch is ticking a few minutes past midnight and the nearby sought adventure destination, the Yoko sports bar is as alive as a dodo. The bewildered taxi driver well in knowledge that there is no party happening looks together with his friend to the back sitting exotic passenger, asking straight and bluntly what he actually is desiring. The responding night owl's appetite chiming rhyme comes swiftly including lesser elegant hand gestures: Bière, bang et peut-être quelques seins!? The morning is a bit too early for diesel, dust and diamonds, but the two locals are in a harvesting roaming mood. The decision is to introduce the guest to a back yard neighborhood beyond the northern city limits and its fried chicken shack at the airport to where make shift houses encroach in to Akanda National Park's swamps. A small stretch of open air bars is inviting enough for the Congo bashing viking's mind to be sweet talked in to a rest stop, "time to lose you virginity on Regab!" However after a few sips of piss he realizes the place replicates a gremlin hunting ground, even deprived of that one transvestite monster in a wedding dress, so a quick, dirty and get ready choice of roadies is conducted. As next they venture out in to the deeper spheres of an area where economic growth benefits are making a detour. Good ten minutes later they arrive at a shack located on a small ridge, built on wooden pylons, with a secured door consisting of more durable material than the surrounding wall. Next step is to apply a special knocking code followed by detailing their visiting purpose. For Shoetef the words are not to comprehend, The door opens exposing two of the tour guide's brothers sitting behind an "oh glory hashapooya" mountain of dried green foliage reaching all the way to the ceiling!*

Libreville never sleeps, never dries up and never stops smoking its shit. The casinos remain open, the birds on the boulevard keep kicking up their heels until sun rise and well you can even end a shindig in the residence of the former president; Omar Bongo Ondimba keeping in mind his slogan, "si present si vivant".

Here breakfast takes a special role when commencing another day with the living. Shoetef decides to put up the feet on the former beloved leader of 42 years' old table while grabbing the red phone and dialing its hot line number, "will this lead him back to Epiney?" It is not connecting. Not even the king toad of the froggy pond who keeps half of Africa economically strangled is keen to answer! Salaude! "What about ….? No? Can I at least get a tee*?"*

Day 77

- Bonjour, may I take place next to you?
- Now I am gob smacked! Last time forgot to ask you to play some Entebbe blues.
- Good to know that your lousy t-shirt is not reflecting on your mental capabilities!
- Alright it is not my forehead but my meat thermometer which gets feverish readings! Bygone healing, please.
- Forget the past. Evil is like a pig wearing lip stick. The real deal is your secretly maneuvering friends successfully gained a fellowship of over 200 million minions which needed digestion. One would argue what happened in Uganda stays in Uganda, but post the mess you escaped from these guys wanted to fine tune official papers there in all glory. However, Africa would not be Africa if not some were too intoxicated in their narrow minded ego's and possibly too scared of the rampage happening… So a rescheduling to Accra came next off the shelf. Of course the curse of Africa being Africa stroke again and the mob desired a more secluded place for their junket. It had to be in a modern designed city capable to accommodate a safe place. Good paved streets and secure private establishments along a promenade with delighting ocean views, but also all possible luxuries for those who officially demonize homosexuality while celebrating success over moral preaching evangelists where further collegiate vowels

can be harvested in ensuring alignment to what they perceive is the appropriate direction for human kind all while they unleash in hiding the beast within them.

- Well, now I feel like an overflowing condom at a Burning Man gig...

- You should, it took years to happen, but then.... Did I mention that they were having a party where reports emerged of one cardinal drinking the beer while shouting hell yeah, followed by excreting the fluids through mouth and nose, back to continuing shouting to loud death metal "hell yeah" while retaking another sip to then dropping it all together and falling back on to his ass where some drug pumped up whores have to lift him up? Must attract you!? It is well known in several circles of interest that rogue elements of the Vatican have been involved in the chase aka a petrified version of Lord Sauron and T-800 exoskeleton combined disguising themselves as smartly as curses from the Necronomicon book?

- And what about the opposing players on the snakes and ladder game board?

- Mais oui! They are likely aware, but follow a different strategy of influencing. They tend to leave others touching the hot stove. A classic example was the tragic Indus valley flooding a few years ago where the West paid the bill! And now to a more localized irritation; you!*

- Firstly I stayed away from Lagos! But somehow I remember a blossoming shadow in Dakar nagging me in not so wet dreams as if a corona flourished itself over zealously while strenuously trying to transformation the gentile beauty in to poison, aiming to kill the visiting, starving, nectar addicted and honey eating sun bird.

- I have been a very successful lady without needing any skin flute players and neither is my golden jewelry fake anymore. Fine quality for a fine lady who kicked the shit out of a desolate and bleak run. I have built a small business empire in disguise

through constructing corporations with official European addresses. And some of our clients tend to be hot-dog gunners who bare handed swipe the fried onions off the bun in favor for mayo!

- So for me to collect all the marbles relating to your knowledge, let me show you a picture of a friend taken in Guinea-Bissau...

- Nah, never seen him. Would imagine him having the same bad taste of local men by wearing black pants and shoes with ugly sporting white socks.

- OK, this guy's theory is a 0.99 in the eternity calculation, the link of knowing to avoid the fury of....

- Do not say that name! Ever! And considering my history, I am no ways the 0.99, but admit those thoughts are an ego booster beyond social media group masturbation. Firstly my belief is that there is a striking possibility that inimical favors can craft characters. Further my finding are concluding that it is searching for carriers who are allowed to be consciously bad, but also float on an observing mental level as if the person had a burning halo whereby capable to execute a sixth and seventh sense. Plus knowledge how to direct potential destructive attitudes without causing harm to themselves nor mentally tormenting the nearby while exercising this all openly and good visibly. Like an African statesman, Arabian sheikh son or an influential South American party powder exporter. Or in an Australian context, that one stinking mongrel of a fly which hoovers unhindered underneath the farmer's wide brimmed hat effortless avoiding any punishment from sewn in corks or the wrathful hand!

- Interesting to hear this all on a day where I am seeking a relaxation on the beach at a Pointe Denis' tranquil bar with stunning city views over the bay and what do I get served, a stalker with an appetite to chop me in to fried masala!

- Show me that picture again as... Yes, definitely. He might well be that third wheel...?

- Well he is definitely not on the slow choo choo train to Franceville!

- Don't get derailed! By the way here in Gabon the passenger trains have air conditioning. Do you have any pictures of other foes?

- Here are another two lacking any delightful ingredients within a bottle of Djino! One of them is as bad as a cheap ass Ugandan Waragi while the other gives you a cough beyond a dunny roll wrapped up roallie*. Both jungle back water monsters who aged quickly, especially health wise. Hold on to your luck of attraction being an evergreen beauty. You are my dear lost mermaid, who became a sexy mystery by not only lurking drunken moray eels out of their crevices for a hiding by big bad sharkie, but also through the good old tough love approach Asians tend to have on their roe faces, just like an octopus being beaten before it can fulfill its ultimate life's goal of deliciously being curried...*

- Ha!

- What?

- As I thought!

- No Cuckoo Klux Klan defying King Kong Khan in a curry?*

- Stop. Hold off burning the kebab skews in your cynical tandoori oven! The white guy's name is Francois. I first met him in Mauritius. He was once so drunk that his loose tongue spluttered out that he was being held ransom by some political influential doctor, who only emerged in the dark when retrieving him like a father. His articulations were perfect, noble, well beyond your obscene vocabulary! Then recently I see him in Banjul on one of the odd off beach bars along the river's mouth where people wearing business attires congregate. With him I saw your Chinese man too. My summary to your dilemma is you got tricked by all, plus obviously by somebody you are not yet aware off. Seems that your calculations are mathematically based on the irrational square root of a minus number. The

Chinese guy is fairly well known business man, including his undiluted interest in alcohol. Conclusively there must be a more sober master mind existing! A hidden double faced personality? A business buffet cook who can stew up the world's elite while still adding his agenda to spice things up? Anyway, overhearing their discussions the two had in Banjul, their thoughts were to initially use a car followed by changing method of travel, meaning motor biking. Recalling vaguely an issue discussed was that scramblers don't carry spare wheels and maybe that is how they left out the guy believing in the bush drums communicating 0.99!?! Anyway in a more clear picture, Francois was known for connections to officials and had sufficient cash to generously bribe in stile as if it was an ice cream wagon serving a pregnant lady! By the way Lucifer's dried and hardened blood drop was never in Dakar as the authorities are too rigorous in being strenuous in their curiosity. It was harbored for longer than anticipated in Casablanca to allow setting up of false paths, which I could imagine that not even his partner in crime knew off. This approached helped out either way; firstly it kept any rats under control and secondly withholding intelligence meant minimizing unexpected disturbances. Who knows? Who wants to know!?

- However the two die within days, but only after a longer taking stint?

- I have a theory for this too. As I slowly was getting really worried, even got the cravings to steal the thing when and while they stood up to leave while congratulating themselves to a plan, but then remembered that rats are not necessarily stupid. My rational guess was they gained learning to tactically distract the pebble rot by tag teaming!

- That makes sense, the stories align until the derailing in Tamale!

- Or before when the vice in its confusion got a keen interest in finding answers by starting to wipe off the mirror's smoke!?

- And now being merged with the unknown 0.99, real bling bling, pregnant and...?

- According to my female instincts there is witch hunt on you as sure as this continent's next round of starvation! From the start your slim body harboring a control center with razor sharp cutting attitude attracted me and somehow the conscious sun rose early of you not actually pro-actively hunting evil down, but its searching of a may I say tasty, cloudy pale ale as its representative to make both happily ever after stoned. And dare may I say you have an unpolished boner with a marrow of resilience!

- Time to wipe off those onions by a shot of mayo!?

Day 78

The night contained a Sanji in need of counseling making fertilization her secondary need. Her stories are long winded, complex with all the behind scenes politics and seemingly being able to maneuver towards the least evil Monopoly players; banks and private funds as targeted income sources. "And what about your planned children..?". Albeit her invigorating to call quits, it seems that she too is captured in greed's quick sand and slowly but surely slipping up to her neck in it. With the upcoming wee hours the serenade talking interruptions are getting a drag and Shoetef decides to do a runner, past the line of whores along the coast line to his apartment where a good humored guard is approachable for dishing out some appreciated silly words. Like many in this trade he too is a good source of knowledge and working in the international airport's vicinity information relating to a low key escape is gained. The resurrected, revitalized or not yet money siphoned off national airline Afrijet departs from a separate terminal whereby only using small planes and thus operates close to incognito.

The electricity is giving itself an early siesta break and thus after a lengthy bath in his own precipitation by walking along the Boulevard Triomphal. Thanks to the tropic's hot midday sun and humidity a physically demanding exercise.

But still better than that confusing post coital ear bashing. The lunch consists of grilled fish and fried banana is enjoyed at a tin shed behind the parliament building. As next he is desiring for a cool off on the beach where sea breeze can give that extra gram of spice to an afternoon session of absolute prime bumming. The path to there is along a polluted stream separating a poor neighborhood with the country's national assembly, followed by the Hotel de Ville and buildings representing French interests. An easy accomplishment of walking and day dreaming to a fill stomach with assistance of being sleep deprived. His arms are happily dangling under the sun until being wolf whistled by two sisters who both are well on their way to happy lands. The leisurely drinking activity is being held at an illegal shed purely serving the purpose of serving the purpose! After ordering a round of beers, hardly capable to enjoy his first shlucking* the prettier of the two grabs him for some passionate pashing*; a slim girl in midst her twenties, bright laugh stretching for miles on her petite cheeks and decorating long beaded dread locks covering her biggest asset of value. Her bum was formed to a sizing and round shape meeting any man's dream of THE perfect ASS. She knew tit and she adored it! As still keen for the beach, he orders a taxi to shift the afternoon session to the Tropicana beach bar, where in dusk light all three are running up and down the beach nude. The girls are needing to continuously pee, so Eve's costume comes in handy, plus sand is better than a mosquito infested drop hole. With afternoon making a farewell with a gorgeous sun set it is time to remove themselves from the lime light. Bypassing further details of home coming the six marinated chops continue with kinky threesome brushing under the shower, whereby the younger sister takes up the liking of voyeurism; all eyes concentrated on her sister… Even when mum inquires of their whereabouts…

Day 79.1 – The Shoetefic Verses For Her

May your dream prince come riding high on a horse; goddess Fortuna be in you favor, opening the path of course and helping to pass the forest trees offering fruits as waiver.

May the love you desire be young, grand and handsome; in mornings eating a peach,

nourishing a body to succumb and charmingly sun set walking with you on a beach.

May your heart's hostage offer comforting wealth; manicure, pedicure you name it all,

children parading without stealth and as climax social news making you a famous ball.

But if you miss the early start by ample thinking; you deprive yourself of potential fun,

conservatism is no pledge for white wedding and a post divorce root beats fate of a nun.

Use your pussy wisely, but be not stingy as spring lamb times end and men sober up!

Day 79.2 - The Shoetefic Verses For Him

When a man shares with his girl a brew, the best is to do it leisurely sexy. When a man shares the magical transformation juice with another hexy*, threesome dreams come true.

When a man shares with his lady a smoke, the best is to do it in the nude. When he simultaneously shares the spice with a second cute, then she too will partake in a joke.

When a man shares other drugs, the best is to ensure a good surrounding vibe. When a man shares it with another subscribe, good chances exist to chill and view wrestling hugs.

But when a man shares boredom, the best is to do it at home if front of the teli. When he falsely openly declares his bedroom as a whoredom, the surprise surpasses a nasty belly.

Keep looking. Keep moving. Keep jesting. But stick to basics and be good at cooking!

Day 79.3 – The Shoetefic Straight Times

Arguably there are some heterosexual tools out there who too should have married their toasters!

Day 777 Dreamliner

Imagine a safe haven with towns decorating fading away colonial buildings aligning to cobbled stoned streets which also entertain beyond palm trees a grandiose masonry presidential palace behind a row of typical red-green-yellow-black colored African national flags, an opposing freshly restored cathedral where behind a mountain stream discharges its waters in to a nicely ellipse shaped bay. Its final path is squeezed in a narrow channel passing derelict structures of the former master's quarters, stores, postal services, shops serving great coffee to tranquil ocean views. Beyond the main settlement palm tree fringed white sand beaches inherit the scenery including steep dropping mountain hugging jungle whereby some peaks poke out with cliffs and wind exposed fishermen wooden houses on stilts. Catholic at heart with all the saints celebrating colorful days including carnival's frivolity, where friendly people might be poor, but never too proud to share home brewed palm wine. It is an island charmingly enjoying itself away from any major cross roads, preserving a health of innocence as international credit cards are neither accepted, preventing its society a fall in to a greed trap of dubious figures who lure at neighboring less luscious shores. A place between neglect of historical achievements and defying modernity with potential as a paradise too chilled out to draw in mean spirits. Welcome to Sao Tome! It is a saudade* place where águas passadas, não movem moinhos* seeking apaixonar com o gostoso príncipe* to heal its mágoa* with beijinhos*.

The first few days are nicely occupied with site visits to Trinidad, the Rocas of Agostinho and Monet Cafe, showering in a rain drench at the Cascatas da Sao Nicolao followed by chilling out on Lagoa Azul. Plus on a tangent venturing out for an inquisitive visit to the Pantufo neighborhood to meet some girls who are as per local's told legends keen in meeting white boys as future husbands. The day's afternoons conclude at the O Pirata bar with a menu containing some pickled lime infused coconut condiment over fat juicy shucked clams.

Due to the island nation's small size a morning spliff on the roof top of the National Museum is a nice way to catch from an unofficial guide a free barbecue invitation. The event takes place next to a corroding airplane above Praia Nazare. It is all about buzios*, the guests cannot get enough of them. However also small fish are grilled making the diet a bit more colorful. But the brilliant tones start to shine when the two head to Parque Popular to meet a couple running a bar allowing the consumption of copious amounts of pot. Plus she is dead drop gorgeous proving there are hidden island treasures still existing. While the big plaza offers an opportunity for local hotties to show off their goodies, it is still low key. Everybody knows everybody and the church messes are not necessarily fully contained to passionate singing of lord praising songs. Each evening at night crowds congregate to a designated club, either Kizomba, Pico Mocambo, Dolores or for tonight Africana. The ride to the steamy dance hall along a small unlit road traversing a neighborhood which can be intimidating as there is just not much happening nor much available in this neck of the woods. Looking at the hot intertwining dancing inside Shoetef decides to first enjoy another island spliff as topping up of rocket fuel for his heat-seeking moisture missile. He then proceeds in asking the most beautiful island blossom to accompany him for some hot Afro-Latino body gluing moves. The surprising determined steps from this rare visitor is making her heart transform in to wobbly gelatin. The hot and horny dancing is amalgamating body juices; skin pores touching each others, arm hairs softly prickling each other, her knees softening up allowing his right leg to place itself between, leading her to firm pirouettes whereby artfully changing the holding hand to allow for closer swinging mingling. The free hand is placed on her slim belly and his breath is tingling her finite neck back hairs. The shared passionate performance is making them forgetting that the actual party is happening on the street between vendors selling home burnt liquor and charcoal roasting stray gone animals. The two are a couple where the skin color variation could not be bigger; him a white pale conquistador happiness smiling beacon with eyes shining fluorescent blue in to the disco light and she proudly framing pure Nubian ebony beauty where the passing by strobe light is swallowed as if no other particles are allowed in her vicinity. The pictures taken at wrong angling light make him look brighter than the sun light capturing his silhouette like a halo's radiance while for her the depiction renders a spectator an idea of how a female grim reaper embossing white teeth scintillation could look alike.

The following day post the hotel mattress soaking up the last chapter of passion, their loving hearts direct them towards the south-eastern coast by a surprisingly local roads knowledgeable taxi driver. Just this time Sod's law determines him being her uncle! "What?" With a small bribe his rima oris changes to an approving smile. The two have now permission to hug, kiss and play on the back seat while winding along the coast towards Micondo where an old colonial farm has been partially restored to previous glory. A two story white painted house is chosen as accommodation. Their room comprises high ceilings where an attached fan represents the only potential romance interfering source. "Damn, where are the palm leaf waving Egyptians when you need them!?". The hotel is near a small town market and ideal closely located to a nearby small isolated beach for pleasuring afternoons. Plenty of wood available, not only the trunk in his bathing shorts.

After some relaxing festive days a decision is chiseled in stone to conduct a day trip beyond the limits of the jungle surrounding a massive stone cock as if the trees are its pubes: Pico Cao Grande aka a virgin yet to be conquered by a porn star's well worn out fuck pot! The pure observance of the massive phallus is getting both again lusting for more frivolous makings beyond what an Apartheid supporter's mind can accept. But love does lead to stupidity and thus they fall prey to the first boat operator and his high price. At least he is ferrying the two over smoothly making the most of the ocean breeze being squeezed through the separating channel. He sails to a back side secluded beach of Ilheu de Rolas where they quickly undress and passionately release the stored up energy. Him lying on the sand, she riding, waves crushing over the copulating genitals offering a welcoming touch of coolness; until a jealous sand fly bites his bum! As next the adventurer curiosity possess them. They walk towards the nearest located building and in to the surrounding gardens where seeing their presence a plethora of dark skinned yellow belly cobra-petra snakes vanish in to dense thick grass. The resort itself is empty whereby Shoetef notices a well maintained pool harboring clear turquoise water reflecting blue colors from its tiny mosaic tiles lining the base. They pass a row of red-purple flowers, then hibiscus bushes waving slender to the meager touch of the gust breaking forest emerging winds and make a left turn, grabbing a few sap sap fruits to ease the walk up the hill. All in perfect harmony which receives only a very minor disruption of a local rastafari selling some dope. And while bearing the feelings of kissing planet's rear, they actually are standing in its human defined center. The erected stone monument over looks the ocean waters towards Porto Alegre, the town which can claim of representing civilization on the confluence of the equator and the zero meridian. They are embracing each other as if an imminent bonding loss awaits. He is feeling like the wood legged sailing Captain Lord of Prime Beef Whistle from Greenwich hemp lands meeting the horizontal equinoctial gate keeping Amazonian matron keen on turning his passion from lonely darkness in to bright day where her kisses reflect warming sun rays. An engaging commitment is made that they will always be together which later is honorably celebrated with a private beach lunch; and of course two cold Rosema long necks to cheer upon. The momentary narrative is pure surrealism of love celebration in front of rocky small ocean pools with blow holes before reaching final terrain grounds. The waves are promoting gentle bubbling in similarity to whirl pools, him sucking the entire environment in to a vortex with her sitting on his knees while observing underneath the palm trees the smell of morning's catch being grilled, a bliss of an eternal dream…

Max 8 Crash

- Good morning darling, how are you enjoying your morning ride?
- Uhhh, oh, water…? Looks like the Pied Piper has finally hypnotized the fattest rat from her burrows! What did you do with the sweet petal rose with the sweetest honey soaked bud where finally an innocent humming bee found its addictive source of content soul buzzing?!?!

- Damn! I got you the Saharan compass to find me and not vice versa! But looks like your cone shell can overmaster it with its devious killer spirit! Damn you!

- No, no, no, just keep on lovingly greasing my Excalibur with your tender fluffy hair!

- You like it? I let some grow as went to investigate the sickest acts on the planet and the only one which somehow is acceptable for me to perform is charizarding. You are now coming home to me baby, so lets do it sicko!*

- Really? For that you drugged and kidnapped me? Would it have been possible to share…?

- I am sorry, but the only thing I will be sharing with you is the stone! I am yours and you are mine. End of story. I am also happy to report that Juan is stored away in a suitable pantry; in an Equatorial Guinean jail together with his dodgy allies. You must have just missed them in Benin. Malabo's chico malo received a tip off of his empire being used as weaponry sales hub without complying to national taxation laws. As a returning accomplishment he ensured that their recent shipment is caught off in Port Harcourt. The relevant authorities' investigations hastily concluded that the freight's purpose was to support the sons of former Biafra fighters aiding their brothers of the Ambazonian independence fighting African People's Liberation Movement. Their outcry escalated in to multi national operation resulting in the arrest of a one armed string pulling Indian slash Mauritian business man at the Hotel Kogo Ocean Resort while attempting to hand over a large amount of cash to his aiding sister, who was waiting on Rio Muni's opposite Cocobeach in Gabon. She too was arrested under protest of declaring herself pregnant.*

- Damn, Aadarsh is still alive! And Sanji, hmmmnnn… I guess with a small luck potion of spare time we should soon be able to party again and this time Juan can invite us to a smashing siesta in South America! Yay, yay, yay!!

- Wait, wait, wait, did you hear me? You Sir belong now to me, the sexy goddess Natalie of whom the future will be shared under the stone's protecting umbrella held by our safety safe keeper…

- Looks like the rising of the sphinx from the ashes? Is there a 2.99? Wait? Who? Does that also mean the damn thing a prehuman civilization carrying asteroid? You know more of the puzzle pieces don't you? Will I rot in nutrition lacking dirt as a leech sucking on any available blood droplets falling through the cracks of an imploding world releasing itself form the out of control breeding humanoid virus?

- Yes, yes and what ever my dualism counterpart of the Taijitu thinks…*

- I believe in my yo-yo-ing yinyang between my legs… OK, OK, sorry! Just please halt on going towards a nuclear explosion fusion of Chernobyl meeting Fuckoshima exceeding Homer Simpson's best reactor management capabilities. So what's the detail in the ghoul's tale?

- As you now know Juan was close to successfully deprive your tan bananas rekindling and joyous reunification with its treasured chocolate fondue; that is to be clear MEEEE! His personal enemy is being scared as bats shit to touch the stone! Next to his religious upbringing with an anthill demonizing church of Bruce being eaten alive from the greed gave him sorrow. After you spilled fuel on to the already charcoaled souls of Sanji and Aadarsh they too kept distance, but still desiring it deeply in their hearts.

- Estar perplexo!

- I have a shared tragedy with them from a place near the Wouri River where shrimps roam as ghosts whereby they most likely are the only cannibals to gift an entire country a name!

- But I met their dad…? He did limp, but that could he is supernatural…? Something is too fishy to even be oyster sauce!

- Twisted twins my dear. And who knows what they were up to in Cameroon with those ghost shrimps desiring fresh meat over

decaying algae! Siblings can confuse people, so why not cause chaos for a conscious piece of shit? The next dot point is answered via the detour that influential Chinese business associations are always seeking to recruit Blue Lanterns comprising suitable historical records and who can prove themselves worthy to rise up to 49er status. The real good ones progress further to "Red Pole" mastery title and beyond to the ultimate enforcing authority of the Dragon Head. With defeating his dad's failure of possession accomplishment Chongstar could have risen from the ashes to Africa's economic King Kong Uno capable to go men-bung against all competing vanguards, order clean uncover executions to those threatening and arrange a worse * fate for anyone mocking him.*

- Me?

- Remember Chiná has developed itself towards modernization whereby developing a wider founded middle class resulting in domestic cheap labor force vanishing. New sources have to be mined whereby not forgetting that their arch enemies have been more or less everywhere beforehand, including Africa. Europe had control of over 90% while India spread its influence along the Indian Ocean foreshores. After Europeans commenced depriving help due to diverging human rights evaluations and Indian families remaining isolated among themselves, Chinese entrepreneurs reassessed the continent's developing potential resulting in start of anonymous operations. The place to celebrate the ribbon cutting too was well designed to mingle tactical planning with concealed hedonistic activities: South Africa's Sun City! Keeping his history in mind this place daringly attracted him in to heavy drinking which also would have served nicely to regain some respect. On the funny side one can imagine that his abducted carbon hostage would have attempted to swing its molecules heavy enough to disgustingly spew graphite over him for his nonequivalent attempt to participate in the evolutionary alpha race!

- Well it did do a nasty retaliation. To finalize this all, anymore gore scheduled? Any revengeful thoughts from, huh, Epiney?

- Ha! Nope. Instead he is waiting for you; in Luanda!

- No ways! Por que eu?*

- Nobody wants you back home! You cannot even fly out from here without being arrested, other than of course to safe haven Angola. And stuffing your sexy gut with bolo natal cake over the past days is now out and over too! The omen is indicating an upcoming major world change whereby opening the gates of rites to Aquarius. A new generation of global strategists are directing current risk adverse leaders towards supporting their concentration in building mole holes in to a mountains while a new epochal manifestation of white sheep herding can suavely be introduced. These new age apostles have roosted and laid infectious eggs. While you can have them hard boiled, the majority will have to accept them scrambled as poached breaches the common egodotcomnism founded sensitive gene wiring!*

- Oh mercy to the savior of the troglodytes. I guess it is the punishment those hatching eggs have as ungrateful action that they did not end as omelets filled with stinking cheese! But why didn't I get fried up by the paragon?

- Because you were born in Africa as a blond blue eye child defeating some of nature's physics and human psychical behaviors which made the stone retrace your first life's screams on a morning after several days of continuous rain tears falling on to barren earth seeking relief from ground goring down pours!

He retrieves the diamond. Her eyes start glittering in the matching colors exposing her soul as an energy field on a concoction of star dust steroids and galactic cocaine infused transcendental desecrating high voltage brewed caffeine excreting continuum is suddenly gifted with mellow female voice chords; "There is fortune for the perceived unfortunate, like our hidden luck at the far end of humanity's cotangent avoiding destructive behaviors done by common over-zealous self loathing wisdom rewriting preachers; who like those vitiated souls in this story will never understand that the luminous meteorite's distinct character was bred on early rejection by the weather where nobody including the grave founders could affirmatively acknowledge its existence of striking beauty beyond a breakfast serve of Asian greens with a touch of salt, sweetish soy sauce melange with mildly throat burning chili flakes; yes indeed it was a Gory Glory Morning!"

14 THE BEGINNING

Mia Charlotte Banter – Hey girls, please excuse me for the ladies. I've surely have now cracked the seal and it looks like the Seybrew will give my first fanny tickle of the day!

Mary Cheng – Never thought that such a disgusting low life can thread a string through the needle hole and sew us together. My mother,…

Admiral Suslaparova – You mean your tiger mother…!?

Mary Cheng – Yes. May god have mercy. Lived all her life in Singapore, never touched anything beyond her beloved husband who if not so close to my dear heart fell rather silly wise as a victim of our national army.

Admiral Suslaparova – I guess meaning not in a war. And the old girl?

Mary Cheng – Her passing too was unnecessary. In a rich country like ours it was this nonsense stuff which governments failed including ours. The idiots were more keen of giving themselves a social etiquette martyr stamp rather than objectively evaluating the global situation. They tried to cushion off their own cubby houses while throwing poisonous darts at each other, controlling the media as means to prevent any questioning of their irrational decisions while failing on implementing adequate treatment response plans. The dogs were shown the master by an organic minuscule, which gave them bark but not bite worthy digestive heart burning. They kept to the kennels pulling the tails in. Walking away from the outside roaming wolf packs while savaging the pups, the weak and those fed with finest Pedigree Pal. Any treats coming from the labs were eagerly and wildly fought over whereby the strongest mongrel then chewed it up as it was his god given toy. Like typical mutts incapable of doing mathematics, therefore just like wild animals went on to shut down hospital services for the needy, while smoking mirrors with subjective derived numerical game plays to force feed through the media's percutaneous endoscopic gastrostomy tube. I was still young, but was planted the seed to work hard. Success can defeat old habits! Society was imminent ready for this transformation and really striving to find the key to unlock humanity's biggest barrier of collective conscious pain.

Admiral Suslaparova – Those are sour words containing a young girls' hidden pain and now finally allowed to be truthfully liberated. Remember you would not be here without a mind, soul and heart of unbreakable steel. So, keep up the self esteem as we girls are stronger than men. They laugh at us because we like to take time to make ourselves pretty. They denounce the horrors of pregnancy. They disrespect us by continuously finding new places, means, interests to accommodate their filthy ball scratching gender segregation efforts. I hate them with passion.

*Mary Cheng – Oh my dear, you are not wrong, but still wrong. I have been desiring to find the right "manly" partner, but many of our guys are so soft; parent's precious little neutered jewels. They even get freaking manicures, vacation paid in Berlin, free university in Massachusetts and when together in the evenings they are out eating tofu burgers with vegan mayonnaise while politely drinking green tea to avoid slurping and burping. Being homo looks cool. They believe the chances of success are done by maintaining a whoring free apomictic tissue spoiling life stile. Ultimately the dream is to be gay as it is perceived by our society like winning the jackpot. I wish we could temporarily at least swap our men out... *sigh**

Admiral Suslaparova – Believe me, the ones we have are not those bear wrestling gods of the acropolis. Their testosterone ends up quickly diluted in fire water! And believe me, would go out with any "Hello Kitty" merchandise wearing K-pop flopping flapping fan star over an aggressive beer belly equipped unshaven Cossack gorilla!

Mary Cheng – I forgot that your part of our union is political influencing. Must admit you have perfected the mix between oligarchy, soviet prescription and double dipping between spying agency interests or more notional to our surrounding of icy cocktail, beach fringing palm trees while fending off hungry sharks. But I wonder what worth you put against a man, none?

Admiral Suslaparova – Must admit that this island allows for luxury in midst of a lovely exotic surrounding. The hotels do accommodate for fine ladies. Just some local attitudes align with laziness which can be seen; and smelled. The men here neither shower or change clothes daily, all while beholding themselves as studs. One could say home sweet home, just in the tropics!

Mia Charlotte Banter – Hey girls, talking about boys!? Here comes the handsome waiter. Baffling, beaming, bodacious, brilliant, big and black, yeeeaaahhhhaaa!!

Mary Cheng – Uuuuuhhhh, don't like black, keep him at bay!

Admiral Suslaparova – Camper trailer trash!

Mia Charlotte Banter – Stop bitching you virgin. And you butch too! We are here to celebrate. Give me a free second to..., come here boy and serve!

Mary Cheng – Here is the data file.

Admiral Suslaparova – Hide it! Be careful as eyes are watching us. Hope you did not forget our agreement to delete anything and everything else. Knowledge is dangerous. Ultimately it can trigger unfavorable social break down as never seen in evolution. Albeit hating men, they still have physical potentials to harvest. Just maintain them stupid. What do you know about freckle face?

Mary Cheng – Good point, techniques are continuously getting smarter applied in the data ocean. I know our partner through some dormitory sharing.

Admiral Suslaparova – And I bet you did not participate on beer bong parties!? She must have met her future money machinery there.

Mary Cheng – No it was seemingly her grannie or grandgran, but guess too breading like bunnies. Anyway she was on some sort of a girls night out and #smirk# the apple did not fall far from the tree. She met this depressed guy coming back from an adventure trying to figure out his tactics towards reintegrating with normal life. He left the following morning, but forgot to take some kind of lottery ticket with him. And bang from there on she was seemingly riding a cable car up the mountain of happiness. By the way it was Mia's slutty idea to contact you through a dating site aiming to find an online bot who was slowly getting bored with the same sales tactics, albeit being paid nicely. Her instinct told her that there must be a held back galloping destitute thoroughbred existing. We first tried as a middle aged wealthy man and quickly got to know your cold personality of no money no honey. Then we ventured with the alternative of alternative.

Admiral Suslaparova – Hmmmnn, don't tell me more. Oh garcon, thank you very much. The tea is for her and the Seybrew, well our happy daisy flower is blossoming and letting lose of her nectar somewhere nearby!

Mary Cheng – Why are you smiling so equivalently enchanting...?

Admiral Suslaparova – What is in my drink?

Mary Cheng – Please stop smiling like a Cheshire cat!

Admiral Suslaparova – All you so called worldly educated are untrustworthy. It does matter if your mother's have spat you out white, black, blue or green; dick, vagina or a toaster between the legs! Hey, hey, hey hands up here!

Mary Cheng – Woah, you don't really think that this isolated place would....

Admiral Suslaparova – Just keep calm or the barrel here ends up as your life's ultimate memory. You should know not to fuck around with strong ladies like me! And why are you erratically pointing in that direction? Stop it.

Mary Cheng – Oh help, Mia is just about to do... Go! Get her! Catch her!

Admiral Suslaparova – Aaaahh damn.... Got here.

Mary Cheng – Are you alright my love? You only had beer? Or were you smoking some of yesterdays pot? Come here, you need to take it easy on yourself. Plus the sun gets you fair skinned girls too.

Mia Charlotte Banter – Sun. Ray! Sun. Ray? Is there a Ray for me today?

Mary Cheng – Albeit being such a lovely place with old English colonial history, pubs serving what you are used to; this is still Africa love. You saw that poor disfigured girl hiding in the kitchen. Come I'll take you back to the hotel room. Can you help please?

Admiral Suslaparova – OK, do not worry with you meagerly slim petite arms. I am strong enough to carry her alone. You check out...

Mary Cheng – Or let the waiter help....? The waiter....? And where is my data file?

15 FINAL NOTE

The drink was not spiked. It was cleared by an observant one-armed bandit.

16 APPENDIX – TRANSLATION AND INTERPRETATION

5 o'clock shadow = Unshaven

A mão livre mimada procurando = The free spoiled seeking hand

Abonsam = Evil spirit home to West Africa

Acanthosis Nigricans = Brown neck, usually comes from insulin resistance which again could be caused by high alcohol consumption

Agent 99 = Barbara Feldon acting as the female counterpart in the 1960s sitcom Get Smart equipped with traits above her boobs (not sure if all men know that there is territory above this territorial line)

Águas passadas, não movem moinhos = Water under the bridge does not make the mill run

Ahora querido amigo. Tranquilo con tuya idioma phrases. = My dear friend take it easy with your language

Al'ama = Blindness

Albtraum = Nightmare

All-drunken Synod of Fools and Jesters = Czar Peter the Great's party club mocking religion

Allez allez vive la vivir, nous demarrons spectaculaire = Go, go, live life, we are taking off spectacularly!

Alors, nous prenons des croissants et café du lait! Le pain ici est plus bien comme le moelleux à moitié cuit carton ghanéen! = Let us just have a nice French basic breakfast rather than English shit, meaning poor coffee like the watery crap Australians drink and toast bread which is as romantic like a broken tooth pick containing some awkward subject matter sticking to it.

Amazighens = Berbers

Anciblotto = The Australian take on the fairy tale of the King of Provino by Giovanni Francesco Straparola!

Ankle biter = Children

Anima mea = A person's soul

Apaixonar com o gostoso príncipe = Falling in love with the right prince

Arabian saddle = A guy resting on a girl, doing 69 position while resting his balls in her eye sockets

Ars talking = Clatter farting

Arschlecker = Ass licker finding it lekker*

Arvo = Afternoon, what else you tumble weed stoner!

Asphalt diving = When a piss head loses his balance and falls head front over on to the tarmac or foot path or anything harder than poking and protruding silicon nipples

Auf nimmer wiedersehen = Not to see you ever ever bloody ever again, most likely to say to an ugly dickwad

Ausziehen Schlampe = Get your gear (clothes) off slut

Avarifeaces = Money hungry scum

Avec un drôle ami = Next best is to share some man love when the wife is on the rags and screaming her wobbly ass off at you for no obvious reason

Avoirdupussies = Avoirdupois means goods of weight

Ba'idi = Foreigner in Amharic

Babar's Kingdom = Fictional elephant with fictional smart elephants in a fictional, you guessed it!! Lucky you just might have 2 IQ points more than writer's toilet seat! Which is 4 points more than a squatter dunny*, however you can gain 6 points back on your congenital deficiency savings account by removing the seat at your home, using and marketing it as means of getting your knees quicker physically stronger...

Babbling = Clatter farting

Baby shower = Man jam, sometimes good to retain a girl's face smooth and milky textured skin

Bag of fruit = Business suit bag of fruit

Bagdrag = Like a tea bag being dipped in to a cup of tea, just a scrotum in someone's face

Bahen-ke-land = Your sister's penis

Bakshish = Tip

Balaenoptera musculuses = blue whales, one large freaking animal and the world's fattest creature too, you do not want to know how many French fries it can eat, or does it eat frogs* like chips?

Ballyhooed = Noisy, sensational, roaring, obnoxious bullshitting around

Baloney pony = Lap rocket

Barnie = Disagreement, fight

Basura = Trash

BCF = Australian warehouse targeting male customer with boating, camping and fishing

Beating around the bush = Not telling the truth

Beef twinkie = Ox's slasher

Beijinhos = Many kisses, mainly on the cheek

Bevie = Drink, beverage

Bhairo Baba = A deity in form of a dog

Bhoot-ne-kaa = Son of a witch

Bian tai = Perverted

Bière, bang et peut-être quelques seins!? = Beer, bong and then maybe some boobs?!

Big wad = Ejaculation

Bikey = Order disobeying guys taking the liking to ride motor bikes, usually in leather gear advertising their gang's logo

Bikkies – Biscuits or bluntly said drug pills

Billabong = Pub for humans, water hole for anybody who does not wear thongs

Blablablant = Blantyre, Malawi's commercial center and as usual in Africa the country's epicenter of bartering

Black stump = Far beyond, remote

Blerrie boudkapping poeskak = Bloody anus chopper full of vagina shit

Blotto = Blind drunk

Bludging blunder = Unnecessary, useless mistake

Blue healer = Trusted anally persisting Australian dog, just like copperoos

Blue heeler = 10 Australian dollar note

Blue waffle = Fictional sexually transmitted disease discoloring and disfiguring a vagina, do not try to google it!

Boa menina = Good girl

Boa noite mulher de príncipe = Good night princess

Bobotie = Sweet tasting mince meat pie, needs some fear challenge for most beef snag poisoned down under brains

Boerewors = Safa sausage which beats any day a $2 Bunnings Warehouse beef snag, in taste that is not the likelihood that a fruit pulp brain slipping out on the accompanying onions

Bog roll = Dunny tissue

Bogans = Urban dwelling red necks who replace their love of game meat for nurturing killer dogs while still amusingly are as fashionable, fat and have a healthy dietary intake like the cookie monster, they usually live in outer metropolitan suburbs and while not mistreating wife, kids or anything else breathing tend to like playing games involving cheap alcohol and/or even cheaper drugs supplied from a friend's backyard laboratory which as such as not yet exploded unlike a police commissioner's son in Western Australia

Boganville = Where the above live and breed, shit and not shave in their own Racoon City type environment

Bolo de mel = (Portugues) honey cake

Bomb chuckers = Broad slang word for Arabs as some do have a jihadi, fatwa or Osama fetish driven passion to kill people through this method, sometimes combined with a martyr urge full in faith that their low IQ equipped mother still remains belief of their childish innocents and on hope that heaven will give them a big fat X-Mas present cake where 70 plus virgins jump out with eagerness to sexually satisfy them, however the reality is more likely a goats sucks up their ashes and poops them out in some rocky outcrop where the next desert wind wipes the shit under the dunes like a housewife sweeping up ant poo under the carpet, while in hell they are gang raped by all the animals which they cut their throats open as halal celebration

Bonheur = Happiness

Bonjour mon amour, ca va? = Good morning my darling, how are you?

Bonjour a la ambassade de Suisse. Nous sommes fermer. Normalement c'est nest pas possible de faire entre en apres-midi. = Welcome to the embassy which is usually closed in the afternoons.

Bonkers = Going crazy, like 200 miles per hour on the overtaking lane, worse
    than the Benny Hill in his best year's chasing topless girls through English
    parks containing manicured lawn

Boogalahs = Testicles

Bottl-o = Bottle shop or for the lucky ones who do not have to bother this place is
    a specific niche of heaven in many countries where grog can be purchased
    or in some cases where feral bogans, red necks, indigenous people and
    other sorts of doll bludgers* obtain the holy juice and run quickly away…

Bon amies = Good friends, in this context corrupted interest groups

Boner = Hard, stiff little man searching for his time of attention

Bongo bongo = Origin in Swahili, wildly seen as a pejorative term, but for some
    Finns an adventurous place with the mythological name of Persläpimaat

Boofhead = A person having an IQ lower than a dunny seat

Borborygmooses = The noise of fluids and gas going through the intestines, just
    decorating an ugly moose face

Bosbefok brak = Crazy mongrel

Boswellox = Shit

Bourgeoise rêver d'ânes de campagne = Snobby upper class dreaming country
    donkeys

Box = Vagina

Bratwuerstle = German sausage, written in Bavarian to highlight the fact of
    Hubert having a small grown Adolf in his pants

Brekkie = Breakfast

Brown eye = Anus

Bubbly = Sparkling wine, bogan champagne, female liberating juice, sweet
    fermented grapes being farted up on as often the stuff contains traces of
    sulphite

Buck aka Buckaroonies = Dollars, $$$

Buckie = Ute

Buckley's chance = Australia's own Robinson Cruiser who escaped as convict on
    was found decades later

Budgie smuggler = Man's bathers, yes those tight ones where you can see the
    outlining of his disgusting clacker doodle doo…

Bufferbred = Dukawalla*

Bulhond = Bull dog, the reference here is towards the breed being recognized as not only stubborn, but also to be commonly known as stupid

Bull-shit-castle = A company's head office

Bunnings Warehouse = We 10% retarder than a croc shit turd hunter on dexies*!

Buongiorno, siete de onorevole anti revolucionista Cinqueli Francisco de Moderna gran Amici leccare de Gelati con Frutta Salsa de Papelito's Culo?!!* = Good day, you Vatican fagstar; lucking he did not ask if he trimmed the rim and polished away the grim dim of his dark lurking suicide owl further known as his chocolate mousse bowl

Burro = Donkey

Burro do preguicoso caralhos = Fucking lazy idiots

Bush chook = Western Australian beer, Emu Export as there is a bird on it! Also known as the local wife basher brand

Bush oyster = Nasal mucus, boogie, the delicacy originating from your nose, best tasting when warm and embraced with slimy touch of green goo to ensure maximum bowel flora happiness promoting a favorable digestive environment

Bush pig = Dirty old country bastard with some liking towards making possums his fury girlfriends (hey better than what happen to altar boys!)

Bushie = Marijuana grown wildly outdoors

Buzz killer = On country roads also known as tire biters

Bychit = You alpha animal behaving like a bull in Russian

C-bomb = Cunt

C-Word = Yeah again cunt

Caballo = The horse or more commonly known in South America for cocaine

Caballo antes de armas = Preference to consume cocaine over going to war, which of course is necessary to be have the treat

Cabsavs' - Cabernet-Sauvignon

Cake hole = Where cake usually ends up, in your mouth you fanny deodorant!

Cala te puta enrabar = Shut up you whore

Canaan = The promised land God gave to Abraham

Canot rapide = Speed boat

Carked it = Died

Carrot = Spliff

Carrying on like a pork chop = Being silly

Carton = Slab of piss

Cao, wo tsoa gou zaizis = Piss off idiots, I can fuck both of you under dogs

Cadeaux = Gift

Carbivore = A person who eats too much carbohydrates, that is the reason why many vego bears are actually beyond well shaped

Carking = Dying

Cattle ticks = Catholics, you guys surely did not think you get away verbally unharmed!

Cavatappi = Italian pasta, cork screw, manga girl's pubic hair growth pattern post nuclear explosion exposure

CBD = Cross-eye Breast Disorder, NOT

Ch'afi = Pimp in Amharic, the language of Ethiopia

Cefa = West African Franc compared and on parity to Franc Francais used in Central Africa whereby they are linked to the Euro meaning remain strong against the English speaking countries' currency like the Nigerian Niari which ultimately is leading to those mainly French speaking nation's economic competition disadvantage

Centrelink = Australian welfare agency, church of doll bludgers as some would say

Cerebro = Brain

Charcuterie = French fine delicatessen which is lovingly sliced, shaven, smoked, spiced and delightfully decorated oink oink oink just waiting for a connoisseur to appreciatively devour; leave the fatty pork knuckles to the Germans and the sausage sizzle to the English!

CHAG = Christian Health Association of Ghana

Charizarding = As part of an act for her to be a chameleon in her genital area, you put her pubes on fire and put it out with your jizz while flapping your arms and high pitching some Japanese dragon defeating mange warrior curses

Cheesoes = Cheese chip snack in Australia

Chewbacca = Star War's fur ball

Chi, chi kati = Hi, with an extra pronunciation for chief muzungu's shaven balls to grow again hair (yes this statement is a load of hog fart)

Chibuku = Traditional African beer, usually home made from sorghum malt and corn, in Xhosa also known as Umqombothi

Chico malo = Bad boy

Chien chinoise = Chinese dog

Chiko = Soft barley toffee

Chingar! Chingado! Chingon! = In Spanish, to be roasted to death by coal, be fucked and troublemaker or problem seeking fucker

Choubaguai = Hideous, the ugliness is as loud as thousand decibels!

Choke the chicken = Male masturbation

Chook = Bird, chicken

Choty goty = Beautiful girl

Christco = Disco playing christian music

Chucky = The murdering doll from a horror movie series, but in relation to spewing, puking and throwing up which means all three together is as violent!

Chuff = Smoking weed from a pipe

Chutney tunnel = colon, where the poo peacefully rests before getting itchy escaping feet

Cigis = Fags

Conques = Five in Italian representing that Italians always surface as a group and don't have the pumbu* to navigate the world alone

Clacker doodle doo = A penis that fucks asses

Clack line = Ass crack

Clapperhappy = Rooting around without giving a rats ass about transmitting diseases around like a happy wart here, a happy wart there, a happy wart for Snow White and a mass grave for Winnie Pooh's fury anal cavity

Clatter farting = Talking non-sense, verbal diarrhea

Clicks = Miles, kilometers

CnH2n+1OH = Learn chemistry and you might get to understand the elementary heart and mind of alcohol

Cocked down = So hard fucked that she (or he or any of the remaining 95 aping and gaping genders) cannot get out of bed

Coldies = Cold beers

Como la mas oscura la chocolate, el mejor el gusto = That darker the hash is, the more potent it is

Cómo me encontraste = How did you find me

Con comme une valise sans poignée = As stupid as a suitcase without a handle

Confiture = Jam

Consente erga obedio et propinquos meos aut futue te ipsi! = Consent to obey and comply or go and fuck yourself!

Contiki = Backpacking company for dumb cunts from Australia and the US

Copperoos = Police or an Australian authority driven man jam sucking animal which unfortunately was not on the to be made extinction list of Captain Cook

Cord togs = The sexy bikini bottoms Brazilian girls wear making every man drool and prey merci mercy for their eyes versa the commonly, but should not necessarily be replicated by blokes as it can cause visual cytomegalo retinitis trachoma which ultimately leads to blindness and never ending mental darkness; it took Steve Wonder only once to look up Aretha Franklin's skirt!

Cotton pony = Tampon

Crack the shits = Getting angry

Cranny axe = Dick

Crass = Extreme, hardcore

Cream skimmers = The lovely top scoop of fresh milk where a small layer of cream can be harvested, thus in this context Caucasian do gooders

Creo = Believe, think

Crois moi = Believe me; like believe me I bet you thought and were already excitingly expecting some dirty female genitalia word from the Zebra poop fertilized underground like siilka in Somali, uke in Swahili or isitho sangasese in Zulu!

Crouts = Common slang for Germans, comes from their love of sauerkraut which actually even the biggest Anglo-Saxon actually does not mind as he likes to devour in Salt'n'Vinegar chips, which recognizably is less healthy and promotes the ugly picture of fat half naked girls roaming the beach esplanade at Brighton even in the middle of winter

Crownie = In this context a special close friend who is a half cookie and a half brownie

Coushiere = Relaxed, comfortable, cozy, hygge(ing)

Cubby House = A child's, usually boy's hide, like a tree house or a forest camp

Cuzzy = Cousin

Daarom daher = Come here immediately in Afrikaans

Dag = Lovable dero*

Dagga = Mull

Dags = Shit

Darjeeling = Himalayan black tea

Darius = Persian emperor disliking Galaktoboureko, but full of custard himself

Décolleté = The sacred gardens of Tittihills

Defo! = Definitely

Delalande's coua = Snail eating cuckoo and just like its slimy invertebrate dinner was too slow to get the fuck out of the debauchery ape man's way! Fried chicken was still unknown to sheet wetting dreams...

Denisovan = Archaic human subspecies; You? Me!?

Dénoyauter caillasseur = A stoned stoner with connoisseur attitudes

Derriere = In French the back, but in this context ass

Deroes = Ignorance prerogative souls or just back yard tin shed living hobbits lacking social skills and any other manners, bum scratching flea carrying urban apes

Dexies = The drug they give to AHDH kids to calm down, but to everyone else woo hoo it pumps those red blood cells up to rim licking Saturn's rings

Dick sticker = Budgie smuggler

Dikbek = Grumpy

Dildotronic = A robot dildo operated by somebody foreign

Dill witted drongos = Idiots

Dip stick = Anal bud tongue massaging douche bag

Dirty Sanchez = Stolen from The Aristocrats, swiping your cock in the anal receivers face artistically drawing an upper lip beard aka mustache

Disco stick = Hairy meat puppet sometimes acting like a muppet on cut strings

Discuple = Excuse me, sorry

Do the Harry = Australian prime minister who went missing, either by the commonly thought ripper snipping wave, but in reality betrayed his communist party friends and was abducted by a soviet chartered UFO

Dog art = Shit

Dole = Australian social welfare pay

Donkie kont = Don't be a donkie kont in not understanding this!

Donner = Beat up

Doobies = Marijuana cigarettes

Doosis = Male cunt ball

Doll bludger = A person who is capable to work receiving social welfare payments

Dome = Head

Donger = Modern accommodation in mining camps, basic clean air-conditioned cheap mass produced logs of en-suite bedrooms

Dopkaas = Dick cheese

Dosh = Money, cash, valuables

Doughball = As intelligent like a piece of bread, so basically you are lucky if the person is toilet trained

Draadtrekker = Wanker

Drankhuis = Pub, drinking house

Drinkies = knocking back a few alcoholic juices or better said time to get pissed

Drinking with the flies = Getting on the piss alone

Droëwors = Dried sausage

Dropkick = Fuckwit

Dragon drilling = When a man is treated like a king by a *Xiaojie* in a hair salon of Dongguan, whereby she licks out his ass

Druggies = Drug addicts, in Tamale they were all of the head on weak weed and lingering around the crowded market, bus station, what ever the dump they call in midst of the CBD

Druggoes = Refer to above – and if you are one yourself then to do a fold in through the space in between just like you do with a MAD mag!

Duffer = Fool in Oznitzkish

Duffing = Stealing in Oznitzkish

Dufus = Idiot

Dukawallas = The English brought in South Asians as second class citizens as demographic and commercial buffer, who in Uganda represented a small minority, but with wealth creating jealousy and racism

Dullsville = A place where there is f-all to do like Mogadishu being famous for a vibrant nightlife, Johannesburg's ghettos for racial peace or Moroni for its fans' pulsing cricket stadium

Dunny = Toilet, loo, thunder box, shit house, the place where a mysterious monster hides to scare shitty annoying yelpers (kids)

(Go) Dutch = Go separate, usually said at a bar by a stingy bastard of a so called mate

Dutchie = Marijuana cigarette

Dwankie == Lame, uncool

Eclaire = Pastry, long in shape and sold in Australian bakeries, they make up a very nice munchie session especially if you can retrieve a rare example containing salted caramel

Eddie = Some dude from the Millionaires show

Egodotcomnism = A long prevailing anecdote as relating to the ultimate generation giving liberal democracy's final death bullet where the choice of freedom transforms away to social common benefiting which will involve a change from earning money hard and justly as means to support your family while living in a neighborhood of choice to an economic environment where earning money is done under the umbrella of affirmative action whereby discrimination of the best qualified is supported due to wide spread jealousy all while depriving everyone from freedom of speech and personal movement liberties all while this new society allows you the free choice to marry your bedroom curtains; in a nut shell socially shared egocentric freedom seeking unforgiving leadership by an oligarchic over monopolistic controlling opinion making machinery.

Eko Akete = Lagos, the place that teaches wisdom as some might say

El acto the poor facto = The eager idiot acting on a retard's command

En jy 'n gesonde = And you are healthy?

Encule la chatte = Fuck that pussy

Enojado = angry

Épouvantable = Awful

Esky = Portable cooler where beer should be stored cold so that even an Eskimo will urinate in ice cubes!

Esquinera = Corner, but in this case a street whore awaiting customers where a road crossing offers larger customer traffic

Este país está más interesado en hacer rica a su querida hija que en cablear un taxi = This country is more interested in getting its daughter darling rich rather than wiring a taxi up, that is satisfying Isabel dos Santos

Et voila = If you had to search for this word, then there is bad news, your cultural linguistic understanding is sub par even compared to a Kalahari bush man and if you first went to look at "Voila", by god the almighty all your culture definitely purely originates from the consumption of strawberry flavored milk shake; give the chocolate flavor at least a go!

Etterkop = Pussyhead

Eustache Dauger = The man in the iron mask who to this day is unknown

F-bomb = Fuck, fuck, fuck, f-f-f-f-f-f-faaarrrrrck

Fags = Cigarettes or gay people depending on context, which could mean that a fag on a burning fag is a queer on heat or for religiously living people in search for highly inappropriate sex act of swords altercation

Fair dinkum = All is mutual content and OK to go

Faire lentement – Go slow, take it easy, chill

Fangita = Venomous pussy lips, like a meat eating plant luring men in to its trap

Fanny = Women's private parts in Australian lingo* (not the ass as sepos* say)

Fazer sexo = Fuck

Fei = Having nothing, Chinese Mandarin derogatory slur for African

Fellas = Guys

Ferengi = Star Trek perv with big ears

Ferme la bouche, tout-de-suite! = Close your mouth right now!

Fils de pute = Children of whores, kind of similar saying to motherfuckers

Fizzing = Disappointing

Flaming galah = Idiot

Flaneur = Strolling to be seen in nowadays urban bogans showing off their limited riches from home but are good contributors to envy in third world countries promoting the picture of silly rich white man and ensuring Mediterranean people smugglers stays well in business

Flatuloquist = A ventriloquist using her skeeza squeeza instead

Floozy = Easy cheap whore

Fok julle naiers, go kak in jou modders poes = Fuck you all, go and shit in your mother's vagina

Fossicking = Searching

Footsak = buzz off

Foozle = Out of dated fuddy-duddy, a person missing the new century like old Menzies loving comb skulls calling a refurbished drinking venue the old tavern name for the god sake to not wanting dusting off the old mold of the past where rats were shitting in the corners where floor boards were dislocating themselves from the rest of the furniture

Fossicking = Gold digging

Foul gin = Stolen from The Aristocrats, drinking a shot out of someone's ass, like in porn guys jerking off in the coal mine shaft and having it swamping out like a flash flooding

Fourchette d'escargot = Snail fork, specifically designed to get those invertebrates out of their cubby house

Fraise = Strawberry

Freckle = Ars bud, an Australian chocolate candy looking like a person's ass hole

Freshies = Fresh water crocodiles, tame lame reptiles compared to the salties

Fritzle Schnitzle = Austrian incest cannibal at his best performance roasting his daughter to 8 Nazi-bazi-turds

Frogs = French

Frostie = Cold beer

Frothie = Beer, yay more of that great stuff

Frothing = Hell keen

Fruit Looping = Fooling around you freckle licking fruit loop!

Ful Mudammas = Fava beans stewed with tahini and garlic

Fully sick cooee = A cool Tarzan cry making gorillas shit in their jocks

FYI = For your information or fuck ya inflammation

Gaan Pluk jou riem = Go and jerk off

Gansha = Mull

Garbo = Garbage, garbage collector

Garden City = Zhuhai, one of China's first economic zones on the Pearl River delta bordering to Macau

Garlic pongstar = Smelly Italian, often also applies too much cheap ass spray deodorant giving your nostrils cancerous tumor growth as prevention measure having to smell these mama boys

Garota podre = Rotten lass

Gaulistan = France

Gazankulu = Former ban(g)tustan homeland in apartheid South Africa of the Tsonga people, north of Pretoria towards Zimbabwe, but still south of Venda

Gham = Uncivilised colored

Gibberdabbadoo = Moralists' disapproving talk, which takes the mickey out of any civilized acting adult, especially those political correctness preaching boofheads

Gidy = Lagos as known for Nigerians

GILF = Grannie I liked to fuck

Ginger minger = Unattractive red head

Glossectomy = Tongue amputation

Gooi = Thrown away

Goffel = Ugly girl

Goggle toons = Television shows

Goodbye = Tire brand merging with time for buzzcation

Goolie = For Australians a rock or stone, but taking in to consideration its other known meaning of testicle

Goon = Chateau de Cask, goon bag is somebody addicted to cheap ass nasty with chemical loaded wine, if grapes could lay a fluid turd, then that would be the product of sale

Gowks = Awkward fools

Graboids = Fictional species of ravenous carnivore sand worm acting as the antagonist in the Tremors sequels with clever Stumpy, albino El Blanco and many other happy wadi pissing deformed maggots

Gran culo = Mighty big asshole which has potential to qualify as a timeless voiding black hole

Grand rue = Major road

Grannie = Grandmother

Grass grazer = Vegetarian, vegan

Gravy train = Free ride, being fed extra rich with doing fuck all

Gray nomad = The oldies roaming the country side in their vans, like a swarm
of rotting flesh imitating the behavior of aquatic oxygen stealing algae in
northern Australia during the winter months between May and October

Gris-gris = Luck bringing gizmo

Grommets = Young surfies

Gronk = A likable dysfunctional person, usually motoric slow or in this case
mentally plucked ever lasting flowers

Guardapolvo atonto es llamativo = The overall as in clothing added as a
misogynistic twist towards a striking level of stupidity

Gun dan = Where the meaning of rolling an egg away basically means fuck off

Gurgler = Throat being used as drain

Gut bikkies = Poo

Gutrot = Blokes beers that qualify as wife bashers

Gweilo = Ghost man, but often to describe a dirty white man, especially thinking
about that the Westerners were smelly stink bags in those days avoiding
washing themselves like a vampire garlic, I guess at least that they didn't
get their blood sucked out and the Chinese still nowadays don't mind
animal blood neither, quite delicious from some critters like snake or fro
a pig made in to sausage, oink, oink, oink…

Haai = Shark

Haaqarrll = Fermented rotten shark flesh, the Icelandic counterpart of yummy
sweet blondies

Hairy meat puppet = Disco sticking with ya dicking, just don't get stuck in the
muck

Hardegeit gomgat = Stubborn Afrikaner redneck

Hazema = Harare and Zirema = in Shona for nothing good aka place of useless
dickwads

Henkersmahlzeit = Last meal before execution

Hexy = Witch (comes from German and Hexe)

Himalayan fruit = Gansha, charaz, Mary J.

Himmel, Arsch und Zwirn = Heaven, ass and thread, Teutonic swearing

Hobo = Feral derelict vagabonding and bumming tramp

Hog wash = Dirty pigs don't get clean

Holvlos = Ass floss, g-string

Home and Away = Can somebody name a drug that makes you wanting to watch this!?

Honkers = Hong Kong

Honkidoori = Same same as above, but with a sprinkle of poppy seeds

Hooning = Driving like a mad cunt, burning out your car tires and preferably attempting to give the local bored old fart of a neighbor a heart attack as he does not deserve better for interrupting your alcohol and drug infused happy times

Huai hun dan = You bad bunch of mixed bad eggs, a road curb whore's son fucked in to livelihood by a bastardized parasite vegetated garden of male customer dicks

Hujambo = Hi, welcome in Swahili

Humbug = Deceptive, wrong leading talk, behavior

Hun = honey, darling

Hundan = Bastard, scoundrel in Mandarin

Hurenson, Hurenseun = Son of a whore

Hypothyroidism = Condition where the thyroid gland is inept to produce sufficient bone growth thyroid hormones

Idiosularmaticism = Small scale village collective retard thinking, as per Urban Dictionary

Idiot box = Television

Incwala = Celebrations of the royal family connecting with its under dogs, poor under dogs, malnourished under dogs, but still have the nice crisp virgin titties for his royalty

Insh'allah ya sadiqu khiana saghiru = May god's will be with you my small betraying friend

Jaan-var tatti licking haraami = Animal shit licking bastard

Jayid = Good in Arabic

Jellybean = They come in all colors, just not white… And sometimes they are so full of sugar killing of any taste

Jellobusters = White fellows wanting to have sex with big girls, preferably black ladies with a decent booty

Jellowogs = Same as above, but with a touch of Italian herbs

Jendi = I am fine, thanks

Jetzt Mal schoen brav lutschen und danach die Rahmsauce geniessen! = Now start to be nice by sucking me off and then also enjoy the cream sauce

Jian nue ren = Bitch, usually used by girls who have gone beyond twisting and wetting their panties

Jig = Jigyassu, inquisitive

Jocks = Male underwear

Jodeterino = Small self loving fucker

John Dory = A fish in Sydney's harbor, great for fish and chips

Jong vrou = Young girl, virgin

Josher = A perverted spook

Jou dom stuk kak von ya oma se bloed poes = You stupid piece of shit from your grandmother's blood bleeding vagina

Jou hol naier bliksam, fok die kak, ek loop! = You ass fucking bastard, fuck the shit, I am out of here

Jou vokken stink vuil geaborteerde fetus damduiker = You fucking smelly gay abortion

Jus soli = Birthright citizenship

Jux = Horny corny

Kack = Use your imagination for this one please, you got more to read

Kang and Kodos = One eyed green bag aliens in Simpsons

Kapuku = Mice

Keen Individual Without Intelligence = Kiwi = Human Biomass made in New Zealand

King Brown = Large sized brown colored glass beer bottle

King kong khan = Kan Kan Kan = A spice blend used in Burkina Faso which consists of a chemical processed stock cube and what ever fish innards stolen from penguins

Kiwis = Knights In Woolen Incredible-Hulk Slippers

Knobstuckling = Female version of knob head

Kohldampf = Does not replicate coal steam as such, but like the steam coming
from a hard element, so does hunger seek the food to satisfy the built
up steam in the stomach; it is just one of those marvelous words of a
rough tree chopping sounding language which cannot be easily
translated

Kpi = Key performance index, used to evaluate if business is on track where
money is not the only defined parameter of success

Krem kop = White man

Kotskop = Vomiting person, vominator

Kumamayo = Mother fucker in Kisswaheli

La hostia esquinera = Taking the holy communion on cross roads with
prostitution

La vie est dure sans confiture = Life is hard without jam

Laji = Trash

Lactoso = Lactating, el rio de leche mujeres!

Lalaland = Dreamworld, not that ride fossicking* stuff of entertainment parks,
nope the shit which happens in your head when fruit looping* is not a
nocturnal pleasant making option

Lamington = Sponge cake with chocolate and coconut flakes

Larrikin = Somebody who does pranks, usually some stupid shit like Steve
Irwin with his eager loving mistreating some poor critter or Crocodile
Dundee, just remember Australians are even shit frightened when seeing
a harmless bobtail

Laylatan saeidat wa dae'aan = Good night and goo bye

Lazy boy = Reclining couch for a single person

L'eau chaude, n'est pas on offerte dans ta patrie? = Warm water does not exist in
your country!

Legba = God of unpredictability and hence the communicator of crossroads in
to the world of the dead

Lekker = Yummi, lovely to eat

Lemon = In this context a car which relates to a driving wreck, basically a piece
of shit on 4 wheels, often to satisfy a boobed human the husband, boy
friend or any other silly dicktated halfwit with some smarts ensures it
looks on the surface shiny, so that the over the moon flying wifie looks

less likely to be random breath tested by the copperoos while fetching her
    kids from school while being off her head

L'enfer oui = Hell yes!

Lentigines = Liver spot merged with a freckle gives you the sun's asshole!

Liquid gold = Devine piss

Lingo = Language in Australian gibberish

Lion kill = 1kg steak, usually you get it for free if the plate is fully completed
    including the chips

Lolo Ferrari = French chick with massive hooters, classic plastic surgeon's trash
    dream

Los tentáculos del diablo son de largo alcance = The devil's tentacles are far
    reaching

Loskind = An apodictic slut

Lubra = Black girl

Luftmatratz = Floating bed

Lurk = Somebody doing illegal stuff

Maagd dogter poeslekkers = Yummi daughter's virgin pussy

Maat = Friend, mate in Afrikaans

Madrugada = Portuguese and Spanish for the time between midnight and dawn,
    the time where spooky ghost come out and give little shitters nightmares,
    yep it does not have to only happen on Elm Street!

Maccas = McDrownald's

Mad-oh = Saying in Lagos for something crazy good

Mafia tart = Pizza

Mágoa = Sadness

Mama Mahu = The divine creator of the world

Mamparra = Idiot

Man jam = Baby shower

Manger = Eat

Mansa Musa = Kim Jong Il, -Un and -Sun combined of the Mali Empire and
    beyond, like his spears replicated North Korean nuclear bombs, just a bit
    more successful making him in to Africa's likely biggest, most powerful,
    testosterone laden piece of cooked bacon!

Mantequilla = Butter

Marché des féticheurs = Fetish market, but not for role playing dominatrixes; to be honest an awful corner of the city where the real animal love of Africa shines, that is a sunny day up a raccoon's ass

Mary J = Mull

Mais oui = Learn some French for this one

Mas = But

Masturvacors = Those using a vacuum cleaner as love toy

Matutu = Minivan, bush taxi, or in bad racist Safa lingo kaffir taxi

Mauvaise herbe = Weed, ganja, smokoluya

Me cago en todo lo que se menea = I shit on everything that moves

Meiensäss = Mountain grazing field where all those Peter Steiner hilarious deviant and Heidi themed pornographic movies are made, like the one where a guilty verdict is done on the fact that a naughty girl had a big fat brown birth mark on her ass cheek!

Melk terting moffie = Jerking off male homo sexual

Melktert = Milk tart, South African pastry delight where egg yolks are beaten fluffy and drowned in milk

Men-bung = Korean slang for mental break down after a series of negative experiences

Merda & merde = shit & shitski

Menier = Mr.

Merde de vache = Cow shit, happy laughing tasteless cow cheese la vache qui rit gone anally feral

Metrosexual = Urban uni sex promoting crap

Mia madre gran puta = My mother the big whore

Middy = Middle sized beer, usually 285ml, but hey this book is not about mathematics, so 300ml will do too

Mierda de vaca = Bull shit

Miknot = Beyond best friends

Milfy = A real cute Mother I'd Like to Fuck, like yay yay yay, but just being too lazy to write it like milfyyy

Millipap = N'shima

Milo = Chocolate powder, best drank with hot milk rather than water

Milton mangoes = XXXX Gold, the Queenslander kiddie basher

Min fadlik = Please

Mitr = Friend in Hindi

Mmoasɛm sɛɛ nyee = Could it possibly mean "Fuck that shit" in Akan, the most spoken language in Ghana…?

Moamba = Palm oil based sauce which can result in a saucy affair

Moerskont = Mum's vagina

Moer-toes = Stuff ups

Mogwai = Not in relation to Tarzan, but in the Chinese mythology they are devils or demons inflicting harm to people

Mohrenkopf = A desert containing nutrition lacking white sugary foam in the inside and a chocolate cover, the word itself means a black man's head

Mompie = Retarded

Mon cheri = An African girl's vagina, nice and black on the outside and when you crack the hard coating a pink cherry swimming in a drop of liquor comes to alight

Mon gracieux flacon d'eau de rosehumain, attendris avec une douche tes jarrets juteux, en ayant lentement faim de chorba de poisson et de felfel mahchi…: My gracious human flacon of rose water, tenderize your juicy shanks with a shower, slowly getting hungry for fish broth and mince meat stuffed capsicum...

Mongrel = Dick wad with rabies, or just a fucked up dog mongrel

Monkey fodder = Fruits you fruit loop!

Mozi = mosquito

Muck hole = Same as chutney tunnel

Muggie = small bug

Mulanje Opapa Mugazi = Vampires from Malawi's highest mountain

Mull = Weed, marijuana

Muster = Rounding up cattle

Myotis punicus = Shouldn't just being a Maghreb mouse-eared bat be enough punishment?

Mziki ezelaki eleng ndeko = Nice vibes cuzzy*

Nargberries = Snow Globes*

N'est ce pas = Isn't that true

Não merda sherlocoloco = No shit Sherlock from the troubled insane

Néanmoins = Never the less

Newbie = The new guy on the block

Nincompoop = A fool, modern day social media fag gone too far by either boring followers or the media platform suddenly abolishing them or creating the final hilarious laugh coming through being caught out cheating with photo shopping

Nippers = Young surfies

Nogal = Of all things

N'oublier par comme nous les deux sont dans le joux = Do not forget we are both in the game

Nutribullet = Atomic blender, no frog on acid speed escaping here

Ocker = Depp Australian slang twang of a yobbo alike

Oechsle = Scale recording sugar levels in wine and as such ultimately the alcohol level

Old girl = Mother

Øl = Beer in Scandinavian lingo

Ojetelito = Little Anus

Omuyaaye = Knowledgeable person, but uses it for evil purposes and his meanness is unpredictable, just a bad fucker like gun wielding druggo gangster

One dayar = Test cricket

Onesie = One piece PJ's, pajamas, when you shit in it, it rubs up your back!

Orkhund = Vagina in Namibian Thornbush whistling

Ozy = In this context an ounce, used when buying a big bag of delicious skunkybeet

Pardon monsieur, mais nous sommes ici dans un pays que les hommes parler anglais. Alors... = Excuse me Sir, but we are here in an English speaking country. Thus...

Pony = Smallest available beer quantity served in Australian pubs, 140ml

Por que eu = Why me?

Protein spill = Vomit

Pu = The goal of Tao, uncut wood, passive state of receptiveness, unending story through just being, aimless goal

Pumbu = Testicles in Kiswaheli

N'shima = Grounded corn paste similar to sticky rice lacking the granularity

Paarl = Red wine from the Cape Colony

Paei mae pii = Sticking up somebody's fertilizer discharge device or possibly just patting a horses back (?), the author honestly does not know as he does not speak this verbalised sign and symbol language; and can you trust everything the web tells you?

PAGAD = People Against Gangsterism and Drugs

Panda chook = Penguins are real smart birds, they managed to find a way living in the same environment like Eskimos but avoiding them (and also cheap ass KFC franchisees)

Pandillero = Gangster in the words of those who defeated the Kings of Aragon

Paragem = Bus stop, bus port and sometimes it is a full service para-gym; a place where excising before breaking your back and making yourself handicapped occurs

Pashing = Kissing with some true amorous passion

Patupap = Cornmeal porridge

Pediculous rakefire = A lice infested and unwanted, mentally damage promoting guest refusing to leave, like those preaching terrorism on foreign soil after actually leaving their war torn bombed clay hut sanitary lacking places

Pendejo = Stupid in Spanish

Pero estais un perro = But you still remain a dog

Pero ya sabes = But you know

Pielkop = dick head

Pineapple = 50 Australian dollar note

Pipe me down = Fuck me hard

Piss = Beer or for some useless dickwads alcoholic drinks

Pissed = Getting blotto, drunk

Polony = Tasteless sausage replicating warm feelings of Poland's vinifera grape extra revolutionary Traugutt

Pourquoi tu ne m'as pas réveillé = Why did you not wake me up

Pozzy = Position, usually in context at an event like footy, but in this case away from any avarifeaces*

Prendre plaisir = Enjoy!

Pueril como un infantiloide = Immature like an infant, or a brain as developed like a raw, green vegetable, salade de crudite

Pumbafu = Idiot

Pusscake = Male Cinderellas, especially Netflix addicted Millenials or in the view of rugby, Australian Football players those who too passionately engage in soccer with wrong methods like drug nutter Maradona's hand of gods goal in 1990.

Pussinimal = Sex addicted hetero man

Put a sock in it = Shut up

Puta = Whore – seriously if you had to look this one up, learn some languages!

Qanb al-Bakstani = Pakistani roallies containing marijuana and opium

Qiongqi = One of the four Chinese evil mythological creatures, some mixture between a dog and ox with wings which devours its preys' hands and feet first

Quaffing Thai badgie = Drink, Bar, Bird… You can take a Thai lady out of the bar, but you cannot take the bar out the lady

Quaggadagga = Half zebra, half donkey with an imaginary dick of an elephant

Qu'est'ce que = What?

Queef = A pink hole fart

Quim = A ladies' vulva

Rabisu = Lurking demon that springs quicker on to its victims than modern dismissal of Akkadian mythology

Raggabrash = Untidy, disorganized

Rainbow kissing = Where a bloke licks out a fanny and keeps the juices in his mouth, while in return jerks off in her mouth and they subsequently swap the fluids through intimate kissing

Rajul aemaa = Blind man

Ramburger = Dick, you dick!!

Rarasa = Highest form of respect

Raw lobster = Authoritarian sea food in a not yet published Sponge Bob episode, but am sure they would kick dero Pat's ass out of the water beyond the skies so that real stars could bully the pink stinking fucker!!

Real McCoy = The real true deal

Red back = 20 Australian dollar note named after a deadly spider which like to lure gray nomads* in camping ground thunder boxes*

Red pancake = When a women is horny and her vulva, lips turn as juicy and blood red like a rare steak, preferably comme une entrecôte de cheval (horse steak)

Red Roof Inn = Shark week, girl flu, menstruation

Red Rooster = Australian chicken take-away which tends to cook the chemically nuked meat so dry that one could be forgiven thinking to be eating untreated white rope

Red sock = When you fuck a girl up the ass and then get her tighten that a-ring followed by pulling out your dick the rectum innards pop out, like inside out of the poo's final journey, which then replicates visually a red sock!

Reffo = Refugee

Regardes-la, un moment, moins une minute, et voila ma serviette hygiénique pour ta souvenir extraordinaire! = Look here, just one moment, it will take less than a minute aaaaannd… here we are, bloody fanny pad for you to keep as remembrance item!

Régime de l'indigénat = Laws and rules the French had for native people in their colonies where any disregard of their superiority was punished up to death

Reichsblut = If you have vinegar deprived potato fried squares flowing through your veins, then I have bad news… You might actually be a Schwab, Preuss or Fries, but behold it could be worse; you could be a jam bun bumming Berliner!

Rellies = Relatives, the same ugly apes as you!

Remote controlled wish mops = Small hairy dogs

Retardigrades = Real tough enduring idiots, like tardigrades on two stilts being as resilient due to their existence everywhere plus also exercising the liking of being near moss giving the saying dumb fucks good its origin of real meaning!

Ridgy didgy = Original, in this situation requires more genuine effort

Rien d'autre = Anything else?

Riff-raff = Local aggros, you have them everywhere in some form

Rip snorter = Fantastic, great, party, you open your eyes up like a true blue Australian when she or he sees a gas barbie burnt steak smothered in what ever $2 cheap ass bottle of suburban dweller enticing shit the Reject Store sells

Roadies = Beers you drink while traveling in a car or any other kind of motorized vehicle or it would be a trekkie!

Roallie = Joint made with pure weed and with short length paper

Rocket Man = Kim Jong-Un as per Donald Trump

Rocky Road = Australian sweet of chocolate mixed with marshmallows, nuts and sometimes even healthier minor components, but yet have to see sperm as one, served in slices

Roos = Just put a kanga in front ya doozie

Rort crook = Cheating thief, fraudulent criminal

Rubber dorito = Condom, come like in a form of a corn chip, sometimes a bit too corny for the horny

Rug muncher = Eating carpet which means girl devouring another ones hairy vulva or in short a lesbian

Ruhrpott = Aka Review, West Germany's industrial belt

Run Forrest, run = Forrest Gump, adult kiddo not only lost his marbles, but also his spare coin for public transport or in modern day terminology his credit card tag function emancipated itself for a real bloody long time like watching Discovery Channel on LSD

Runners = Diarrhea

Rustydusty = Buttocks in sepo* lingo

Saali kuttayi chutia = Bloody dog bitch fucker in Hindi =

Sacre merde = Masquerading of holy shit

Sacrebleu = Poke in to the wounds of Jesus Christ!

Safa = South African

Saharian goggles = The wind blows heavy in the desert and makes visibility close to impossible, however with a turkey slap* without the slapping you still might not be able to see, but no sand should come in to your delicate eyes neither!

Salaam wa sabaah al-khayr = Peace and good morning

Sales pute = You dirty whore!

Salisbury = Harare, oh yes so apartheid stile, but neither did cricket originate there!

Salope = Bitch

Salaude = Pork & Bastard or where oink goes woof

Sapiosexuality = When a brain or intelligence is seen as 'sexy', acknowledgment that a person with a small wiener can feel great again (even if his IQ is somewhere between a freshly dislodged banana's foreskin and a polished toilet seat)

Sarkhund = The male counterpart of orkhund, just instead of the whistling, they fart talk through the capability of moving their hemorrhoids and bigger these are the deeper the meaning gets until somebody stores a push bike up their cavity to be crowned as assholedom of assholeries!

Saudade = Longing for love while in melancholy feeling incomplete

Sausage sizzle = A place full of horny blokes but no sheilas

Savoir vivre = Know how to live

Schwarze Fraeulein = Black Lady

Schweinsbesteiger = Disrespecting word for a great soccer player meaning pig fucker

Schwobe = The belittling of Germans by the Swiss originating from the Schwabs who populate the Southern Nazibazimacht influence, and hence representing the main exposure of the nervous neutrality destructive anxious Swiss

Se = Knowing

Sebastianic sword = When a lad's cock reaches the long levels beyond refined appealing magnificence that fucking himself is a pleasure beyond any worldly possible proposition

Sekhmet = Egyptian goddess with a pussy cat face

Sepo = Americans, originates from their international executed behavior aligning to a septic tank

Septic states = The land ruled by peckerwoods, hillbillies and white trash with names like Rusty Kuntz, Mike Litoris, Dick Swett...

Servo = Petrol or gas station

Seti = Lady in Amharic

Seulement si te ne le fais pas = Only if you do not….

Sewi mogesi = Silly man in Amharic

Shwaboe-shnaboes = German dicks

Shackle dragger = Australian, from the era of convicts put in to shackles

Shamozzle = Unnecessary problem, mess, which could and should have been easily dealt with, but somehow didn't, like a fat kid should not be in a candy store if the door width would have been constructed narrower!

Shark bikkies = Children swimming in the ocean

Shindig = Party, often under planned and then cranks up beyond

Shlucken = Beer bukkake

Schluckenlager = Windhoek Lager aka national beer of Namibia

Shmuck = As per Wikipedia pejorative term meaning one who is stupid or foolish, or an obnoxious, contemptible or detestable person

Shudra = 4ht and lowest social class in India, the laborers, of which also the Dalit or Harijans (untouchables, rubbish collectors and processors) belong to

Shukran = Thanks in Arabic

Smudge fudgers = Taking up a liking to colon candy

Slab = Carton of beer, usually containing 30 cans of juicy wife basher

Slit sluts = Derogative word for Oriental long hair cats

Slym sloot = Female cum

Smize = Smile with your eyes

Smoko = A break at work

Snag = If you think Vegimite is true blue tucker* at its worst which you can shove in to your gut, then you have missed out on the typical beef sausage, full of cholesterol sky rocketing promoting artificial meat waste mixed with what other crap a butcher can get on the cheapy to create a texture and taste consisting of saw mill dust and fat

Soccerella = Neymar at Russia world cup 2018 doing elegant pirouettes on his pedicured feet while falling on his manicured hands indefinite times better than a middle aged upper class bogan on a $10 dollar bottle of dry white (wine) – like playing up as if their crown has fallen down to the floor while attempting to gain attention, followed by support for an obnoxious outcome while bystanders are inertly churning in disbelieving hope that Godzilla rocks up, eats them by chewing slowly and spitting their ugly coupons (faces) out

Sook = To sulk, whingers, copying whining Pommies deprived of green mushie peas

Space docking = Stolen from The Aristocrats, shitting in to a vagina and as it takes a bit to squeeze out that sausage the process looks similar to a spacecraft docking on to a home base like the Death Star

Spit = A girls taking a cock from behind while sucking another one off, looks like a spit on the roast

Spliff = Marijuana cigarette

Spoof = Fudge sickle custard, man jam

Sprung = Dishonesty caught red handed, done very visibly

Spyt kakking = Throwing up, vominator on power ups

Sikki = A day's rest from work due to a virtual illness

Single barrelled pump action bollock = dick

Snow globe = Same as wrinkle purse

Snow leopard = Mature lady

Soft cock = Male who is scared to be tough, testosterone Cinderella

Später = Later in Crout lingo

Spaiker = Fuck yourself

Spastic eagle = A girl who has a dick on her mouth, one up the slit, one in the clacker plus one in each hand being shaken through the 5 individuals moving forwards and backwards just like a spastic eagle!

Spastocrats = Priests, greenies rejecting smoking weed, women having difficulty in finding dick, religious mob, pampered Millennials and any other prerogative individuals preventing others having a good time

Spornosexuals = Men full of themselves, that they work out like nutters to show their abs off on social media where muscles are more important than doing up their teeth, which basically opens the competition door for other scrotum waxing male prawns (great body, ugly face)

Sprog = Kid

Squeezing the beetroot = A girl heavy on the rags, painfully losing a lot of blood

SSB = A favorite of Australian wives, especially in the arvo and before picking up the ankle biters from school, Sémillon and Sauvignon Blanc

Staatssicherheit = Nazi-bazi bad boys ensuring state safety by slaughtering any non Aryan life forms

Stoke = Pleasing

Stoned pony = Same meaning like riding a high horse

Stronzo = Arshole in Italian

Stubbie = Beer bottle as further described below, it is sooo gooood, you cannot
    give this great invention enough space to allow for its golden glorious gut,
    bubbling along like you do after consuming it!

Stubbies = 330ml to 365ml beer bottles, stubby holder is then the condom or
    cooler around it to keep the golden juice nicely cool with maximum oral
    pleasuring experiencing while mass murdering them

Suspercasparism = Critical thinkers who are suspect of clowns who avoid eating
    soup

Swaksinnige = Imbeciles, you get stupid people with any color, even in blue,
    stupid Avatars who waste 2 hours and 42 minutes of your life!

Suig piels = Sucking dicks or cock suckers

Tai niu bi,...bi, bi., bi = Fucking awesome, you pussy, pussy, pussy

Taijitu = The appropriate name for the yin and yang symbol

Tais-toi = Shut up!

Tarajueh = Fuck off in Arabic; as you do if you don't have the money for a high
    maintenance Lebanese doll or cannot find a willing beast as Plan B sex
    partner

Tassie = Tasmania

Tats = Nope, not a nick name for Tutankhamun

Te = The power needed to meet Tao's aimless goal

Tee = T-shirt or what; an elephant's trunk?!

Tea = In this context dinner, supper, la cena

Tej = Ethiopian honey wine similar to mead and just a bloody awful in taste as
    well as causing a headache

Telhas teeze = Kiss my ass

Thunder box = Drop toilet, WC without water to flush

Tiens mon dieu = Oh my god hold it!

Tighs = Tight stocking or leggings, in short gutter stile Gucci, but does make
    those more proportionate upper middle class cat haven asses shine!

Tinned ass = Rich

Tinnie = A can of piss

Titkop = A looking alike and full of fat like a tit

Tits on toast = Breakfast served in a brothel or by a scantly dressed lass or a fat
guy with plenty of man boobs!

Theek = Fine in Hindi

TLC = Tender, Love, Care or Thick Love Cunt!

Tomba! Kuma mbuziko! = Fuck you goats cunt! (in Swaheli)

Tool = Usually applied to young useless blokes, a year or 2 or in some extreme
cases 10 elder than school leavers hunting down juicy fresh food who are
often partially engaged as Woolies (Woolworths) till bills and strapped of
cash, possibly even too young to legally buy booze attracting these young
losers, and those even older are droolies, but they usually hide themselves
under the umbrella of the nice guy neighbor with a secretly kept flask of
Rohypnol for a hearty pedo bear session...

Tour d'amour relais = A nice hard enduring pushing fuck stint like riding the
bike up Col du Tourmalet in the Pyrenees to succeed at pass height in
gaining the maillot jaune (yellow shirt)

Tout la-bas et tout droit = All out there and straight ahead

Tozz feek, kol khara ya ibn el sharmouta = Fuck off, eat shit you son of a bitch

Trannybag = Grand mother with a dick who is soooo fat it cannot see the testi
pimple

Trekkies = no, not Captain Kirks talkative mob, it is a load of stubbies which
accompany you when traveling around which often is walking or driving,
but not like swimming because you would then be a bloody shlucken
freak

Trots = Diarrhea

Ts'omi = Fasting

Tu est plus beau que dix milliards couchers soleil = You are prettier than a billion
sunsets

Tucker = Food

Turkey slap = Comes from an episode of the academic intellectual promoting
Australian Big Brother series where a guy slapped his dick in to a girl's
face; and if mentally pictured it looks like a ...!!!

Twilight monkeys = Homo sexual men

Ty che suka blyad = What the bloody mother fucking fuck in Russian

Ugukwinya = Swallow!

Uie = U-turn

Va te faire foutre = Go fuck yourself in French

Verdad coños = Real, true cunts

Verdomp = Damn in Afrikaans

Vetala = An evil spirit hijacking the corrupt individuals destined for greatness and feeding on their pure seen ambitious life's blood, slowly sucking them fully out before discarding the soulless converted to some ball licking evil jackals to be then doggy style fucked for eternity!

Vete a la mierda coño = Fuck off cunt!

Vinnige = Quick

Violet Crumble = An Australian chocolate bar made of crisp easy breakable caramel tasting sugar exploding filling

Você está uma babaca = You are an asshole

Você não é um bockie branco = You are not a Boer (white bock)

Voila = Check "Et voila"

Volksnaehe = Being close to people, populous, a politician that can fart in a crowd and still be hugged by the white sheep

Voluntold = Force applied to make somebody volunteer for something he does not want to do, but usually understands the benefits, a successful mechanism used by ass licking managers when it comes to meeting corporate staff related kpi's like the big bull shit called development plans

Voorhuid voorspel drup besmette stinkgat = Foreskin foretelling dripping stink hole

Vrotbek = Bad breath

Vrot gracht = Rotten channel aka the stinking shit canals of Amsterdam

Vrot in a tronk = Rotting in jail

Vrystaat vernier =Shifting shitting spanner

Waco = Place in Texas where a religious mass murder took place

Walkie = Usually giving your pet dog a physical opportunity, plus he can then get rid of some of his shit which does not end up in your own pedicured back yard

Wally = Fool

Wɛ akɛn waa = Fuck that shit in Gadangme

Weenier = Small penis

Weinsteiner = Touch a women's bosom just like Harvey did before ending up behind bars

Weisswürstel = Bavarian breakfast snag, sausage which is eaten with sweet puke promoting mustard and ok, a pint of real holy juice aka you don't take your beer with you to Munich!

Welcome = In this context for the blissfully intelligence ignorant reader "whale cum"

Whelping toupée = Natural hair

Wetterschmöcker = Old witch craft of men in Muotathal Switzerland to predict the season's weather

Whacka whacka = Idiot talk

Whakky tabacci = Gansha

Wheel of Gooner = Wheel of fortune for the urban poor where a bag of cheap liquor is swung around on the clothes hanger while those still capable to juggle their beer guts on stilts take turn of luck in getting a free shot until where the bad ending of all is gone goes ugly where before all are gone means the a bashing of pissbot titans

Wife basher = Cheap local piss making men not so love their wives

Wisecrack = Smart ass

Wikus van de Merwe = Main actor in the movie District 9, "they are all prawns"

Willy Wagtail = Australian bird, many find them cute but the darn things are rude bad tempered little fuck turds

Winchester Geese = Mainly older single ladies, but also some as young as 10 who were under the reign of the bishop of Winchester under his "prison" law exemption from common law in London; many were found in the cross bones graveyard of having died perinatal and conclusively with the saying of getting bitten by one meant contracting a venereal disease the women were very likely The Catholic churches' fun time playmates, at least before seemingly a liking for young altar boys came more fashionable…

Wogs = South Europeans

Woop-woop = Beyond, far, going out of the city in to the bush

Worm food = You, me and one day even Lenin

Wormwood = In this context whites feeling sorrow to the sight of African poverty, however still remaining deep in their hearts absent in going beyond the surface in fright learning that there own existence is not only temporary, but full of luxury

Wrinkle purses = Testicles

Wunderbar und wunderschön = Just fucking great, get it!?!

Wuss = Weak person

Xevioso = The Vodun spirit of thunder

Xiao jies = Prostitutes

Ya shar mu taigh = You bitch in Arabic

Yabber = A lot of talking

Yaddi = Talk

Yalla = Go!

Yansh = A girl's buttocks in Nigerian slang

Yard ape = Children

Yarn = Extended chat, often used to talk about the good old past and then reminiscence how things were better followed by evolving to a whinge festival… Or the smarter conversations move back in to positive as a new cold stubby has been brought out by a loving wifie

Yarning jibber = Nice story, usually exaggerated bull shit

Yarpie = South African Boor, decaffineited Bantu bushman as many men and most likely also their wives have horrible poorly maintained beards while still complaining that their black counterparts all smell and have lazy, social rotten attitudes

Yobbo = A person with low values, crude, gross, urban cave man

Yocto = 10^{-24} meter

You'll be apples = You will be fine and innocent like a piece of apple pie or aka apple cake pussy in Dusk till Dawn

Zahiristan = A fictional state in the German book "Das Ende der Wahrheit" which means the end of truth

Zar* = A malevolent spirit

Zatknis = Shut up in Russian

Zhuhou = Noble man in the Zhou dynasty, a time where the land slowly threw all its social and traditional ingredients in to a soup pot

Zinger = A spiced up burger offered at Kentucky Fried Chicken parlors, promotes people desiring to transform towards more culinary sophisticated zomoebas

Zit = Pimple

Zomoebas = Brain eating basic cell critters